I0573545

The Family Secret

Roberta C. M. DeCaprio

A Wings ePress, Inc.

Paranormal Romance Novel

ings
ress, Inc.

Wings ePress, Inc.

Edited by: Jeanne Smith
Copy Edited by: Heather O'Connor
Executive Editor: Jeanne Smith
Cover Artist: Trisha FitzGerald-Jung
Images from: Pixabay

Wings ePress Books
www.wingsepress.com

Copyright © 2022 by: Roberta DeCaprio
ISBN-13: 978-1-61309-515-7
ISBN-10: 1-61309-515-5

Published In the United States Of America

Wings ePress Inc.
3000 N. Rock Road
Newton, KS 67114

What They Are Saying About
The Family Secret

Roberta C.M. DeCaprio got me again...on a paranormal, no less. *The Family Secret* grabbed me at the very beginning and kept me reading and reading. I had to find the answers posed in the novel, and the journey was a wonderful trip throughout. My compliments to the author.

—Dorice Nelson
Author of: *Clan Gunn: Gerek, Saratoga Summer 1963*, and *Lost Son of Ireland.*

Roberta C.M. DeCaprio writes a plausable paranormal, unique, leaving no circumstances to doubt...only to the imagination. If anyone could make you believe time travel is possible, it would be she. And what a journey she wove, each page of *The Family Secret* building into a novel I couldn't put down.

—James C. Lemke
CEO and President of River of Orange Productions, LLC;
Screenplay writer and graphic novelist of *Sweet Raven.*

Dedication

I dedicate this book to those loved ones
I have lost in recent years:
My mother, Carmela DeNofio DeCaprio
(April 24th, 2020, due to Covid 19).
My maternal grandmother, Helen Formichelli DeNofio,
who was the inspiration for the grandmother in this book.
My great-aunt, Annie Formichelli Barone,
who taught me the power of the St. Jude Novena.
My cousin, Curtin Phillipson, who only graced
this earth for four years.
Writer/Poet/Mentor, Lyn Lifshin.
And three dear friends:
Writer/Actress, Kathryn Phillips-Spira,
Tammy Walker Almy, and Dino DeCherro.
Lastly, to my editor, Jeanne Smith.
Thanks for all the tutorial help and your expertise in
making *The Family Secret* a page turner.

* * *

In some families, not even death is final.
Nor are skeletons the only things in their closets.

Prologue

October, 1930, Anglewood, New York

It was a day Sophia Pettrocini would never forget. It started out as the usual Saturday, helping her father in the family-owned business, but it would end in a most unusual way. This day would be the beginning of all that would happen in the days to follow.

Just ten, and short for her age, her black hair braided in two pigtails that hung to her waist, for some reason Sophia consistently wore a pink, gingham jumper. She always said she liked the way the hem swished around her knees as she ran down the stairs to Nawna's apartment.

Nelana Caralena Pettrocini was her paternal grandmother who had come to live in America just before Sophia was born. She was a good woman, especially to Sophia, who loved to sew and make soap with her grandmother. But Nelana had her own opinions, and sometimes her views clashed with those of Sophia's mother, Maria. This was why it was important for Nelana to have her own living quarters. The arrangement worked for the most part, ensuring everyone's privacy.

Sophia found Nawna sitting at the table in her small kitchen, which always smelled like garlic and freshly baked bread. Upon hearing her granddaughter enter the room, Nelana closed the lid on the cedar wood box she was looking through and locked it. "And so, *bambino*, my baby granddaughter comes to see me."

"I'm not a baby anymore, Nawna. I am ten now." Sophia fingered the floral designs and the raised letters spelling out her grandmother's name on the box. "Why are you always looking through this?" Once, she'd caught a glimpse of what her grandmother kept in the locked box: a pair of rimless glasses and a black diary.

"Is that any of your business?" Nawna teased, crushing her granddaughter in a warm embrace and kissing her several times on the cheek. "And you will always be a baby to me, no matter how old you are."

Sophia returned the affection before plopping down in a nearby chair. "Do you have anything good to eat?"

Nawna raised one thick brow. "Again, you have not had your morning meal?"

Sophia shook her head. "Mama needed to nurse Angelo and change Vincenzo, so I came down here."

"Ah...good thing you have me or you would starve," Nawna said, her grin of few teeth spreading across her plump face. After Sophia stuffed herself with sausage and Italian bread smothered in tomato sauce, she helped her grandmother wash the dishes. "Now your papa waits for you in the store."

Every Saturday, Sophia helped her father in the Cutler Street bakery her family owned, relieving her mother, who worked there during the week, along with performing her various other wifely duties. She didn't know how her mother had any time to donate to the family business, baking the bread and rolls sold in the shop, while raising three kids...nursing Angelo, only a few months old, along with caring for Vincenzo, just a toddler and still in diapers, plus Sophia, who at times demanded attention in other ways. Nelana made the pies and soap, but most of the work was on Maria

Pettrocini's shoulders. Taking pity on her mother, Sophia helped out on Saturday afternoons.

"Come, let me bless you for the day." Nawna made the Christian sign of the cross on Sophia's forehead, then kissed her on each of her cheeks. "That is for all that you do good today." She turned Sophia around, lifted her skirt and gave her a pat on the behind. "And that is for anything you think of doing bad."

Sophia giggled. "That didn't even hurt."

"Ah, not like when your mother uses the wooden spoon, huh?"

She turned to face her grandmother. "That can really sting, especially if Mama's very mad."

Nelana shrugged. "Well, she has got to keep you a nice girl. Now and then a hand to your bottom is how it is done." She kissed Sophia again. "Now go, your papa waits for you to help, but do not eat too much candy this time." Nelana waved a hand in the air. "I warned him not to sell the candy, too." She shook her head. "This will change many things, cause *problemi*, problems. But would my son listen to his mother?"

Sophia didn't understand what things would change. How could selling candy cause a problem, unless you ate too much and got sick, which is what happened when she'd consumed an abundance of coconut creams. The severe stomach ache she suffered and the enema her mother gave her afterward to relieve the pain would be forever etched in her memory.

When she entered the bakery, her father was washing the large front window, getting it ready for a new display. "Fill the jars on the counters with peppermint sticks, Sophia," he instructed. "And make sure the lids are on tight."

The day progressed and grew warm...warmer than it should be in New York for the month of October. Sophia was just about to take a break, go for a drink of lemonade to quench her thirst, when the door opened and a man in a black cape, top hat and shiny boots entered the store. Accompanying him was a little girl, slim and fragile. A crop of red curls adorned her head, the ringlets framing a delicate face. Two large round blue eyes stared in excited wonder at the jars of candy lined up on the counter.

"What would ye be wishin' for, *wean?*" The man's baritone voice resounded through the tiny shop, his words rolling off his tongue like a melody.

The youngster pointed to the jar Sophia had just filled.

"Aye, the peppermint sticks, is it now, *a leannan?*"

The little girl beamed. "Yes, Da."

The man turned to purchase the candy, pulling a coin from his vest pocket. "I would be pleased to purchase a peppermint stick and a few loaves o' yer bread, at me lovin' wife's request."

Sophia smiled and handed the child the candy while her father wrapped the bread and took the man's money, or *bawbee*, as he referred to the coin he had handed Antonio. She could hear her father chatting with the man, but paid no further attention to their words, so intent was she on the pleasure that filled the little girl's face. With every lick on the peppermint stick, the child's eyes rolled heavenward, her expression one of pure joy.

Sophia giggled. "You must really like peppermint."

The little girl responded with an exuberant nod and took a large bite. But when her eyes rolled again, it was not out of pleasure, but from sheer panic. Somehow a piece of the candy had lodged in her throat and she was choking.

Sophia's heart sank to her toes and she rushed to the little girl's aid, striking her hard on the back. But the child's airways stayed obstructed, her face first turning red and then a frightening shade of purple. "Papa, Papa," she screamed. "She's choking!"

Antonio Pettrocini's portly form moved with liquid speed across the shop, his chubby arms wrapping around the child's abdomen. With an upward push, he freed the candy from her throat. It shot with a force across the room, landing beside the caped man's booted toe.

Stunned, the child's father stared down at the candy for a moment, then looked over at his daughter, who by then had wet herself, messed the floor, and was crying loudly.

"You are fine now," Antonio consoled, patting the child on the top of the head.

The caped man reached his daughter in two strides, gathered her into his arms, and sobbed right along with her.

"Sophia, get the mop," her father ordered, making his way behind the counter and returning with two glasses of water.

After the man and his child regained their composure, he took Antonio's hand in both of his. "'Tis a *braw*, brave act that ye have done, *mo bhuidheag*, me friend. And I bestow me blessin' upon ye."

Her father's face turned crimson, the blush rising to his ears. "That is not necessary."

"Aye, 'tis very necessary. *Mo nighean*, me lass, is me heart and me best beloved in life, as I am sure yer *wean* is to ye," the man said, his eyes filling again with tears. "And so to yer wee lass, and to her first born daughter, and so on, and to the lads they will marry, I bequeath a blessing."

What he proclaimed made no sense to Sophia and when she had a moment alone with her father later on in the day, she questioned him. With a casual wave of his hand, he dismissed her. "The man was overwhelmed with appreciation and didn't know what he was saying. Now we have work to do and will talk of this no longer."

She had her suspicions about her father's dismissive attitude concerning the situation and explained the turn of events to her grandmother. Nawna smiled, reached for her cedar wood box, and shooed her upstairs. Later that night, Sophia snuck out of bed to eavesdrop on her parents as they sat talking in the parlor.

"I know the man you speak of, Antonio," Maria said. "I have heard he possesses supernatural powers and can cast spells."

Antonio's tone was weary. "And where do you hear such things, Maria?"

Maria's voice trembled. "The women in church, they say he is from Scotland."

"And, so we are from Italy. America is a melting pot."

"But the other women say he is a wizard with powers too frightening to speak of."

"Then do not speak of them," Antonio said flatly.

Exasperated, Maria sighed. "Antonio, you are not listening."

"It is you who must not listen to everything a bunch of old women say," Antonio snapped. "Idle talk can ruin lives."

Maria's voice rose an octave. "It is the truth, Antonio, whether you want to admit it or not and he has cursed our child."

"Be quiet, woman, keep your voice down," Antonio warned his wife. "Our daughter is blessed, not cursed. That is what the man said and that is what we must believe." He sighed and added, "That is what we must always believe, because it is too late to change."

"You can believe whatever you want, Antonio, but I will be in church tomorrow and every day thereafter, to say a novena to all the saints for our daughter's soul." She pointed a finger at Antonio. "Your mother warned you about selling candy in the store. For once in your life, you should have obeyed her words."

Sophia tiptoed back to her room, knelt to say a prayer, climbed into bed and pulled the blanket over her head.

Part One – Nela

The Blessing Train

One

April, 2007, Anglewood, New York

The quiet woke me.

That may sound strange...how could the stillness be loud enough to wake anyone?

But it was.

In fact, in an ironic way it was deafening, which was disturbing.

The unnatural silence concerned my cat, Mrs. Beasley, as well, because she jumped on the bed and licked my face with her abrasive tongue. Not a sound could be heard, and along with my cat, I wondered why.

Living on a busy thoroughfare above my beauty salon for five years, I've become accustomed to the traffic. Main Street, Anglewood, New York, is a block away from Shire Downs Medical Center and only an exit away from the Thruway. Ambulance sirens, motorcycles, trucks and cars speed down the street at a constant flow.

No longer do the noisy commuters keep me awake.

But tonight—or should I say Saturday morning—as I glimpsed my clock and noticed it read 2:00 a.m.—not hearing the activity did keep me from falling back to sleep.

The silence brought an eerie calm to the room and I had a quick and distressing thought that the end of the world had finally arrived, or more realistically, I somehow had suddenly gone stone deaf. But then the mattress dipped and I heard the springs squeak as Guylan rose from the bed, his bare feet padding across the hardwood floor.

I gave Mrs. Beasley an affectionate scratch behind the ears and put her down on the floor beside the bed. Turning to face the opposite end of the room, I found Guylan standing in front of the window. He had opened the drapes and was gazing down at something on the street below. The full moon hung like a giant, gold coin in the sky. Its light cast a glow, illuminating his perfect form...broad shoulders, straight back tapering to a narrowed waist. Though I couldn't make them out in the darkness, I knew they were there—two very deep dimples—set at the base of his spine, one above each firm, round buttock cheek.

He was standing in what I call *pirate fashion,* with knees straight and feet placed far apart. He was like a modern-day buccaneer, as naked as the statue of David, standing defiantly by the window...but why?

"Guylan, what is it? What's wrong?" I called out in a soft voice. Even a whisper was an affront to the dead calm.

He remained as silent as our surroundings.

I suppressed the thought that our wedding preparations were giving him cold feet. That often happened; it did to my friend, Becky Hall. Allen proposed, gave her the ring, and when the plans got underway, he got as skittish as a frightened horse and broke the engagement. Becky was devastated. Two years later, she's still pretty messed up over it all.

Could Guylan be having second thoughts now, and not know how to tell me?

I twirled the ring he'd given me at Christmas around my finger, the tension tightening every muscle in my body, and gave an anxious little cough. "What's wrong, Guylan?" I asked again, not sure I really wanted to hear his answer.

He turned to face me. "Nothing, Nela." Pausing, he glanced back out the window, then again at me. "Everything's fine."

My suspicions were not appeased. "You don't sound so convincing."

He inclined his head, straining his ears for the usual night sounds. "It's so quiet. Why does that happen when..." his words caught in his throat.

"When what?" I interjected, my heart pounding

He turned back to look out the window. "I'm not sure, Nela. I'm not sure about anything anymore."

"What is it, Guylan...what's bothering you?" I prodded further, praying to myself it wasn't our upcoming nuptials.

Once again, he turned my way. "Nothing, all is fine," he said, his voice much surer than a second ago. "All is fine," he repeated, convincing himself as well.

I sat up, the blanket falling to my waist, and felt his eyes scanning my naked breasts. A thrill ran through me and I ached for his touch on them. Reaching for the covers, I raised them with an invitation for him to return.

He made his way to the bed and drew me into a warm embrace.

I caressed his face, tracing his full lips. "Suppose you tell me what's going on?"

"What makes you think anything is going on?" he muttered in a defensive tone.

"Well, something's disturbed your sleep."

He placed a hand across my backside. "This is what disturbed me."

"You're lying, Guylan Quinn," I whispered. His finger made tiny circles on my buttock cheek. It tickled and I bit my lip to keep from giggling. "Stop trying to distract me."

"Am I...distracting you?" he whispered into my ear, his lips nibbling on a lobe.

"You know you are," I groaned, wrapping a leg around his waist and closing the small gap between us. "But I won't be swayed. Tell me what troubles you."

"Right now, the fact that you talk too much," he teased, moving his lips to suckle one of my nipples.

I arched my back as he drew me into his mouth. The way his tongue flicked across and around the hardened peak sent waves of ardor tingling through my flesh. "This is totally unfair," I muttered, drawn to his affection like a magnet.

He broke for an instant to look up at me, his voice solemn. "Life isn't fair, Nela."

His answer stunned me for a moment. "What's prompted you to say that?"

He sighed, his fervor cooling. "Lately I've been reflecting profoundly on a few things."

"Like what?" Along with being sorry the passion was stilled, I knew he needed to speak his thoughts. But inside I grimaced at the possibility he no longer wanted to marry me.

Guylan's voice cracked. "With my work at the animal clinic, I see how precious life is...a sick cat or dog fights for its life; the owner hopes, by some miracle, I can save their beloved pet. And, oh how I try. But when I can't, the sorrow, the emptiness and heartbreak wrack me for days. Deep within, I always think I could have done more. For some reason, I feel I could have done more in many instances."

"What instances?"

"I'm not entirely sure, I just feel inside there's something *more* for me to do, a grander scheme of things."

I pushed a dark curl from his forehead, somewhat relieved it was his job he was profoundly reflecting upon and not our marriage.

"Maybe I'm not cut out to be a veterinarian?"

"That's not true," I protested. "I've seen how good you are with the animals. You've cured so many. Being a veterinarian is your calling." With gentle strokes, I caressed his shoulder. "Living would seem too long if you harbored your lifelong desire."

"And is life long enough to harbor a secret from the one you love, Nela?"

Alarm rippled along my spine. There was a secret I was keeping from Guylan, but not because I wanted to. I just didn't know how to explain the situation to him. Now I worried my guilt showed and he suspected I was hiding something from him.

I was ready to spill all, bare my heart and soul, when he sealed my lips with a kiss. "No more talk," he whispered against my mouth. "Just love me."

His phallus penetrated my womanhood and the bubble of silence burst. The blare of an ambulance siren shrieked in the night, simultaneous to the explosion of his passion within me.

Everything, again, was as it should be...or was it?

~ * ~

When I woke, Guylan was gone. I scooted over to his side of the bed and inhaled the scent of him still lingering upon the pillowcase. In the last year, he'd become such a part of my life...the most important part, and I couldn't wait to be his wife and start a family with him. Gazing at the clock, I groaned, not wanting to rise and leave the cocoon of our lovemaking. But my grandmother was set to arrive within a week for two days, and I had so much to do. I rose from the bed with the anticipation of Gram's visit, after not having seen her for an entire year, and squelched the dreamy state enveloping me. I spun into multi-task mode, making a mental list of the things I needed to do, as I hopped into the shower.

I worked the Saturday hours in my salon...a perm for Mrs. Dunn, a touch up for Karen Stiles, and several haircuts and trims, before heading to the mall to purchase a new dress, with shoes to match, for Gram. I was also meeting my mother for dinner, in the hopes of pawning off on her the purchase of the groceries I would need so Gram could cook her traditional Saturday evening meal.

Mom, always on time, was waiting for me in the corner booth at Duncan's Café. She wore a casual, yellow linen blouse and jeans that hugged each curve of her slender build. Her medium-length dark hair was pulled back into a high ponytail. Gloria O'Riley still turned men's heads and my father knew it.

My mother's chocolate eyes crinkled with a smile as she waved me over to the table. I plopped down in the seat opposite her and sighed. "What a day! I haven't stopped since this morning." I took the menu she handed me. "Sorry I'm late."

She shook her head. "Nela, I dare say, you're going to be late to your own funeral." She scanned the menu. "The stuffed pork chops look good."

"And you look tired, Mom," I said, concerned.

She met my gaze and placed the bill of fare aside. "I guess I am, a little."

I searched her face, my own much like hers since I'd inherited the Italian looks—dark hair, eyes, and olive complexion— from my maternal ancestors. My two younger sisters, Hannah and Alana, favored the paternal side of the family, the copper curls and green eyes of the Irish relatives. "After working thirty years as a paralegal, you should be retired by now."

Mom reached for her water and took a sip. "I can't do that just yet, Nela, not with Alana still in college."

My youngest sister had been a change of life baby for my parents and just now was in her last year of college. I leaned forward in my seat. "How about cutting down the hours, then?"

She shook her head. "Since your father's heart attack and early retirement, there just isn't enough coming in to handle what's going out." She frowned. "And don't you be saying a word of this to your father, either. He's been depressed enough at having his wings clipped...he doesn't need to feel responsible for me as well."

"Why don't you two sell the house, buy something smaller, easier and cheaper to maintain?" I suggested.

"And where would Hannah live while she waits for her husband to return from Iraq?"

For a moment, in my worry over my mother, I'd forgotten Hannah and my niece Cara occupied the basement apartment while my brother-in-law fought overseas.

My mother bit her bottom lip. "Hannah can't afford anything since she and Joe lost their business, and I won't have my granddaughter growing up in a bad section of town or attending a school with gang activity."

I reached out and took my mother's hand. "I just worry about you, Mom."

She forced a smile. "Well don't, I'm fine." She narrowed her eyes and changed the subject. "Have you gotten something for your grandmother to wear?"

"Yes, at Barkley's, a beautiful blue dress and shoes to match," I boasted.

"And the groceries for the weekend?" she prodded.

I cast my eyes downward, as I'd done when I was a child and confronted by her. "Not yet."

She chuckled. "Can I take a wild guess here and assume it was a task you'd hoped to pass off on me?"

I raised my gaze to meet hers, again seeing the dark circles etched beneath her eyes. "I can manage it myself."

"Nonsense, you probably wouldn't get the right items anyway," she teased.

"Don't you think it's time I learned? I mean, I'll be getting married myself within a year," I said in my own defense.

The two of us broke out in simultaneous laughter.

Mom extended her hand. "Give me the list."

I hesitated before reaching into my purse for it. "Are you sure?"

She smiled. "You can start your wifely culinary lessons after grandma's visit."

I sighed, relieved, and found the list.

"Now," she said, reaching for the menu, "what about the pork chops?"

~ * ~

Gloria made her way to the car and sat for a moment, staring into space. A week ago, she'd found a lump in her left breast. As soon as she could, she'd made an appointment with her gynecologist for Monday. What would lie ahead of her after seeing the doctor? Would she need to see a specialist? Would she need chemotherapy, radiation? Could she handle the sick, weak months of recovery?

Since Brian's heart attack, she had been the main breadwinner, and although her husband's early retirement check was an ample one, it wasn't enough at this point to completely carry them through.

Oh, the inconvenience of it all, putting everything on hold for the healing. She sighed. *Then again, cancer isn't convenient at any time.*

Feeling herself slipping into a fearful state, she pushed her thoughts to the positive. The lump could be just a fibroid, a cyst; she mustn't get ahead of the situation. Adamant about her regular doctor visits and routine self-examination, Gloria was sure, should there be a real problem, she was catching it on time, at an early stage.

"So, I plunge ahead and believe for the best," she whispered to herself.

But the hardest part would be telling the family.

~ * ~

Guylan sat in the park across from the animal clinic where he worked. The bench he occupied gave him a bird's eye view of the fountain and the surrounding rose garden. Since the weather had warmed, he found it relaxing to take his lunch away from the antiseptic smells and bustling chaos of the clinic. Saturdays were even more hectic than usual, and the park afforded him a place to think, which he needed to do.

Early that morning, while he slept at Nela's house, he'd been awakened by the stillness, the silence that accompanied the caped man's appearance. From the window he looked down to the street below and found the stranger standing on the sidewalk, looking up.

He thought back to the first time he'd seen the man. It was about a month after Christmas. He had had dinner with Nela and her family, sort of an informal engagement party with a few of Nela's closest friends. By the time dessert had been served, gifts opened, and guests thanked and bidden goodnight, it was quite late when he arrived home.

He parked the car in the apartment complex lot and noticed the man with the top hat and cape standing on the corner, beneath the street lamp. It was a cold, blustery night, not fit for loitering, especially in that part of town, where it was rare anyone would linger on the street. The man's presence bothered him and when he got up to his apartment, he phoned the police. But by the time the authorities arrived, the man had gone.

Two weeks later, he was sitting in a booth by the window at Melton's Coffee Shop on Greenly Boulevard, when he spotted the man standing across the street. He threw a five-dollar bill down on the table, reached for his coat and fled out the door.

Once more the man had vanished.

Now, taking the last bite of his peanut butter and banana sandwich, he felt again like he was being watched. He stood, scanning the park. A woman on the next bench read a book, a man and his son played ball near the oak tree, another woman walked her dog...nothing unusual or out of the ordinary, and yet the hairs on the back of his neck rose. No longer hungry, he dropped his half-eaten sandwich in the trash container and looked around the park one last time before he made his way back to the clinic.

Two

Monday was the beginning of the work week for most folks, but for me it was the second day of my weekend, since I worked in the salon on Saturday. Guylan worked on Saturday too, taking Sunday and Monday off. On Sunday nights, we ordered Chinese take-out, eating our shrimp egg rolls and beef chop suey sitting on the couch, watching a rented movie. Mrs. Beasley waited with wide eyes for one of us to drop a morsel of shrimp, walking off in a cat-huff when nothing fell her way.

Guylan was quiet and withdrawn. Again I worried, as I had done the night before, that he was having second thoughts about getting married. At this rate, my obsession with his frame of mind was going to cause my skin to break out as it often did when I became stressed over something. "A penny for your thoughts," I said.

He swallowed his food and smiled. "You won't get much for your money."

"I think I will." I set the egg roll I'd been munching on down on the paper plate in my lap.

He frowned. "Why do you say that?"

I sighed and wiped my fingers on a napkin. "It seems you've been somewhere else as of late, the last few weeks especially." I uncurled my leg from beneath me and set the plate down on the coffee table. "In fact, I've noticed the difference in you ever since our engagement dinner." I looked down at my left hand. "Ever since we announced our marriage plans."

"Nela—"

I cut him short. "If you're having second thoughts about marrying me, Guylan, you need to tell me." There, I'd said it...now I cringed inside as I waited for his answer.

He leaned forward, placing his food plate beside mine and reached for the remote control to pause the movie we were watching. "Is that what you think?"

I gave him a taut nod.

He took my hand, brought it to his lips and kissed it. "That couldn't be further from the truth."

"Then what is it, Guylan? What's wrong?"

He took an audible breath and sat back, keeping his hold on my hand. "Do you remember the other night, when everything went quiet and you woke to find me staring out the window?"

"Yes." With a frown, I added, "Why was it so still?"

"It happens when he comes," Guylan whispered.

I moved closer to him. "When who comes?"

"The man." He hesitated, casting a quick glance out my living room window.

I followed his gaze.

"The man who has been following me," he finished, his blue eyes returning to look deep into mine.

A chill traveled down my spine. "Someone's been following you?"

He took a deep breath. "Since the night of the engagement party."

I slid closer to him on the couch. Whoever this man was and whatever he wanted, he now knew where I lived. "I think we should call the police."

"The thing is, Nela, I don't really have an accurate description, since I've never really seen his face, just him at a distance. After the dinner at your house, when I first spotted him, I called the police once I got inside my apartment. But by the time they arrived, the man was gone. I did give them a statement and they said if he continued to stalk me, I was to notify them again. But other than that, there's not much more the cops can do. I mean, the man's really done nothing wrong, other than creep me out."

"Well, at least it will be down on record more than once he's been following you, should—"

"Should I turn up missing or murdered," he interjected.

I shuddered. "Don't say that."

He sighed. "Okay, tomorrow I'll go down to the Fifty-third Precinct and give another statement to someone there."

"Why do you suppose everything goes so still?" I asked, uneasy now in my own home.

He frowned. "If only I knew, Nela. If only I knew." He brought my hand up to his lips again. "I'm at least relieved I've told you about it." He smiled. "We should never have secrets between us, Nela."

"No, never, Guylan," I agreed, still keeping silent the one I hid from him.

~ * ~

After the trip to the police station, Guylan headed for the library to do some medical research. Patches, a brown and white, longhaired Dachshund, was nearing sixteen and needed her spleen removed. Not an easy surgery for a dog to rebound from, but even harder for such an old one. Concern about the animal coming out of anesthesia was one of the main worries. While Guylan was searching in the medical section for the volume he needed, the air filled with a subtle energy. Once again, the stillness enveloped him, but as quick as it had come, it left. A moment later, a library assistant approached, handing him a folded piece of paper.

Old roots before new ones, it read.

"Who gave you this note?" he questioned the assistant.

"The man sitting there," the young man said, pointing to an empty chair at a table in the corner. "Well, he was there, only seconds ago."

His heart raced. "What did this man look like?"

"He wore a black top hat, shiny black boots and a cape," the assistant said.

Guylan looked down at the note and read the words again: *Old roots before new ones.* He blinked, baffled. Having grown up an orphan, he didn't have old roots. There was nothing to link him to his past except the ring he wore on his right hand. He glanced at the ring and studied the raven mounted on the onyx, its bill heavy, the feathered wings long, its tail graduated and wedged shaped. Engraved around the stone were the words *Corbie Xenos.* He'd looked up the word *Xenos* and discovered it was the Greek word for *foreigner* or *stranger.* What *Corbie* stood for, he hadn't a clue, since all his attempts at finding the meaning were in vain.

And what of the new roots?

That could be in reference to his up-and-coming marriage to Nela, but how would the caped man know of Guylan's plans? The blood drained from his face.

"Are you all right, sir?" the assistant inquired.

"Yes, thank you," he lied, sitting down on a nearby chair. He forced a faint smile to reassure the assistant, who by then looked stricken with concern. "I'm fine...really."

The assistant nodded and returned to his duties.

He crumpled the paper and dropped it on the table beside him. For a moment, he stared at the crinkled message, his mind desperate to solve the riddle written upon it. When he was growing up in the orphanage, word games and riddles were a favorite pastime. Sister Margaret allowed crossword puzzle books to those touting excellent grades, an incentive, no doubt, for others to improve. Guylan hadn't thought of Sister Margaret in years. She had to be at least seventy-five or eighty by now. In her younger days, her memory had been as sharp as a knife and her wits quick. The children could never con her into anything, and they had all tried, including Guylan. If Sister Margaret were still alive and as attentive, she just might be able to shed some light on this new riddle.

I guess there's only one way to find out.

He looked again at the ring, then sighing, he picked up the message, stuck it in his pocket and headed for his car, driving to East Sagamore Street and St. Bernard's Home for Boys.

~ * ~

The main foyer smelled as he remembered, a mixture of lemon floor polish and spray disinfectant. The high ceiling that had looked to him when he was a child as though it reached heaven was yellowed and stained, the paint peeling from recent water damage. Making his way down the corridor, he rehashed the times he had walked the same path, fear gripping his heart. At least once a week, if not more, he had been summoned to Mother Superior's office for misbehaving.

The elder nun, tall and ominous looking, would first make him explain in detail his offense, then she'd have him reflect on how he could improve his standard with Almighty God. It was all a very drawn-out affair, to afford him the time to agonize over what was to come next, which was to drop his trousers, bend over the desk, and feel the sharp pain of the ruler across his bare thighs.

The day he broke Ronnie Fargus's nose for destroying the robin's egg he'd rescued from a fallen nest, Mother Superior's wrath swelled to unbelievable proportions and her discipline tactics took a new turn. Almighty God's standards made room for Father Samuel and his *board of education*. The two were called upon by Mother Superior to deliver the punishment he deserved.

Father Samuel believed a sound beating was one enduring the test of time, and demanded Guylan drop both his trousers and undershorts to the ankles. The painful paddling reddened his bared backside beyond comprehension, as well as humiliated his pride. To add to the mortification, Ronnie Fargus was allowed to watch. The enemy's smug smile and satisfied delight peered from beneath the large bandage across the bridge of his nose, incensing Guylan even further.

"Do you think you've had enough, young man?" Father Samuel bellowed.

Guylan gulped the sobs of pain and embarrassment that rose to choke him. "Yes, Father."

The *lint eater*, as the children had nicknamed Ronnie for the fact that he picked lint from his navel and ate it, had no regard for animal and insect life. Many times, Guylan had caught Ronnie pulling apart ants, leaving their bodies all over the sidewalk, little insect legs twitching. When Ronnie deliberately smashed the bird's egg Guylan had saved from a fallen nest, it was the last straw.

"Are you ready to apologize to Ronnie, Guylan?" Father Samuel snapped, giving him another swat, this one harder than the others.

"Yes," he muttered, reaching to pull up his pants, his insides jiggling from the intense beating.

Father Samuel stilled his hands, making him stand naked from the waist down in front of Ronnie. "I didn't hear your apology, my child."

Weren't they taught all things great and small were created by God? Shouldn't Ronnie be apologizing, too? But that wasn't about to happen and Guylan's face was as hot as his backside under Ronnie's scrutiny. "I'm sorry," he choked out in a hoarse tone, once more reaching for his trousers.

Again, Father Samuel stopped him. "And you will never use your hands as a weapon again?"

More hypocrisy. Wasn't his punishment dealt to him by the weapon held in the priest's hands? "Never, Father," he promised, pulling the hem of his shirt down to cover his nakedness.

"Very well, dress yourself then," Father Samuel commanded.

But he and Ronnie didn't stop fighting and they'd both receive many such beatings throughout the years at St. Bernard's. Guylan was sure the two of them had worn out Father Samuel's *board of education* and had a running tab going at the emergency room.

Ronnie needed someone to keep him in line and that's exactly what Guylan did. Why he'd thought it was his duty, he would never know, but looking back, he believed Ronnie feared him enough to keep from running amok. The fights they got into stopped Ronnie from being more of a dill weed, for lack of a better word, than he already was.

How many years had passed since then—almost twenty-six? And yet, replaying the long-ago scene still brought tears of shame to Guylan's eyes. Instead of breaking Ronnie's nose, he should have broken the little weasel's neck. Ronnie turned out to be an elected official. His road to fame had begun in college when he married a councilman's daughter. Guylan spent the first two years of higher education at the same community college Ronnie had chosen and knew first-hand the nightly escapades the dill weed had behind his then-fiancée's back. The poor woman, not at all attractive, was used by Ronnie for his career. Had she known about the other women, she'd have had her father run Ronnie out of town on a rail instead of awarding him a prestigious position.

Guylan shook his head to free his thoughts. Taking a cleansing breath, he turned the doorknob and entered the outer office.

The young woman at the reception desk smiled. "Can I help you?"

He hesitated, looking around the room...the walls were the same shade of green, the linoleum still black and white checked. Even the same shades adorned the windows. Bringing his attention back to the young receptionist, who waited for an answer, Guylan returned her smile. "Yes, please, is Sister Margaret still in residence here?"

"Yes, she is." The young woman glanced at her watch. "She'd be in the staff lounge right about now, taking a coffee break." She reached for the intercom's receiver. "Should I page her for you?"

Staff lounges, paging systems, coffee breaks instead of afternoon tea...St. Bernard's *had* changed somewhat with the times, even if the décor remained the same.

"Yes, thank you," he agreed.

"And your name, sir?"

"Tell her Guylan's here to see her...Guylan Quinn."

~ * ~

Sister Margaret had aged with much grace, her large blue eyes as vibrant and expressive as Guylan remembered. She wore a different habit, one that didn't cover her hair and face as much as the previous style. Often, he had wondered about the color of her hair.

16

Now, gray strands streaked auburn curls peeking out from the scarf wrapped around her head.

Holding out her hands to welcome him, Sister Margaret smiled. "My heavens, what has it been...nearly twenty years since I set eyes on you last?"

Guylan was pleased to see she was just as sharp. "Yes, to be exact."

She stepped back and surveyed him. "You left this place a gawky, eighteen-year-old boy and have returned a strapping man." She squeezed his hand. "Has life been good to you, Guylan?"

He shrugged. "I can't complain."

She giggled. "I've learned it does no good."

Her mirth made him chuckle, too. "No, it doesn't."

"Come," she said, leading him into Mother Superior's office. "Sit and tell me what you've been about."

That room hadn't changed either. The large desk, the one he was bent over to receive his punishments, was still in the same corner. He made his way to the chair Sister Margaret offered, waiting for her to take the seat opposite him before he sat.

She crossed her legs and arranged the skirt over her knees. "Still have a bit of trouble feeling dressed in the new clothes." She smiled again. "Guess I'm from the old school. Now..." she made a gesture with her hand for him to proceed.

"I co-run an animal clinic on Wattling Street," Guylan began.

Her eyes widened. "Then you're a veterinarian?"

He smiled. "Yes, that I am."

She slapped her knee with a hand. "I knew you'd go into a field that helped animals, the way you always cared for stray cats and injured birds." She reached over and gave his arm an affectionate pat. "Good for you, Guylan."

Like a young boy again, he was happy for her praise. "Thank you, Sister."

"And why haven't you come around to see me sooner?"

"I guess..." he hesitated. "Other than you, Sister, St. Bernard's was a time I wished to forget."

"Was it all that bad, Guylan?"

"There were some good times, I will admit, but they were few and far between. So, when the time came for me to walk through the doors of this building and out to freedom, a surge of relief coursed through me and I swore an oath to myself I'd never come back." Speaking of that day aroused the old fears and uncertainties he'd endured. "Finding a job, a place to live and paying for college became nearly impossible to do on my own," he admitted, perhaps for the first time in his life. "I was discouraged, hungry, tired, and I resented how unprepared living here left me for the outside world. I was alone, frightened, confused and had no one to turn to...no one who cared."

"I'm so sorry you felt that way, Guylan." Sister Margaret's voice softened. "I cared. I always did. Many times I wished I could tell you how much, and what you meant to me."

Thinking back, he realized she was speaking the truth. Sister Margaret had read him bedtime stories, mended his clothes, made pancakes on Saturday mornings because it was his favorite meal, and when he caught the measles, chicken pox, or the flu, she swabbed his feverish body down with alcohol, staying by his bedside throughout the night. She had been the closest thing to a mother he would ever have.

This time he reached for her hand, giving it an appreciative squeeze. "I believe you would have, thank you."

"And then there's God, Guylan. He knew what you needed before you did."

"Yeah, well, He sure let me get to the end of my wits at times."

"But He did supply your daily needs, I'm sure," Sister Margaret said.

"True, my needs have always been met."

"Well, then what more does one need than his daily bread? Why worry about a cold glass of lemonade quenching your thirst in July when it's January?"

"You have a point," he agreed.

"Tomorrow is yet unborn, Guylan. No need to worry till it arrives." She searched his face. "Now suppose you tell me the real reason you've come here today."

He drew a deep, ragged breath. "Do you know anything about my family, Sister?"

Sister Margaret's brow shot up in surprise. "You've known right along your parents died in a car crash when you were a toddler."

Guylan's gaze wavered before returning to her face. "I came to St. Bernard's when I was three?"

Sister Margaret nodded in agreement, her features growing tense.

He steadied his voice. "But I couldn't have come alone."

"No, you didn't come alone," she replied.

"Then who...who was it that brought me here?"

Sister Margaret's mouth twitched, and then curved with tenderness. "A woman in her late forties brought you. Her soft blue eyes were so full of sorrow and...and...fear."

He leaned forward in his seat. "A name, Sister. Did the woman have a name?"

Her brows set in a straight line. "There wasn't a need for her to speak her name."

Guylan combed his fingers through his hair and stood, making his way to the window. Looking out at the sloping lawn, he envisioned making snowmen and sliding in winter on his sled. Come summertime, he'd flown a kite. In all truth, this was home, or the one he had grown up in.

"Why is knowing so important now, Guylan?"

He turned to look at her, growing impatient. "Because I believe it's my right." He sidled closer, softening his tone. "I'm getting married a year from this May, Sister, and I think it's important, for when I start my own family, to know my roots." It wasn't the entire truth, but not an outright lie either. "Didn't you catch the engagement announcement in the paper?"

Sister Margaret's tongue moistened her lips with a nervous sweep. "It was in the paper?"

"The Sunday edition, in fact, with pictures and all," he said.

"No, I didn't see it, but I hope that..." her voice trailed off and she stared, lost in thought for a moment before forcing a smile. "Well, so you're getting married. How nice for you, Guylan. And your future wife, she's of your faith?"

His eyes locked with hers. "Yes, she's a Catholic as well. Nela's from a big family...they're a loving bunch and when Nela looks about the church she'll see their smiling faces. She'll hear their good wishes as they raise their glasses in a toast to our happiness at the reception."

"I truly hope I'm included," Sister Margaret said. "To be the one that smiles for you."

He searched her face. "I'd like that, Sister."

Sister Margaret became uneasy under his scrutiny. "I'm sorry things can't be the way you want them, Guylan, but we should all feel blessed for the things we do have."

"And do I even have my real name, Sister?"

Sister Margaret sighed. "The woman who brought you only said to call you Guylan and to give you that ring you're wearing," she said, her eyes going to his hand, "when you turned eighteen."

He swallowed the emptiness invading his heart. "Then how did I come by the last name of Quinn?"

Her tone softened. "Quinn is Mother Superior's family name." She smiled. "Most of you didn't have a last name and we nuns used our surnames so Social Security cards could be issued." Sister Margaret tilted her head sideways. "Do you remember your best friend, Andy Beechum?"

Guylan nodded. "We're still very close to this day. In fact, I've asked him to be my best man."

"Well, his last name came by way of Sister Catherine. Beechum was her family's name."

He held up his hand. "And there was nothing other than the ring?"

She looked away. "It was a long time ago, Guylan."

He came down on one knee in front of her, forcing her to look at him. "There was something else, wasn't there?"

She shifted in her chair. "Some things are best left alone."

"Please, Sister, what can it hurt to tell me now?" he pleaded.

Her voice broke with emotion. "A lot, Guylan. I never wanted any part of it and neither do you."

His tone hardened. "Let me be the judge of that."

Sister Margaret bit her bottom lip. "There was something...a book."

He frowned. "What kind of book?"

Her voice wavered. "One Mother Superior demanded I immediately burn."

He glanced down at the nun's hands, folded in her lap. "Why would she ask you to do such a thing?"

"Because of its content." Sister Margaret shivered. "But I couldn't burn it, for a reason I can't explain." She made the Christian sign of the cross. "And I will speak no more about it."

Guylan's heart raced. "Where is this book now?"

"Let's just say, for the good of all, it remains on holy ground," she said.

He stood. "How long will it take for you to get it?"

Sister Margaret's blue eyes darkened. "There are a few channels I must go through first, so about a week, but...I won't..."

"I need that book, Sister," he interrupted, reaching into his pocket and handing her a business card. "As soon as you have it in your possession, contact me."

She stared for a moment at the card he held.

"Please, Sister," he begged again, softening his tone.

"Very well, Guylan," she conceded, taking the card. She raised her gaze to meet his. "But whatever happens is on your head; I won't be responsible. I didn't want to be then, and I don't now."

Three

The week flew by and the time for Gram's visit arrived.

I glanced at my watch...it was almost midnight. In a matter of seconds, it would be the first Saturday in May. I sat down on one of the terminal's benches and waited for my grandmother's train to arrive. *The Blessing Train*, as Gram called it, had, for the last three years, brought her home for a forty-eight hour stay. Within that time, she enjoyed a reunion with the closest members of the family. It always seemed to me not enough time, but as I was aware of the fact that not everyone was as fortunate, two days each year would have to do.

The large clock sitting in the park across the way struck midnight and Gram's train came into view, amazing me at how it appeared. Gram descended the steps, looking around for a familiar face. I waved to her and she smiled the same smile I'd grown to love and cherish, and missed for the last year.

The rose brocade dress she wore, once vibrant and rich looking, was faded and wrinkled, the veil of her pillbox hat frayed. And although alert, she appeared fragile and pale. Always, when she first arrived, this was the case. But later on, with the love and warmth of family surrounding her, Gram's transformation was astounding.

I strode over to her, giving her a big hug and a kiss atop her head. This wasn't hard to do, since I'm five foot five and Gram's only four foot eleven. "I've missed you so much this past year, and have tons to tell you."

Her thin lips, void of the usual magenta lipstick, curved into a broad smile. "And I'm anxious to hear it all, but first..." she looked down at her crumpled dress and frowned. "I need to freshen up a bit. I've been wearing this old thing for ages."

My grandmother has impeccable taste in style. Sunday's church outfit was always a lesson in fashion. The jewels, hat, purse, gloves and shoes, all had to complement the rest of the attire. At the end of the service, Gram would stand in the church foyer with a few lady friends, chatting and posing, showing off her ensemble.

"I knew you'd say that," I said, "so I took the liberty of buying you a new dress. It's a soft, pale blue shade with shoes to match."

Gram's voice rose with her excitement. "Oh, Nela, what a thoughtful gesture." But her joy became subdued when she took in the poor condition of her nails and touched the snarled curls falling from beneath her hat. "All gussied up in a new dress and still I'll look a fright."

I believe my grandmother's sense of style influenced my career choice to become a cosmetologist and open my own beauty salon. As a child, I watched her give herself a manicure every Saturday night. She was meticulous in the way she would file the almond-shaped nails to just beyond her fingertips, push back the cuticles and then apply the bright red polish. When she would play the piano, her fingers were a striking contrast against the white keys. Her toenails were not to be neglected, either. They'd be adorned with the same shade, and peek out from her sandals, squared in proper form to avoid becoming ingrown.

I took Gram's arm and escorted her toward where I had parked the minivan, but she stopped short at the terminal window to read a flyer posted there. "The woman making this announcement, this Dana Clair, has opened a music school." She turned to look at me.

"She was one of my pupils, Nela." Gram smiled. "Nice to know she followed up on what I taught her."

"I agree. It must make you very proud."

"More pleased than proud, that I helped to mold her career," Gram said.

I assisted her into the passenger's seat. "Would you like me to open the shop, give you a manicure, new hairdo...the works?"

Gram's face brightened. "That sounds perfect. You're just too good to me, sweetie."

"It's the least I can do. I remember all the times you were there for me, helping out with tuition and all."

She shrugged. "It's what family does for each other, Nela." Then she frowned. "But aren't you usually open on Saturdays?"

"Not this Saturday. This weekend all I want to do is be with you." I ran around to the driver's side of the car and after making sure both our seat belts were fastened, I started the ignition.

Gram smiled and turned to look at me. "You know, Nela, I miss the times when you and your two younger sisters were small and would come to visit. All the cookies we made and the Christmas trees we decorated throughout the years." She sighed. "I wish I could make it back here more than once a year, but I should be grateful. Some aren't as lucky."

"I know, Gram...I know," I sympathized. "But even to see you for just the two days that we do, we're happy. Each year we look forward to this reunion. And next year we'll be able to see Gramps too."

Her face brightened. "That's true, next year will be Henry's five-year anniversary, and from then on he'll be allowed to join me each year on the first Saturday in May." She giggled like a school girl. "I am so excited for that time to come. He's promised to take me dancing at the Hallston Lodge."

I smiled. "That's where you two met, right?"

"Yes, I can't believe it's been over sixty years." Her voice softened. "And that dear man still makes my head spin."

"What's the secret to a happy marriage?" I said, blushing a bit at the thought of what my grandfather did to make Gram's head spin. I knew they were very much in love, but picturing their intimacy was mortifying.

"Trust, love and a sense of humor," Gram admitted, and then her voice saddened. "But there were times that weren't so happy... like when my mother-in-law came for a visit. My mother and my father's mother had their differences, but they initially got along, even loved one another. My grandmother knew when to mind her own business." She narrowed her eyes. "But Henry's mother was notorious for butting her nose in where it didn't belong. I truly believe that woman could scare the devil himself."

"She was that bad?"

"Worse than anything you could imagine; very possessive and bossy." Gram folded her arms over her ample bosom. "She wouldn't let Henry go about his life, had to always have the last word and her word was always right." Gram shook her head. "And I tried to like her, Nela, really I did."

Guylan's parents had passed away when he was a small boy, so I wouldn't have to cope with in-laws, though I was sorry for him, not having a family. "What made her act so domineering?"

"I think her actions stemmed from the fact that she was widowed at a young age and left with five boys to raise, your grandfather being the eldest. He was several years older than his brothers and helped his mother with their rearing, kept them all in line. I believe Henry's position in the family contributed to her acting more like a jealous wife toward him than a mother."

"And when you came along and took Gramps from her, it was just too much for her to bear," I concluded.

"Yes, I believe so," Gram agreed. She shrugged, using both shoulders and briefly closing her eyes as elderly Italian women do. "But your grandfather, thank heavens, stuck by me. Henry made everyone, especially his overbearing mother, know I came first and foremost in his life, and that meant a lot. Marriage is hard, but with the right partner it all seems to work." Gram smiled. "You'll see what I mean when it's your time."

"My time *has* come, Gram." I felt the excitement bubble up inside of me when I thought of Guylan's compelling blue eyes, his firm features, the confident set of his shoulders. "His name is Guylan Quinn and he's asked me to marry him." I raised my left hand and wiggled my finger to show her the ring, a beautiful emerald cut set on a thick, gold shank with diamond accents adorning each side.

Gram clapped her hands together in delight. "Oh Nela, my little Nela, how exciting for you." Her plump face melted into a buttery smile. "And he's swept you off your feet?"

I giggled at her exuberance. "Yeah, he's done that for sure." The lovemaking we shared entered my mind and this time the unwelcome blush that heated my face was because I replayed my intimacy with Guylan.

Gram frowned. "Has he got a good job, Nela...one that will support a family?"

"Very good, Gram. He's a veterinarian."

"A man who has a heart for animals will have a heart for other things as well." She nodded, satisfied. "Yes...yes, that's a good profession, lucrative and constant...almost everyone has at least one pet in the family."

I laughed again. "You sound like a financial planner."

She shook a finger at me. "A good relationship tends to stay good when the finances aren't strapped. Always remember that, Nela."

"I'll remember, Gram," I agreed.

"And when is the big day?" she probed.

"Next year...May fourth, 2008, at noon, St. Michael's Church, so you and Gramps can attend. And I've chosen the Hallston Lodge for the reception, so I guess you'll be dancing at my wedding."

Gram's soothing voice probed further. "Does he know about us...the family blessing?"

"No. Not yet, anyway."

"Well, you've got to tell him, Nela." Her tone changed to one of calm authority, the same tone she'd used to admonish me when I was a child. "If he can't cope, if it will disturb him, he's not the fellow for you."

I frowned. "You don't have to chastise me, Gram. I know what I have to do."

"I don't like the annoyance in your voice, Nela. Conduct yourself in accordance. No matter how big you get, I'm still your grandmother and you need to respect that."

I sighed. "I'm sorry."

"How long have you and this boy—"

"Guylan, his name is Guylan," I broke in, reminding her.

"How long have you and *Guylan* been together?"

"It's been almost a year. I met him last June when my cat, Mrs. Beasley, developed a urinary tract infection." I smiled. "He gave me the ring at Christmas."

"I can't believe you'd accept his proposal without telling him about the family blessing."

My fingers gripped the steering wheel tighter. "I tried many times, believe me, Gram." I sighed again. "But it's just not an easy thing to explain. I mean, it's a blessing for our family, but an outsider might think the whole situation is rather creepy."

"I'm ashamed of you, Nela, letting it go this far without telling him what to expect," Gram scolded further. "And if you're afraid he won't want to marry you after he learns the truth, then you don't trust his love. Without trust you have nothing."

"How did you explain things to Gramps?" I asked, taking her focus off me for a time.

"I just told him—as a first daughter, I was blessed with something beyond imagination, then I preceded to tell him how it happened, the whole wonderful experience...and it is wonderful, Nela." She added, "Truly it is."

"Are you trying to convince me or yourself, Gram?"

She puckered her lips. "That doesn't even justify an answer."

I cleared my throat and asked the question that hadn't seemed to matter to me before I met Guylan, but was my main concern now. "What did Gramps do when he learned it would also extend to him, if he married you and stayed married to you?"

Gram shifted in her seat. "At first, he laughed, thought I was joshing him. Then he thought I was crazy...we argued about that. I remember kicking him out of my parents' home, telling him 'this was how it was and if he couldn't handle it, then he wasn't the beau for me,' and I slammed the door, went up to my room and sobbed my heart out."

My interest mounted. "Obviously you two worked things out."

"True, we did. He came back the next day and apologized, told me he didn't want to go through life without me. We talked and talked," she smiled, "and kissed and hugged. In time your grandfather learned to take the whole situation in stride. And he even began to see it as a stroke of luck for him, too."

"How'd my dad take it?"

"Your mother has never told you?"

"She's never uttered a word."

"Ah, well, Brian O'Riley, the stubborn Irishman that he is, walked out when he learned the truth and didn't come back after the first night, as your grandfather did." She shook her head. "Nope, he let your poor mother suffer for at least two weeks."

My eyes widened. "Two weeks! Poor Mom, she must have been a wreck."

"Oh, she was a real mess...cried day and night, wouldn't eat and when I finally got her to take a bowl of soup, she threw it right back up."

"No wonder she's never talked about it," I reflected aloud. "But clearly they worked things out as well."

"Yes, but the two tormented themselves in the process...your mother making herself sick and weak and your father getting himself drunk every night and calling the house, breathing into the phone and then hanging up."

I frowned. "There wasn't caller ID service back then, so how'd you know it was him making the prank calls?"

"He admitted to it later, after he and your mother made up. In the end, it was your grandfather who really straightened things out."

I giggled, knowing Gramps as I did...no-nonsense type of guy, slight in stature but big in personality. "What did he do?"

"Well, he found out from one of the neighborhood boys, who happened to hang around in the same crowd as your father, that Brian was getting himself drunk at a place called Lofty's Bar and Grill. After receiving yet another prank call, your grandfather hightailed himself over to the bar and confronted Brian."

"Why haven't I heard any of this?" I said, annoyed. After all, my parents knew I was going through the same dilemma with Guylan.

"Ah, well...like I said, your mother probably doesn't want to rehash a sorrowful time, and your father would like to forget the embarrassment," she said in their defense.

I frowned again. "Why would my father be embarrassed?"

Gram rearranged the disheveled-looking hat upon her head. "Well, your grandfather...he did a little more than just confront Brian."

My curiosity got the best of me. "Don't stop now, Gram."

She screwed her nose up. "Nela, I'm not sure your father would appreciate you knowing what happened."

"I promise, Gram, I won't say a word, really...cross my heart and hope to die," I vowed, sounding like I did at thirteen when I pried from Julie Claymore what she'd seen her older sister, Evelyn, and Bobby Miller doing on the couch one night when their parents weren't home.

"Your grandfather, as I said, having reared his younger brothers, taught your father a lesson...sort of...well, sobered him up with a bit of discipline so he'd listen to reason."

I was almost afraid to ask, but too curious not to. "What do you mean by *a bit of discipline*?"

"Well, Henry went to Lofty's and found your father drunk as a skunk. He took Brian by the arm and escorted him to the car."

I had a feeling *escorted* wasn't really the word for how Gramps got my father to the car, but I remained silent.

"Henry drove Brian to the abandoned barn out on Route Ten," Gram paused. "How your grandfather explained the goings-on to me was simply that he knocked some sense into Brian, as any father would an unruly son."

"Define *knock some sense*."

There was a long silence.

"Your grandfather gave Brian a licking," Gram at last admitted.

I frowned. "A licking?" Then the meaning dawned. "You mean he beat my father?"

"Well, no, not beat...more like spanked," Gram muttered.

"But my father had to have been at least twenty-two years old."

"Yes, well, your grandfather told him if he was going to act like a child, he'd be dealt with like a child, and then Henry proceeded to remove his belt and give Brian's bared behind a good thrashing."

"Holy shit," I blurted out. "Bare-assed to boot?"

"Now, Nela, there's no cause for profanity," Gram scolded. "Conduct yourself in accordance, young lady."

"Sorry Gram, but are you saying my father decided to marry my mother because Gramps worked him over?"

"No, of course not," Gram snapped. "The spanking was only to sober your father up enough to listen to reason. Henry then explained to Brian what his initial reaction had been when he had learned of the family blessing, and how he dealt with it."

"Well, I guess all my problems are solved," I said in a sarcastic manner. "All I've got to do is have Dad beat up Guylan."

Gram crossed her arms over her chest. "Not beat up...spanked, and I shouldn't have told you that story."

I softened my tone. "I'm sorry, Gram. I'm really glad I learned all this tonight."

"Truth be told, Nela, Henry could have thrashed Brian from here to East Missouri, and if he wasn't a *keeper*, it wouldn't have made a difference."

"What's a *keeper*?"

"A *keeper* is a man who will understand a situation and go through life beside you in spite of it. They're the ones worth the effort because they make an effort in return. And they're out there... otherwise none of the first daughters in the family would have married. I guess that's how you can tell if you've got the right one," she added softly.

"Well, I guess I'll soon see if Guylan's a *keeper*." I sighed. "I've invited him to the reunion, thought I'd let him meet you and see how wonderful you are, fall in love with you as everyone does, and then spring it on him."

Gram clicked her tongue. "Good luck with that strategy, Nela."

"It's far better than a spanking."

"I just hope your young man doesn't feel betrayed or tricked."

I bit my bottom lip and turned into the salon parking lot. "So, do I, Gram...so do I."

Four

"Mmm, that feels so good, Nela," Sophia DelFino purred, as her granddaughter vigorously scrubbed the staleness from her hair. "When you were little, I would wash your unmanageable curls the same way. Your whole head would shake, and you'd close your eyes as my fingers made your scalp tingle."

"Then I have you to thank for my success. All my customers comment on how wonderful they feel after I've given them a good head wash. I only use the pads of my fingers, though, so as not to damage the scalp."

Sophia looked up into her granddaughter's angelic face. "I'm so glad, my darling, everything in your life is working out."

"Now, if I can just be honest with Guylan. He's been going through a difficult time with something himself."

Sophia frowned. "Has he confided his troubles to you?"

"He has, but with all his worries, I'm even more concerned about how he'll take knowing our family's secret."

Sophia clicked a disapproving tongue. "You aren't starting out very well in the trust department, Nela." She sighed. "Well, if he's a *keeper*, it will all be fine."

"And if he's not?" Nela countered.

"Then you're better off without him."

"I suppose," Nela said and rinsed the shampoo from Sophia's hair, adding conditioner. "This needs to set for five minutes." She gave her grandmother's arm an affectionate pat. "I'll get the manicure table ready while you soak."

Sophia closed her eyes. Her talk with Nela about the blessing brought to mind how it had all begun...in her father's bakery, when she was just a small girl. That warm October day had changed her life, as well as the lives of all the first-born daughters and their husbands to come.

"Gram, do you still want that manicure?" Nela said, breaking through her thoughts.

She opened her eyes. "Wild horses couldn't stop me."

"Then let's get going. I've got your favorite flaming red shade, and while I apply the polish, I'll catch you up on the family gossip."

After the beauty treatments were finished, Sophia followed Nela upstairs for a cup of tea. She swallowed the warm brew and smiled. "Ah, I've missed the heat flowing down my throat, my lips puckering with the hint of the lemon."

"It's funny what we take for granted."

"Savor everything, Nela, even something as small as drinking tea." She pushed a wayward curl aside from her granddaughter's face. "You really do take after my side of the family."

"Everyone sees the resemblance I hold to Mom."

"You are more like her now than ever, especially in that photo," she said, indicating a photograph of Nela and Guylan sitting on the buffet table. "Your beau is handsome."

"That was the picture we put in the newspaper to announce our engagement," Nela explained.

Sophia studied Guylan's face. "Those eyes, they're such a deep blue. Where have I seen eyes like his before?" Shrugging, she smiled. "Oh, well, it will come to me." She stood and stretched her arms above her head. "This old body of mine is so stiff and clumsy. I'm not used to being bogged down anymore."

Nela glanced at the clock on the wall, the one Sophia had given her with the timepiece inside the belly of a fat baker. "It's four in the morning, Gram. Would you like to get some rest? The others won't arrive until around nine."

"I've rested enough, sweet girl. But you go ahead and take your sleep."

"I'd rather spend the time with you." Nela stood and made her way to the entertainment center. "I bought this movie at a garage sale." She popped the disc into the DVD player. "One I think you'll like, a Hepburn and Tracy film."

"I'm anxious to see it, then," Sophia said as she walked to the sofa. "Those two were always my favorite. They just had some sort of magic chemistry together."

Nela chuckled. "Yeah, in real life they were having an affair."

"It's not right for us to judge, Nela." She kicked off her new shoes and put her feet up on the ottoman.

"I suppose you're right, Gram." Nela curled her legs beneath her and snuggled down next to Sophia.

"What have I always taught you?"

"To conduct myself in accordance," Nela said.

Mrs. Beasley joined them on the couch, her little pink nose sniffing the air, the hairs on her back rising.

Sophia locked eyes with the feline, taking it to task. "I guess you'll just have to get used to me all over again." She reached over and scratched the cat behind the ears. Mrs. Beasley relaxed and she chuckled. "That's a good girl." Then she reached for Nela's hand. "This is just like old times, my little darling...just like old times."

~ * ~

Guylan was surrounded by the silence again, along with a presence. Someone was watching him. He sat up in bed with a start and glanced over at the clock...it read 4:00 a.m. He pulled back the blanket and went to the window, looking down to the street below. The man with the top hat and cape stood on the corner, under the street lamp, gazing up at the window.

"You bastard! Who are you and what do you want?" he whispered. "Why don't you leave me alone?"

The stranger tipped his hat and strode away.

He closed the drapes and made his way back to bed, willing sleep to come. He had an early morning consultation at the clinic and later in the evening, dinner at Nela's.

Tonight, he was finally going to meet her grandmother.

Five

The sound of a pot crashing to the floor woke me. I sat up and looked around the room, startled.

Gram stood in the archway. "I'm sorry, Nela, for waking you. The pot just slipped out of my hand."

I rubbed my eyes and stood, stretching the stiffness from my bones. "What time is it?"

"Almost eight, and I want to get the tomato sauce going so it will have a long time to simmer before dinner."

Still a bit groggy, I followed her back into the kitchen and watched her rummage through the food in the refrigerator, moving a carton of milk to the top shelf and placing a lone apple in the bin drawer. "Did you get the hamburger for meatballs?"

"Should be right up front," I said.

Gram reached for the eggs, opened the carton and placed each one in the special egg section on the refrigerator's door. "Nela, I simply don't understand how you can live so unorganized." She turned to face me. "If a woman doesn't take pride in her own home, no one else will."

I frowned. "Because the eggs are in the carton instead of on the refrigerator door, I'm classified as not proud?"

"You're grasping at semantics," she snapped. "You know perfectly well what I mean." She grabbed the hamburger and went to the sink. "Your sarcasm doesn't wash with me. It didn't when you were a little girl and it doesn't now."

I remembered what did wash as a little girl—my mouth—out with soap whenever I sassed Gram.

"Conduct yourself in accordance, my dear," Gram warned.

I sighed and made myself a cup of tea and a piece of toast. While I munched on the stale rye bread, Gram busied herself around the kitchen, making her famous meatballs and tomato sauce with stuffed artichokes. The sun's rays streamed through the kitchen window above the sink, shining its heat on Gram's face. Her flesh began to warm and glow with a healthy hint of color, the gray hair suddenly turning a beautiful shade of silver. Though I'd seen the transformation before, it never ceased to amaze me how Gram thrived once back in her element.

"You've gotten all the groceries right," Gram praised. "I lack for nothing here." She turned toward me and smiled. "Which is good. I won't have to send you back to the store."

I returned the smile and kept quiet the fact that my mother was the real shopper who had stocked my kitchen two days ago with everything Gram would need.

"While I make the garlic bread and scrambled eggs for breakfast, you go and take a shower, Nela," Gram instructed.

I nodded and left her to do her thing in my kitchen.

I closed my eyes as the hot water cascaded down my back, and thought of a way to tell Guylan about our family blessing. Would he think it was a blessing? Or would he think my family was a bunch of freaks and take off running for the hills? After learning the way Gramps and my father had taken the news, I wasn't quite sure I wanted to put Guylan through the ordeal. Though I thought him to be a *keeper*, what would I do if I found out he wasn't?

I opened my eyes and looked down at my feet, curling my toes under to grip the wet porcelain of the tub. Some things are just not possible to accomplish. Would getting Guylan to understand my family's secret be an impossible task? Or would he embrace the difference and look at it as an adventure?

I stepped from the shower and dried myself, glancing at my naked reflection in the mirror. I turned from side to side, surveying my body. I wasn't a model, but the package was better than average... slender waist, full, perky boobs, arresting facial features. Wouldn't Guylan feel fortunate to have me as his wife?

I groaned and applied after-bath cream on my legs. Guylan wasn't a shallow man...that's what had made me fall in love with him. He was all about sharing and caring and wanting to be best friends as well as lovers. With him I could have a relationship like my parents and grandparents shared, the kind I'd yearned for and dreamed about all my life. Guylan was Prince Charming without the chauvinism, protective without being controlling. He valued honesty; how would he take the fact I hadn't been honest with him?

I sighed, realizing another aspect...I wasn't getting any younger. In December I would be turning thirty-four, and my biological clock wasn't just ticking...it was clanging loud and clear. If I didn't marry and have a child soon, a daughter, the blessing would end with me. This fact filled me with resentment. Yet, the burden of being the oldest was often cast upon me.

Growing up in a household with two younger sisters and a full-time working mother, I was always hearing: *"You're the oldest and should know better...we're depending on you to watch your sisters, to know what's right, to work along with us in caring for this family."*

I was just a kid then, too, but I carried a lot of weight on my shoulders. Now, nothing has changed. I sympathized with my grandfather and how it must have been for him, helping to raise his brothers. Next time I saw him, we were going to have a long, overdue talk.

It was unexpected when Gram opened the bathroom door, pulling me from my thoughts. "Nela, where do you keep the oregano?"

My first instinct was to cover myself with the towel.

Gram laughed. "You've got nothing new to me, sweetie. Who do you think it was who cared for you when your mother was expecting

Hannah and she was put on full bed rest?" She reached over and tweaked the cellulite living on my backside before repeating her question. "Where do you keep the oregano?"

"In the cupboard to the left of the sink, bottom shelf," I said, slipping on my panties.

Gram frowned. "I might be able to reach it. If not, I'll holler."

She shut the door behind her and I finished dressing.

~ * ~

Hannah hadn't slept well since Joe had been deployed to Iraq. The bed was just too large, empty and cold without him. For weeks after he'd left, she refused to change the bed coverings, keeping his scent upon the sheets and pillowcase.

She missed his arms around her, rubbing her breasts as she fell asleep, awaking to his kisses and the sensuous foreplay leading into passionate lovemaking.

When he left, a part of her had ripped away; her sense of belonging was lost with him being so far away and gone for so long. She had hoped, as the many months dragged on, it would get easier, but in truth she feared for his welfare now even more than she had in the beginning. She had grown up with Joe West. He'd been there through so many aspects and changes occurring in her life. He'd stuck out the trials, never left her side and wanted nothing more than to spend his life with her.

Hannah stretched and climbed out of bed. If she dallied, she'd never get to Nela's to see Gram. She opened the bedroom door and shouted down the hallway to her daughter. "Cara, you up?"

"Five more minutes," Cara snapped. "And don't keep ragging on me till then."

She rolled her eyes in frustration. Guiding a teen-child was exasperating at times, even more so without the other parent around to help.

"I'm getting back what I did to my own parents," she grumbled, making her way to the bureau. Atop the chest of drawers sat a picture of her and Joe on the boardwalk in Wildwood, New Jersey. She remembered the day as clearly as if it had happened yesterday.

It had been warm and humid, the smell of the ocean wafting on an occasional breeze.

Then she thought further back to the day she had met him...in Cooper's Market, where he worked bagging groceries. She'd gone in with her mother for feminine napkins, and their eyes met when she placed the box on the counter to be cashed out. Embarrassed to the ends of her hair and wishing the floor would open up and swallow her whole, she gazed elsewhere, but her eyes were drawn back to his. He flashed a lopsided, bad-boy grin and that was all it took...she was hooked, couldn't resist. But what chance did she have, a shy girl from Holy Cross of Christ School, with a jock from Temple High? Yet, a week later, to her enormous shock, Hannah found him sitting on the Catholic school steps, waiting for her to be dismissed.

He stood, hands shoved in his pants' pockets, flashing her that wry grin. "I'm Joe West."

The blood rushed to her head. "I'm Hannah...Hannah O'Riley."

He arched a blond brow. "Nice to meet you, Hannah O'Riley."

His dark eyes penetrated her soul, melted her heart. "What are you doing here?" Her voice sounded as erratic as her pulse. "And how did you know where I went to school?"

He removed a hand from a pocket and pushed aside the blond curl that had fallen across his forehead. "I wanted to meet you, and you were wearing your school uniform when you came into the store to buy—"

"Okay, okay," she interjected, not wanting him to finish his sentence. She frowned, as a mixture of anticipation and apprehension washed over her. Why would this guy seek her out? Was this a trick Marjorie Benson was playing on her? The upper classman had lost her seat to Hannah as music club chairman, and maybe this was how she was getting revenge.

"Why me?" she blurted out, then flinched as soon as she'd spoken the words.

Joe's eyes twinkled with a mischievous glint. "Because I think you're cute."

Her heart danced.

"Thought maybe you'd like to go have a pizza with me," he added.

"Now?" She felt a bit faint.

"Yeah." He reached for her backpack and slung it over his shoulder.

"Well, I can't. I just can't..." she stammered. "My parents, they would never let me...I mean, they don't know you." She swallowed hard. "I don't know you."

He shrugged. "What's to know?"

"Well, you could be a...a..."

"A thief, a murderer, the local rapist?" he finished the sentence for her.

"God, no," she gasped. "I didn't mean—"

"Didn't you?" he interjected. "Isn't that what parents always warn their daughters about when a guy is interested in them?"

She frowned. "You're not making this easy."

Joe chuckled, taking a step nearer. "Nope, and I don't intend to, Hannah O'Riley."

She raised her chin in defiance. "You don't intimidate me, Joe... whatever your name is."

"West, Joe West, and I'm not trying to intimidate you, Hannah. Just want to get to know you." Again, the devilish grin appeared. "Maybe even, eventually get to kiss you."

"Ugh," she shrieked aloud, but was thrilled inside over the kiss part. "Go east, young West," she quipped.

He screwed up his face. "Very funny, Hannah banana."

She stuck her tongue out at him.

He chuckled again. "Good comeback, very mature."

She flipped her long hair over her shoulder and reached for her backpack. "Leave me alone."

He tightened his grip on the satchel. "Can I at least walk you home?"

And that was how it had begun.

What proceeded then was every parent's nightmare...she understood now, as a parent of a teenaged girl. She lost her virginity at seventeen on Halloween night, 1993. It was the beginning of her senior year and she and Joe made love in the back seat of his clunker, a 1980 Chevy Camaro. For two years they had kept from going all the way, but that night he was dressed like a swashbuckling pirate, in tight black pants, a shirt opened to the waist, an eye patch and cape adding to his handsome looks. And when he said, *"I would love you now, señorita,"* her resolve and strict Catholic upbringing dissolved.

In spite of the cramped quarters, her one foot propped atop the front bucket seat and the other hitting the rear window, she opened herself to Joe. He pleasured her whole being, filling her with an intense and driven urgency she had never known existed. Her sweaty back stuck to the seat's vinyl covering, lips swollen and sore from his demanding kisses, and thighs moist and sticky with the aftermath of their lovemaking.

It was something she wanted to experience over and over again for the rest of time, this being the beginning, the greatest night of her life, a dream come true. But the day she had to tell her parents she was pregnant, that dream turned into a nightmare.

What would she do if Cara ever dropped a bomb like that on her?

Hannah had to quit school and get a G.E.D. instead of graduating with her class. Joe had graduated the year before, but he was never good in his studies and couldn't get a job that paid enough to support a wife and baby. The two of them struggled. If it weren't for her parents allowing them to live free in the basement apartment and her grandmother bringing them meals, they wouldn't have survived.

Then Joe joined the National Guard and when his training period ended, further education was paid for. He chose a trade college, where he learned carpentry and masonry. He started a construction company of his own and as business increased, they were able to rent a small house a few blocks away from her folks and buy a used car. Everything seemed to flourish and, just as they'd decided to purchase a home of their own, Joe was called to serve his country. With Joe gone, the business began to crumble. Soon all was lost, and once again Hannah had moved into her parents' basement apartment.

"Oh, JoJo, your Hannah banana misses you," she whispered, grabbing clothes from a drawer and heading for the shower. She met Cara in the hallway. She pushed aside a strand of strawberry blonde hair from her daughter's forehead. "Still have a sore throat?"

"Yup," Cara mumbled.

"Then you take the bathroom first," she offered, "and I'll fix you a warm water and salt gargle for you to do after your shower."

Cara curled up her nose. "Uck."

"It will help, trust me." Hannah set her clothes on a nearby kitchen chair and made her way to the cupboard for a glass. "And before you take anything to reduce a fever, I want to take your temperature."

Cara frowned. "Thermometers make me gag."

She sighed. "Please don't be uncooperative today, Cara, there isn't the time."

"I said thermometers make me gag," Cara repeated and slammed the bathroom door.

Hannah sighed again. What did Joe always call Cara, Star Shine? She rolled her eyes and whispered, "More like Star Shit."

~ * ~

Alana stood beneath the shower spigot, head back and eyes closed, as the warm water cascaded down her neck.

The shower curtain opened, followed by a soft request. "Mind if I join you?"

She turned to face her lover and smiled, stepping back to make room. Face to face the two stood, the warm water sandwiched between their breasts, Beth's tinier than hers, with nipples a darker shade of rose.

Beth's hands rested on Alana's hips, pulling her closer. "I'll miss you while you're at your sister's."

Alana looked deep into Beth's amber eyes, their tender gaze stirring her senses. "Come with me, then."

Beth dropped her eyes to Alana's mouth. "Not today. You need to tell them without me there."

"I've already told my sisters," she admitted.

"And you don't think they've already said something to your parents?"

She shook her head. "They're good at keeping family secrets."

Beth, a head taller than Alana, bent to kiss the tip of her nose. "And what about you, are you keeping any family secrets?"

Alana's heart raced. She had only kept one from Beth...about the blessing. But she needed to take one coming-out at a time. Clearing her throat, she changed the topic. "How did you begin when you told your parents you are...you have..."

"An alternative lifestyle," Beth interjected with a smile.

"Yes," Alana said.

"It's not as if I had the plague, Alana," Beth teased.

"I know, it's just I've only come to accept what I am, myself. How do I make my parents and my grandmother understand?" She sighed. "Coming from an Italian/Irish/Catholic household...well, this isn't going to be easy."

"It never is, no matter what type of household you come from," Beth reflected. "Just start with the truth, Alana. No one can deny you the truth." Beth's hand wandered down to the juncture of her thighs. "Have you washed here yet?"

There was a tingling in the pit of her stomach. "No."

Beth's long, dark lashes swept down across her cheekbones; her reply was breathless. "Then let me do it for you."

Alana, powerless to resist, spread her legs wide in response and smiled.

~ * ~

My mother, my sister, Hannah, and my niece, Cara, arrived around nine. Cara's metamorphosis after her recent fourteenth birthday was comparable to Dr. Jekyll and Mr. Hyde. The dreaded teen years had infiltrated her innocent body like an enemy army, the alteration turning the sweet little girl we all knew and loved into a moody, self-absorbed bitch.

My mother hugged Gram, holding long onto the embrace. "Mom, I've missed you so much."

Gram kissed her only child and wiped the tears from her eyes. "Gloria, you look tired."

"Gee, I'd better return that expensive eye cream," my mother joked.

"This isn't a laughing matter, Gloria."

"Work's been hectic," Mom said.

Gram frowned. "I thought you said last year you were going to retire."

My mother shook her head. "Just couldn't do it, Ma, with Alana still in college."

"That's what happens when you have a baby late in life...you're old when they're still young," Gram quipped. She searched her daughter's face. "You need vitamin C. Go into the kitchen and pour yourself a tall glass of orange juice."

My mother obeyed as though she were still a child.

Gram turned her attention to Hannah, and gave her a hug. "And how's things with you, Miss Hannah?"

When my sister was little and visited Gram, she had loved poking around in an old trunk filled with clothes. Hannah, dressed in a drop-waist dress adorned by a feathered hat upon her head, would put on a show for Gram. It was the *Miss Hannah Show*, starring Hannah O'Riley. From that time on, Gram always called my sister, Miss Hannah.

Hannah sighed. "It's been a hard year, with Joe in Iraq and my daughter not giving a crap for what I say."

"Being a single parent can't be easy," Gram sympathized. "And I'm sure you're scared for Joe, as well as missing him."

"All true," Hannah agreed.

"But you're a smart gal, honey, and you have to pull it together. I'm positive you've got the right stuff," Gram encouraged.

Hannah flopped down beside Cara on the sofa and sighed again, pulling from her purse a digital thermometer. "Yeah, right. I can't even get my daughter to take her temperature."

Gram turned her attention to Cara, who sat sulking. "Aren't you feeling well, Cara?"

Cara shook her head. "I've gotta sore throat."

"This is the third time in two months," Hannah explained. "Friday, I took her to the doctor, and he doesn't want to administer antibiotics as quickly as he did before. The new mindset is not to squelch the immune system. Constant use of antibiotics won't give the system a chance to become strong. So he told me to keep track of her temperature. If it gets too high, then he'll prescribe something."

Gram agreed. "Sounds like a wise plan to me." She turned to Cara. "It's obvious you have a problem with all that?"

"The thermometer under the tongue makes me feel like puking," Cara mumbled.

Gram turned away from Cara and toward me, giving a wink of her eye. "Nela, do you still have that special thermometer?"

I instantly knew what Gram was about to do. "Yes, in the bathroom medicine cabinet."

Gram made her way to the sofa and took Cara by the hand. "I know just how to solve your problem."

Cara followed behind Gram, turning to cast a smug look at her mother before entering the bathroom.

Hannah and I looked at each other, burst out laughing and together counted aloud backward from the number five. Three... two...and on the number one, Cara raced from the bathroom and flung herself onto the sofa.

"Did you get your temperature taken?" Hannah inquired, struggling to keep a straight face.

"No," Cara snapped.

"Gram's way won't gag you."

Cara folded her arms across her chest. "Yeah, well, I'm not doing it *that* way either."

Hannah prodded further. "Why not?"

Cara's cheeks turned scarlet. "Because, Great-Gram wanted to shove the thermometer up my butt, the baby way. I'm too old to have it done like that."

Gram came into the room, hands on hips. "Your mother was your age when I took her temperature that way."

Cara gasped. "Really, Mom?"

Hannah began to explain. "I had been sick with the flu for days and my parents had to attend Aunt Alana's kindergarten moving up ceremony, so Gram came to take care of me."

Cara's voice rose an octave. "And you just let her do it to you?"

Hannah shrugged. "I didn't have much choice. I was as sick as a dog, lying half-dead on my belly in bed, when Gram came into my room, ripped off the blanket, yanked down my pajama bottoms and inserted the thermometer."

Cara shuddered. "This family is weird."

My mother laughed as she entered the room. "Oh, honey, you have no idea."

Cara's eyes widened. "No one's touching my butt."

"And that's part of your problem with this child, Hannah," Gram scolded. "If you had taken her over your knee a time or two when she was younger and reddened that part of her anatomy, she'd be more civil to you now."

Gram cast a glance my way and I stifled a smile, remembering the story of Gramps and my father she'd told me earlier. I guess you're never too old for a spanking.

Hannah sighed, exasperated. "Things are different now, Gram, than when Mom was a kid. You can be hauled away on child abuse charges if you do stuff like that to your children."

"Hauled away for giving your own child a well-deserved spanking?" Gram asked, appalled.

Hannah continued. "The child experts are finding such discipline causes sexual issues, bed wetting and other anger problems in a kid's life as they mature."

Gram turned to my mother. "Gloria, have you got sexual issues, do you wet the bed or have anger problems because your behind got whacked when you were bad?"

My mother sat back in her chair and crossed her legs. "Can't think of any."

"There, you see," Gram said.

Hannah held up her hands. "I'm just telling you how it is now, Gram."

"How come you didn't spank us, Mom?" I asked my mother.

She folded her hands in her lap. "I didn't have to. One look from your father and you girls obeyed. And when your father wasn't around, I threatened to call him."

"I remember, when I was older, being grounded from the mall," I said.

My mother arched a brow. "That worked, too."

Gram shook her head. "You had Brian standing with you, Gloria. Hannah's doing this all alone for now." She pointed to Cara. "You can't let that child run amok."

My mother stood and went to Gram. "Come on, Ma, I'll help you set the table."

Gram nodded and the two left the room.

Hannah grabbed the digital thermometer from her purse and handed it to her daughter. "Under the tongue, now!"

Cara shook her head and clamped her lips shut.

My sister's rage turned her cheeks red. She glanced my way. "Do you think, between the four of us, we could manage to take her temperature Gram's way?"

Another ploy...instantly I went along. "I don't see why not."

Cara's embarrassment turned to raw fury. "You're all sick!"

"No, you're sick," Hannah countered. "And the only way you're going to get well is if you let me take care of you."

"Your grandfather and Aunt Alana are due to arrive here at any moment," I added. "I don't think you'd like it much if they found you lying face down on the sofa with your pants—"

"Okay, okay," Cara interrupted, grabbing the thermometer from her mother. "This really sucks." She glared at her mother. "Don't blame me, then, if I puke all over Aunt Nela's floor."

Six

Guylan's efforts to save Patches, the elderly Dachshund, paid off. The little dog woke from anesthesia, coming through the surgery to remove her spleen with flying colors. "Call Mrs. Granville, Betty," he instructed his assistant. "And let her know Patches is awake. She's not out of the woods yet, but so far, so good."

Betty nodded in agreement. "There's a call for you on line four."

Guylan pulled off the latex gloves and threw them in the trash bin. "Please put it through to my office phone."

Sister Margaret's voice on the line was hurried. "I've got the book, Guylan. Can you meet me at the little Italian café on Logan Street, Villa Maria's, in two hours?"

He glanced at his watch. Already it was nearing noon, and there were several patients left to see. "It looks like I'll be here till around four; can you meet me by four-thirty?"

Sister Margaret sighed. "If that's the best you can do, but not a moment later, Guylan. The less time I have this book in my possession, the better."

He frowned. "It can't be all that upsetting, Sister."

"Upsetting would be a *nice* word for it, Guylan," she retorted. "Just be on time."

He hung up and an icy chill crept down his spine. What sort of book had his birth folks left that warranted Mother Superior to demand it be burned and disturbed Sister Margaret?

The loud buzzing of the intercom brought him from his thoughts. He pressed the button. "Yes, Betty?"

"Your next patient is in exam room three, Dr. Quinn."

"Thank you, I'll be right in." Again, he glanced at his watch and hoped he could stay focused on the day's work instead of wondering what the hell was in that book.

Seven

After breakfast, Hannah sat on the back porch, smoking a cigarette.

"Those things will kill you," Nela commented, joining her sister on the porch swing. Hannah exhaled a puff of smoke and Nela waved a hand in front of her nose, feigning a cough. "Not to mention the rest of us, from the second-hand smoke."

"Well, right now, with Joe fighting a war and me being here with the kid from hell, I'll die if I don't smoke." She dropped the cigarette in a glass of water on a nearby table. "You need to get an ashtray."

"You need to quit," Nela said, giving a disgusted look at the floating cigarette butt.

Hannah screwed up her nose. "Bite me."

"No thanks. You're full of nicotine."

"And you're full of shit," Hannah countered.

"Speaking of...where is brat face?" Nela teased.

"Taking a nap on your spare room bed." She lit up another cigarette.

Nela moved to the wicker chair opposite her. "How'd you explain to Joe about the family blessing?"

Hannah sat back in the swing. "Well, you've got to remember, I met Joe when I was Cara's age." Her eyes widened. "God, that's a scary thought. I was my daughter's age when I met her father." What she and Joe had done circled her thoughts. Maybe she should lock Cara in a barred tower and throw away the key? She shook her head to clear it. "Anyway, when Mom explained the whole thing to me, I went running to blab it all to Joe, and in our own little flaky teen brains, we thought the whole thing was rather cool. It didn't really affect us, since I was daughter number two, and after a while it just became something we both grew up with." She glanced out the window, the second-story enclosed porch affording her a view of yards and gardens. "And Cara was born into knowing, so she doesn't think twice about any of it."

Nela sighed. "Wish it were as easy for me to tell Guylan as it was for you to tell Joe."

"You haven't told him yet?" Hannah turned to look at her sister.

"No, not yet, but he's coming for dinner tonight. I plan on telling him then, after he's met Gram."

She laughed. "Well, good luck, big sister."

Nela chewed her bottom lip. "That's the same reaction I got from Gram."

"What'd you get from me?" Gram questioned, stepping out onto the porch.

Nela waved her hand casually in the air, brushing the subject aside. "We're just talking about Guylan."

Gram sat beside Hannah on the porch swing. "Yes, well, it's a tad too late for any other course of action, so we might as well be supportive of what lies ahead and conduct ourselves in accordance."

Nela frowned. "I guess so."

Gram reached over and gave Hannah's arm an affectionate pat. "What's swirling around in that pretty brain of yours, Miss Hannah?"

She sighed. "I'm worried for Joe. I watch the news, and every day our guys are getting killed by suicide bombers in that hell hole. I'm scared Joe won't come back."

Gram sat back and crossed her short, stubby legs. "Your worrying won't add an ounce of prevention to what happens. What will be, will be. But, prayer, doing the best you can on the home front and not watching the news will get you through."

Hannah looped a long auburn curl around her ear. "I worry about the home front, too."

Gram cocked her head sideways. "Why is that, Hannah?"

Tears welled in her eyes. "It will all work out, Gram." She forced a smile. "You won't have a time with us all for another year and I'm not going to spoil this day with my troubles."

"What is it, Hannah?" Gram probed. "I want to hear everything."

She swallowed the tears burning the back of her throat. "When Joe left, the construction company he'd started was beginning to grow and we weren't doing too bad. We even thought about buying our own home. But now, with him being gone almost a year, the company's died and all our hopes and endeavors have been smashed." She took another cigarette from the pack and stuck it between her lips.

Gram leaned over and ripped the filter-tip from Hannah's mouth, throwing it in the glass. "That won't help, honey."

Hannah clasped her hands in her lap. "I've had to leave the house we were renting and move into the two-bedroom basement apartment at my parents' home. And because I have no skills, I work for minimum wage at a deli warehouse." She stood and moved to the far end of the porch, looking down at the row of silver trash cans lining the side alley below. She swallowed the lump of fear and loneliness hard. How she missed Joe.

"But you do have a skill, sweetie," Gram said.

She met her grandmother's gaze, throwing her hands in the air with her exasperation. "What, Gram...what's my skill?"

"Do you still have the accreditation certificate for achieving ten years of classical music and composition at the Sophia DelFino's School of Piano?"

Hannah nodded. "But that's not going to get me anywhere."

Gram gasped. "I beg to differ, young lady. I founded that school. It was certified by the state of New York and many of the pupils I taught have received recognition for their achievements."

"Because they all went on to a higher education," she pointed out.

Gram's voice was stern. "Look, Hannah, you're a concert pianist, versed in the finest works in the classical repertoire, as well as the legacy of the composer. Not all piano teachers delve into the craft with such extensive content."

She rolled her eyes heavenward. "Yeah, Gram, I'm sure today's kids care that Mozart was one of seven children, took to playing the piano at four years old, produced an enormous output of music in his short life, yet died penniless." She sighed. "Yada, yada, yada."

"But they should care," Gram countered. "If they're playing the man's creations, they should know his first name was Wolfgang and understand that his enthusiasm for music was boundless. They should learn of the heartbreak he suffered when he fell in love with Aloysia Weber and lost her, only to marry her sister Constanze instead, the two going on to have seven children, with only two surviving infancy." She searched Hannah's face. "This was a man who walked the face of the earth as you and I do, and with such a passion for music, all else he endured could not pull him from his dream of being a composer. Two hundred and seventeen years after the man's death, his songs are still being taught, still being played, still making hearts swell. This is what music appreciation is, Hannah, and you have that to give."

Hannah bit her bottom lip to keep her emotions in control.

"But where would she work, Gram?" Nela asked.

Gram turned her attention to Nela. "Remember the flyer I discovered in the terminal's window, the one about my former student, Dana Clair?"

"I remember."

"Well, she might be Hannah's answer." Gram turned to Hannah. "She's just opened a studio on the corner of Seventh and Pine, not more than a block away from Cara's junior high school. If you could land a position there, you'd be able to drop Cara to school on your way to work. There's no doubt you'd be paid twice what you make at the deli warehouse, and after school Cara could walk to the studio, do her homework or read in the lobby, and accompany you home at quitting time."

"Sounds too perfect," Hannah groaned. "This Clair woman probably wouldn't even give me a second look."

Gram frowned. "Well, with a negative attitude like that, probably not. But if you go into the studio on Monday morning and tell her where you studied, and that you're my granddaughter, I'm sure Dana will listen."

"You never know till you try, Hannah," Nela added.

Hannah wiped the tears lacing her lashes with a swipe of a hand. "You're right. And I have this Monday off from work, too." She frowned. "Let's hope Cara's feeling well enough to go to school."

"Right after dinner, you take her home, make her gargle with warm water and salt and take a couple aspirin, rub menthol on her throat, and before she goes to bed, give her an enema."

Hannah's mouth gaped wide. "An enema? She has a sore throat, how's an enema going to help?"

"Cleanses away the germs from the body, ridding the system of infection, and the fever breaks," Gram said. "My mother cured me from fever many times with an enema. It works every time."

"Like Cara's going to go for that one," she said, not even wanting to imagine how she'd get her daughter to agree to such a process.

"She's a child, Hannah...your child," Gram said. "You have to take control and do what's best for her. If you don't, she'll be the one in charge, and heaven forbid that should happen."

It was then that Brian came to the door. Hannah thought her father was still a formidable man, in spite of his recent heart attack. Standing at six feet tall, with a thick shock of auburn hair framing a handsome, freckled face, he was the quiet strength of the family.

He opened the screen door and motioned Sophia inside. "Gloria and I are waiting to have the traditional game of Canasta with you."

Gram stood. "Well, now, deal away."

~ * ~

Alana joined me and Hannah after Gram left. Her short, copper curls bounced as she made her way to where Gram had sat. Alana stretched and yawned. "I'm so glad this semester is nearly at an end. After graduation, I'm thinking of going someplace where I can help starving children."

"Stick around, you may need to feed Cara," Hannah wisecracked.

"No, I'm serious," Alana said. "I've been doing a lot of thinking about the world's hunger situation and I would like to go with my friend Beth and see what I can do to help. Maybe go to Guatemala or Africa."

"Beth...*thee* Beth?"

"Thee one and only Beth," she snapped.

"You haven't told Mom and Dad yet that you and she are... are..." Hannah's voice trailed off.

"Lovers, mates," Alana supplied. "No, they don't know yet." She stood. "I'm pretty good at Canasta. Think I'll see if they could use another player."

After Alana left the porch, I turned to Hannah. "Guess we upset her."

Hannah shrugged. "She's going to have to thicken her skin sooner or later if she wants to live her life the way she desires."

I sighed. "Why does everything have to be so complicated?"

"You're thinking of what lies ahead of you with Guylan, aren't you?" Hannah said.

I narrowed my eyes at her. "Oh, you think you're so smart, knowing what's in my head."

Hannah reached for a cigarette and lit it, taking a long puff. "It's not hard to guess, Nela." She swished the smoke in her mouth and blew out a ring. "And if you don't get your act together, the family blessing will end with you."

I laughed to cover my annoyance. "In this day and age, a woman doesn't have to be married to get pregnant."

"True." Hannah's tone was low, patient. "But have you thought of the possibility you might not be able to get pregnant?"

"Why wouldn't I be able to get pregnant?" I said, light bitterness in my voice.

Hannah drew on her cigarette and blew out the smoke before she spoke. "Well, look at the female track record in this family." She proceeded to explain. "Great-grandma was in her thirties before Gram was born and she had several miscarriages before the other two boys came along. Gram tried to get pregnant for seven years before Mom was born, and after, she had three miscarriages. And Mom waited years before she got pregnant with you and had to be very careful when she finally did. Three years later, she was on full bed rest with me and I was born premature. Then it took nine years before Alana came along." She put out the cigarette and stood, looking down at the yard below. "I got pregnant after the first time, wouldn't you know. I mean, Joe and I were just kids. But when Cara was three, we tried for Joe's boy…he wants a son so bad. And it never happened." Hannah turned to look at me. "Cara's fourteen and still nothing's happened."

The pattern was clear. "I get the picture."

"Alana's still having female trouble, even after she had the one ovary removed last summer. But the blessing doesn't pertain to anyone but you, so the pressure's off me and Alana."

"Thanks for pointing that out," I snapped.

Hannah softened her tone. "I didn't mean to upset you, but the truth is you're not getting any younger, Nela."

I stood to face her. "Don't you think I have thought of all that?" I rubbed my hands over my face in my agitation. "And then there's the added possibility I'd have a boy first, and couldn't have any more." I opened my arms wide. "But what's the answer here, Hannah? We can't predict these things."

Hannah reached out and embraced me, the smell of stale smoke lingering in her hair and clothes. "I know, I know," she sympathized. "It's all a crap shoot."

Our conversation was brought to an end by Mom's call to us to join them all in the kitchen. When I entered the room, Mom motioned for me to take a chair beside her, and then indicated the one to my father's left for Hannah. Gram sat opposite me and Alana to her right. "What's this all about?" I asked, searching my mother's solemn expression.

"I have something I need to tell you all." My mother glanced at my father, who in turn, looked deep into her eyes and rubbed her shoulder.

A strange feeling enveloped me, a sensation someone might experience in waking to find a dreaded nightmare was real. I didn't want to hear the rest of my mother's words, because somehow, I knew...with the way she looked so tired...they wouldn't be bringing good news. I bit my bottom lip and braced myself for what was to come.

"Last week," Mom began, fiddling with a deck of cards stacked on the table. "Last week," she repeated, gathering the courage to finish her sentence. "I found a lump in my left breast."

My father remained quiet, but I saw him stiffen; the muscles at his jaw throbbed and I worried for his welfare. Not too long ago he'd suffered a near-fatal heart attack. How would my mother's news affect his own health?

My eyes roamed the table. Hannah, with her already fair complexion, looked paler. Alana's emerald green eyes welled with tears, her full lips thinning. Gram, with the sunlight from a nearby window casting a glow onto her silver hair, sat with large, brown eyes fixed on my mother. Folding her hands upon the table, one thumb moved back and forth over the other.

"Should I wake Cara?" Hannah asked.

My mother shook her head. "You can explain things to her later, after my doctor appointment on Monday, when I know more."

"Good, you're already on this, then," Gram said, relieved.

"I'll come with you," my father proclaimed, the vein down the center of his forehead bulging with the concerned wrinkle of his brow. His fair complexion had colored to a deep red with his agitation.

"Brian, I don't want you to tax yourself or get upset," my mother advised.

"Gloria, I'm fine," he assured her. "And I'm not going to let you go through any of this alone." He forced a smile. "You were there for me."

"Both of you calm down," Gram chimed in. "First, it could be just a fibroid. My side of the family has been prone to have those fatty tissues." She leaned forward. "I'm glad you are aware of your body's changes, Gloria. I'm sure whatever the situation, you've caught it in time."

My mother forced a smile. "I'm sure of it too, Mom."

My father's hand traveled up to rest on my mother's hair. He stroked the thick, dark curls. I knew what he was thinking...if she needed chemo, the beautiful crop of ebony adorning her stunning face would be gone.

She turned to look at him. "We'll get through this, Brian."

My mother was a trooper, always making things easier for her family. "It will all be all right, Mom," I added, knowing deep down she had to be frightened.

"Damn right it will," my father said, pulling her closer and kissing the tip of her nose.

I admired my parents' relationship and the glue holding them together. I'd always hoped one day I'd experience a love like theirs. For a selfish moment, I thought of my own dilemma with Guylan. Would he be as supportive of my situation?

"There's more for you to do on this earth, Gloria," Gram announced with an air of confidence. "Trust me on this."

"Do you truly know such things, Gram?" Hannah asked, leaning forward in her seat.

I caught my sister's eye and understood what had fueled her question. If Gram had an insight, could she know what would happen to Joe? Hannah worried about how he'd come home to her...walking, not walking, or in a casket. My insides shuttered at the thought of the latter.

"Just trust me," Gram said again, ignoring Hannah's question.

"I have some news to tell everyone, too," Alana offered, her eyes wandering around the table to each of our faces.

I knew what she was about to divulge, and inside I groaned, resenting that she'd use this time as an opportunity to *come out*. She was always a selfish girl. Being the youngest, we all spoiled her, let her have her own way more times than not. And now, she needed to be the center of attention again, but of all times. Then again, what better chance would there be? With everyone so upset and frightened for my mother, the news of Alana's new lifestyle might not seem so drastic, or so she hoped, I'm sure.

Gram's polite nod encouraged Alana. "We're listening, my dear."

Alana took an audible breath. "I'm gay."

Gram reached over and gave Alana's hand an affectionate pat. "Good for you. Staying positive is always best. You'll be a good comfort to your mother."

Alana frowned.

I stifled a laugh.

My mother's eyes widened. "That's not what she means. She means she's—"

"I'm in love with Beth," Alana cut in.

If my mother's news hadn't given my father another heart attack, Alana's would. The forehead vein looked like it was ready to pop. "Beth...your roommate, Beth?"

"Yes," Alana said.

"Brian, don't get so upset," my mother consoled, caressing the side of his face with the back of a hand.

He ignored her. "What the hell are you thinking, Alana? Or aren't you?"

Damn it, Alana! Why did you pick now to tell them?

Hannah read my thoughts, as she often did. There was a bond between us that Alana and I didn't have. "Ya know, little sister, this wasn't really the time to bare all," she admonished.

Gram, picking up on today's meaning of *gay,* glared at Alana. "I'd like to bare something...your little behind, and then redden it till you can't sit. Maybe that will knock some sense into you."

"I second that motion," my father agreed. "And when you're done, Sophia, I'll take over."

Though the whole thing was anything but funny, I again stifled a laugh, remembering earlier Gram telling me about my father's spanking from Gramps. I was sure Dad was thinking along the same lines and considering the outcome of a sound spanking.

Alana, eyes filling with tears, shifted in her chair. "I can't believe how you're taking this. I mean, it's not like I've got the plague."

"I think I could handle the plague," my father snapped.

Alana broke down in sobs. "I'm sorry if I'm different, if I'm not what you want me to be. But this is how things are and if you can't accept me for what I am—" she stood, her chair scraping along the linoleum floor.

My mother reached over and halted her escape. "Sit, Alana."

Alana hesitated.

"Please, honey," my mother pleaded. "Walking away from a situation never solves it."

Gram's demeanor softened. "She's right, Alana, and I'm sorry for snapping at you the way I did. I should have conducted myself in accordance."

Alana hesitated before she reclaimed her seat. "I know my way isn't yours and I understand how this shocks you. I'm sorry for that, really I am, but I'm still me, still the same person I was twenty minutes ago. I'm still part of this family and I still love you all." She struggled with the next words. "But now, I love Beth, too."

My father covered his face with his hands.

My mother rested her head upon his shoulder and Gram sighed.

Hannah and I caught each other's eye and everyone remained silent, until Cara walked in to the kitchen.

Still groggy from her nap, Cara's eyes scanned the room. "What's going on?"

Eight

Villa Maria was a quaint café. Red checked cloths covered the round tables and matching curtains adorned the windows. Each drape panel was pulled back with tie cords, allowing the late afternoon light to nourish the plants hanging on hooks and resting on sills.

Guylan spotted Sister Margaret sitting in a booth to the far end of the eatery. Her navy-blue dress and scarf trimmed with white stood out among the other patrons' clothing. He took the seat opposite the elderly nun and forced a smile. "Thank you, Sister, for all your help."

"You might not thank me in the end, Guylan," she mumbled, pushing a package wrapped in a brown paper bag across the table.

He began to open the package, but she reached out to still his hands. "Not here. Not in front of me," she said in a lowered voice.

He raised his gaze to meet hers. "What in God's name is in this book that's gotten you so spooked?"

"Not in God's name, Guylan," she responded, her voice quivering. Her eyes went to the package he held, and then returned to his face. "Be careful," she said, and stood.

"Wait." He stood to face her.

She shook her head and made her way to the door, leaving him staring after her in stunned silence.

"Can I help you, sir?" A waiter approached.

He shook his head and walked past the attendant, out the café door and to his car. Placing the package on the seat beside him, he debated whether to open it there or at his apartment. He touched the paper wrapper, and then pulled his hand away. In a final decision, he started up the car and drove home, bringing the package to his tiny den and placing it upon the oak, roll-top desk he'd rescued from a garage sale. With trembling fingers, he unveiled the book from its paper container, staring for a moment at the raven etched on the front leather cover. Bringing his hand up to the volume, he compared it to the one on his ring. It was an exact copy.

The immediate hush in the room caused him to hesitate before opening the book. He knew the unnatural quiet meant the caped stranger was nearby. If he were to stand, make his way to the window and look down, he knew he'd see the same figure that had haunted him for months, gazing up at him from the street corner.

He traced the outline of the raven's body, the leather's grain worn and smelling musty. After opening the cover with care, he ran his hand over the smooth, yellowed page that held the family name of MacRaven. Another page showed a family tree. At the top was the name Ian MacRaven, wedded to Katrina McDougal. From their names branched out Sean MacRaven, wedded to Fanny McFarlin. Sean's son Daniel MacRaven wed Jennifer Casey and their son Quentin MacRaven wed Adorna Hawthorne. From there, another name branched out...Olena MacRaven, wedded to Zackery Sincloud. It appeared there was a second offspring from Quentin and Adorna, but the entry was crossed out with a heavy, black ink line and Guylan couldn't make out the name. From Olena's name came Xavior Sincloud, wedded to DeYonna Grayson, and then lastly, two more from Xavior's name, Audra and Guylan Sincloud.

His eyes rested on his name. "My name is Guylan Sincloud," he whispered. "And I have a sister...or I had a sister." He felt numbed and jubilant all at once. Then he turned to the page with the heading,

Blessings Bestowed. Here was a list of family names. He read each one, stopping at the group he recognized: *Sophia and Henry DelFino, Gloria and Brian O'Riley.* A cold chill crept down his spine.

Why are Nela's family's names written in this book?

Below the names there was a decree written in beautiful script. It read:

> *I bestow upon the head of these families a*
> *blessing carried on through each generation from*
> *first daughter to first daughter and also bequeath*
> *the blessing to their husbands. This award is for*
> *a service performed to me or for a member of my*
> *family. I decree the blessing will take place upon the*
> *first Saturday in May of every year, at the time of*
> *Beltane, when the veil is thinned between this world*
> *and the one of the hereafter, making the journey*
> *passable. Then these families will unite for a time of*
> *forty-eight hours in a joyous reunion.*
> *Signed, Quentin MacRaven.*

His stomach churned.

What the hell was all this about, and what service had Nela's family done for Quentin MacRaven?

Turning to another page, there was an index, listing spells and remedies in alphabetical order...ones for *aggravating instances, ailing body parts, bothersome warts,* and so on, right down to *yeast infections* and *zoning problems.*

Reading on, he also discovered a section dedicated to the *mystical mysteries of magic,* a *book of secrets.* When the cell phone rang, he nearly jumped out of his skin. Its tone broke the eerie silence surrounding him, pulling him from his thoughts. Slamming the book shut, he reached into his pocket for the phone.

"Are you still planning on coming for dinner?" Nela asked.

He glanced at his watch. It was nearing seven; he was already a half hour late to arrive at Nela's house. "Yeah, sorry honey, I just got involved in something," he apologized.

"How much longer do you think you'll be?"

He stood. "I'm on my way."

"Oh, and Guylan," she added. "After dinner we need to talk, in private. There's something I need to tell you."

He eyed the book in front of him. "Me too, honey...me too."

~ * ~

When Guylan arrived and I met him at the door, my stomach rose to my throat. I did my best to squelch the anxiety. This was Guylan, my Guylan, the man who in the last year had become both confidant and lover, not to mention my best friend. Why, then, did I think he would be an ogre once he learned about my family's blessing?

At the dinner table, I sat Guylan beside Gram, knowing she'd win him over with her stories and sense of humor...and she did. By the end of dinner, Gram had allowed Guylan to convince her to play a piece on the piano.

We all followed Gram into the living room and sat around the piano, which stood in the corner, covered with family photos. Gram opened the lid and slid her fingers over the keys, warming up with scales and little ditty tunes, as was customary for her. The classical piece she chose was Mozart's Piano Concerto No. 21, a slow-moving melody known to lull the listener into another dimension. For just a few moments, the piece shifts from a serene tune to one with uneasy traces. Then the major and minor keys intermingle together to reassert the tranquility of the principal once more.

Hannah and I glanced at each other, a quiet understanding passing between us. There was the connotation of a lesson in Gram's lyrical entertainment, bringing us to focus on the quiet before the storm. After the havoc, everything will even out and we'll all move ahead with our lives, no matter the outcome. We would endure my mother's breast lump, Dad's heart attack, Alana's sexual preference, Joe being in Iraq, Cara's teen years, and Guylan's attitude toward the family blessing. In any instance, we would all survive, and that was what mattered most.

After Gram's little recital, Hannah was the first to leave. She hugged Gram, the embrace long. "Thanks for the job tip, Gram. I'll go to see Dana Clair first thing on Monday."

Gram caressed Hannah's face. "You'll do fine, Miss Hannah, just don't give up." She placed a hand over her heart. "Take yourself to the center of your balance and move out from that quiet place with your confidence refreshed, then conduct yourself in accordance." She embraced Cara, looping a long strand of hair behind her ear. "Do you know who you were named after?"

"Aunt Nela, who is my baptismal godmother. Caralena is her middle name," Cara said.

"Well, that's true, but Caralena was my grandmother's middle name as well," Gram said.

Cara frowned. "Wasn't she a witch or something?"

Gram laughed. "Well, she had something mystical about her and conjured up premonitions of things to come, but I wouldn't go so far as to call her a witch." She gave Cara a kiss. "Be good to your mother, child. She needs your support during this difficult time."

When Hannah hugged me, I whispered in her ear. "Good luck de-germinating Little Miss Star Shine."

Hannah giggled. "Maybe I'll just bake a laxative into cookie dough. It worked for Byron Foster."

When Hannah and I were in high school, Byron had robbed the girls' lockers of desserts stashed in lunch bags. Hannah and a few other girls, who had been the victims of Byron's sweet tooth, baked up a batch of chocolate chip cookies, substituting the chips with a chocolate laxative.

I laughed. "Be careful how much you use. Byron was out of school for three days and looked like he'd lost five pounds."

When I shut the door behind them, I couldn't help but feel positive for Hannah. I was sure she'd land the job at Dana's music studio, and be on her way to financial security. When Joe came home from Iraq, she might even have a little nest egg saved for them to start over.

I caught the tail end of my mother's conversation as I re-joined the family at the kitchen table. Mom was explaining to Guylan why we were holding the reunion in my cramped flat. "It's tradition to have the yearly reunion at my house, which is much bigger than Nela's. But because an old oak tree fell through the kitchen window after the violent storm we had two weeks ago, we're having reconstruction done...everything is a mess."

"Gram loves to cook," I added, "and everyone knew a torn-up kitchen wouldn't suffice, so we moved the plans here."

"And you're a wonderful cook at that, Mrs. DelFino," Guylan praised. "I've never tasted tomato sauce so delicious."

Gram beamed. "Please, call me Gram, and the trick is to simmer the sauce with the meat all day." She smiled. "Let me explain to you, Guylan, that for Italian folks, the grandmother's home is the family gathering place. On Sunday, Gloria would bring the girls for the *rounds* before returning home, and what this meant was a stop at Gram's house for after-church dessert. The girls, wearing their black patent leather shoes, little pink toppers during spring months or faux fur jackets with matching muffs during the winter time, would run into the kitchen. In no time, their coats would be removed to reveal their polka-dotted Swiss dresses beneath, as they reached for the rich, homemade Italian pastries waiting on the table for them. We'd all sit around, chatting and drinking cups of steaming hot chocolate, or a glass of cold lemonade, weather depending." Gram sighed. "Such times were the best."

My mother chimed in. "Then once I got all the girls home, and changed from their Sunday clothes, I'd fry meatballs, simmer sauce and we'd have ziti and homemade Italian bread." Gloria laughed. "I always called non-Italians *those Americans*, which was so silly. I was born in the United States, I am an American, too."

"An Italian-American," Gram corrected. "Americans did things differently than we did. They went to the market. We bought from the milk man, the vegetable vender, the baker or we made our own bread and grew our own vegetables in a garden."

My mother chuckled. "Wasn't it your mother who hated going out for too long because there was no one left home to watch the house?"

"My mother was the same," my father added. "And she was Irish." He shook his head and smiled. "I remember, after my brother and I devoured all our Easter candy, we were made to take castor oil."

"Your mother was a wise woman, Brian," Gram said. "Too many sweets disturb the natural flow of things in the body."

The heat rose to my face and I cleared my throat. "I'm sure Guylan doesn't want to hear about such things."

"No, it's okay, Nela. Really," he assured me. "I like hearing about your family's ways." His expression saddened. "Growing up in an orphanage, not ever knowing your parents or what their family home life was like, can make for a lonely existence at times."

"Well, you're lonely no longer, Guylan," Gram said. "Once you marry our Nela, you'll be a member of the family, too."

"Yeah, enter at your own risk," Alana grumbled.

My father cast a threatening glare her way, the same one he had used when we were children.

"Excuse us," I said, reaching for Guylan's hand.

Everyone knew what I was about to do.

Gram gave Guylan's arm an affectionate pat and smiled. "Make sure you're back in time for dessert. I made a pecan pie."

He licked his lips. "I love pecan pie."

Gram gave him a playful wink. "I know."

Guylan followed me downstairs to the beauty salon and sighed, contented. "Your grandmother is a sweetheart and is aging so gracefully." He flashed me a mischievous smile. "They say if a man wants a preview of what his wife will look like in her older years, all he needs to do is look at how the mother and grandmother turned out."

I stopped to flick on the light switch.

He took a seat at one of the hairdryers and looked around the room. "It's strange in here at night."

I knew fully what he meant. The usual bustle by the sink or at the comb-out counter was constant during work hours...women talking all at once, the phone ringing, dryers blowing. Now it was quiet, the silence almost eerie. I sat on a chair opposite him. "And do you like what you see?"

"You mean with your mom and grandmother?"

I nodded.

He smiled. "Yeah, honey, I do. Your grandmother and mother are very beautiful women for their age." He sat back in the chair, bumping his head on a dryer cap.

I stood and pushed the plastic drying bubble aside.

"How old is your grandmother, anyway?"

"She just turned eighty-seven," I said.

"She doesn't look that old," Guylan reflected.

I returned to my chair and met his gaze. "That's because she was only seventy-nine when she died."

Nine

Guylan stared at me in silence, his blue eyes wider than I'd ever seen them.

I remembered Gram saying she'd started with the wizard story when she explained the family blessing to my grandfather, so I followed her lead. I cleared my throat and squared my shoulders. "My grandmother's father opened a small bakery when he came to this country from Dugenta, Italy. Aside from the bread and pies, it was known for its peppermint sticks." I paused, searching Guylan's face a moment before going on with my story. "One day, a man came into the store with his small daughter. The little girl loved peppermint sticks and when her father bought her one, she ate it with pleasure. But suddenly she bit off a large piece and began to choke."

He sat forward and opened his mouth to speak.

I held up a hand to stop him. "But my great-grandfather saved the day. He came to the child's aid and wrapped his arms around her waist. The candy dislodged from her throat and flew out of her mouth, clear across the room."

He sighed, relieved.

"And the girl's father, who turned out to be a wizard," I added, moving on quickly with the rest of the sentence, "was so grateful his daughter's life had been saved, he bestowed upon my great-grandfather a blessing."

He frowned. "Wait—back up there a minute—did you say a *wizard* bestowed a *blessing*?"

I nodded, my stomach knotting. "It was known in the community this man had some sort of supernatural powers, and so he was called a wizard."

His frown deepened. "And what kind of a *blessing* did this *wizard* bestow, Nela?"

I forced myself to speak in spite of the panic rising to choke me. "He placed upon the family the ability to return after death."

Guylan swallowed hard and sat frozen.

I took an audible breath. "Please, let me finish the story."

He nodded, remaining silent and staring at me like I had two heads.

"The blessing came with stipulations, the first being it could only work on the first daughter of the first daughter, and so on. Second, the awakening would only happen after the fifth anniversary of the person's death. Third, it would only occur once a year, for a forty-eight-hour period on the first Saturday in May at Beltane, when—"

"The wall between the afterlife and this one was at its thinnest," he finished the sentence.

I gasped. "Yes, how did you know?"

"What was the rest of the blessing, Nela?" he choked in a hoarse voice.

"If the woman died while still married, whether before or after her husband, after his death the husband would also return."

"Good God in heaven," he whispered.

My voice shook. "It's obvious my grandmother has already received the blessing. When my mother passes, it will be given to her, and when I expire, it is bestowed to me." I clasped my hands in my lap. "And you," I added, closing my eyes to control the spasmodic trembling in my stomach. "I'm telling you the truth, Guylan."

"I know you are, Nela; that's what's so frightening."

I opened my eyes and met his gaze. "You do? I mean you don't think I'm crazy?"

"No, I don't."

I narrowed my eyes. "But you do think it's frightening?"

"Don't you?"

I shrugged. "I guess if I were first hearing about it, I would."

His lips were pinched together, the muscles at his jaw throbbing. "Did your grandmother ever tell you what the wizard looked like?"

"He wore a top hat, boots and a cape..." my words caught in my throat with the look on Guylan's face. "What...what is it?"

"You've just described my stalker," Guylan said.

"How can that be? I mean, the man would be over a hundred years old by now."

"True, but there's no doubt we're not dealing with the normal realm here, Nela."

"Point taken," I muttered.

"And I believe there's more here than either of us realizes." He ran his fingers through his hair. "Why didn't you say something sooner? I thought we weren't going to have secrets between us."

"I didn't know how you would take it, going through your own problems, and I didn't want to add more." I frowned. "And look who's talking about keeping secrets. You failed to tell me what the stalker looked like."

The silence between us increased with frightening intensity.

He stood. "I've got to go, Nela."

I reached for his arm. "Guylan, wait. Aside from keeping secrets from each other, there's something very intense going on. What do you think it all means?"

"I don't know, but I mean to find out." He stepped back from my grasp. "How does your grandmother return each year for a visit?"

"She comes by train...*The Blessing Train.*"

He straightened his collar and made his way to the door.

"Guylan, don't leave, not like this," I pleaded. "We need to talk things out."

He turned to look at me. "I can't do this now. I need to think."

"Wait, please," I begged, standing and approaching him. "Over the phone you said you had something you needed to tell me."

He glanced out the window, and then back at me. "I'm not Guylan Quinn."

My eyes widened. "What are you saying?"

"Sincloud...my last name is Sincloud," he whispered. "I found out this afternoon."

I blinked, baffled. "I don't understand...how did you learn all this in one day?" I motioned to a chair. "Please, sit. Stay and talk to me."

"Not now, Nela. Not now...not now," he stammered.

One last time I tried to detain him. "Please, Guylan...give us a chance to deal with all of this together."

"I can't until I know everything, the whole truth," he said, glancing again out the salon's front window.

"I swear to you I'm telling the truth, but if you'd like proof, come with me tomorrow night to the train station. At midnight, Gram's train will arrive and you can see for yourself—"

He interrupted with, "Not your truth, Nela...my truth."

"Guylan—"

"No, Nela. I've got to go. Forgive me, but I can't do this now," he whispered, turning his handsome, somber face from me as he stepped out the door, slamming it shut behind him.

Sickened, overwhelmed with despair, I relocked the salon's door. At the foot of the stairs, I shut out the lights and climbed the steps to my flat, anguish searing my heart.

It was my mother who met me at the top of the stairs. She searched my face, the tears welling in my eyes. "Oh, Nela, he didn't understand."

I shook my head and walked into her embrace. "He said he couldn't deal with this now."

"Neither could your father right away, but he came around." She enfolded me in her arms and held me tight.

"I heard Gramps had a hand in that," I said.

She chuckled. "Should we enlist your father's help, then?"

I laughed through my tears. "Not this time."

My mother stroked my back with the palm of a hand, as she'd done when I was a child to soothe me from the hurts of the world. But I wasn't a little girl anymore and this time the hurt went too deep.

"You're an incredible woman, Nela. I think Guylan knows he'd be letting go of an awful lot," she whispered. "Give him some time."

I had nothing more to say; my energy had drained along with my hopes and dreams. I just nodded in agreement and went to the bathroom for a tissue. On my way back from having a good cry, I passed the back door. Gram and Alana were talking on the porch.

"Are you sure this is what you want, Alana?" Gram asked.

"It is, Gram, and next time you visit, I'd like you to meet Beth. I know you'll like her." Alana smiled. "She's absolutely incredible, really gets me...understands and appreciates the person I am."

A stab of guilt pierced my heart. I hadn't really been there much for my youngest sister. The twelve-year difference between us hadn't made us as close as Hannah and I were. Maybe I should call Alana more, take her out to lunch, become involved in her life. The final year of college wasn't easy. Neither was discovering you belonged in a same-sex relationship. All in all, Alana had to be going through a difficult time and could use my love and support.

My thoughts were interrupted by Gram's voice calling my name. "Nela, come on out and sit with us."

I opened the screen. "I didn't mean to listen in."

Alana shrugged, pulling up the zipper of her hooded sweatshirt. "What's the difference? There's nothing more to hide now."

"I guess not," I said, plopping down on a nearby chair.

Gram's eyes surveyed me. "Guylan's left?"

My voice came out in a suffocated whisper. "Yes."

She stood and made her way over to me, wrapping her arms around my head, smashing my face against her bosom. "I'm not feeling this is the end of things, Nela. I just think Guylan needs a bit of time to digest it all."

I sobbed.

She turned my face up to look at her. "He'll be back...trust me on this."

Ten

Guylan walked to his car, screams of frustration at the back of his throat. His mind, spinning in a thousand different circles, was having a hard time comprehending anything that had transpired. Tonight, he had sat at a table and eaten beside a dead woman...a nice woman, but deceased just the same. Nela called it a family blessing.

Blessing or curse...the work of Quentin MacRaven?

Nela should have long ago told him, but then again how could he be so bold as to admonish her for keeping a secret from him when he wasn't telling her the truth, either. "Correction," he mumbled to himself. "I'm still trying to find out the truth."

But his excuse didn't wash, because he had kept from her the note he'd received while at the library, the visit to Sister Margaret and the mysterious book. Now he was beginning to understand why the elder nun had kept it locked away all these years.

Sitting in the driver's seat, he slapped his forehead with the palm of his hand, wishing somehow to knock the parts of the puzzle into place. It only managed to add a headache to the whole situation. Confused, he stared out the windshield, spotting a piece of paper stuck beneath a wiper. He opened the car door and ripped the paper free, leaving the door ajar for light. Written in the same handwriting as the first note, this message simply gave an address: *1147 Glenpointe Drive*. Without hesitation, he started the Camry and drove the twenty minutes to the Hillsdale area of town, a wealthy, gated community. When he came upon the house number indicated in the note, his mouth dropped open.

The sprawling, gray stone mansion was like a miniature castle, with its turrets, balconies, columns and stained-glass windows. He pulled into the driveway and stopped before the call box on a post. Reaching out from the window, he pressed the red button.

"And whom shall I say is calling?" a man's voice responded.

"Guylan Quinn," he said.

The large gate opened, as though the occupants were expecting him, and he was allowed access onto the grounds. He drove down the remaining length of the driveway to the circular area in front of the double doors. His heart raced as he made his way up the marble staircase flanked by matching lion statues. At the top, he was met by a short, stocky man wearing a tuxedo, no doubt the butler. The man welcomed him inside with a gracious wave of his arm, as Guylan crossed the threshold.

"My Lady is waiting in the parlor area, sir," the butler's voice droned.

Guylan arched a brow. "And who is your lady?"

The butler gave him a quick bow. "Lady Olena Sincloud, sir." He inclined his head politely. "Please, follow me."

Guylan was led to the left of the large winding staircase. The floor tiles gleamed with the light of the hanging chandelier, and the wall tapestries were of the finest quality. He halted before a large portrait of a man, deep blue eyes peering down at him from beneath a black top hat. Flowing from the man's shoulders was a black cape over a ruffled white shirt. Belted tan breeches tapered to knee-length, above shiny, black boots.

His breath caught in his lungs. "Quentin MacRaven," he whispered.

"So right you are, sir," the butler agreed as he opened a set of double doors and stood aside for Guylan to enter.

The room was done in shades of red, from light crimson to the deepest burgundy. A fire was burning in the white stone fireplace; a portrait of a young girl with large blue eyes and a head full of red curls hung above the mantle.

"At last you've come," a soft, female voice said from the corner of the room.

Guylan turned to see a frail, elderly woman sitting in an armchair by the window. The light from the Tiffany lamp illuminated the pure white hair piled atop her head. She studied him with the same blue eyes as those of the child in the portrait.

"Can I bring you anything, ma'am?" the butler inquired.

The woman smiled. "Would you like a cup of tea or a glass of lemonade, Mr. Quinn?" When he remained speechless, she prompted, "Perhaps a glass of brandy would do you better?"

"No...no, thank you," he managed to choke out.

She nodded and turned to the butler. "Nothing for now, Harrington." She waved her hand casually in the air. "Leave us, please."

Harrington inclined his head politely and left the room.

The woman motioned for him to take a nearby seat. He made his way closer, his eyes never wavering from the deep blue ones looking back at him.

She smiled again. "Do you know who I am, Guylan?"

He paused, then cleared his throat. "You're my grandmother."

~ * ~

It was only 8:00 when everyone left. I felt like I'd been up for days. I undressed and climbed into bed, the pain of losing Guylan washing over me again and again. As bone tired as I was, sleep was impossible.

I made my way to the living room, where I found Gram sitting on the sofa, savoring a cup of tea. She looked up when I entered the room. "Can't sleep either?"

I shook my head and plopped down beside her.

She took another sip of her tea. "Have you a sleep suppository in the medicine cabinet?"

I giggled, in spite of the way I really felt. "No one uses that kind of sleeping method anymore, Gram."

She shrugged. "A pity...it's fast and safe by passing into the intestinal tract and causing less ill side effects. Expecting the liver to digest too many medications can bring on lots of trouble later on in years."

"Well, we're a pill-popping generation now," I informed her, placing my bare feet upon her lap.

She began to massage my toes. "When you were small, I'd give you feet and back rubs all the time."

"I remember. It always put me to sleep."

"Do you think it will it help now, Nela?"

I sighed. "I guess it can't hurt to try."

She rubbed the instep of my left foot with her thumb. The sensation was heavenly. I leaned back and closed my eyes.

"Life is full of letdowns, Nela. And each time we're disappointed, it seems like the ultimate blow, till the next time and the next and the next."

"I don't think I can bear any more," I whispered.

"You'll be surprised what the human heart can endure," she said and hummed a tune.

I opened my eyes to find her staring at me. "What are you humming?"

"Oh, something I heard another woman on the train singing. She was from the year 1793 and quite astonished by all the changes in the world." Gram sighed. "She had several generations traveling with her...nice family."

I gasped. "I always thought our family was the only one blessed by the wizard."

"Now, how does that make sense, Nela? Why would I need a whole train to transport just me?"

I frowned. "I never thought of it that way. I guess I just took it for granted you were the only traveler."

We both burst out laughing.

"Really, none of it makes much sense," I added.

"Well, now, there are lots of things we take for granted that don't make sense," Gram said, massaging the instep of my right foot.

"Like what?" Her gentle kneading relaxed my body for the first time all day.

Gram's fingers moved over my toes, where she bent and flexed each one. "The way soap is made comes to mind."

I giggled. "Why's that?"

"My grandmother, the thrifty woman she was, always made our soap in the springtime. I'd help her gather the ashes from the winter fires accumulated in all the wood-burning stoves. My parents owned a large, two-story house at the edge of town. The front half of the downstairs was for the bakery, my father's office and store rooms. Behind the store was a two-bedroom apartment for Nawna, my paternal grandmother. On the second floor, there was another flat... quite large with three bedrooms, a large living room, dining room and eat-in kitchen. This is where my parents, my two brothers and I lived. I'd start by cleaning out the wood-burning stove in the bakery... there were two, one in the shop and one in my father's office. Then I moved on to help my grandmother clean the two in her apartment. There was one in the living room and kitchen. Upstairs there was a stove in the kitchen, living room and dining room. The ashes were stored in large, terra cotta pots, handmade by an Italian man who had a pottery shop three doors down from our flat, and kept in a dry spot until it was time to make the soap. Then my grandmother would take an old pickle barrel and line the bottom with twigs and hay. This was so that, when she poured water through the wood ash, it wouldn't leak out the slits. We called the barrel a *hopper*. If the solution was thick enough to float an egg, we were in business. If the egg sunk to the bottom, the water had to be poured through the ash again."

I listened intently, finding the procedure interesting. "Great-great-gram sure went through a lot of work just to have soap."

"Oh, that was just the beginning. All year long, the fats and drippings from beef and pork were saved and put into jars stored beneath the kitchen sink. When it was time to make soap, a large pot was placed on an outdoor fire and the lard was boiled to make lye soap for cleaning. Then she'd add the ashes, perfumed oil and salt to the mixture, and press it into molds."

"Why was soot used?" I wondered aloud.

"For the alkali. There's a potassium-based alkali in the wood material." Gram frowned. "But what always struck me as rather ironic about the whole procedure was the grease from hog fat. If dropped on your clothes, it left a nasty and often permanent stain. And the soot from the stoves, if touched, would dirty and blacken the flesh as well as your clothes. Yet those two elements, when combined, became the essential ingredients in producing something that cleansed."

"I bet there are a lot of strange things like that in life," I reflected.

"Oh, there is no doubt about that, Nela."

"Like the process of inoculation...injecting a strain of a disease to prevent catching it," I said.

"Yes, Nela, that's another good example," Gram agreed.

"Gram?"

"Mmm."

"The wizard who bestowed the blessing, what was he like?"

"He wore a top hat, cape and boots. His very presence filled the room, and beneath his hat, dark, thick hair hung to his shoulders, framing an arresting face. And those eyes: large blue ones, the same eyes as his child, but when he stared at me, I could swear his eyes turned pale blue, almost white and transparent." She inclined her head with her memories. "I can still see his purposeful stride as he entered my father's bakery; boot heels clicking on the wooden floor."

"A man similar to that description has been following Guylan since our engagement dinner."

Gram frowned. "Has he notified the authorities?"

"Yes, a few days ago."

Gram's frown deepened.

"He's gone to the police, given a statement, but you know how these things go...the cops can't do anything until something happens."

"In this case I'm glad for once," Gram admitted. "To mess with something like this isn't wise."

"But why, and for what reason would the wizard be tailing Guylan?"

"I'm not sure, Nela, but there is a purpose for everything, especially the things we can't explain."

I bit my bottom lip. "I believe Guylan knows more than he's telling."

"What draws you to that conclusion?"

"He wasn't all that shocked when I told him about the blessing... in fact he knew about Beltane...literally finished my sentence for me. And then he said something really weird. He said his name wasn't Guylan Quinn, but Guylan Sincloud."

"Sincloud, Sincloud," Gram repeated. "Why does that name sound familiar to me?" She shrugged. "Oh well, it will eventually come to me. And this is the first you're hearing of his new name?"

"Well, yes. It happens that he just learned it himself, but he wouldn't divulge how."

"I don't think you and Guylan are starting out very well in the trust department, Nela."

I sighed. "It appears that way, doesn't it?"

Gram's lips thinned. "You need to call Guylan in the morning and talk all this out with him."

A cold chill crept down my spine and I shivered. "What do you think is going on, Gram? I mean, outside of the two of us keeping secrets?"

"I don't know, sweetie, but I'd say there's a lot more to Guylan than even he knows. He's certainly much more than a *keeper*."

My heart leapt. "What more could he be?"

"He's your fate, Nela, your true soul mate, and I'm getting a strong sense the two of you are destined for each other."

"Can you predict someone's destiny, Gram?"

She looked down at my feet, silent for a moment, and then raised her gaze to mine. "Sometimes it's just a revelation I get."

"Like with Mom's lump?" I probed.

"Yes, like that. I don't know the exact outcome; I just know Gloria's got more time here on earth."

I swallowed hard. "How much more time?"

"I don't know that, Nela."

"How about Hannah's husband, Joe. Can you feel anything about him?"

"Not now...not yet," she added in a soft tone.

Her gentle massage caressed my ankles. It felt so good, so soothing. I scooted down further, reclining now on the sofa, and closed my eyes. "How are you able to use your body each time? I mean, why isn't it...after all this time—"

"Worm food?" Gram interjected.

I cringed at her word choice, but then again, Gram was never one to sweet talk. She called it how she saw it.

"I'm not real sure myself, Nela. Perhaps it has something to do with the spirit replenishing the body as it is joined to it. However it happens, what this family has been given is a rare and wonderful blessing and I'm not about to be questioning the gift. What I do know is my body must return each time to the hallowed ground to which it was commended, or my spirit will not have a way to walk about and be seen in this dimension."

"What's it like to be—" I hesitated, feeling awkward about asking her my next question, almost like you would when trying to find out someone's income.

"What's it like to be what?" Gram said, waiting for me to finish my sentence.

"The way you are, you know...living-impaired," I said, opening my eyes to see her reaction.

She chuckled. "Nice way to put it. What took you so long to ask me these questions?"

I shrugged. "The first year you came back, we were all so excited to see you again after five years, and the time flew by so fast, none of us thought to ask until after you were gone. The following year, we discussed asking the question and agreed we'd do it together, at a family meeting, but then Cara got food poisoning and we spent most of your visit in the hospital."

Gram's brows furrowed. "Yes, I remember how scared we all were for Cara's welfare."

"So true, and because of that whole situation, we didn't think it was an appropriate subject to breech."

"And so now you feel it is the opportune time?" Gram said, massaging my heels and moving again to my arches.

"I guess it's as good a time as any," I said, closing my eyes once more, feeling very tired.

Gram hesitated, and then she cleared her throat. "Well, let me see...where to begin," was all I heard before I fell asleep.

Part Two–Guylan

The Attic Portal

Eleven

May, 2007, Anglewood, NY
The MacRaven Mansion

Olena Sincloud smiled, her ruby lips spreading over even white teeth. For a woman her age, at least in her late seventies, I thought she was well preserved, but then again, I had the distinct suspicion I wasn't looking at your average elderly person.

"Yes, I'm your grandmother," she admitted in a soft tone, the deep, blue eyes filling with tears. "Welcome home at last, Guylan."

I sat and stared, my mouth agape.

"I'm sure you must have many questions," she said, ringing a bell for Harrington.

"That's an understatement."

Harrington opened the parlor's double doors, and I remained silent as he set two goblets of brandy on the table beside Olena's chair. She reached for the one nearest her seat and indicated with a slight inclination of her head for me to take the other. "I know you said you didn't want the brandy, but I insist."

I took a sip of the amber liquid and let its heat and sweetness glide down the back of my throat, savoring the richness. After Harrington left the room, I found my voice. "Why was I given up?"

Her fair complexion colored. "It was necessary to do at the time, for your safety."

"And just what was it I was being kept safe from?" I probed, my voice growing stronger.

"Not what, but from whom," she said and sighed. "I know you must be very resentful—"

I interrupted her. "Resentment is putting it mildly."

Olena sighed again and took another sip of her brandy. "Will you at least give me a chance to explain?"

I chuckled. "Why, Grandmother, I'll give you all the chance in the world. It's an explanation I've been waiting to hear all my life."

Olena studied me. "You're the spitting image of your father, my son Xavior. You even become vexed the same way as he did."

"Suppose we start with him, and my mother," I said, sitting back in my seat. "How were they killed?"

"They weren't—they were murdered." She glanced at the hands she held in her lap. "Audra along with them...she was only seven."

The blood drained from my face. "How...how were they murdered?"

"The authorities found them all dead in their beds." She raised her eyes to meet mine. "Their throats cut."

My stomach churned and I swallowed hard against the bile rising to choke me. "Where was I?"

"You were with me," she said. She pulled a linen handkerchief from her pocket and dabbed at the lone tear that had slipped down a cheek. "It's hard to have a son predecease you. It's just not natural for a parent to bury a child." She closed her eyes in her anguish. "I'd lost my mother about ten years prior, and as grief-stricken as I was over her death, it was nothing compared to what I endured losing my son and his family. Every time I am made to think of that time, I bury them all over again."

I sympathized with her, and leaned forward in my seat, reaching out to take her hand. "I'm so sorry."

She entwined her bony fingers with mine. "It's so good to have you home again, Guylan."

"Why was I with you on that night, Olena?"

"Your parents were attending Audra's piano recital and you, a rather rambunctious little fellow at the time, would have disrupted the entire evening. Xavior asked me if I'd take you back here to the mansion to sleep overnight, since they would be late in returning. DeYonna was somewhat skeptical about letting you spend the entire night. She was in the process of weaning you, but still breastfed you just before putting you down to sleep." She cleared the emotion from her throat. "And then you wouldn't leave without Luna, the German Shepherd Xavior found a year prior, on the night of a full moon. Your father loved such heavenly happenings and had stepped onto the front porch to view the large, golden orb better. It was then he spotted a dog lying on the lawn, injured and dying. For weeks he nursed her back to health; in fact, you watched him." She searched my face. "Do you remember any of this, Guylan?"

I shook my head. "But the subconscious is a strange thing. I must have stored the incident away somewhere deep within, and perhaps it was the catalyst for my love for animals and the need to want to heal them."

"Xavior named the dog Luna," Olena continued, "and she took such a shine to you. The two of you became inseparable. So, when I took you to my home that night, you insisted the dog come along as well."

I stood and made my way to the fireplace, looking up at the portrait of Olena as the very child who had choked on a peppermint stick long ago and was saved by Nela's great-grandfather. In turn, Olena saved my life and I met Nela, fell in love and asked her to be my wife. It was all predestined to be, but why?

"Was the murderer ever caught?" I asked, turning to look at Olena.

"No, but I know who did it." She folded the handkerchief with trembling fingers and placed it on her lap.

"How do you know?"

"He left a calling card, a raven's feather stuck to the front door. It meant nothing to the police, but Quentin, Zackery and I knew the raven's feather was Mortimer MacRaven's signature," Olena said.

I frowned. "Who is Mortimer MacRaven?"

"He's my father's brother."

My frown deepened. "Then why didn't you tell the cops?"

"I couldn't."

"What do you mean you couldn't? The bastard murdered my family. He should have paid for what he did," I snapped.

"I agree, but to explain to the police what he was..." Olena's voice trailed off.

My pulse raced. "Suppose you explain it to me, then."

Olena cleared her throat. "When the *Geis,* the Druidal ancient training created and granted by a warrior patriarch, was given to Quentin by his chieftain father, Mortimer grew jealous. One night he broke into Quentin's library and found the family book of secrets. He cast a spell upon himself to receive great power and riches, but because Mortimer was unskilled, something went terribly wrong with the incantation. All he managed was to conjure up evil, selling his soul to the dark fae."

My knees went as weak as a blade of grass and I returned to my chair. "What the hell is the dark fae?"

"Worse than your most horrible nightmare," Olena said. "They are the residents of the dark side of the fairy world and will stop at nothing to kill off humanity so they can rule the universe. Summoning them, as Mortimer did, was the total opposite of Druidic tradition, which at all times maintains spiritual balance, treating and holding the natural world—animals, trees, stones and star lore—hallowed and with respect. Druidry seeks answers to eternity, believing in the immortal soul and its connection of the mind, body and spirit. The universe, the land, as well as relationships and sexuality are held sacred. Mortimer's deal with the demon fae was against all the things Quentin and the MacRaven family stood for."

I shifted uneasily in my seat. "Paganism...it's all pagan."

"Actually, you're very wrong, Guylan. There are many variations of Christian denominations and groups belonging to the Druid heritage and society. Druidism is practiced in Ireland, Wales, northern France and Scotland, with several hundred groups worldwide." She waved a hand in the air. "But, let me get back on track...to Mortimer. He went to Quentin for help, but by that time the deal had been set and nothing could be done." Olena picked up the goblet of brandy and handed it to me. "I think you should take another sip before you faint."

I gulped down the last bit of liquor from the glass. "What did all this have to do with my parents?"

"For years, Mortimer had the powers and riches he asked for, but one can't dodge a deal with evil. As each day passed, the demon fae haunted him, reminding him the time grew closer for him to pay his dues, and Mortimer didn't want to comply." She paused, downing the last of her brandy as well. "Again, Mortimer asked Quentin for help, and again nothing could be done. Quentin refused to have anything to do with the dark side."

"So, Mortimer took his revenge out on my family?" I concluded.

Olena's eyes saddened. "He knew that would be the ultimate way to hurt Quentin and the rest of us, since Xavior had already received the *Geis*. But most important for him was being able to offer such a powerful soul to the dark fae. It would appease them and another deal could be struck that would buy Mortimer more time."

My heart raced. "So, Mortimer lives now...off my father's soul?"

"More or less, yes," Olena said.

I swallowed hard against the lump in my throat. "Tell me more."

She stared past me, into space. "It was a hot July night, hotter than any I can remember since. The air was humid, thick and still. Too still," she added, her gaze resting on mine. "You cried most of the night, aggravated by the heat and wanting to feed from your mother. You broke out in a rash all over your chest and bottom. I had to soak you in chamomile bath milk to keep you cool, and dress you in only a diaper. Your little arse was so raw, I should have kept

the diaper off as well, but you weren't completely toilet trained."
Olena paused a second before she went on. "The night gave way
to a thunderstorm, which frightened the dog. I ended up having to
put Luna out back, in the gardener's shed, because she pranced and
howled. After Xavior arrived home from Audra's recital, he called
to say the storm had knocked out the power in his part of town
and not even a fan could be used. I offered to have him come to the
mansion, but his reply was Audra was already asleep and he didn't
want to disturb her. Little did I know it would be the last time I'd
ever hear my son's voice." Her eyes glistened with tears. "My guess
was Xavior left the windows open about the house to catch the small
breeze brewing after the storm, and Mortimer was able to enter
through a downstairs opening." Olena clenched her hands into fists.
"How he navigated through the house, unheard and in the dark, still
haunts me. I don't think Mortimer visited Xavior and his family but
a handful of times, so to know the layout, especially in the dark..."
her voice trailed off and she shuddered. "I guess evil has its way of
getting beyond ordinary obstacles. He was also clever enough to
make it appear to be a home invasion...a robbery. After he murdered
them in their beds, he ransacked the house. I believe he was also
looking for the ring and the book of secrets." Her voice broke off into
a sob. "Audra must have awakened and tried to hide. Her body was
found on the closet floor."

The horror of the deed made me physically ill. I hid my face
in my hands to control the raw emotion emerging from what I was
imagining happened that night.

"Then Mortimer must have gone looking for you, since you
were next in line after Xavior," she said. "Everything in your nursery
was turned upside down." She choked out the last of her words. "If I
hadn't taken the dog with me that night, they might all still be alive."

I raised my gaze to hers. "Why is that?"

"There was something very special about Luna, besides her
being an excellent watch dog. She slept beside your crib, watched
your every move. Somehow, she managed to escape from the shed
and make her way across town to the house she shared with Xavior.

It was her howling on the front porch beneath the door with the raven feather stuck upon it, which alerted neighbors to call the police. Luna felt something was wrong and that's why she headed back to your home, but arrived too late. I know if she had been in the house that night, she would have alerted Xavior to Mortimer's intrusion."

"Thank heaven I was with you," I said.

"So very true, Guylan. And if you were to stay alive, I had to hide you. What better place than one where evil would be hesitant to tread but a—"

"A Catholic orphanage." I finished her sentence.

"Yes, holy ground, but not just any Catholic orphanage," she said. "One where I knew you'd be watched over and loved by a family member."

I frowned. "I don't understand."

Olena stood and walked over to the large bay window. "It was the best I could do under the circumstances. Leaving you was hard enough; you were all I had left. I wanted to make sure you were cared for by someone who would look out for you with her heart. So, I entrusted your care to my sister, Anya MacRaven."

My frown deepened. "I don't know anyone by that name."

"It wasn't the name she went by in the convent." She turned to look at me. "You would know her as Sister Margaret."

Twelve

My ears rang; splotches of light flashed before my eyes.

"Guylan," Olena called to me. "Take a deep breath." She made her way to her chair and rang for Harrington.

The next time I opened my eyes, I was lying on the sofa, a cold compress on my forehead.

Olena sat in her chair, watching me. "How are you feeling now?"

I sat up, the room spun for a moment and I swallowed hard, taking the glass of water she'd offered me. I took a swig and leaned back against a pillow. "Why didn't Sister Margaret tell me?"

"She wanted no part of the family and fled from us when she was only sixteen to join the nunnery, said she had to pray for all our souls. But my father always kept tabs on where she was, how she was faring. Just before Xavior was murdered, Quentin received news from one of his contacts that Anya had returned to the area and was at St. Bernard's in Anglewood." Olena's mouth was tight and grim. "When we realized the murderer's identity, Quentin instructed me to take the ring, the book, two more things Mortimer was after, and you to St. Bernard's Home for Boys."

"Why didn't Mortimer harm you and Quentin?"

"Quentin was quick to cast himself into a suspension chamber where Mortimer couldn't touch him. I entrusted Luna's care to my dear friend, Myrtle Johnson. Many years later, I learned the dog had run away on the night of a full moon and was never found. And your grandfather, Zackery Sincloud, and I fled to northern France, where we stayed with a group of Druid priests until we could escape to Scotland. Somehow, Mortimer found us and ambushed Zackery as he traveled back from meeting a contact." She shivered. "Every part of him was ripped to shreds, like a pack of wolves—or something much worse—had descended upon him, tearing him to pieces. The two men traveling with Zackery were spared, no doubt so they could relay to me who it was that had murdered my husband." Olena paused to compose herself. "I didn't think any more could be taken from me than already had been, but when I buried the love of my life, I buried a part of me as well."

How would I feel if I lost Nela? I cringed inside at the thought as I again consoled Olena. "I'm so terribly sorry."

"So am I, Guylan." Olena sighed. "I was then hustled off to Caledonia, Scotland, where the MacRavens still have family and Druidic ruins dot the moors. That's where I've been living all this time, on the grounds of a monastery," she concluded.

"Why did you come back?"

"I was summoned by my sister. She notified me of your visit and the questions you were asking. I knew if you were coming around with such questions, you had to have seen something, felt something. So, I got on a private plane owned by a dear friend, carrying a gut feeling you were in danger, and returned to the States as soon as I could."

"But why...why am I in danger now, after all these years?"

She reached into the same pocket where she kept her handkerchief and pulled out a newspaper clipping, handing it to me. "Because of this."

I opened the folded paper to reveal the engagement photo of me and Nela.

"You're the spitting image of Xavior. It isn't hard to see you're his son, and Mortimer knows his time on earth is coming to a fast end. That newspaper announcement alerted him to your whereabouts. Since you're no longer guarded by holy ground, you're an easy target."

"Why didn't you come for me when I was a child, take me with you to France?"

"It would have been way too risky. As it were, Mortimer found us and murdered Zackery. Being with Anya was the only real solution, and when I handed you over to her care, I made a deal with her. I promised you would never be a part of the MacRaven gift and I'd never return for you, if she would take you and keep you safe."

I looked at the ring on my finger. "Why then, did she give me the ring?"

"That was what she promised to do if I kept my word," Olena said. "I knew one day you'd need it for protection. I believe Anya did as well."

"And the book...why did you give her the book?"

"To keep it from Mortimer. In the wrong hands, the book and ring could be used for something other than good. The evil Mortimer possessed would transmit the bad, changing the book and ring's powers from what they were originally destined to be."

I looked down at the raven-crested ring I wore. "What powers does this ring hold?"

"You'll learn all in good time," Olena whispered.

"Mother Superior told Sister Margaret to burn the book. Why do you think she didn't?"

"I'm not sure myself. All I can think is, in spite of Anya's disgust for what our father is, she knew in time it would be essential for him to speak to you, once you grew to be a man, and the book would help you achieve what needed to be done."

"Which is what?"

"Again, all in good time, Guylan."

I took an exasperated breath. "Then I assume Quentin MacRaven is still alive." My mind began to calculate his age. "He's got to be about—"

"A hundred and seven." She finished the sentence for me. "And he continues to live in a state of suspension."

My eyes widened. "But I saw him several times."

She frowned. "You couldn't have."

"But I did," I protested. "He's been following me for months, dressed as he is in the portrait hanging in the hallway. It's the reason I went to Sister Margaret." I explained to her about the silence accompanying each of his appearances, and the note I received in the library. "It was in the same handwriting as the one I received tonight, giving this address."

"I was under the impression Anya told you to come here when she brought you the book, which she admitted to doing." Olena's expression hardened. "It looks as though I've gotten here just in time."

My head began to throb. "I don't understand any of this."

"Everything will be explained to you soon, Guylan, but right now I need the book Anya gave you."

"I left it at my apartment."

Olena reached for the bell and summoned Harrington. When he entered the room, she gave him instructions to fetch the book.

I stood in protest. "I'll get the book."

"That would be way too dangerous at this point," Olena informed me in a stern tone. "Now, give your keys to Harrington and you come with me." She stood and reached for my hand. "It's time you met your great-grandfather, Archdruid Quentin MacRaven."

My eyes clung to hers. "He's here?"

Olena gave a taut nod. "Where else would he be?"

Reluctantly, I handed my keys over to Harrington and followed Olena up the large staircase to the second floor. The well-crafted cherub and flowers carved into the thick oak banister must have been costly. Rich-hued, Oriental carpeting paved the path to another staircase. The paneling on the walls and the expensive artwork made my modest wallet scream. I couldn't help thinking how I'd been made to pinch pennies all my life, eating macaroni and cheese for supper every night and renting cold water flats, when all the while my family was rolling in wealth.

Olena read my thoughts. She stopped short in front of me and looked up into my eyes with a challenging gaze. "How do you think you came by the scholarship to medical school?"

I frowned, annoyed. "Through my good grades and extra hard work, that's how."

"Well, you were a smart one, I'll give you that, but there were smarter. It was the nice lump of money I donated to the college that really saw you through."

My eyes widened in astonishment. "I don't believe you."

Olena shrugged. "I don't care if you do or don't, it's the truth, as well as why you were singled out by a certain Horace Manchester searching for a roommate to share his very nice three-bedroom apartment...and only asking you for a quarter of what the rent really cost." She turned and made her way up the last set of stairs. "And then there was the bank position you worked part time at while in your last two years of college."

The heat stung my face. "Are you saying you had something to do with me being hired?"

She cast me a glance over her shoulder. "The bank is one of the many businesses the Sincloud family owns, Guylan." She stopped at a door, her large blue eyes locking with mine. "You were watched over and compensated...grant you, not as you would have been if you lived here, nor could the family's money do much for you while you were growing up at the orphanage." Olena took an audible breath. "My dear sister wanted you to appear as all the others so there'd be no animosity expressed toward you by your peers. But you were never in danger of being homeless, starving or unable to reach your goals once you left St. Bernard's orphanage."

"Am I supposed to be grateful for that?" I snapped.

She shrugged again. "Be whatever you feel you should be, just know you weren't left out in the cold...never were you abandoned."

I combed my fingers through my hair and glanced around the narrow hallway. "Why are we in an attic?"

She reached for the knob and turned it. "This is Quentin's chamber." Pushing the door open, she stepped in and flicked a wall switch.

I was at a loss for words at what I saw. The room was large and the windows were stained glass. Walled bookshelves, from floor to ceiling, were filled with leather-bound books of all sizes. To one corner of the room sat an antique mahogany desk and chair, with a Tiffany lamp and a quill pen, inkwell, an opened journal and a photo album atop it.

"Everything is just as he left it thirty-five years ago," Olena said, making her way across the large room to a curtained wall. She pushed aside the green, velvet drapery to reveal a glass encasement.

I neared the large container, my heart racing at what I saw inside.

"He looks quite peaceful, don't you think?" Olena whispered. "But grant you, looks are deceiving. Within, my father is troubled. He knows there is much to say and do, in so little time."

My voice failed me as my eyes wandered over the suspended form inside. Naked, except for a small cloth covering his genitals, Quentin MacRaven floated inside the glass coffin. He was a tall man, broad shouldered and hardy looking, in spite of his age.

"Who's looked after him all this time?"

"Harrington's father, Manning Harrington, Sr. He was the curator of a museum and hid Quentin's chamber among the other antiquities stashed in the basement. In return for his help, I paid Manning a monthly stipend and allowed him, his wife and son to live here in the mansion. Now the son has taken over. Since his wife's death ten years ago, and his daughter's departure to Australia, Harrington has brought my father back to the mansion." Olena glanced down at her father in the encasement. "As long as he stays in the chamber, he'll continue to look seventy-two, the age he was when he climbed in there."

"Unbelievable." I gasped, placing a hand on the glass case. Energy like an electrical current coursed through me, crackling and sparking like a downed power line. I pulled my hand away, the hairs on the back of my neck standing on end.

"Remarkable, isn't it?" Olena said in awe. "Nothing can touch him; not even time."

"Can he get out of this thing?" I walked around the glass container, glimpsing Quentin MacRaven from every side.

"No. He's too weak, been in there too long."

"Why did he choose to stay here, enter this...this glass chamber, instead of escaping with you and Zackery?"

"He needed to stay here for you, to keep the powers alive within you. If the connection were broken before you were skilled, all would be lost."

I raised my gaze to hers. "Again, you talk of powers and skill."

"Quentin will explain all that to you."

I frowned. "I thought you said he's too weak to get out."

"He is, or was, but now he can transmit as a hologram using the energy that's just entered the room."

My frown deepened. "And what energy would that be, Olena?"

Her lips thinned. "Yours, Guylan...it's your energy Quentin can use."

Thirteen

Mortimer MacRaven stood beneath the street lamp, looking up at the apartment windows on the second floor of the brownstone. The stench of his rotting soul overpowered the spring scents of the many flowers lining the walkway. He swallowed the taste of death lingering on the back of his tongue. It wouldn't be a peaceful passing by any means. In all truth, it would be quite the contrary, and it loomed closer with each fleeting day. He could feel his strength waning; when he glimpsed into a mirror, he saw the light in his eyes fading. Yet, in spite of the changes his body was undergoing and the pending torment wrenching his heart, all was not lost.

He pulled the newspaper clipping from his pocket. "Ye look so much like yer da," he whispered.

And like Xavior, ye too will die, but this time I will keep yer soul for meself.

His time with the dark fae of Dublin, Ireland had taught him a most useful skill, the ability to take another's soul. But he only needed one—Guylan's—in order to possess the power he craved.

He returned his gaze to the apartment building, Guylan's windows dark now with his absence. Earlier, his great-nephew had carried with him the MacRaven book of secrets, a hallowed possession he'd coveted for years. Tonight, Mortimer would win two victories: the extension of his life and the MacRaven powers.

He smiled to himself as he made his way across the street.

No...all is not lost, not by any means.

~ * ~

Nela woke with a start.

"Everything's just fine, sweetie," Gram consoled, giving Nela's foot an affectionate squeeze.

She blinked her eyes into focus. "I guess your foot rubs still have the power to put me to sleep."

Gram chuckled. "Next you'll need a back rub, if you stay the night sleeping on this couch."

Nela stretched her arms over her head and yawned. "And you were just about to tell me what it was like to be—"

"We've done enough talking for tonight, time for bed," Gram interrupted.

Nela removed her feet from her grandmother's lap and set them on the floor, glancing at the clock on the entertainment center. It read ten o'clock. She stood and stretched her back. Gram was right; already the muscles across her shoulders ached. "It's not all that late, so I think I'll try calling Guylan."

"Do you think that's wise, Nela?"

She turned to look down at her grandmother. "You're right. It would be better if I went to see him."

"That's not what I meant, young lady," Gram scolded. "I think you should give him the chance to come to terms with all you've told him."

She shook her head. "Guylan and I have never gone to bed mad at each other."

"That is an essential element in a good relationship. It's a lesson my mother taught me and one I passed on to your mother. In turn, she's taught you, and I'm happy you abide by it...except this is a different circumstance."

Nela frowned. "Why is it different?"

"You two didn't just have a disagreement...he's not angry with you over something you said or did that he didn't like. He's astounded, confused and maybe even a little frightened over what you've revealed to him. He needs time to regroup, think things over, and weigh the pros and cons of this situation without you looking him in the face."

"I can't stay back and wait, Gram."

Gram stood. "Very well, then, go get dressed so we can be on our way."

"What's this *we* stuff?"

Gram raised a defiant chin. "I'm coming with you, of course. I got you into this circumstance, it's only right I help to get you out."

"Gram, I—"

"This is not up for negotiation, Nela." Gram gave Nela's behind a quick slap. "Now, off with you...get dressed!"

~ * ~

The air left my lungs.

Olena moved closer. "Oh dear, you don't look very well, Guylan."

I managed to squeeze the words out, past my closing throat. "Just tell me I didn't hear you right."

"You've heard everything I've said, just as I've said it. Quentin needs your energy, although at this moment you don't look as though you've much left."

I braced myself against the wall.

"Perhaps it would be wise for you to sit," Olena suggested. "Harrington's already left for your apartment and I dare say, should you faint again, I'll have to leave you lying on the floor."

I took a deep breath and made my way on shaky legs to the chair I'd seen by the desk. After taking a moment to collect my bearings, I forced myself to speak again. "You can't be serious."

"I've never been more serious in my life," she stated. "You are his only hope. For that matter, you're the only hope any of us has at this dire moment."

A newfound strength surfaced, along with my annoyance. "I know nothing of this family's *hocus pocus*, and I don't want to know."

"It's not a case of what you want," she countered. "But what you are destined to do, for Quentin, for your parents, Audra, and even yourself."

My stomach churned. "My parents and sister are long dead and gone, nothing will change that. And I've done pretty well on my own till now."

"That is where ye are wrong, Guylan," came a deep voice from the opposite side of the room.

I turned to see Quentin MacRaven standing beside the green velvet drapery shielding his glass coffin. I cast a glance inside the case, and still the man's body floated within. "How...how did you do that without me feeling anything?" I stammered, surveying his glowing presence with wide eyes and a racing heart.

"He's just attaching himself to the currents of energy in your body and projecting a hologram through your eyes," Olena explained. "It's how he can talk with you, train you in what needs to be done."

Train me to do what?

Quentin MacRaven stood tall and imposing outside the container, garbed in a gown and robe. Both garments were virgin white, a white so pure and dazzling, my eyes watered with its brilliance. The gown was fastened around his middle by a girdle, a large crystal encased in gold at its center. Round his neck he wore the breastplate of judgment and below that was poised a serpent's jewel or the *Glain Neidr*. On his head he wore a gold tiara and upon each of the two fingers of his right hand sat a ring, one of plain gold and the other the chain ring of divination. This was all being explained to me by Olena as I collected my wits.

I cleared my throat and straightened my shoulders. "I see you've changed your outfit from what you wear to intimidate me. Was this all done to impress me, scare me into doing what you want? If so, your parlor tricks won't work."

The old man's face wrinkled like paper with his frown. "Och, nay, how could I have done this before, lad?"

I chuckled. "Oh, come on, MacRaven. You've been stalking me for months, only wearing the hat and cape." I cocked my head sideways. "But something is missing...ah, the dead silence."

Quentin cast a quick glance at Olena. "Did ye know o' his sightin', daughter?"

"Yes, Da," she admitted. "He just told me of them when we were downstairs."

Quentin turned his gaze back to me. "'Tis not I, Guylan, ye have seen. I could not appear to ye outside this room and I have not worn the clothin' ye described in years. Not since I have been made an Archdruid." The old man sighed. "Ach, me worst fears have finally come to pass."

My pulse beat with erratic spurts. "And what were those?"

"'Twasn't me ye saw, *mo ghile*, me lad," MacRaven replied.

I locked eyes with the apparition standing before me. "Then who..." The words caught in my throat as the answer to that question finally dawned. "Mortimer," I whispered aloud.

"Aye," Quentin agreed in a bitter tone. "*Mo bhrathair*, me brother's come back."

Fourteen

Sophia reached for Nela's arm. "Nela, I don't feel right entering Guylan's apartment with him not at home."

Nela turned the key in the lock. "Not to worry, Gram. I do it all the time, and Guylan doesn't mind, or else he wouldn't have given me a key."

She followed Nela through the door. "But what are we accomplishing by sitting in an empty apartment?"

"I want to be here when he comes home." Nela flicked a nearby switch and cast a glance at her watch. "Where do you suppose he could be at this hour of the night?"

"Now, don't get your imagination all fired up," Sophia warned, moving to sit in the armchair by the bay window. "He's probably doing what your father did, getting drunk. I just hope he's smart enough to take a cab home."

Nela took a seat on the sofa. "Guylan would never drive drunk; he has too much respect for life...his and others."

Sophia looked around the living room. "At least he's clean, neat for a man; has good taste in décor as well."

Nela giggled. "He was brought up by nuns, Gram, what would you expect?"

She sniffed the air. "Maybe I spoke too soon. Do you smell that?...Like something is rotting."

Nela inhaled. "I don't smell anything."

Sophia stood and pointed to a door at the far side of the room. "It's coming from that room in there."

"That's Guylan's den." Nela stood and made her way to the door.

Sophia followed close behind.

Nela opened the door and gasped. The caped man was sitting at Guylan's desk, reading a large book. She shut the door and motioned for Sophia to follow her into the living room. "He's here."

"Who's here?"

"Guylan's stalker. He's broken into the apartment," Nela whispered.

Sophia grabbed Nela by the arm and pulled her toward the front door. "We need to get out of here; he may be armed."

"Halt where ye stand," boomed the voice behind them.

Nela's feet froze.

The caped man neared, moving to stand between them and the front door. "Well, well, ye must be Nela?" He pulled a crumpled newspaper clipping from his vest pocket and held it up. "I recognize ye from the announcement." He searched her face. "Though, I must say, the photo does not do ye justice, lass."

Sophia looked deep into the man's eyes—they were eyes she'd seen before, yet different. "Do I know you?"

He chuckled, his top lip curling into a sneer. "Nay, 'tis not me ye know, woman, but *mo bhrathair*, me brother."

Her eyes widened, a rush of recognition washing over her. "Yes, I remember now."

"He is the reason ye are here this Beltane." He pointed to the sofa. "I command ye now...the both of ye, to sit."

The two of them walked like robots under his control, their feet betraying them.

"What do you want?" Nela swallowed hard. "Is it money? If so, I'll give you all I have on me."

The caped man threw his head back and laughed. "I have more money than I know what to do with."

Sophia reached for her granddaughter's hand.

"What then...what do you want?" Nela repeated.

"A soul, Miss O'Riley. I have come for the soul o' yer precious Guylan." He snickered. "Perhaps yer own as well."

~ * ~

When Nela opened her eyes, she shot a look at her surroundings and frowned. She didn't remember how she'd gotten from Guylan's apartment to the dank, dungeon-like room where she now found herself. The stone walls were coated with a green mold and the windows were boarded up...the only light, a bulb attached to a wire hanging from a wooden beam. Her eyes sought the dimly lit chamber for her grandmother and found the elderly woman locked in a glass cell.

"Gram, can you hear me?" she choked out.

Gram put her hands to the glass, her words muffled. "Nela, are you all right?"

She attempted to go to her grandmother, but discovered she was restrained. Her right wrist was cuffed to a wood-slat headboard. The mattress she laid upon, dusty and stained, reeked of mildew.

She was clad in nothing but a hospital-type robe, the back open and the hem just reaching her knees. Her face heated at the thought of the caped man stripping her of all her clothes and re-dressing her in the skimpy gown. Each time she sat forward, her bared backside scraped against the bedding's course, tattered covering. The filthy stuffing oozed from the torn material, littering the dirt floor, and the thought of bed bugs or fleas, coupled with the horrible stench, made her gag.

"Nela, are you all right?" Gram repeated.

"I...I think so," she stammered. She pulled at the handcuff with her free hand, to slip the restrained hand free, but her efforts were in vain. Though she had a tiny wrist, it wasn't slim enough to slide from the iron band. "What happened?"

"I'm not quite sure. There's something about his voice that commands obedience, and he was able to demand we follow him here." Gram scanned the room from her glass prison. "Wherever *here* is."

The caped man appeared out of nowhere. "Ye are in the basement o' me mansion," his voice bellowed from the doorway. He made his way over to Nela and sat at the edge of the mattress. The stalker's shirt, unbuttoned to the waist, revealed ancient rune-like symbols tattooed down the center of his chest. Hanging from a thick, silver choker chain around his neck was a charm in the shape of a raven.

He caressed Nela's cheek with the tip of a finger. "Guylan is a lucky lad to have ye, *mo nighean dubh*, me black-haired lass." He grinned, showing a row of large, rotting teeth. "But now his luck has run out."

"Who are you and why do you want to harm Guylan?" she demanded.

"Och, how rude o' me." His eyes scanned the length of her. "Let me introduce meself." He inclined his head politely. "I am Mortimer MacRaven, Guylan's great-uncle."

"You lie. Guylan doesn't have any family; he's an orphan," she snapped.

"Perhaps I should explain," Mortimer said.

A rush of fear and rage raced through her body, as his story unfolded. She had no doubt this man was capable of murdering Guylan's parents, and now planned on exchanging Guylan's soul for his.

"And ye, lass, are along for added insurance," Mortimer concluded. "Until I can rob Guylan o' his soul, 'twill be the one ye have I'll be takin' for good measure. 'Twill be a spare until the main one is ready." He threw his head back and laughed, the wicked cackle sending chills down her spine.

"So, let me get this straight...I'm your rebound soul?"

Mortimer leaned forward, bringing his face up close to hers. "Ach, ye have summed it up just right, lass." He kissed her lightly on the tip of the nose. "'Twill be yer soul that will be keepin' me alive until I have the soul and power I deserve."

Nela jerked her head aside, her flesh crawling with the feel of his lips. She could smell the horrible stench Gram had mentioned earlier. It reminded her of rotting meat. And giving him a closer look, which she was compelled to do since his face was so near hers, Mortimer MacRaven didn't look as young as he had from a far glance. Beneath the pale flesh, blue veins ran like tiny roads on a map across his forehead, down the temples, to the cheeks and neck. In his transparent blue eyes, she saw the faces of evil, several tiny cameos with angry and snarled expressions, all mingling in fury around the opaque orbs. She swallowed the rising fear and nausea threatening to shatter her resolve and spew from her mouth.

"*Mo ghraidh*, me dear Nela, Guylan should be receivin' the note I sent him just about now." He cast a crooked smile. "If he is any sort o' *a duine*, man o' worth, he will be here to save ye as I planned. 'Twon't be long before everythin' falls the way I hoped 'twould."

"And what are you planning to do with my grandmother?"

One of Mortimer's dark, bushy brows rose. "Do? Why should I do anythin' with her?" He cast a quick glance at Sophia, pacing in her glass cell. "Her soul is o' no use to me, and will return to the afterlife in twenty-four hours." He turned back to look at Nela. "But her body will remain here, where 'twill shrivel and decay."

Nela shuddered with the thought, her stomach churning.

"And without her body as a host," Mortimer continued, "she will never be able to cash in on her *bheabachd,* blessin', again." He rocked with depraved laughter and stood. "I will be leavin' the two o' ye alone now, give ye a chance to say yer goodbyes." Leaning over Nela, he pushed aside a tendril of hair from her forehead. "Ye see, lass, I am not completely heartless, only soulless, and soon not even that."

After Mortimer left the chamber, tears welled in Nela's eyes, slipping down her cheeks. She inhaled the stale air surrounding her and called out to the one she loved so dearly and feared the most for.

"Gram, how am I going to get you out of that glass enclosure to set you free?"

"First, dry the tears, Nela, and pull yourself together. If you stay strong, don't let your fear get the best of you, you'll have a chance at survival."

She wiped her eyes with the back of her free hand. "But Gram, if you stay in that cube until after midnight..." her voice trailed off with the thought of her grandmother's body decaying into dust before her very eyes.

"There are no *buts* about it, Nela. What you're going to do is buck up and not crumble under pressure," Gram interjected with a sternness in her voice that meant business. "Now, take a deep, calming breath and conduct yourself in accordance."

Fifteen

I sat at the antique desk to collect my wits. With the thought of Mortimer MacRaven, the man hell-bent on my demise, being the one stalking me these many months, I had to force air into my lungs. "He would be old too, wouldn't he?"

"He will be ninety-seven," Quentin said. "But no doubt he is usin' the spell o' a *shimmour*, a guise to look younger. The dark fae do it all the time."

I glanced at the family photo album lying on the marbled desktop and with a finger, traced the familiar raven symbol on its cover.

"'Tis the family's crest," Quentin said, his presence moving closer, his light casting a magical glow upon the book of photos.

I held up my hand and looked at the ring's crest, vibrating, coming to life with the man's presence. It was an exact image to the one on the book Sister Margaret had given me earlier, and now to the one on the photo album. "What does the raven mean?"

"Me great-great-grandfather's name was Ian MacCorbie. *Corbie* is the Scottish word for raven. When Ian came o' age, he left his clan against his family's will to join the Druids. The family, an angry lot they were with Ian's choice, renounced the lad and with their declaration o' disownment, took from him the MacCorbie name. They wanted no part o' Ian's spiritual choice, that bein' a time when witches and those dabblin' in the supernatural were hunted down and burned at the stake. Word came to Ian that his family proclaimed him dead by means o' drownin' in order to save their own skins and avoid retribution from the authorities. This saddened and disturbed Ian, the young lad that he was, and the Archdruid took pity upon him. After ordination, the high priest gave to Ian the ring ye wear, with the words *Corbie Xenos* engraved along the sides. *Xenos* in Greek means *foreigner* or *stranger*," Quentin explained.

I nodded. "Once I looked up the word and learned its origin, but I couldn't find what *Corbie* meant."

"Ian was then considered a stranger, a foreigner to the MacCorbie clan, and so the name he was given by his new family o' Druid priests was MacRaven," Quentin said.

"And what is the meaning of the raven symbol?" I probed.

"The raven is considered to be the oldest and wisest o' all animals. If a person has the wisdom o' a raven, 'tis said that one possesses the supernatural powers o' a *seer* and has the second sight." Quentin moved to stand on the opposite side of the desk. "The raven represents the sun...healin', the sign o' creation, protection and prophecy as well as transformation."

I looked up at him and our eyes met. In his I saw, for only a moment, great wisdom and strength, and then a flicker of sadness. "Can raven magic be a dark power as well?"

Quentin gave a taut nod. "Aye, lad, it can also mean a moonless night and death. The *Bean Sidhe,* Banshees, take the shape o' the raven, their cries on a roof top are an omen o' death for one in the household livin' below." He sighed. "Och, on the dark side, the raven is the totem o' Goddess Morgan le Fay, a pan-Celtic sorceress. She is called the Queen o' *Dubh Sidhe*, the dark fae queen."

"And that's where Mortimer has gone, to that dark side."

Quentin's lips thinned. "Och, aye. For many years now, me brother has been in a *droch aite*, bad place."

I combed my fingers through my hair. "There's something that baffles me. If he's been gunning for me all this time, and now finally found me, why has he hesitated to do away with me? He's had more than enough chances."

"He needed to direct ye here first, so ye would have the chance to learn who ye were, what ye are."

"What am I?"

"In yer veins runs the blood o' a powerful clan and the supernatural abilities to do things ye would never imagine yerself capable o'. Ye have the gift o' second sight, as well as healin' powers and the ability to bequeath a blessin'," Quentin explained.

"Like you've done for families, giving deceased loved ones a chance to return for two days a year at Beltane?"

"Aye." He smiled. "I see ye have already read the book."

I nodded. "A few pages here and there."

"Not to mention yer engaged to the daughter of a family Quentin's blessed," Olena added.

"I'm sure that family is favored above the rest, since Olena would not be here today without such intervention," I reflected aloud.

Quentin nodded, his smile broadening. "Ye speak the truth, Guylan, and I am pleased to hear ye have joined yerself to that family. They are good people, trustworthy and carin'." He cleared his throat and brought the conversation back to the business at hand. "As ye stand here today, ye have not a clue how to use the powers, since ye have not had the opportunity to be taught by Xavior. Mortimer knows this. Until ye have had some trainin', he will not make a move."

"Then ignorance is bliss. Leave me untrained and I'll stay safe."

"It doesn't work like that," Olena said.

I frowned. "Then how does it work?"

"Me own *tannasq,* spirit, is dwindlin', Guylan. Soon the light o' this world will be gone from me and 'twill be the mists o' the afterworld I'll be enterin'. All that keeps me here is ye, and me obligation to pass to ye what ye need to know in order to defend yerself against Mortimer." Quentin took an audible breath, at least to my mind's eye...where he dwelled, it appeared that way. "I have reason to believe me brother, from his time with the dark fae, has learned to rob souls. His will soon be doomed, and 'tis yer own soul he will be wantin'."

"But he wants a powerful soul, so he can be what you are, right?" I countered.

"Aye, to a degree, but a soul is still a soul and right now an untrained soul is better than the rottin' *tannasq* he has," Quentin said.

Again, I frowned, confused. "Then that brings us back to my original question. Why hasn't he taken it from me by now?"

"Because he's not interested in your untrained soul, he'd rather wait till yours is ripe," Olena said. "And while he waits, he'll snatch another's."

A knock at the door interrupted my next question. It was Harrington. He'd returned from my apartment.

"I saw the devil himself, I did." Harrington's stubby fingers twitched nervously. "He appeared out of nowhere and snatched the book from my hands, then tied my wrists and ankles with rope, gagged me and put me in the closet, leaving the door ajar just enough for me to see everything going on in the sitting room." He shivered, his watery gray eyes darting from me to Olena, then to Quentin as he spoke. "Then the girl arrived."

I jumped on his words. "Girl, what girl?"

"A pretty one, sir, with long black hair and large, dark eyes. I saw her as she came through the door. She let herself in with a key and an older woman followed."

My heart sank to my toes. "That's my Nela." I frowned. "Why would she and her grandmother be coming to my apartment at such a late hour of..." my words caught in my throat as I remembered how I'd left things with her and our pact, *never to go to sleep mad at each other*.

"And then that caped devil came from the other room, with the book beneath his arm, and commanded they sit," Harrington rambled on, his long, skinny tongue licking his dry lips.

"Mortimer used voice control," Quentin said.

"And the two women followed him out the door with no question about it, just tagged along like a puppy to his master." Harrington took a deep breath. "As soon as I was alone, the ropes fell from my wrists and ankles and I was free, but before I left, I spotted this note on the floor beside my foot." He pulled an envelope from his pocket and handed it to me. "It is addressed to you, sir."

I opened it with trembling fingers and found the answer to the question I had been about to ask before Harrington interrupted us. It was written in the same script as the other notes.

Whose soul would Mortimer use while mine was being trained?

The answer...he would take Nela's.

Sixteen

Olena Sincloud watched her grandson's face turn pale for the third time that night, only this time his strength amplified instead of weakening and he bolted to his feet, making his way to the door.

"Och, where do ye think yer goin', lad?" Quentin snapped, his form growing more solid.

She knew it had to do with the adrenalin rushing through Guylan's body. His determination to run to Nela's aid was recharging his energy and that burst was flowing into Quentin's body, increasing the old Druid's strength as well.

Guylan turned, his blue eyes flashing with rage, and answered in the same, sharp tone. "I'm going to help Nela."

"Help her do what, Guylan?" Quentin said, softening his own words.

"Get away from that fiend…he will not take the only family I've known," Guylan bellowed.

And those words, *the only family I've known*, echoed in Olena's heart. Nela was all Guylan had, the only person he had ever loved and who loved him in return. He knew of no parents, grandparents or siblings…all he had was the heart Nela had given him and now that was being threatened.

"Harrington, bring up the brandy," she said.

"Yes, ma'am," Harrington agreed.

"I don't want any more brandy," Guylan shouted. "What I want is to get the hell out of here and to my Nela."

His face turned red with his anger, as Zackery and Xavior's had done in the throes of their rage. So much like his father and grandfather was this young man standing before her, her heart ached. It was almost as though the two had come back from the dead, altered, but basically the same—the same wealth of dark hair, the same shaped nose, the same confident profile: squared jaw and strong chin. But the eyes, they were hers and her da's, the MacRaven eyes, an unfathomable cornflower shade of blue, large and round, smart and assessing. And right now, they were like summer lightning, flashing with fury. She dismissed Harrington and shut the door behind him.

Guylan turned on her and spat out his words with contempt. "Get away from the door, old woman, or I'll remove you myself."

"Guylan, sit down...now!" Quentin bellowed, pointing to the chair. The Tiffany lamp upon the desk hummed with the vibration of his voice.

There was only one other time Olena had seen her da as mad as he was now. It was a few years after the choking incident at the bakery. Quentin, from that time on, had kept a closer eye on her and Anya, worrying and fussing over them to no end. Their mother scolded Quentin, asked him to ease up at being so overprotective. The day he complied with his wife's wishes, Anya, then only six years old, developed a persistent cough. Olena got into the herb cupboard and concocted a potion. She added the blend to Anya's tea that night, in the hopes it would heal her younger sister.

Instead, Anya almost died, vomiting until nothing spilled from her mouth but green bile. Olena confessed to giving her sister the herbal remedy and Anya was rushed to the hospital. There she stayed for three days and Olena was sent to stay with her Aunt Sheava, her mother's sister, while her parents kept a vigil by Anya's bedside.

The day Anya came home from the hospital, Olena was overjoyed, but her happiness was not to last. The days of not knowing if his youngest daughter would live or die had taken a toll on Quentin. Before bed that night, he entered Olena's room, a lethal calmness in his eyes, sat at the edge of the bed and pulled her over his knees. Her nightgown was pulled up and thrown over her head, and the flesh of her tender, young arse felt Quentin's wrath.

When her mother had come in to soothe her, she sobbed. "Why did you let him do that to me?"

Her mother, with tears in her own eyes, pulled her close and held her tight against her bosom. "'Twas necessary to do, because we love ye, me dear daughter, and Anya as well."

The raw pain didn't feel like love until she became a mother herself. It was then Olena knew her parents had spoken the truth.

She walked over to Guylan and placed a hand on his arm. Looking deep into his eyes, she wondered if Anya had guided him with love when he got out of line. Did he know...did he feel the love? Was her sister able to show Guylan any affection without looking like she favored him? She smiled and made a silent gesture toward the chair.

He obeyed, taking his seat with a scowl on his face and his arms crossed over his chest.

"Now, lad," Quentin continued, his temper somewhat composed, "will ye sit there like a *clot-heid*, fumin' because ye could not get yer own way? Or will ye be listenin' to me plan?"

Guylan, the MacRaven stubborn streak etched upon his face, turned to look at Quentin. "I'm listening."

"Without the book o' secrets, I canna train ye as I would like, but I know someone who can," Quentin said.

Guylan relaxed his pose and leaned forward in his seat. "Who do you know?"

"Your da. Xavior can teach ye," Quentin said.

Guylan's dark brows pulled into an affronted frown. "Do you have dementia, old man? My father's been dead for thirty-five years."

Quentin's mouth thinned with displeasure. "Aye, he is dead to us in the here and now, but he was alive back when."

Guylan chuckled. "I haven't got time for this crazy talk, not while Nela's life is in danger."

"But the element o' *time* is exactly the answer," Quentin pressed.

Guylan's agitation grew. "How is time the answer, other than the fact we're wasting precious minutes of it when we could be helping Nela?"

Quentin moved closer to Guylan. "None of us is locked into any certain time; ye have seen this for yerself with the blessin' I have bestowed upon Nela's family. Not just the dead can be journey takers, but the livin' as well."

"And where are *we* living supposed to go?" Guylan replied, annoyed.

"If 'tis possible for us to travel this universe beyond the eternities, between life and death, then 'tis also possible to jump from present to past, and even into the future."

Guylan, exasperated, threw his hands up. "What in God's name are you babbling about?"

Quentin took a deep, calming breath. "Have ye never heard o' time travel?"

Seventeen

Just when I had begun to think the evening couldn't get any more bizarre than it already was, I was proven wrong. "Time travel," I all but screeched. "What kind of an insane solution is that?"

Quentin scowled. "'Tisn't an insane solution at all, lad. In fact, time travel is the only source we have to fix this mess."

I felt my rage mount to undesirable proportions. "If you were capable of doing this, why didn't you do something right after my family was murdered? Why didn't you take yourself back a few days and prevent it?"

"I needed someone with powers to remain here, be the balance," Quentin said.

"Then why not send Olena through?" I probed and then narrowed my eyes. "Or aren't women equal to men in this case?"

"Nay, the female gender is no barrier, if she were able to do the work." He sighed. "But me powers escaped this daughter." He smirked. "And the other daughter, who inherited the gift, ironically has no use for them."

My eyes widened. "Sister Margaret has your powers?"

Quentin nodded. "I was helpin' her fine-tune them when she became a wee bit *camstairy*, obstinate, ran away and joined the nunnery." He sighed again. "And without certain properties and elements in the equation, like the energy to help navigate through time, lastin' *coil*, troublesome circumstances and repercussions could arise."

I threw my hands in the air again, out of frustration, fatigue and bone-seeping worry for Nela...take a pick, it was all there, swirling around inside of me. "Of course, there are always consequences, aftermaths, or some life-threatening cost." I narrowed my eyes. "I can hardly wait to hear what the downside is for me."

"Well, then, that bein' said, I shall tell ye," Quentin replied, struggling to stay calm. "A person ye know in the here-and-now must also connect with ye in the past, to keep ye weighted or grounded to yer original origin. Without this attachment to yer own time period, ye will not be able to return."

I couldn't even believe I was having this conversation, but then again, I was conversing with a hologram, a figment relayed from my own energy, so why not talk the absurd? "You mean I could just freeze in that time frame?"

"Not freeze, but stay and live it out all over again," Quentin corrected.

"Which means I would be living in this time, my present day, as a man of seventy-three years old," I calculated.

"Aye, 'tis the truth o' it," Quentin agreed. "On the other hand, if Mortimer is stopped, not only would yer parents and Audra be alive, but Nela would be safe from him as well."

"But I could lose having a life with Nela," I countered.

"True again," Quentin said. "Unless—"

"Unless what?" I interrupted.

"Unless I send ye back as a babe sleepin' in a *crèche*, nursing from your mama's breasts and messin' yer *clout*, a lad the age ye were when the murders happened. In that way, should I not be able to draw ye back, ye will just relive yer life, only this time with a family."

I frowned. "I know if something is altered, the results may be as well."

Quentin gave a taut nod. "Ye may or may not meet Nela."

"So, if I stay, Nela could die at the hands of Mortimer. If I go and remain, I'd be too old for her, and if I am a toddler, I may grow up without ever meeting her." My frown deepened. "Either way, those are not very good odds on Nela's and my behalf."

"I fear 'tis the truth o' it, lad," Quentin admitted.

I was torn by conflicting emotions and needed a moment to think. I stood and paced the room, thinking back on the time I'd already had with Nela. Would it last me a lifetime? Would I always remember her...the way she smiled, the sound of her voice? How could I live without ever again holding her in my arms, feeling her seductive, young body, uptilted, full breasts and curved hips melting against my naked flesh?

I closed my eyes, miserable, grief and despair tearing at my heart. Until now, outside of Sister Margaret, Nela was all I'd had in the way of family. My eyes shot open. "Sister Margaret," I shouted.

"Aye, what of her, lad?" Quentin said.

"She's who I know here that would also be in the past," I said, hope resounding within me.

But Quentin immediately squelched that hope. "If ye return as a child, Anya would have no contact with ye. She disowned her family, wanted no part o' us. There is a slim chance ye would ever have the opportunity to meet her, as little as ye would be and needin' an adult to brin' ye to the orphanage."

"But if you send me back as a grown man, I could just wander over to St. Bernard's myself, act like I was a handyman wanting to donate my time to fixing up the place for the children. God knows the building was—still is—in constant need of repair, and that would give me an excuse to see her."

"The plan might work for ye to see Anya, but not to gain Xavior's trust to warn him o' Mortimer's attack," Quentin said. "'Tis not likely, in such a short span o' time, Xavior would become a close enough friend to ye to allow ye to be sleepin' in his home. And 'tis where ye would need to be, in that house on the night o' the murders."

I wandered restlessly around the room, realizing while we all debated on what course of action to take, Nela was being terrorized by Mortimer. With my thumbs pressed hard against my temples, I was hoping to pull from the depths of my brain the answer, when Olena placed a restraining hand upon my shoulder.

"What about me?" she said softly. "You know me here, and I am in the past."

I locked eyes with her, forgetting for a moment she was even in the room. "Yes, why didn't I think of it myself?"

She smiled. "We never think of the obvious." She pointed to the family album on the desk. "That's something else that might help."

I frowned. "How can a photo album help?"

"In there are pictures of Xavior, your mother, DeYonna, Audra and you...even Luna. If you look at them, hear me speak of them and get to know them, when you see them in the past you might have a chance at staying grounded."

I glanced to where Quentin's form stood. "Could it work?"

"Aye, between Olena bein' there and ye havin' knowledge o' yer family, it could," Quentin agreed.

I hurried to the desk and reached for the album, opening the book to the first page. "Tell me, Olena, and be quick about it, everything you can about my family."

~ * ~

Nela shivered. The skimpy gown she wore didn't offer much warmth in the damp dungeon where she and her grandmother were being held hostage by Mortimer MacRaven.

Gram's voice came muffled from behind the glass walls of her cell. "Can you jimmy a wooden slat free, Nela?"

She wiggled the wooden slat of the headboard with her free hand. It rattled a tad but stayed secure. "It's not budging."

"I had a bed with just such a headboard when I was a girl," Gram said. "And one day I was jumping and fooling around, and accidentally kicked a slat in half." She moved closer to the glass. "You have to hit it just right with your foot, in the center of the board in order to split the wood. Could you manage to get your foot above your head, like when you do a somersault, and give it a kick with the flat of your heel?"

"I think so." Nela hadn't taken five years of gymnastics and three years of kickboxing for nothing. Though it had been many years ago, she was still pretty nimble and able to do a split and a somersault, not to mention still having muscular legs. She brought her legs up and the hospital-like gown rose to her waist, leaving herself displayed. She straightened her legs and with her free hand, arranged the gown to cover her body.

"Never mind, Nela, it's only us girls here," Gram said. "Now, try again."

She scooted down as far as her restrained arm allowed and again doubled her knees to her chin. With a foot, she kicked the slat of wood she was secured to. The first blow sent shocks of pain through her leg. She hit the slat again, nearer to the center. Still, it held. Pain routed to her thighs and lower back. She took a deep breath and kicked again, throwing more of a thrust from her hips. The wood split and shattered.

"Good, Nela, now wiggle the broken board till it breaks free."

She got up on her knees, inhaled a deep breath and called upon every ounce of strength she could muster. With all her might, she pulled down on the split board, yanking it free from the headboard. The wood hung from her wrist like a stake. She ran to her grandmother's glass cell. With trembling hands, she searched the clear panes, moving up and down, side to side, to find a way to open the cubicle.

"Never mind about me." Gram pointed to a boarded window that had a piece of wood hanging. "That board is rotted, should easily come free." She then pointed to a barrel in the far corner of the room. "Climb up on the barrel and get out the window."

Nela shook her head, still looking for an opening in the glass prison. "I won't leave without you."

"Yes, you will," Gram snapped. "Now go, Nela...go while you can."

"Halt," a voice demanded.

Nela's body jerked to a standstill with the command, hands frozen in fists at her sides.

"The only place ye are going, *mo ghradh*, me dear lass," Mortimer bellowed, "is straight to *ifrinn*, hell!"

Eighteen

"This procedure can't be rushed," Olena warned me, turning to the first page of the photo album. "You need to look at their faces, focus and listen to the little innuendos I have to share about each one, in order for this plan to work."

Focus and listen. Would that even be possible with my thoughts on Nela and what she was enduring at the hands of a madman? In spite of my inner turmoil, I forced my attention on the picture of my parents on their wedding day. "Good heavens," I commented, "They're just kids."

"They ran away, eloped right out of high school," Olena said. "They met in the eighth grade, were inseparable from that time on. Zackery and I, and DeYonna's parents suggested they wait a bit, go to college first and get a job under their belts before they took on marriage and the responsibilities it entails. But as you see, they didn't listen. DeYonna's parents died shortly after she wed Xavior, her father from a stroke and her mother a few months later from a massive heart attack, so in a way it was good she had a husband and all of his folks to be her family." She sighed. "It was also very fortunate my husband was CEO of a bank and could give Xavior a position that could support a family, because Audra was born a year later."

"'Twas a wee bit like mother like son, would ye not agree, daughter?" Quentin chimed in.

"It's true. Zackery and I eloped as well, so I couldn't very well fault my son's actions. Zackery was thirty, but I was only eighteen when we wed. Although my parents adored Zackery, they wanted us to wait and have a longer engagement. I gave birth to Xavior by the time I was nineteen. When I was twenty, a tumor was discovered and I had to have a complete hysterectomy. Thankfully, it didn't turn out to be cancerous, but I was rendered barren. Had I waited to marry and conceive, I'd never have borne a child."

"This must have made Xavior all the more precious to you," I said.

"And then to have him taken away..." her voice trailed off.

"Did my mother have any siblings?"

"I believe she had an older brother. Presley Grayson was his name. He had been sent away somewhere, institutionalized for a mental illness or something of that type when DeYonna was only four or five years old. She didn't remember anything about him and her parents never talked much either, so I didn't feel it was appropriate to pry." She turned the page to a photo of my mother, long, dark hair curling around her shoulders, holding a baby in her arms. The infant was wrapped in a pale, blue blanket, just the tip of a round, dark-fuzzy head visible. "Here you are with DeYonna, a few hours after your birth," Olena explained.

My interest flowed as I studied my mother's face for the first time in my life. I was amazed at her beauty...the slender white neck and delicately carved bone structure. Her face was a perfect oval, her nose exquisite and dainty. Yet there was an inherent strength about her features, a sparkle in her large green eyes, and she had a determined chin, raised high and proud as her full lips smiled for the camera. Her hair shone, loose tendrils of it framing her face. She took my breath away. I heard myself muttering something to the effect of, "I can see why my father fell in love with her, didn't want to take the chance of losing her."

"Yes, she did leave Xavior spellbound," Olena reflected.

"DeYonna was *canty*, lively, cheery, the most tender and carin' woman I've ever met," Quentin added.

"She gave herself over in a complete manner and without reservation to her family, always thinking of better ways to make a happy and loving home for you all," Olena said. "She wanted a houseful of children, and had she lived, there is not a doubt in my mind you and Audra would have had at least a few more siblings." She chuckled. "Plus, my son couldn't keep his hands off her. Whenever they were together, she wasn't far from his reach and he'd either have his arm around her shoulder or be holding her hand. Once I asked DeYonna if Xavior's affections stifled her. She cast me a dreamy look and smiled, then said she welcomed his attention at any time of the day or night and hoped for more."

"Wow," was all I could manage to whisper.

Olena turned the page to a picture of my father, and I blinked, astonished at the strong resemblance we had to each other. Looking back at me from the photo were my blue eyes, my squared jaw, my straight nose, my wealth of ebony, unruly hair.

"Uncanny likeness, wouldn't you agree?" Olena said.

"Almost eerie," I concurred.

"If you really want eerie," Olena added, "your mannerisms are identical, which is mind-boggling since you hardly had the opportunity to see how he moved, the way he held himself when he walked. You become vexed like him, you even sound like him. It's just something in the genes, I guess, because you are a carbon copy of a man you've barely known."

"What was he like?" I was eager to know everything about him.

Olena's voice trembled with the reminiscence. "Strong in character, tender in love, compassionate and sensitive at heart. He worked hard at managing the family business as head of Sincloud Bank and Trust. He took over quite well when his father retired, never faltering in his duties, and making a difficult transition for Zackery, easier."

"I was trainin' him to take over for me as well," Quentin added. "He had the gift, was tuned in to the dynamics and symbolism o' the craft. He would have been a remarkable Archdruid, leadin' the clan for many years to come. And when it was time, Guylan, for ye to take over, Xavior would have instructed ye well."

"Death is never fair," Olena said. "But to have Xavior and DeYonna, two remarkable people, have their lives taken from them, snuffed out in such an unnecessary and ruthless manner," a sob escaped her throat. "Well, I can't help but choke on the injustice of it all."

I felt the same and I hadn't really known them. I could only imagine the grief Quentin and Olena harbored. Another page was turned and there I saw a photo of a sweet-faced little girl, amber curls and large blue eyes, holding a doll close to her heart.

"She took my copper locks," Olena said. "And my temper too, I am ashamed to admit." She chuckled. "She managed to get into everything and tax everyone's patience. I believe she got a hand to her bottom more often than not."

"I was the same," I admitted, remembering the many trips to Mother Superior's office.

"But what a large heart she had," Olena added. "She appreciated hugs and kisses, adored her baby brother and loved playing the piano."

"Was she any good at it?"

"She was brilliant for her age," Olena said.

Lastly there was a picture of Luna, lying on an oval rug beside a crib, head on paws and ears perked.

"Your special dog," Olena said.

"What made this dog so special?" I probed.

"Do ye know what a *kelpie* is, Guylan?" Quentin said.

I glanced his way and shook my head.

"A *kelpie* or *each uisge*, water horse, is a shape-shiftin' creature from Celtic folklore that haunts Scotland's rivers and lochs."

"And you believe Luna was a kelpie?"

"Xavior did," Quentin said.

I frowned. "Why…I mean, if such a thing existed, it haunted the waterways. What would it be doing on land, guarding a little boy?"

Quentin shrugged. "Och, *croich gorn*, yer guess is as good as mine, lad. I only know Xavior felt Luna possessed a supernatural presence." He chuckled. "And given the fact I am who I am, 'twas not for me to quibble."

"I have to admit, there was something in the animal's eyes," Olena confessed. "The way she looked at you when you spoke to her, like she understood. Many times, I believed she did."

I gazed back at the dog's picture and focused on her eyes. They appeared almost knowledgeable, wise, as they peered up at the camera.

"There's no doubt in my mind," Olena said, "if Luna had been at the house when Mortimer broke in, everything would have been different."

There was no longer any doubt I had to travel back in time and change the events that happened that night, but a frightening thought struck me. "How, as a toddler, will I have the ability to change things?"

"That brings us to the next step, Guylan," Quentin said.

I combed my fingers through my hair. I could wait not a moment longer to hear this next installment. "Which is?"

"If ye are to control things, have a better influence on the situation, then ye must at all times maintain yer adult intellect," Quentin said.

I shot him an incredulous glance. "Let me get this straight, I'll have a three-year-old body, sleep in a crib, suck milk from my mother's teats and crap in my pants, but I'll still have a thirty-eight-year-old brain?"

"Aye, that ye will, lad," Quentin said. "A wee bit o' an injury to yer pride, I grant ye, but necessary to accomplish the mission."

I smirked. "More than a wee bit." I became overwhelmed with the concept we were contemplating. How was I comprehending any of what had happened tonight, let alone reasonably decipher it?

"Ye must strive to see Olena, yer link to the present. The more people ye encounter from this era also livin' in the past, the stronger yer adult intellect will be. *Cuimhnich,* remember, I told ye there was a chance ye could get lost in the past?"

I nodded.

"Well, not enough contact with people ye know from this era would be how losing yerself would happen. Ye would begin to forget ye were who ye are and yer grasp on where ye really belong," Quentin explained.

I swallowed hard and cleared my throat. "And how do I return?"

"I will discuss that with ye now." Quentin extended his hand to me. "Remove the ring ye are wearin'."

I frowned, confused, but obeyed, handing him the ring.

He cupped it in his hands, making the raven crest glow a fiery red with the heat of his energy...or I should say, the energy he drew from me. When he held the ring close to my face, my eyes watered. I turned my gaze aside.

"Come near, lad," Quentin said.

I shielded my eyes and stood, making my way nearer to the hologram.

"Now, open yer mouth," Quentin instructed. I was ready to protest, but he held up a finger to silence my objections. "There is little time left for us to accomplish this task. It nears midnight."

I kept my silence and opened my mouth.

"Wider," he demanded.

I obeyed.

Grabbing the side of my lower lip, Quentin pressed the raven crest to the inside of my right cheek. My flesh sizzled and I stiffened with the shock of pain. Quentin then mumbled a few words I didn't understand and caressed with his finger the outside of my cheek. The pain ceased. I searched with my tongue for the shape of the raven branded in the soft tissue and found it raised and foreign, but already healed.

"That insignia will be yer compass, how ye will navigate through time. The raven is a messenger that will call to ye about life's creation. 'Tis a magical bird that will awaken yer spirit, show ye how alive the supernatural is within this world, what is available to ye, if ye seek and learn. Ye will feel the mystery and power manifested by an energy ye will need to bring ye from the dark and into the light." Quentin said, handing the ring to Olena, "She will keep it safe for ye."

"How do I use it?" I said, lest I find myself at Valley Forge with George Washington or watching the fall of Rome.

"Ye will think of the year ye want to visit and then press the insignia with the tip o' yer tongue."

"Let me recap here," I said, moistening my lips. "It's 1972 I want...July...?"

"Twenty-ninth," Olena was quick to add. "It was a Saturday."

"I think 'twill be better for ye to be gettin' yerself back a day or two before, to become more familiar with yer surroundin's," Quentin advised.

"So, I'll want Thursday, the twenty-seventh of July, 1972?"

"Aye," Quentin agreed. "When ye get that date in yer mind, press yer tongue to the raven crest etched in yer cheek and ye will be off."

I squared my shoulders and took a deep breath.

Quentin turned his attention to Olena. "Open the attic portal, *a leannan.*"

Olena walked over to one of the floor-to-ceiling bookcases. She reached beside the shelves and pulled on a decorative wall sconce. The ledge moved and a door was revealed...the door to the past.

I felt my mouth slacken with astonishment, a wash of heat and energy coursing through my body. I glanced inside at what loomed ahead and found a long, dark tunnel.

"Now, leave us, Olena," Quentin demanded.

Without a word, Olena left the room.

"Why did she have to leave?" I said, my eyes never leaving the mystic portal.

"I thought ye would be more comfortable if she were not here," Quentin said.

I turned to meet his gaze. "Why is that?"

"Ye will not be able to travel through time dressed as ye are."

I looked down at the white shirt and jeans I wore. "What is it I'm supposed to wear?"

Quentin arched a brow. "Why, nothin', *mo ghile*, me lad. Ye canna travel through time hampered by cloth."

My brows shot up. "You mean I have to be—"

"Naked." Quentin finished the sentence for me. "As naked as the day ye were born."

Nineteen

"Not even a stitch?" I implored.

"Nay, not a one, or else ye will not make a smooth transition."

From the smirk he tried to stifle, I got the impression he was thoroughly enjoying my reaction.

"But what happens when I show up on the other side, or wherever I'm going to emerge, wearing nothing but my birthday suit?"

"Och, *dinna fash* yerself, *mo ghile*. Since ye will only be but three years o' age, I *dinna* think it much matters," Quentin said, this time chuckling.

I frowned, annoyed. "I'm glad this is so amusing for you."

"'Tis how 'tis done, *mo ghile*. There must not be anythin' to interfere with the energy's flow." Quentin's smile faded and again he got down to the business at hand. "The threads within the cloth can entangle ye, stop ye short and freeze entry. Ye will then be stuck in limbo, not goin' forward or backward."

I sighed and removed my clothes. When I slipped off my briefs, I held them for a moment bunched in my hands. "Nothing," I inquired again, not meeting the hologram's gaze.

"Nothin'," Quentin countered. "And I'll be sayin' goodbye to ye now as well, lad. When ye return, I will be long gone on to me reward and embraced again in the arms of *mhuirnin*, me darlin' wife, Adorna."

"Then I'll see you next in eternity," I said, feeling a bit sad I would never have a chance to know him.

"That ye will," he said. "Now, step to the frame o' the portal."

I dropped the underwear to the Oriental-carpeted floor, squared my shoulders and neared the door, gazing into the empty abyss ahead.

"Close yer eyes, me *braw*, brave lad," Quentin instructed. "Relax yer arms, let them fall to yer side, and take a deep, cleansin' breath."

With a racing heart, I obeyed.

"After ye walk through the portal, 'twill feel like ye have stepped off a high cliff. *Dinna fash* yerself no matter how frightenin' the sensation or how strange the sounds. No matter what ye hear, never, under any circumstance, open yer eyes until yer body stops movin' and ye land on solid ground."

Too overwhelmed to speak, I just nodded my reply.

"While mentally recitin' the date ye wish to travel to, push the tip o' yer tongue against the raven brand marked on yer inner cheek and take a step forward," Quentin coached.

Again, I did as I was told.

In an instant I heard a *whooshing* sound humming in my ears. My body dropped at a rapid speed, to only God knows where. Louder the noise echoed through my head, my flesh first growing very hot, then cold, and then hot again. I felt my bones and muscles shrink in size and weight. Every nerve ending tingled, every fiber of my body was being altered. People were talking, softly at first, then louder. Music played, drowning out the voices, and then thunder crackled in the distance. Birds sang and I heard the rushing waters of a waterfall, all the while falling farther and faster.

I strained to keep the tip of my tongue rooted to the raven brand etched on my inner cheek. With my eyes clenched shut, I recited over and over in my mind, *July twenty-seventh, nineteen hundred and seventy-two.*

And then I hit something soft, the impact causing my body to bounce against something hard. I opened my eyes to peer out from between mahogany bars to a bright, cheery room done in blues, greens and yellows. Stuffed dogs and cats of all sizes and colors sat on wall shelves, plastic trucks and cars filled an opened toy chest that sat beside a chest of drawers. And on the walls were pictures of whimsical choo-choo trains with happy faces.

Raising a hand to touch the bars, I noticed my fingers. They were small and pudgy. I pulled back and glanced down at my body. My muscular chest had been replaced with a diminutive, round abdomen. At a further glimpse, my hard, athletically structured legs were now short and plump. Between my thighs sprouted the tiny stub of my manhood framed by two miniature sacs. I inhaled and got a whiff of something putrid. The stench gagged me and I pinched my button-shaped nose with a minuscule thumb and forefinger.

"Not a pretty smell is it, Guylan?" a woman's voice questioned.

I raised my gaze to the beautiful, dark-haired woman with large green eyes peering, perturbed down at me. I recognized her from the pictures I'd viewed earlier.

Mother!

With a knee, she hit a lever of some sort from beneath where I lay and the bars lowered. She reached for something at the foot of the cubicle and held it in the air. "This wouldn't happen if you'd only learn to go potty in the toilet."

Mortified, I realized it was a dirty diaper she was holding; obviously, my dirty diaper.

"Now don't you move a muscle, lest you soil your sheets, too," she cautioned, turning to throw the messy pants in a large trash can. The top of the silver dispenser swung inward to receive the smelly bundle.

My mother returned with a white container and placed it at the foot of the crib, which was what I realized I must be lying in. Pulling from it a soft, pleasant scented cloth, she grasped my ankles with a free hand and raised my legs high, lifting my behind clear off the mattress. To complete my shame, she thoroughly wiped clean my buttocks. After slathering my bottom with the emollient-coated cloth, she tossed it in the trash and drew out a fresh wipe from the container. Taking my tiny manhood between her thumb and forefinger, she pushed back the foreskin and cleaned my genitals.

I swallowed the humiliation, keeping in perspective I was only a child of three to her. I was the baby boy she had cared for since birth, and not a thirty-eight-year-old man who had just traveled back in time.

Lifting me from the crib, she set me down on the colorful, braided rug decorated with more train characters. I stumbled, not yet used to standing on such small limbs, and sat down hard on my behind.

"Still a bit sleepy, I see." She reached for me, setting me once again upon my fat, little feet.

I spied Luna, curled in a corner of the room on a dog bed. I pointed at the animal and opened my mouth to speak. I wanted to say, "There's the dog," but instead, all that escaped from my lips was, "Nice doggie."

"Yes, she is a nice doggie," my mother agreed, pulling from the chest of drawers an outfit for me to wear.

Luna stood and made her way over to me, licking my chin with her long, large tongue. I wiped my wet face with the back of a hand before petting the dog's head.

"Be nice to Luna, Guylan," my mother warned. "No pulling her ears."

I would never hurt an animal, I wanted to shout, but all that came forth was, "I like Luna."

"Good, because she loves you," my mother said. "You're her boy and she'll always protect you."

Luna nudged me, sniffed me all over, and when her dark eyes looked deep into mine, I sensed her wisdom. Could it be Luna knew I was a time traveler and the reason for my visit?

You must help me save my family.

Luna barked and wagged her tail.

I hugged the animal's large head and kissed her, realizing she understood.

Again, she licked my chin.

"Time to get dressed," my mother interrupted.

For this I was thankful, since standing unclothed was becoming more and more awkward. I made my way to where she stood and reached up for the clothes.

"First you've got to do pee pee in the potty, and then take a bath." She took me by the hand and led me out the bedroom door. I was paraded naked down the hallway to the bathroom, which was already occupied by a little red-haired girl sitting on the toilet.

"Mornin' Guy Guy," she chirped, knotting the material of her skirt in her hands, no doubt to keep it from falling in the commode and getting wet.

I stared tongue-tied, humiliated by the fact I had interrupted her during toilet time, and I was standing bare to the bone in front of her.

"He's a bit groggy this morning," my mother said, placing me on the cold seat of a child's pot that sat next to the big one. "Now do tinkle like Audra, Guylan."

Bedside me, I heard Audra's urine trickling down into the toilet's basin. "Now you do it, Guy Guy," she encouraged.

I looked down at the plastic lip that stuck up from the pot's seat, no doubt to keep urinating little boys from spraying the floor and wall.

"Come on, Guy Guy," Audra cheered me on. "It won't hurt you."

"You can do it, honey," my mother chimed in. "Go pee pee like a big boy."

I could if you two weren't in the room looking at me.

My mother turned her attention on Audra. "Hurry now. Dad's waiting downstairs to drive you to piano practice before he has to get to the bank. You want to do well at the recital, don't you?"

Audra nodded and stood, holding her skirt high on her hips as she slid off the toilet. Bending to reach the toilet paper hanging on a dispenser roll, she bared herself entirely to my view.

Respectfully, I turned away.

"Make sure you wipe yourself well, Audra," my mother said, turning on the tub's faucet.

"I know, I know, and then wash my hands with soap and warm water after," Audra recited.

My mother smiled. "You're a smart girl."

"Do you think Guy Guy is smart?" Audra pulled up her white panties and flushed the toilet.

"Yes, I do," my mother said, adjusting the temperature of the water filling the tub.

I smiled to myself.

Audra climbed up on a small footstool so she could reach the sink's faucet. "Then why does he poop in his pants?"

I frowned.

My mother came to my defense. "Because he doesn't know any better yet, but he's learning."

"He better get smarter and learn soon," Audra commented, wiping her hands on a nearby towel.

My mother shut the tub's faucet. "He will in time, Audra. But what I hope for you both is to know the importance of being kind. I want my children to grow to be people of value."

I smiled again. *I am a kind person with values. I care for animals, I love a good woman, and I respect life.*

My mother tilted her head as she reflected on the words of her next sentence. "I think it was Albert Einstein who said a man should try not to be a man of success, but a man of value."

"Who's Albin Einsteen?"

My mother chuckled. "Albert Einstein, Audra, not Albin Einsteen," she corrected. "He was a very smart man, a scientist who is best known for his theory of relativity."

"The theory of what?" Audra probed.

"I'll explain it to you further when we have more time," my mother said. "We can look it up in the encyclopedia when you come home."

Thirty years from now, Audra, all you'll need to do is Google old Albert's name and an online encyclopedia, like Wikipedia, will tell you his theory of relativity.

"Did he have lots of friends?" Audra continued.

"I haven't the foggiest idea," my mother said. "Why do you ask?"

"Because I think having lots of friends makes a person valuable," Audra said thoughtfully.

Audra, you little philosopher...you're going to love the innovation that lies ahead.

"And if Guy Guy doesn't do better than his very best, he won't have any friends. No one wants to play with someone who makes a smelly, yucky mess in their pants," Audra concluded.

I squared my little shoulders and bore down with my stomach muscles, producing a long, loud stream into the pot.

Audra's eyes widened. "Mom, he did it...he did pee pee in the potty."

Defiantly I raised my chin and locked eyes with my sister. "I *am* smart."

"Yes, you are," Audra said, getting down on her knees in front of me. "Like Einsteen."

Einstein, and not quite, although every man has to start out somewhere.

I reached out and gently touched her smooth, creamy complexion.

She smiled, her large, azure eyes crinkling at the corners. "You're a good boy, Guy Guy," she whispered and kissed my forehead. "You'll have friends, don't worry."

My heart instantly fell in love with this sweet-faced little girl and I shuddered inside to think of her dead on the closet floor, her throat cut.

I won't let you die, Audra. I'm here to save you...all of you, and then you can see firsthand the technology of the future and be an Einstein yourself one day.

"Audra, Daddy is waiting," my mother reminded her. "Now give me a kiss and a hug and off to piano practice you go."

I swallowed back the tears threatening to choke me as I watched my mother and sister embrace each other. Audra placed one more kiss on my cheek and skipped out of the room.

I turned to look at my mother, readying my bath with a rubber duck and floating dinosaurs, and my heart went out to her as well. This was the family life I'd missed out on all of these years, the close-knit nurturing and unconditional love a mother and father feel for their children. And although Sister Margaret gave me the best she was capable of, it wasn't anything close to the warmth and devotion radiating from my mother.

I blessed the day and the second chance I'd been given to grow up with parents and a sister instead of as an orphan, as well as an opportunity to save them all, and my Nela too, from an early grave.

My mother lifted me from the pot and hugged me close to her heart. "What a good boy I have." Gently she placed me in the tub. "Now let's get you all washed up, nice and clean so you can wear your big boy underwear with the superheroes on it. Then we'll have breakfast together and we'll read stories and..."

"I wuv you, Mama," I interjected, taking her face between my two, small hands.

She smiled and planted a kiss on the tip of my nose. "I love you too, my baby boy, never forget or doubt it."

Twenty

I'd never in my wildest dreams thought going back in time was even remotely possible or that I would ever have the chance to experience a day like today, with my mother. Growing up in an orphanage, there's not a special person who dotes on you. You belong to no one and yet to everyone. You get the same amount of ice-cream and pizza on your plate as everyone else does. At night, you're given the same hug, if you're lucky enough to get a hug, before you go to bed. And when you're bad, you're doled the same punishment, whether you deserve it or not, to avoid favoritism. Never are you looked upon as an individual with different needs, hopes or desires. You're just one child in a group of many, sheltered, fed and clothed until you're old enough to be sent out on your own. We'd all learned very quickly to look out for ourselves.

When Sister Margaret took a group of us to the park, I would watch the interaction between the mothers and their children populating the benches and swings. I remember one day, Sister Margaret became friendly with one young mother holding a child, and offered to take the boy while the woman coaxed her older son from the swings. When the child realized his mom had left him in

Sister Margaret's care, he stiffened his legs and screamed at the top of his lungs, his little arms outstretched and calling for his mother. No matter what effort Sister Margaret made to console the small boy, he wasn't happy until he was back in his mother's arms, hiding his red, tear-stained face tight beneath her neck.

I had certainly never understood the child's behavior...until now.

After giving me the most fun-filled bath, with rubber toys floating about the bubbles and singing songs as she washed me clean, my mother dressed me and held my hand as we walked down the hallway to the staircase.

The house, a 1930's cottage, was decorated in warm colors. The second floor had three bedrooms and a bath. The bathroom appeared to have been recently remodeled, because in place of the cast iron, clawfoot tub there were a modern tiled shower, sink with a vanity and cupboards beneath. The almond-colored toilet matched the sink and tub, blending well with the beige and white tile combination on the walls and floor.

The staircase led to the foyer, and to the right of it was my father's den. French-style glass paned double doors were half-opened, and peeking in, I spied a large desk, a piano, and many bookshelves stacked with books. To the left of the staircase was the living room, furnished with a television, sofa, two matching chairs, a rocking chair and ottoman. The large, three-bayed window seats were surrounded by built-in shelves, where my mother displayed a collection of Hummel figurines and various other knick-knacks. The brick fireplace sat adjacent to the windows.

The dining room was situated off the living room, and light from another three-bayed window seat bounced off the crystal chandelier hanging above a round, oak dining table. On one side of the room, there was a matching china cabinet and on an opposite wall a buffet table.

The kitchen could be entered from either a hallway off the foyer or from the dining room. The large, yellow flowers on the wallpaper made for both a warm and cheery atmosphere. I knew this room was the core of the house, where the family gathered the most, and I thought of Nela's folks. All the times I was invited over to join them at dinnertime, everyone helped out in the kitchen, laughing and teasing each other. I got the same warm feeling now from my mother's kitchen, and I didn't take my eyes off her as she busied herself making breakfast.

Off the kitchen, there was a half-bath and laundry room combo. A short hallway from the opposite side of the kitchen led to the basement door, the back door and a patio. I could see the entire fenced back yard from the large windows beside the table, where my highchair sat against a wall.

While my mother prepared me a slice of toasted bread slathered with grape jelly, I played with the round-shaped cereal she'd placed on the chair's tray. Those that fell to the floor, Luna happily devoured. I drank from my own special cup. It was a two handled mug with a capped top. A small funnel protruded from the lid like a hard straw. It was decorated with kittens and dogs chasing a ball of yarn all around its base. My mother called it a *sippy cup*, and told me to drink all of my orange juice so I would grow up strong and handsome like my father.

I made a mess of myself, in spite of my efforts to stay clean. My chubby little boy hands weren't at all coordinated. I dripped orange juice down the front of my shirt and got grape jelly stuck between my fingers and in my hair.

"Oh, Guylan, you're such a mess," was my mother's response as I was led away to be stripped a second time and given another bath. This time when placed on the potty chair, I needed no persuading. Nature really called and I was able to leave quite a present for my mother to empty. She was ecstatic and even called my father at work to tell him of my accomplishment.

"Daddy's proud of you too, sweetie," my mother relayed as she hung up the phone.

My face heated with the thought of my father possibly boasting of my achievement to his colleagues. Would the same co-workers be around when I worked part time at the bank? In fact, would I still work at the bank?

Throughout the day, I was never out of my mother's sight. She read me stories about trains, trucks and steam shovels while I sat on her lap, inhaling the rose scent of her perfume. I prefer Tolstoy, Clancy, Mailer and Twain, but she had me mesmerized by the way the words rolled off her tongue, perfect bow-like lips forming each syllable. Her low, soft voice lulled me into a contentment I had never known existed. My heart filled with an overwhelming love and admiration for the woman who'd given me life, her beautiful face the focus of my day. I couldn't stay near enough to her and ate up the attention in volumes.

I was given a hotdog cut into tiny pieces on a plastic dish for lunch, drank another *sippy cup* full of apple juice, and then my mother readied me for an afternoon nap. The big-boy superhero underwear I wore was replaced by a diaper and together we laid in the large hammock out in the yard. My mother, resting on her side, undid the buttons of her crisp, white shirt and bared a breast.

Drawing me close, she angled the swollen teat level with my mouth. "Drink, baby, and sleep for a while," she whispered.

For a moment, I just stared up into the soft green of her eyes, stunned. The last nipple I suckled belonged to Nela and definitely not for the same reason. Feeling awkward and a little like I was betraying my fiancée, I pulled back.

My mother caressed the side of my face with the tip of her finger and smiled down at me. "Too big are you now to nurse?"

I remained silent, keeping my eyes locked with hers instead of gawking at the full bosom exposed beneath my chin.

Back and forth she rubbed my cheek. "One day this soft, little chin will be rough with razor stubbles."

What would you do if you knew I'd only shaved this morning?
"And you'll be taller than me."
I'm taller than Dad.
"But for now, you are just a wee lad, as great-grandpa Quentin calls you, and you need a nap." She teased the side of my mouth with

the tip of her mound. "Drink," she urged, rubbing my back with the hand she had around me and rocking the hammock back and forth.

The day was warm, a slight breeze tugged at the curls falling across my forehead, and weariness washed over me. Moving my lips to surround her swollen areola, I took her into my mouth and drew onto my tongue the nectar oozing from the rosy peak. It slid warm and sweet down the back of my throat. One of my hands lightly fisted against my chest, the other moved to hold the ample flesh of her breast.

"That's my good boy," she said softly, her hand moving from my back to tenderly rock my diapered bottom. "Now, close your eyes and sleep."

I couldn't fight the moment...I didn't want to. I snuggled closer to her, inhaling the aroma of her skin mixed with a summer day. The comforting rhythm of her heartbeat vibrated against the palm of my hand and I drifted off into the best sleep I'd ever had.

~ * ~

I woke in the nursery, Luna lying beside the crib on the round, braided rug.

It was my father who came into the room to tend me. He was a broad-shouldered man with thick, black, wavy hair. When I looked up into his deep, blue eyes, I swore I was looking into a mirror.

He cast me a broad grin. "You ready for dinner, sport?" He undid the sticky tabs on the diaper. "Let's just make you presentable enough to dine with the ladies."

To my horror, not only had I totally soaked myself while I slept, but when the warmth of the diaper was removed, my tiny phallus sprang upright.

He chuckled. "Like father, like son."

While my father cleaned me up, I worried I was beginning to lose myself within this time period, as Quentin had warned. If I didn't see Olena soon, I feared I'd continue to possess a toddler's body and revert to having a three-year-old's mind. Not only would I be unable to return to where I belonged, but much worse...I'd be incapable of preventing Mortimer from murdering my family. Everything would play out just as it had thirty-five years ago, all of them gone from me again, this time Nela as well.

Lifting me from the crib, my father held me over his head, high in the air. "If I didn't know better, sport, I'd say you looked concerned over something." He lowered me enough to be able to playfully nibble on my chubby baby-belly, and then he moved to my neck, making a razing sound against my flesh. The silly noise and vibration made me giggle, and my father's blue eyes twinkled. "Now, that's more like it."

I wrapped my arms around his thick neck, smelling the spice and citrus scent of his cologne. I knew the brand; it was my favorite and I had splashed on a handful just that morning...or was it yesterday morning?

My frown returned. That was what I had failed to ask Quentin: how did past time parallel with the present? For all I knew, Nela could already be—

"Are you hungry, sport?" My father interrupted my thoughts. "Mama's made fried chicken, your favorite. She cooked it especially for you, in celebration of you doing poop in the potty."

I can hardly wait to see the festivities when I get an A in school.

All through dinner, I brushed the tip of my tongue lightly over the raven brand etched in the flesh of my inner cheek, hoping that if I felt the raised mark, it would somehow help me to keep an intellectual grasp on my mission. Staying focused and alert was even more essential now, since the day in question loomed closer.

Luna waited patiently for a morsel of food to drop, sitting in her usual place beside my high chair. I locked eyes with her and I knew she'd picked up on my dilemma.

A stroke of luck fell my way when my mother brought us into my father's den to look up Albert Einstein in the encyclopedia, as she'd promised my sister earlier in the day. When I took in the masculinely decorated room, I noticed Luna making her way to lie beside a table where a picture of Olena and Zackery sat.

Following her, I pointed to the framed photo and shouted excitedly, "Me want, me want."

"That's a picture of Gamma and Poppy," Audra explained. "They live with Great-grandpa Quentin in a really big house on the other side of the bridge."

"Me want Gamma," I shouted again, frustrated that my baby tongue prevented me from saying more than a few, choppy sentences.

"Would you like to talk to her on the phone?" my mother said.

I nodded. Quentin said I had to connect with someone I knew from the future; he didn't say I had to set eyes on them. A phone call just might do the trick, giving me the reinforcement I needed to exercise and ensure my adult mind.

My mother made her way to a large, oak desk by a set of windows and picked up the receiver of a green-colored phone. Dialing...no push button, no cordless...she phoned Olena Sincloud. "Guylan would like to talk with you, Gamma. He's something important to tell you," my mother said and handed me the receiver.

I blinked, baffled, not knowing what she meant. All that concerned me was hearing Olena's voice. I held the heavy ear and mouthpiece to my own ear, thinking of the convenient, compact cell phone I used at home, in my own time.

"Hello, Guylan," Olena chirped. "What is it you have to tell me?"

It worked! The sound of her voice, carrying now a much younger tone, strengthened my resolve and gave me the boost I needed.

"Tell Gamma you did poop in the potty," my mother coached loud enough for Olena to hear.

"I did poop...poop in potty," I muddled, relieved even though my tongue didn't work, my brain did. Hopefully, with this short blast of recognition, I'd stay centered for a while longer.

Olena pretended to be pleasantly surprised. "In the potty now, like a big boy?"

"Yup," I said.

"I am so very proud of you, Guylan," Olena praised.

I beamed with pride and handed the phone back to my mother.

After all, praise was still praise, and in everyone else's opinion, today I had certainly earned it.

Twenty-one

Friday morning dawned bright and very humid. I woke to the dull droning of the fan that sat on a table adjacent to the crib. Sticky and wet, I cried out for my mother.

It's funny how one can get used to having things done for them. Being a child had its downside...absolutely no privacy, and outside of the time I slept, I was never allowed a minute to be alone. But on the upside, the utter and complete pampering, not doing a lick of work or having a care in the world, wasn't the pits either.

My mother bathed me, dressed me, fed me, played with me and rocked me to sleep. My father made me laugh, wrestled with me and made me feel secure. Both loved me, as well as my sister. I marveled over all the attention, especially since it was something I had never had. But I also struggled every minute with the fact I couldn't allow myself to become too self-absorbed. If I became fully indulged in my newfound youth, I could very easily lose track of whom I really was and where I belonged.

My mother complied with my wish to speak to Olena again, my grandmother overjoyed with the gesture. It was better than nothing, hearing her voice over the phone, but I could feel myself becoming too comfortable with my surroundings, and quite frankly, it scared the hell out of me.

After my afternoon nap, I was outfitted in a pair of denim shorts and a T-shirt that read across the chest in big, blue letters, I'M DADDY'S BOY. On my feet, I wore socks picturing dancing bears, and a pair of denim sneakers with white laces. My mother strapped me into the child's car seat behind the passenger side and seat-belted Audra beside me. It was the first time I had been out of the house since I arrived, and the warm breeze blowing in from the open window soothed my sticky flesh. I closed my eyes and inhaled, enjoying the ride.

When my mother brought the car to a stop in front of Sophia DelFino's School of Piano, I nearly jumped for joy. I had met Sophia DelFino in my present life, so seeing her here in the past would definitely help the cause...or so I hoped. But, as I thought deeper on the matter, I began to worry. I had met her as a deceased soul; was there a possibility she wasn't *eligible* to be a connection?

My mother carried me with one arm across the parking lot, toting a diaper bag on the other shoulder and holding Audra's hand. The woman was forever multi-tasking, and had a way of making it all look so easy, though I doubted that was the case. Because she worked so hard all day, I showed her my appreciation, but in my current state of being, all I was able to do was tell her, "I wuv you," and give her a wet, sloppy kiss. It seemed to do the trick, but somewhere deep inside of me I sensed she was a volcano ready to blow.

My mother set me down just inside the front door and I looked around the gaily painted room...a light blush shade with white wicker furniture placed about. Pictures of students playing the piano graced the walls. Audra proudly pointed out the one of her.

I admired the hardwood floor, knowing how hard it was to get the wood to shine. A few summers ago, I helped a co-worker from the animal clinic sand his living room wood floor and it was very time consuming, not to mention messy.

Sophia DelFino greeted my mother with a hug, her silver hair now black and pulled up into a thick bun. She was slenderer and taller, but the latter could have been because I was so small. She bent to take me in her arms and I hugged her, remembering the delicious meal she had prepared for me the last time I had seen her.

"My, my, how you've grown," she said, giving me a kiss on the cheek.

A small twinge of strength surged through my body and I held tight to the energy.

"And those blue eyes..." she went on, turning now to my mother. "Someday they'll make a special gal swoon."

That would be your granddaughter.

My mother chuckled. "Right now, we're working on potty training. He's not to the point where I can bring him out without backup," she said, patting the diaper bag. "Audra caught on so much easier."

The heat rose to my face. *Please, spare the details. Has my dignity not been compromised enough?*

Sophia set me down next to my mother. "Well, don't get discouraged. Boys are always harder to train than girls. My mother always said I was a breeze, but my two brothers were nearly four years old before they were completely trained."

My mothered sighed. "Well, he's turned three and I'm hoping he catches on soon. We've been trying to get pregnant again, but I really don't relish having two in diapers."

Upon hearing my mother admit this fact, I gazed up at her. Could she even now be expecting? If so, that would be another life Mortimer stole.

Inside, I cringed.

Sophia gave my mother's arm an encouraging pat. "All things work out for the best." She gestured with her hand toward a door to the far right. "Please, make yourself comfortable in the lounge. There's fresh coffee made," she then smiled down at me, "and a changing table, should one be needed."

I won't need one!

Sophia extended a hand to Audra. "Shall we get going on your songs?"

Audra nodded and walked away with Sophia, jabbering about what she was planning to wear on recital night.

My mother led me into the lounge and sat me down at a kid-size table and chairs; taking from a shelf a pop-up book, she began to read. I pretended I was interested, touching the ball on the page and smiling up at her. "Ball is bouncing," I said.

She liked my clever interaction and returned my smile. "That's right; the ball is bouncing down the hill. What color is the ball, Guylan?"

"Red," I said.

"And what color is the dog?"

"Black," I said.

"And where's the big, yellow letter B?"

I pointed to the letter and my mother hugged me.

"What a smart boy," came a familiar voice.

I cast a glance at the doorway and my eyes widened with shock. I nearly fell off the chair as I looked into the woman's dark eyes. *How could Nela be here, in the past...all grown up and pregnant?*

Twenty-two

"How are you feeling, Mrs. O'Riley?" my mother asked. "Sophia told me you needed to take it easy."

"Please, call me Gloria," the woman responded, taking a chair beside my mother. "I have my good days and my bad. This happens to be a good day." She smiled down at me. "And how old is this precious boy?"

My mother reached into the diaper bag for a tissue and wiped the drool from the side of my gaping mouth. "He turned three in April."

"He's smart for his age," Gloria commented.

My mother briefly glanced my way with adoring eyes. "But his speech isn't as fluid as Audra's was at his age."

Gloria laughed. "Typical man...doesn't waste words."

My mother joined in. "Isn't that the truth. And are you hoping for a girl or boy?"

"My first hope is for a healthy baby, of course, but I'm partial to wanting a girl. My reasoning has to do with a family tradition."

I know the one.

"And I've only five more months to go," Gloria sighed. "My due date is the week before Christmas."

Nela will be born earlier, on December twelfth.

"I just wish the morning sickness would stop. My friend Rita is as far along as I am and her nausea stopped months ago." Gloria shrugged. "I guess everyone is different."

"That's so true," my mother agreed.

"I'm just blessed to be pregnant at all. Brian and I have tried for so long." She sighed again. "In my family, all the women have troubled pregnancies. My mother and grandmother had a few miscarriages, and I think that's what frightens me."

My mother reached over and gave Gloria's hand an encouraging squeeze. "I have a feeling all will go well."

Gloria smiled. "Thank you. I pray it will, too."

I stood and moved closer to Mrs. O'Riley, placing my hand on her belly.

"Guylan, no," my mother snapped, reaching for me.

Gloria O'Riley stilled her hand. "No, it's fine. I don't mind, really."

I moved closer and laid my head on the mound that was my Nela. Warmth rushed through me, and I know Nela felt it, too, because she kicked within her mother's womb. My strength was replenished, my mind strong and clear.

"Oh, my," Gloria gasped.

I raised my eyes to hers and smiled.

"Did you feel the baby kick?" Gloria said.

I nodded, my smile growing. "Nela," I said.

"Nela," Gloria repeated softly. She turned to my mother. "I actually like that name. Nelana was my grandmother's name and if the baby is a girl, I could name her after my grandmother and call her Nela for short."

My mother giggled. "Imagine Guylan coming up with a nickname for your baby."

Can you imagine I ask her to marry me? Because I will. I mean, I did.

Gloria turned her attention back to me. "If this baby is a girl, I promise you I'll call her Nela. Would you like that?"

"Yup," I agreed and placed my head once again upon Mrs. O'Riley's baby-bump. She gently stroked my hair as I embraced my beloved *fetus-fiancée* growing beneath her mother's heart.

~ * ~

When we all arrived home, I witnessed my mother's anger for the first time.

In her defense, I must say, the temperature had to be in the high nineties. I had broken out in a prickly-heat rash all over my chest, thighs and buttocks and was completely miserable. Audra was cranky too, breaking into either tantrum fits or dramatic sobs over everything that occurred.

The last straw came when my sister asked for a root beer ice pop and was told to wait a few moments, just long enough for my mother to moisten a few cotton balls with calamine lotion to dab on my rash.

Audra stamped her foot. "But I'm hot and want an ice pop now," she demanded. "Why does he always come first?"

"Because he's a baby," my mother explained, her face flushed with the heat. I could see her patience growing thin. "And the rash is hurting him."

"Well, I don't care," Audra snapped.

"You should care, Audra; he's your baby brother. Do you want him to suffer?" my mother said through clenched teeth, lifting me to her hip and heading upstairs to the nursery.

Audra screamed from the bottom step, with hands on hips. "Then I'll just get the damn ice pop myself."

My mother trembled with rage.

The volcano was ready to blow.

In a flash, with me still in her arms, she ran down the stairs and placed me on the floor. Then she reached for Audra. Grabbing my sister by the arm, she bent her over a knee and gave her a hard slap across the bottom. "That one's for being selfish." Then she doled out the second slap. "That's for using a swear word." The last slap brought a cry from Audra. "And that's for being disrespectful."

When my mother loosened her hold, my sister stepped back, hands rubbing her backside and tears streaming down her face. "I get embarrassed when you spank me on my tushy."

You don't know what embarrassment is till you've received a bare-assed beating from Father Samuel and his board of education.

"Well, you make me ashamed to think my daughter is so unkind," my mother retorted.

Then my poor, exasperated and overwhelmed parent did something that left Audra and me stunned. She sat down on the floor, covered her face with shaking hands and cried.

I stood and made my way to her, wrapping my arms around her neck. Audra came to her, too, sitting down next to my mother and laying her head against her chest.

"I'm sorry, Mommy," Audra sobbed. "I didn't mean to be unkind."

My mother gathered Audra into her arms. "I hate spanking you...I hate it, hate it, hate it," she wept openly. "But sometimes you just push me too far, Audra." She wiped her nose with the back of a hand and kissed the top of Audra's head. "I love you so much."

Through her tears, Audra choked out, "I love you too, Mommy."

Moved by their affection...hot, miserable, and covered with a rash, I began to wail as well. You know the saying...*you'll feel better after a good cry?* Well, it's true. I let loose with everything that had built inside of me the last few days—all of it. From the strange and mystical things I'd learned and experienced to the immense worry for my family and Nela. I choked on the fear I'd fail and they'd all die in spite of my efforts. Coupled with the possibility I'd never get back to my own time, my frustrations escaped in volumes at the top of my lungs; all the while, I was hanging on to my mother's neck.

Luna, plopping down beside us, threw her head back and began to howl, too.

The four of us, intertwined, let free the sorrows in our hearts.

It was then my father came home from work, walking through the front door with a cheery, "Hi, my loves, I'm home." He stopped short, his mouth gaping wide, when he discovered all of us sitting on the floor, sobbing in unison.

Twenty-three

I always classified a hero as the fireman who saved a baby from a burning building, or the soldier who gave his life for his country, not the husband who was able to dry everyone's tears and set their world right again. But after that day, I changed my mind.

My father, dressed in a very nice, black work suit, got down on his knees and opened his arms to his sorrowful family. We tackled him, and one by one he kissed us, joked with us and turned a horrible moment into one I will never forget.

I've known what it is to put in long hours at work, especially on a hot summer day, and so my father had to be beat as well. Yet he never complained, just set to the task of making things in the house better for everyone else. He ordered a pizza for supper, so my mother didn't have to cook and heat an already hot kitchen with the stove. While we waited for our meal to be delivered, he marched my mother upstairs to take a cool shower, got Audra her ice pop and coated me with calamine lotion. I looked like I had pink spots.

After supper, he turned on the sprinkler and let Audra and me run through the twirling spray of cold, tap water. We screamed with delight each time it hit our backs, the coolness soothing to hot skin.

Luna barked and played as well. Even my parents got in on the fun, chasing each other around the yard like carefree children. I watched my father catch my mother, pull her wet, tanned body into a loving embrace and kiss her. She responded, wrapping her arms around his neck and deepening the kiss.

At St. Bernard's I'd remembered none of this. How was it something so amazing, so beautiful, could just be wiped clean from my memory? Or did I remember in the beginning, and cried at night for my mother's comfort, my father's strong arms and my sister's smile? Sister Margaret never spoke of those early years. Why would she want me to remember, when in truth she was hiding me from what I was, who I was. And now my heart broke for me, for the little child I once was, ripped from the people I loved and would never see again.

Overwhelmed with emotion, I marveled at the way my parents melted in each other's arms. At this time in their lives, they were only twenty-eight...younger than I am, or was before I arrived there. The way they feel for one another is how I feel about Nela. Never can I get enough of touching her, kissing her, making love to her. And in this very moment, I prayed I wouldn't be too late to save her from Mortimer, with all the time I'd already spent here to save my family. I hoped with all my heart, when all was said and done, I didn't unbalance everyone's lives too terribly and I'd be able to go back and have a life with them all.

My father dried me with a large, downy towel and re-dressed me in a pair of blue-checked shorts and a white tank shirt. I reached out to touch his face. He turned his lips into my palm and kissed it. "I love you, sport."

"I wuv you, Daddy," I said, my heart swelling with pride to be his son. This was the man who could teach me the family's way and mold me to do magical and wondrous things. I could not fail in my mission here, but how would I accomplish what needed to be done?

My father carried me back downstairs on his shoulders and I mentally called out for Quentin's help.

Quentin MacRaven, if my energy is still connected to yours, help me to complete what it is I've been sent here to do.

By the time my father had stepped onto the bottom step, the doorbell rang.

"Company's here," Audra screeched and ran past my father to open the door.

My father reached out a hand to stop her, a frown creasing his brow. "What were you told?"

Audra stepped back, her lower lip protruding into a pout. "To check first who was on the other side."

My father reminded Audra. "That's why I had a peephole placed down low. Now, look and see who comes to visit."

She moved toward the door, looking back at my father before she gazed out the peephole.

Audra took a look and then returned her gaze to my father, her face beaming with delight and a large grin spreading over her lips. "It's Gamma Olena and Great-grandpa Quentin."

My father returned her smile. "Well, let them in."

I smiled too, realizing Quentin must have heard me, and in fact might be actually looking out for me.

Quentin was the first to enter, looking exactly as he had when I saw him as a hologram, but minus the Archdruid garb. In a lightweight pair of beige pants, a V-necked orange, short-sleeve shirt, and with a knapsack on his back, he reached up to take me off my father's shoulders.

I recognized my ring with the raven signet, which he wore on the middle finger of his right hand.

Quentin's eyes locked with mine. "And here he be, the wee lad I came to congratulate for makin' a mess in a pot instead o' in his *clout*. 'Tis a right o' passage, me laddie, that meself included went through."

I wrapped my arms around his neck.

After Olena finished giving Audra kisses and hugs, she turned her attention to me. "And are you going to keep that baby all to yourself, Da?" She reached up to tousle my hair.

Her touch sent rivulets of electricity through my body; my mind became crystal clear and strong. I could tell from the way Quentin smiled he knew what was transpiring.

Thank you, Quentin.

"Well, Da?" Olena said.

"For the time bein', aye, daughter. This wee lad and I have some business to discuss, now that he is on his way to bein' a man."

My mother entered the room and kissed Quentin's cheek. "He has a way to go, Grandpa."

"Still and all, he is on the right path and we need time to bond." He looked at me. "Is that not the truth o' it, laddie?"

I nodded. "Yup."

Olena laughed. "And so, are you happy now, Da?"

Quentin smiled. "Aye, that I am."

Olena hugged my mother, and along with Audra, the three of them walked hand in hand to the kitchen.

I heard my grandmother say, "We were watching the news report on the television and out of the blue, he comes in and says he wants to visit Guylan."

"And where's Mom's other half?" my father joked.

Quentin shrugged. "Last I saw Zackery, he was out in the yard, sprayin' the little beasties eatin' his tomato plants."

My father shook his head. "That garden of his is becoming an obsession."

"'Tis what happens when a man no longer has a job to go to each day that dawns," Quentin remarked. "Zackery retired at fifty-two, a wee bit too young; should have worked a few more years. At fifty-eight he is anythin' but idle brained and is still robust in health."

"He and my mother wanted to travel," my father said, coming to his father's defense.

Quentin arched a gray, bushy brow. "Och, and where do they go?"

"Give them time...Dad's only been retired a few years."

"And I can tell ye, lad, in a few years still, the two o' them will be sittin' on their arses, watchin' the shows that come on the tube, because they fear they will miss out on what the grand-bairns are up to." He narrowed his eyes. "Truth be told, I did want to come and see this lad tonight. Somethin' just called me to him, but yer mother missed the wee ones, and after I saw her sulkin' about most o' the day, I decided to put an end to her misery."

My father gave Quentin an affectionate pat on the back and laughed. "So, then, let us men go to my den to bond."

"Aye," Quentin agreed, still holding me in his arms. "Point the way and the wee lad and meself will follow."

Luna joined us, sitting on the floor beside my father's desk.

Quentin opened his backpack and pulled from it a bowl and a bottle of water.

"Come, Xavior, and sit at the desk, with the lad on yer lap," Quentin instructed as he handed me over to my father. After removing the backpack from his shoulders, he pulled from it a bowl and a bottle of water. Carefully, he placed the items on the desk so he could pour the water into the bowl.

My father took a seat at the desk. "I didn't know we'd be doing oracle training tonight. Maybe I should bring the baby to DeYonna."

"Nay, he must stay," Quentin protested. "He is part o' this."

My father frowned. "So soon? Isn't it a bit early for him to—"

"Och, no, lad. 'Tis never too soon," Quentin said, sitting in a nearby chair and gesturing to the bowl of water. "Now, tell me what ye see."

My father took a deep breath and gazed into the bowl.

I did the same, remaining quieter than any toddler actually would.

The water began to swirl like a tornado, turning gray, then black. A white mist passed over the tumultuous eddy, calming the water. Once it had stilled, a vision took shape. The scene played out slowly, like a virtual reality tour, the camera filming the staircase, moving up the steps, turning into my parents' bedroom, then a quick glimpse of them lying on the bed. Blood was everywhere, staining the wall above the bed, the pillows beneath their heads, their clothes and blankets.

My father gasped in horror, tightening his left arm around my waist, and covering my eyes with his right hand. "Merciful Lord, what the hell was that?"

I squirmed free and cast another look at the bowl, but the vision had gone.

My father's lips thinned. "What the hell am I seeing? Why did you want my son to see this?"

"'Twill be yer fate and he is part o' it. 'Tis he that brought it forth; he has the sight," Quentin explained.

My father twirled me around in his arms and cupped my face beneath his chin. "No, it can't be true."

"Och, aye, 'tis, Xavior, and ye need to heed the sign," Quentin said.

I searched my father's terror-filled eyes. "Mortimer," I whispered.

His face turned sheet-white. "When?"

"Tomorrow night," I said.

"Ye must get yer family away from here, and then deal with *mo bhrathair*, me brother, yerself," Quentin said.

I hugged my father around the waist. "Luna stays...with you."

My father sat paralyzed in his chair while Quentin absorbed the water in the bowl with a piece of heavy gauze. He placed the bowl and cloth in a plastic bag he'd retrieved from his sack and packed everything away.

"Come lad," Quentin said, slinging his backpack over a shoulder and lifting me from my father's lap. He stood me on the floor. "We need to do one more thing." He took me by the hand and led me to the doorway.

I turned around and caught a glimpse of Luna moving closer to my father, who sat petrified in his chair. The dog laid her head on his lap.

Quentin led me into the foyer and sat me on the bottom step of the staircase. Quickly he rummaged through his pack and pulled from it a small, clear plastic bag. He opened the bag to reveal two plump blueberries. "Eat one, *mo chridhe*, me heart," he coaxed.

I hesitated, knowing full well blueberries make me sick.

"I know why ye are hesitatin'," Quentin said.

I narrowed my eyes. "How?"

"'Tis the way o' it and there is no time to explain the *how* o' it now. Just trust me and know 'tis the only way yer ma will listen." He took a berry from the plastic baggy and held it out to me. "Not pleasant, but necessary."

I fingered the raven crest on his ring and for the first time wondered why my father wasn't wearing it. He was nearly done with his *Geis*...the Druidical training.

"'Twill be yers one day, me *braw*, brave lad. Olena will hold onto it for ye," he said, reading my mind.

My gaze met his, sure now that all along he'd known the events that would play out, and kept from my father the ring and book of secrets so they wouldn't fall into Mortimer's hands.

"Why didn't you stop it?" I whispered.

"I could not till now, laddie. 'Twas yer help I needed."

Instantly, I popped a berry into my mouth. From experience, I knew it only took but one to make me sick. Within a few hours, I would be very ill and feeling miserable. But, if my sacrifice meant my family and Nela would be safe, then so be it.

Isn't every destination always about the journey anyway?

Quentin started to reseal the bag when I stopped him. I reached for one more berry...just to make sure everything turned out right.

Twenty-four

I read an article once when I was in my time: blueberries rid the body of toxins. In my case it was *toxic*, ridding my body of everything I had eaten within the last two days. By the time the grandfather clock in the foyer struck the hour of 2:00 a.m., I was experiencing the effect of eating the blueberries. I should have quit at only accepting one, but I'd wanted to make sure my effort wasn't in vain. Now I hated myself for being so damn heroic. One blueberry, I'm positive, would have done the job sufficiently.

The stomach pains woke me, hence the reason I heard the clock chime the early morning hour. Within a matter of minutes, the pain increased, giving way to nausea. I swallowed hard and stood in my crib, leaning over the rail. Better to vomit on the floor than where I slept. What shot up from my stomach and sprayed out of my mouth reminded me of all the exorcist films I'd viewed, where the possessed person projectile vomits just before their head begins to spin around.

I showered the dresser beside the crib and the surrounding floor with chunks of food, the smell gagging me and making me hurl again. I rested my forehead on the rim of the bars and took deep breaths to calm myself, but in a matter of seconds the pain returned and this time the other end of my anatomy rebelled. I expelled waste enough for ten men on a diet of prunes. My bowels literally exploded, filling the diaper. Watery stools ran down my leg and pooled around my bare toes like a backed-up sewer.

Luna, by this time, had moved away from me and made her way to the door. She sniffed the wretched stench and began to bark.

I began to cry.

My mother was the first to enter the nursery, slipping down over her naked thighs an oversized T-shirt she'd hastily donned, her shoulder-length, dark curls in disarray. My father followed, wearing only underwear briefs.

"Oh, God," he groaned, covering his nose and mouth with a hand.

My mother neared the crib and I vomited again, this time the mess running down my chest.

"Baby, my poor baby," she said, lifting me from the crib. She kept me at arm's length and set me on the floor, stripping me to the bone.

I burst from the other end again, defecating on the floor.

"Why is he so sick?" My mother's tone shook, her brows furrowed with concern as she reached for the container of wipes and made a feeble attempt to clean me. When her efforts failed, she carried me to the bathroom, runny bowels dripping down my legs and leaving a trail along the way. She stood me in the tub and took the shower head down from the wall holder, adjusting the water to a warm temperature, then sprayed me all over.

My father, gagging and gasping, was left to clean up the nursery.

How my mother and father managed to get me and the nursery clean without getting sick themselves, I'll never know. It has to be the unconditional love parents have for their children. I only hope when it's time for me to care for my own children, I'm as dynamic.

After my father scrubbed the crib clean, it was too wet for me to reclaim, so I slept in their room, in a portable playpen lined with quilts.

But none of us slept.

By 4:00 a.m., I had soiled three more diapers and had the dry heaves.

My father, realizing he wasn't going to sleep tonight, threw on a pair of jeans, a T-shirt and sneakers. He ran downstairs to the kitchen for a chunk of ice.

While my mother coated my parched lips with the cold cube, I lay limp in her arms. Now and then I'd stick out my tongue for a lick, just enough to moisten my mouth.

Her large, green eyes, filled with worry and fear, looked down at me. "He's dehydrating, Xavior."

"We should check him for fever." My father left the room and returned with a thermometer. He held it between a thumb and forefinger and shook his wrist. I opened my mouth, raising my tongue to receive it, just as my mother turned me face down across her knees and undid the diaper. She saw me as a toddler, unable to hold the implement in my mouth. Aware now of where I was getting the thermometer, my face grew hot with humiliation. I cringed when she inserted the tip, a whimper escaping my throat.

Her knees, pressing against my stomach, rocked me back and forth. "Hush, my sweet baby, Mama is here."

Audra walked into the room at that point. "What's wrong with Guy Guy?"

"We don't know yet, honey," my father said.

"Are you keeping track of the time, Xavior?" my mother said, holding my buttock cheeks together so the thermometer wouldn't slip out.

"Yes, De, another minute to go," he said.

Uncomfortable, weak and mortified to the roots of my hair, I began to cry.

Audra got down on the floor and looked up into my face, attempting to comfort me. "Don't feel bad, Guy Guy, I had to have the thermometer stuck up my tushy when I was small, too." She stuck out her tongue. "When you get big, like me, you can use the thermometer that goes under the tongue." Then she rolled her eyes and made a crazy face.

In spite of everything, I laughed.

"Thank you, Audra, for trying to make him feel better," my mother said softly.

If you only knew what I was doing for you...going through all this to save your life, Audra.

"Time," my father said.

My mother removed the thermometer and handed it to my father to read while she re-diapered me.

"He has a slight fever," my father announced. "The reading is a little above 101, which for a baby isn't too high."

My mother put me over her shoulder and rubbed my back. "Still, I don't like it. I'm going to give him a dose of liquid baby aspirin and then I think we should take him to the hospital."

Hospital! I'm only having an allergic reaction to blueberries. It will pass, it did before, when I was six and ate a blueberry muffin one morning for breakfast at the orphanage.

"Hurry and get dressed, Audra," my mother said. "We need to get Guylan help."

"Okay, Mama," Audra agreed, and rushed off to her room.

"I'll go and help her get her things together," my father said.

My mother frowned. "What things?"

"Books, a few toys, the outfit she plans to wear for the recital and a pair of pajamas," he said. "And I'll settle in Luna as well."

My mother gasped. "Good heavens, Xavior, do you think we'll be at the hospital that long?"

He shrugged. "One never knows, De; better to be safe than sorry."

My mother bit her bottom lip. "I suppose you're right."

"I'll prepare a diaper bag for Guylan, too," he offered, rushing out of the room.

She sighed, the weariness etched on her face, and laid me on the bed. Quickly she stripped off her nightshirt, standing a moment naked before my eyes.

She dressed in record speed, slipping into panties and bra, shorts, a T-shirt and sneakers. Then she wrapped me in a blanket and headed downstairs.

I shot a glance at Luna, who sat at the foot of the steps, while we waited for my father and Audra. If it were possible for a dog to wear a worried frown, then Luna had one on her face.

Mentally I sent her a message I'd be okay.

She barked a response as we all exited out the front door.

~ * ~

I continued to cleanse my colon two more times after arriving at the Shire Downs Medical Center. The smell and mess got the attention of the receptionist and my case was moved ahead of all those waiting prior.

I was undressed, poked and prodded in every hole, nook and cranny by several learning interns. Again, my temperature was taken. The nurse grabbed my ankles and lifted my legs high, performing the task much more roughly than my mother had done earlier.

After a few tests were taken, I was dressed in a shirt with an opening up the back and straps around the waist and arms. These straps secured me to the hospital crib, no doubt to ensure I'd stay still while hooked up to the IV inserted in my left arm. Too weak to protest, I lay limp and numb, a bone soaking fatigue washing over my entire body.

The day went by with agonizing slowness and my flesh itched and burned from the rash I developed. My father and Audra made many trips to the hospital cafeteria for something to eat, bringing back something for my mother as well. The food smelled delicious, although I'm sure, being hospital food, it was a little better than mediocre.

I was moved to a private room by 3:00 p.m. Audra sat and read to me, her little hands holding up the book for me to see each picture after she read the page. For a time, we all slept, Audra and my mother in a recliner beside my crib and my father in a chair at the foot.

At around five, my father took Audra down to the hospital cafeteria to get dinner, bringing it back up to the room. Again, I watched my family as they ate. My stomach had settled by now, as I knew it would, and I could feel the groans of hunger gnawing at my insides.

"Shouldn't we call Olena and Zackery and let them know we're at the hospital with Guylan?" my mother said.

My father shook his head and continued to eat his burger, which was beginning to look very appetizing to me, hospital food or not.

"But they're his grandparents and have a right to know," she persisted.

My father took a sip of his soda before he spoke. "Until the tests come back and we know more, there's no point in worrying them."

I knew the real reason for the secrecy. If Mortimer somehow caught wind of what had happened, he'd deviate from his plans. This had to be dealt with tonight. My father obviously wanted it done... so did I.

"You're probably right," my mother agreed.

"What about my recital?" Audra said.

My father handed her a French fry from his plate. "I've packed your clothes and when the time nears, I'll take you."

Audra's lips stuck out in a pout. "Isn't Mommy coming, too?"

"Sorry, pumpkin, but Mommy needs to stay here with Guylan. We wouldn't want him to be all alone, now, would we?" my father said.

Audra shook her head, her face a picture of disappointment.

I felt terrible, ruining her big night, especially when she'd worked so hard. But being sad over not having both parents watch you play piano isn't as bad as being dead.

"After the recital, I'll take Audra to my parents' house to sleep. It will be too late to drag her back here and she should sleep comfortably in a bed," my father said.

My mother agreed. "You shouldn't come all the way back here either, Xavior." She picked at the tuna sandwich on her plate, putting a piece in her mouth. "And then there's Luna to consider, too."

"After I packed Audra's things, I ran downstairs to fill Luna's bowl with dry food and release the catch on the doggie-door," he said. "So, she's fine."

Nice going; you thought of everything.

"Still and all, it's best you stay at the house and sleep comfortably in a bed, too." She gestured to the recliner. "There's only room for one to sleep here."

"If you're sure, De."

"Yes, very," she said.

Good going again with making her believe she made the decision for you to stay home.

Around seven, while my mother took Audra into the bathroom to help her dress for her big evening, my father walked over to the crib and released a side bar.

He bent to kiss me. "You get well, sport, and leave the rest to me."

I whispered. "Come back."

He smiled and tweaked my nose. "I plan on it."

"Luna will help."

"I always knew she would," he said.

Audra skipped into the room and twirled around to show me her dress. "Do I look pretty, Guy Guy?"

"Pretty Audra." She smiled, giving me a kiss, and then gave one to my mother.

"You'll be a hit," my mother encouraged, blinking back the tears welling in her eyes.

My father went to her and held her close. "Everything's going to be fine, De, not to worry."

She forced a smile and they shared a long, deep kiss.

After my father and Audra left, thunder rumbled in the distance. My mother walked to the window and looked out at the approaching tempest. "It looks like a storm is coming. I sure hope Xavior and Audra aren't caught in it," she mused aloud. Turning toward me, she smiled. "Sleep now, Guylan, it will all be over soon." I raised my right hand to her and she came near and released a crib side bar, stroking my face with her cool fingers. "Just close your eyes now, baby. Mama is here with you. I'll always be with you, so you have nothing to be afraid of."

Promise?

"I promise," she whispered, not realizing she'd read my mind.

Slowly, I closed my eyes.

Twenty-five

Xavior had to force himself to concentrate on Audra's recital. His little daughter had worked hard, practicing nightly on the piano, to be the best she could be tonight. It was sad enough her mother couldn't be here to see her accomplishment, but then to have a disinterested father as well. He sighed, filled with guilt, but it couldn't be helped. Right now, all he could focus on was the vision he'd seen in the water: a bloodbath...he and DeYonna lying in bed with their throats cut. God only knew what had happened to his children, because he couldn't bear to see any further. He feared for his family...they were in mortal danger. Whatever insane reason Mortimer had for wanting all of them dead, he didn't have time to learn. He just needed to stop his great-uncle, and save his family.

He shivered, returning his attention to the evening at hand, and glanced at the playbill, looking for his daughter's name. Audra was up after the boy who was now on stage. Hopefully he could persuade her to leave after her own performance.

~ * ~

DeYonna looked down at her sleeping son, his thick, dark hair curling around his tiny ears, and her heart swelled with love. Why had he gotten so sick? She sighed, hoping the tests taken today would shed some light on the problem. But already she saw her son improving, the color coming back into his cheeks. She hated seeing children sick, with tubes and needles stuck in their chubby little arms. She always cried when the telethons aired on television, with kids as young as Guylan in wheelchairs, their heads hanging, unable to control their arms. Or the cancer kids, bald and hooked up to machines, their eyes orbs of pain and sorrow.

No, it was all wrong!

Children needed to run and play, to laugh and be happy, not be bogged down with illness and disabilities. It was their legacy to be healthy and vibrant, enjoy their lives and grow to experience all the wonderful things ahead of them, not stare death in the face.

She rubbed her neck and stretched her back. It had been a long day. She made her way to the recliner and laid back, her thoughts wandering to Audra. How was her recital going? Did she remember all the right chords, play the right keys? She hated the fact that she couldn't be there to applaud her daughter's achievement. But she was torn between her children: to stay here with a sick baby, or watch her daughter play piano. She knew she had made the right decision, but her heart still hurt to be missing Audra's big night.

She turned to glance at her sleeping son and smiled at the weird faces he made while he dreamed. She was so blessed to have both her children, and Xavior. DeYonna placed a hand on her belly, massaging it gently. Soon there'd be another Sincloud, and after things settled down, she'd break the good news to Xavior. In spite of Guylan's mysterious illness, she was a very fortunate woman. Her children were basically healthy, didn't have to struggle through life with a disability as some children did, nor did they battle a terminal illness. She had a husband who loved her and she loved him in return, and a new life grew beneath her heart.

What more could anyone ask for?

~ * ~

"But Daddy, Mommy says it's rude to leave before the others play their songs," Audra protested.

Xavior was at her side backstage now. Audra's performance was finished, and he was readying her to leave. He took a deep breath, remaining calm through her objections. "I agree with Mommy wholeheartedly, pumpkin, but with Guylan sick in the hospital, Daddy has to get you to Gamma's house before it grows too late."

The thunder rumbled loudly. Audra shivered. "I don't like thunder and lightning."

"Then let's get you safely to Gamma's, before the storm really hits," he coaxed. "And I haven't told her we were coming, so it will be a surprise."

Audra's face brightened at this news and she happily allowed him to lead her by the hand out the door.

On the drive to her grandparents' home, Audra chatted away, excited about the night. He listened halfheartedly, concentrating more on making good time across town and back before the rain fell. He didn't like driving at night in the rain, especially with the kids in the car.

When Olena opened the door, Audra yelled, "Surprise," and he had to spend the next hour sitting at the table drinking coffee, explaining to his parents everything that had happened.

Quentin remained quiet, his eyes never wavering from his grandson's face. Xavior shifted in his seat under the older man's scrutiny; he was suspicious Quentin had had something to do with Guylan becoming sick...but how? And how much more did his grandfather know about what would happen tonight?

Quentin leaned in and whispered, "Och, no sense in rehashin' the matter, lad. Just be gettin' yerself home and take care o' what needs to be done."

Xavior swallowed the lump in his throat.

"And what needs to be done, Xavior?" Olena said, offering him a cookie.

"Luna," he lied, taking a bite of the shortbread treat. "I need to tend to Luna. She's been alone since early this morning."

"And she hates thunder, like me," Audra added, reaching for another cookie herself. "So, she shouldn't be all alone."

He kissed his daughter at the door and held her close for a long moment. Would he survive this night to ever see this child's face again?

Quentin walked him to the car. "*A bheanachd*, me blessin' upon ye, *mo ghile.*"

He gave a taut nod. "At least DeYonna and the children are safe."

"And they will be needin' ye to care for them," Quentin said, "so ye will be needin' this." He handed Xavior the book of secrets. "Look to the page concernin' the dark fae and *deanhan*, demon possession. Read aloud the incantation and memorize it with yer heart, then when ye come eye to eye with *mo bhrathair*, me brother, recite it with conviction and righteousness."

Xavior looked down at the book he held in trembling hands. "I don't know if I can do this, Grandfather."

"Ye can and ye will, lad," Quentin said sharply. "The things we must do are rarely easy." His face saddened. "Tonight, Mortimer is *dhiobhail*, the devil himself, and I must *cuir stad,* put a stop to him. Do ye think it is easy for me to know his life will be snuffed out? He was me bairn brother, the one I helped me mother care for, the child that once looked up to me with admiration. Then his greed replaced his sense of value, love and devotion for his family. He became jealous o' me powers, resented and despised me." He sighed. "So now I must help ye with this task, but by no means is it easy."

"I'm sorry, Grandfather."

"Aye, I am as well, Xavior." Quentin sighed again. "Now, stretch out yer right hand, lad."

Xavior extended his trembling hand and Quentin placed the raven crest ring on his middle finger.

"As ye are recitin' the spell, raise yer hand and aim the raven insignia at Mortimer's heart. Over and over, ye must speak the words with not one falter, so memorize them well. If ye do this correctly, the raven crest will glow...a deep, rich, crimson like the true blood o' the MacRaven clan. The heat will burn through Mortimer's evil heart, to his black soul, dissolvin' the dark fae's hold upon him and he will crumble to dust." Quentin laid a hand on Xavior's shoulder. "Keep yer eyes focused, ye mind sharp, and ye conscience clear."

He searched Quentin's face. "Did this already happen, Grandfather?"

"Aye, lad, once upon a time ago, when ye was not forewarned. The consequence was tragic."

"Was that the vision I saw in the water?" he probed.

"Och, aye, but take heed, laddie. In some families, not even death is final. Nor are there only skeletons in their closets."

His stomach tightened. "Then we all died, even the children?"

"Nay, not Guylan," Quentin whispered.

The blood drained from his face. "What is he, what is Guylan?"

"He is yer son, come to save ye all." Quentin sighed. "Work with the second chance ye have been given, Xavior. Such a chance is rarely bestowed. And *cuimhnich*, remember all ye have been taught, who ye are and what ye can do. Ye have become a strong Druid, acknowledge yer power and use it wisely. Win this battle and then come back to collect yer daughter."

Xavior squared his shoulders and took a deep breath. "Then I believe I'll see you again tomorrow."

Quentin smiled. "Aye, lad, plan on it."

Twenty-six

Lightning lit the pitch-dark sky; thunder boomed, cracking near the house. Xavior just made it inside to the kitchen before the rain fell in torrents. He flipped a switch by the door and placed the book of secrets on the table.

Luna came running from the living room to greet him, toenails clicking on the kitchen linoleum as she danced back and forth. He knelt and pulled the dog against him, cradling her head as he spoke in a calm tone. "It's all right, girl, the thunder isn't going to hurt you. Truth be told, it's the least of our worries." He pulled back and looked deep into the animal's wise, chocolate eyes. "I'm going to need your help. So, gather your wits about you and work with me here."

Luna licked his face and barked.

"Good girl, now let's get things ready for when evil comes calling." He stood and reached for the book. "First things first," he said, taking a seat and turning to the page his grandfather had instructed. Over and over again he read the incantation, becoming familiar with the words and meaning.

The unfruitful works of darkness have no domain amongst the good. So, I banish thee to hell, where thee rightly should...burn away to ashes...blown aside by gale and gust, bones and flesh, mind and spirit, now nothing more than dust.

He committed to memory the passage so the words would flow from his heart, strong and bold, his tongue a mighty sword to fell the enemy.

"No longer will this menace hurt my family," he whispered, gathering the book and making his way upstairs.

He hid the book beneath a quilt on the top shelf of the bedroom closet and pulled down the spare pillows DeYonna stored there. He fashioned the pillows beneath the bed's blanket to resemble sleeping bodies. He did the same in Audra and Guylan's rooms, since Mortimer would pass by their doors first. Just as he finished preparing the trap, a flash of lightning lit the room. Soon to follow came a house-shaking clap of thunder, knocking out the power. Grabbing a flashlight from a hallway cupboard, he made his way downstairs. As soon as the rain let up for a moment, he opened wide all the windows in the dining area. "Welcome to my home, you bastard."

Again, he climbed the stairs to the bedroom, crouching in a corner with the flashlight in his left hand and Luna by his side.

Together they waited for Mortimer.

When the grandfather clock in the foyer struck midnight, Luna raised her head and perked her ears. A low growl rumbled from her throat.

"Stay, girl," he commanded in a hushed tone, placing a hand upon the dog's back. "You need to be quiet. We don't want to do anything to warn him."

Luna cocked her head sideways and whined a response.

Another clap of thunder shook the house and Xavior shivered, swallowing the fear rising to choke him. Wiping sweaty palms upon his thighs, he inhaled as Mortimer's heavy, booted footsteps fell on the stairs and neared the bedroom where he hid.

The enemy's large, dark shape entered the room, walking to the bed. Mortimer stooped forward to remove the blanket. When he discovered the pillows beneath instead of his victims, he shot a glance around the room.

Xavior stood and flashed the light in Mortimer's eyes.

Like a deer caught in headlights, Mortimer remained wide-eyed and stunned.

He raised his right hand and leveled the ring to aim at Mortimer's heart. With a voice shakier than he'd like, he recited the incantation.

"I command yer tongue to cease," Mortimer shouted above Xavior's words, backing away from the ring's scarlet ray of light.

Over and over, Xavior chanted the words, blocking out Mortimer's command, listening only to the inner strength welling within him. The red beam grew stronger, slicing through Mortimer's form and knocking him against the chest of drawers.

Mortimer gasped and collapsed to the floor.

Xavior angled the ring and the flashlight to where he saw Mortimer fall, expecting to see a pile of dust, but there was nothing heaped upon the rug. Mortimer had vanished.

He continued reciting the incantation, sounding out each word louder and bolder, and searched the room with the flashlight. Cautiously, he stepped from the corner and moved to the foot of the bed, shedding the light around the room.

Luna growled behind him and he spun around to see a large, black bird perched on the window's ledge. The massive raven spread its wings and soared over his head, attacking his skull as it passed. He lost his balance and fell backward. Blood trickled down his forehead and into his eyes. He wiped it away with the back of his hand, and stood, searching with the flashlight for the bird. The giant raven swooped down a second time, clipping him in the back of the neck. The blow sent Xavior to his knees and he lost his grip on the flashlight. It rolled beneath the bed. He waved his hand around, aiming the ring's glare at every corner of the room and reciting the spell.

The sound of wings flapping filled the room. He stood, spinning around to find the bird with the ring's light. The raven slammed into him again, hitting him in the middle of his back. The impact was hard, and once again he was knocked to the floor. He lay face down, gasping for breath. Then a green light radiated from where

Luna stood barking. Xavior rolled onto his back and sat up. The glow grew stronger, brighter. Shading his eyes, he stood, bracing himself against the wall. The apparition grew taller, wider, until it filled the opposite side of the room. In its midst stood a dragon, green scales down its back, amber eyes catching sight of the raven. With a swoop of its long, reptile-like forked tongue, it captured the bird and moved to face Xavior.

The raven wiggled and screeched in the dragon's grip, but was no match for the mighty beast.

Xavior leveled the ring and aimed the light on the raven's chest, reciting the spell. A crash of thunder resounded through the house, the windows shook in their casements, and floorboards trembled beneath his feet. The bird's high-pitched shriek rang in his ears, then it exploded; bits of feathers and dust floated in the air.

The dragon's shape shrunk, its light faded, and in its place stood Luna.

"Luna, my heavens, Luna," he whispered.

The dog barked and ran to her master, pushing him to his knees and licking the wound on his head. He laughed and hugged the dog close to him. "We did it, girl. We saved our family. Mortimer can never hurt us. He can never hurt anyone ever again."

~ * ~

Nela stood frozen, her eyes locked with his.

"Aye, lass, ''tis hell yer goin' to," Mortimer roared, grabbing her by the throat and slamming her against the wall.

Her feet dangled in the air, her bared backside scraped against the stone slab, bruising her flesh. Calling upon every ounce of strength she could muster, she tried to raise her arm and stab Mortimer with the stake still attached to her wrist. But his voice, his very command, left her paralyzed.

Mortimer's face neared hers, the foul stench of his breath warm upon her cheek. He angled his mouth over hers and inhaled, siphoning the life from her body. Her heart raced, her lungs collapsed, a roaring, whirling tone rang in her ears, louder and louder until she thought for sure her head would burst.

But instead, Mortimer's body split in two, his eyes bulging till they popped from their sockets, hair and nails growing longer and longer before they shriveled and dissolved. The flesh fell away from his bones and crumpled. Nothing was left of him but a pile of dust beneath the clothes he'd worn.

Nela gulped for breath and screamed, waking with a start.

"You were having quite a nightmare, sweetie," Gram said, massaging her feet.

She shook her head to clear it. "Oh, I had the most God-awful dream." She sat up and cringed, pain shooting down her spine.

"I knew you'd get cramped sleeping on this couch." Gram gave her leg an affectionate pat and smiled. "Off to bed with you now, where you can stretch out and get a good night's sleep."

Nela swung her legs off the sofa. "I don't know if I'll ever close my eyes again after such a bad dream."

"Sometimes it helps to talk about it."

"I can't while it's still so fresh in my mind…it would be way too frightening." She glanced at the clock on the entertainment center. "But I would like to call Guylan before it gets too late. We made a pact never to go to bed mad."

"Let it go for tonight, Nela."

She turned to look at her grandmother, "But Gram…"

"No *buts* about it, Nela. Let it go tonight and wait for Guylan to call you."

She bit her bottom lip. "What if he never calls again?"

Her grandmother reached over and pushed aside a curl from her forehead. "He'll call. When he's ready, he'll call. Trust me on this."

Twenty-seven

Sunday morning dawned bright, the sun's rays streaming through the opened slats of the window blinds. My stomach pains had ceased, along with the vomiting and diarrhea, and I'd been taken off the IV fluids. Now, I sat on my mother's lap while she spoon-fed me gelatin from a plastic container. Occasionally my eyes wandered to the door, hoping my father would enter. During my bath and the morning exam, I thought of nothing but his safety, worried as I was he hadn't survived Mortimer's attack.

My mother, oblivious to the danger my father faced, only cared about my health; she held me, now that I was off the tubes, close to her heart, rocking me and singing softly.

Oh, for a chance to know what happened. Where is a cell phone when you need one?

Around noon, my heart swelled with joy as my father's broad-shouldered, masculine form walked into the hospital room. I stood and raced to the foot of the crib, holding my arms out to him. His warm smile melted me inside; I was so glad, so thankful to see he was alive.

"All's well, sport," he whispered in my ear. "The monster's dead."

"Up, up," I said, practically climbing the footboard of the crib to reach him.

He handed my mother the duffel bag he had slung over a shoulder, saying, "I brought you a change of clothes," and gathered me into his strong arms.

I held him tight, feeling loved and secure, happier than I'd been in a long time.

He gave my diapered bottom a pat and kissed the side of my neck. "And how's my boy feeling today?"

My mother stood on tiptoe to kiss my father's cheek. "He's so much better, Xavior. I believe we'll be able to take him home by tomorrow morning, after the doctor reads the test results."

"Has he been able to eat anything?" He took a seat on a nearby chair and placed me on his lap.

I leaned back against his chest, my ear to his heart, and listened to the wonderful rhythm of life flowing through his body. He was alive...they were all alive.

I had a family.

"I was able to give him a bit of gelatin earlier, and so far, he hasn't gotten sick from it. I'm going to breastfeed him in a bit, see if I can get him to sleep. He was very restless throughout the night."

My father rubbed my stomach, moving his gentle strokes to my left thigh and down to capture my foot. Raising my tiny toes to his lips, he kissed each one. "I want him home. I want all of us to go home."

My mother moved closer and kissed my father on the top of his head. "What on earth? You're hurt, Xavior."

"It's nothing, De. When the lights went out from the storm, I tripped on a scatter rug, bumping my head on the dresser."

I looked up into his eyes, knowing full well he was lying. His wound was from battling Mortimer. How did my father slay the beast? I realized he'd never tell a soul. My mother would never know what had happened that night, how close they all came to dying.

He winked at me and I tried to wink back.

My mother continued to ruffle her fingers through his hair. "Looks nasty, did you think to put an antiseptic cream on it?"

"Yes, I'm fine," he said, closing his eyes as she stroked his temples and moved to caress his cheeks.

She sighed. "See what happens when I'm not around to take care of you."

His eyelids flew open and he smirked at me. "How true; I am quite lost without you, De."

My mother knelt beside the chair, gazing deep into his eyes. "I'm pregnant, Xavior."

The play of emotion flashing over my father's face was priceless...shock at first, then happiness, then last of all, pure awe. All this transpired in a blink of a moment, his love and devotion for my mother at the core of it all, shining through in volumes.

He reached for her, pulled her to him, and then lowered his mouth on hers.

I watched their lips fuse together, tasting each other's sweetness, drawing long upon their fervor and deepening their love. My heart ached for Nela, and in thinking of her warmth, the thrill of the passion we shared, a great relief washed over me. With Mortimer dead in this time, he could never be alive in the future, and Nela was safe, too.

My father pulled back and searched my mother's face. "How far along are you?"

"Only a few months. I found out for sure a day ago, but with Guylan getting sick, I hadn't the time to tell you." She smiled up at him. "Are you pleased, Xavior?"

"You know I am." He traced her full lips with the tip of a finger.

"Me too," I chimed in, making them both laugh and turn their affection on me.

Olena and Zackery brought Audra to the hospital around noon. They all joined in on the congratulations. It was the first time I had set eyes on my grandfather. He looked like an older version of my father. I had a glimpse of how I'd look when I was in my fifties.

Zackery Sincloud was good with children, reading to both of us the books Audra brought, while Olena talked with my parents about the new baby. We each had a turn on his lap, laughing at the way he mimicked animal sounds.

"Do the cow again, Grandpa," Audra urged, giggling when Zackery complied.

I was thankful this kind, loving man hadn't been murdered, ripped to shreds on a back road in France.

After my grandparents left and my father took Audra to the cafeteria for food, my mother bared her breasts and fed me. I drew the nourishment from her, the sweet warmth filling me with contentment, the rose scent of her flesh familiar and comforting.

She caressed the side of my face as I nursed. "Soon you'll be an older brother, a big boy, no longer a baby. You'll drink from the sippy-cup and use the potty."

My eyelids grew heavy, fatigue overtaking me.

She laughed and began to rock me. "Ah well, we won't worry about that right now, will we?"

I curled up against her and fell asleep.

~ * ~

The tests results came back negative for any virus or disease, which I knew would be the case, and by Monday afternoon, I was dressed in street clothes and taken home.

Luna was overjoyed to see me, licking my face so hard I ended up sitting on the floor. I sensed she'd have a lot to tell me, if she were able to talk. I could see it in her eyes.

It all got quite scary, didn't it?

She heard my thoughts and barked a response.

Thank you for saving my father.

Luna wagged her tail and licked me again.

My father took the day off from work so he could be with his whole family, something I thought he'd never take for granted again as long as he lived.

Olena and Zackery came for a visit; Quentin joined them, and we had some time away from the others when he took me by the hand. Together we walked to the back of the yard. "I am truly sorry, *boidheach*, me beautiful boy, ye had to go through the *flux* the way ye did." He sighed and rubbed my stomach. "Yer poor, wee *wame*. If there was a better way to do it, ye know that I would have spared ye the *fash*, trouble."

I raised my arms to him.

He chuckled and picked me up, kissing me on the forehead. "All is forgiven, then?"

"Yup," I said.

He glanced around the yard, taking in the rose bushes and inhaling their scent, as it wafted on the light, summer breeze. Then he looked up at the oak tree, where a blue jay was singing its song. He smiled. "'Tis a good day to be alive."

I smiled.

After a dinner of roast beef smothered with gravy and mashed potatoes, fresh green beans from Zackery's garden, and Olena's homemade apple pie, everyone was pretty sated. I was served beef broth with unsalted crackers, which tasted like cardboard, and a sippy-cup of iced water. It was an unfair situation, the aroma of my mother's food teasing my taste buds and leaving me hungry for a real meal.

I was put in the playpen beside my parents' bed to sleep. My mother still wanted to keep an eye on me, in case I fell ill again. In such close proximity to her, and under her watchful eye, I was unable to leave for my own time. Perhaps it was just as well. I was still in a weakened state from all I'd expelled and hadn't yet been allowed to replace.

The night brought cooler weather and my mother covered me with a lightweight blanket. Curled beneath it, I relaxed, eyes closed but not yet dreaming. My parents, however, believed I was asleep.

My mother giggled softly. "My, Xavior, is all that for me?"

Curious, I opened my eyes. Peering above the blanket, out into the dimly lit room, I caught a glimpse of my father's naked form. Between his thighs his desire for my mother stood hard and at attention.

I smiled to myself. *Like son, like father.*

He slipped beneath the covers and from their bed I heard the most delicious noises; sounds I recognized and missed. Their groans, the squeaking of the bedsprings, the sighs of release and moans of satisfied fulfillment ignited thoughts of Nela. I pictured her long legs spread wide for my pleasure. I yearned to touch her, kiss her, and make love to her. With such aching desires and passionate longings heating my body, my tiny phallus grew hard beneath the diaper cloth.

"Oh, De, you're amazing," my father muttered, breathless. "You're so hot, so wet."

I don't want to know this about my mother...she's the woman who changes me, bathes me, and uses her teats to feed me.

Wasn't it blasphemy or sacrilegious or something to be privy to your parents' intimacy? Right then, the information overload was causing *me* dire physical effects.

"Hush, Xavior, or you'll wake the baby," she whispered.

Her words gave me an idea and I purposely stirred.

"See," my mother said. "He's waking now."

Guilt claimed my heart for cutting short their lovemaking, but if they continued, I feared my mother would find the diaper soaked with something other than urine, if that were physically possible for my baby's body to do. Mentally, I knew it was and I was on the brink.

"Maybe he needs changing," she said, sitting up and reaching for the robe at the foot of the bed.

No, don't touch me now...please, not now.

"He's fine, De," my father said, taking the robe from her hand and pulling her back against him. "Let him alone, he'll go back to sleep. He's just...just *adjusting* to his surroundings."

That's it, Dad...as man to man, you know the score and what I'm trying to adjust to.

He kissed her. "You go to sleep, too."

She yawned and sighed. "I suppose you're right."

I lay awake long after my parents had fallen asleep. In the quiet of the room, I thought of my adult life. I missed my job, my friends, and most of all, my woman. My tongue gently probed the inside flesh of my cheek for the raven mark and I sighed, relieved to still find it branded there. It was the key to the door I would go through next, my ticket and passage to move on.

I've accomplished what I was sent here to do. Now, I must leave. Tomorrow morning. Better still, tomorrow night I will depart from this segment of my life...my time here is done.

Twenty-eight

Tuesday, July 31st, 1972 was hot at daybreak with a little breeze. All of us were thankful the humidity had broken. Because it was actually cooler outside than in, Audra and I played in the yard, dressed in our bathing suits: hers a yellow two piece trimmed in white and mine a blue pair of trunks.

My father went to work, happy, I'm sure, for the central air conditioning in his office, and my mother opened the sprinkler so Audra, Luna and I could run through the cold tap water and cool off. We ate ice pops and drank fruit-flavored drinks, played with a large, colorful blow-up beach ball and blew bubbles, Luna chasing after both. My mother donned a halter top and short-shorts and sprawled out on a blanket beneath the oak tree, attempting to read a book while her children played.

She was a stunning woman, as vibrant and cheery as Quentin had explained. I *got* what my father saw in her. In fact, I understood totally a man's commitment toward his wife and children, and was excited inside for the chance I'd have to experience the same with Nela. In many ways, Nela reminded me of my mother...dark-haired and slender built, long legs that looked dynamite in heels. And after what I learned last night sleeping in my parents' room, just as passionate.

I took a slow and probing look around me, since I knew it would be the last time I'd ever be this age again, or have the opportunity to experience life from this perspective. In the years to come, I'd no longer be the youngest. The fetus my mother carried beneath her heart would be the new baby in the family. As humiliating as some of what I'd endured was, in many ways it was also comforting. I didn't need to worry about a thing, not even wiping my own nose; everything was done for me by one of my parents.

Never again would my sister feel uninhibited around me... using the toilet as I sat in the potty chair, undressing and dressing in front of me or walking in on me as she pleased while my mother washed and dressed me. Our genders, as we aged, would make us self-conscious and modest to such familiarity...our innocence gone and replaced by what's politically correct.

My parents' youth and vigor would fade as well. Now, they ran up and down the stairs, sometimes toting a child in one arm or on their shoulders as they went. But as the years went by, that would change. No longer would they be young parents with young children.

Even Luna would age, settle down and lie about the house in a lazy frump. I'd seen it in my line of work as a veterinarian. Elder dogs lost that puppy energy, didn't bark as much, didn't run around long with children. Some had arthritis, others went deaf or developed poor eyesight, their watchdog days a thing of the past.

It would never be the way it was now, ever again.

So, I absorbed the day fully, smelling the aromas of my mother's kitchen and tasting, savoring everything she fed me. I listened and enjoyed the sound of Audra's child-like giggles, my mother's soft, youthful voice, and Luna's bark. I curled my toes in the grass, my fingers in the frizzy locks springing like copper snakes from Audra's head, reminding me of Medusa, and rubbed a cheek on Luna's shiny coat.

I hugged my mother, climbed up onto her lap, inhaled her scent and marveled over the loving caresses she bestowed on me. And although I was ready to leave this era, it was a bittersweet decision.

After a lunch of peanut butter and marshmallow sandwiches, my mother dried Audra and me, dressed us in matching sunsuits and laid us down together in the hammock for a nap while she sat reading a few feet away on her blanket. Luna lay in a hole she'd dug, as dogs will sometimes do to keep cool, at the far end of the yard. A quiet place where the trees thickened and little children weren't allowed to roam. Even a dog needs a break now and then. It was a perfect afternoon, and I was just about to close my eyes when the doorbell rang.

Audra leapt from the hammock and yelled, "I'll get it," running through the kitchen to the foyer.

"Wait," my mother called after her, placing her book aside and standing. For an instant, she was torn between leaving me alone in the hammock, with the risk of possibly falling, or running after Audra to stop her from opening the door to someone she didn't know. It was something I'd heard my parents warn her about several times.

My mother opted to gather me into her arms before trailing after Audra. In making that decision to protect me, she was too late to stop Audra from flinging open the front door, admitting an intruder into the house.

My mother's flip-flops flapped against her heels as she ran through the kitchen. Holding me tight in her arms, she rounded the corner and hurried through the hallway joining the foyer. She stopped short at what she saw, the blood draining from her face.

"Who are you?" she choked out, putting me down on the floor.

He stood by the door, clothes stained and ragged, bloodshot eyes roaming the length of her.

"What do you want?" She pushed me to stand behind her left leg.

He neared, the stench making me gag. Thin, with dark, straggly hair hanging matted to his shoulders, he held Audra tight against his chest. One arm was around her stomach and in the other hand he held a knife...under her throat.

My mother gasped. "Please, whoever you are, I'll give you anything you want. Money, jewelry, just please, please *don't* hurt her."

Audra's eyes were wide with fear. She didn't move a muscle, didn't make a sound, but the tears slipped down her cheeks. The front of her sunsuit was wet. Urine trickled down her sun-tanned legs to her feet, and dripped off her cotton candy-pink polished toes. It made a small puddle on the floor.

The intruder's lips curled into a crooked smile, revealing rotted teeth. "You don't recognize me, DeYonna?"

My mother shook her head.

"Why I'm your beloved, older brother, Presley Grayson." He walked over the urine puddle, nearer to my mother.

"Presley?" My mother pushed me further behind her.

His tone was condescending. "That's right, DeYonna. Your big brother has come for a visit." He glanced around the room. "Looks like you've done all right for yourself, marrying that banker and all."

"You know Xavior?"

Presley nodded and smiled. "I met him briefly, quite by accident, of course. Last week I was walking by the bank and noticed they were giving away coffee and donuts to the public, as a promotional thing. Since I hadn't eaten for days, I thought a donut and a cup of coffee would hit the spot, and then the craziest thing happened." The sweat from his forehead trickled into his eyes and he blinked it away. "The bank's manager shook my hand, brought me to his desk to give me information about the types of services the bank offered, and there, sitting on his desk was a family picture." His laugh was a deranged cackle. "I couldn't believe my eyes, and I'm proud to say I recognized you immediately, De. And when your loving husband mentioned your name, my hunch was confirmed."

"How did you find out where I live?"

"I followed your hubby home one night and hid in the bushes. I've been watching the house all weekend, waiting for him to leave so I could talk to you alone." He laughed again. "Thought the folks got rid of me for good, didn't you?"

My mother took an audible breath. "I was only five years old when you left, Presley. I hadn't a clue what happened to you." She held out shaking hands. "Please, let me have my daughter. I'll take the children next door to the neighbor's house and we can talk things out."

She moved closer to Presley and he backed away. "No one's going anywhere."

"Fine," she agreed. "Then let me put them down for a nap and I can fix you lunch. You must be hungry and thirsty."

He licked his dry lips. "That does sound good."

My mother stepped closer. "Then let me take my daughter."

Presley Grayson brought the knife closer to Audra's throat. When the blade hit her flesh, my sister whimpered. "I'm sorry, Mommy, for opening the door."

My heart went out to the frightened child, tears welling in my own eyes. In the midst of all her tremendous fear, she still felt anguish over having been disobedient.

My mother's voice trembled as she attempted to reassure Audra. "It's okay, honey, everything will be okay." Then she turned her attention back to Presley. "Please, let her come to me. Can't you see how scared she is?"

He ground out the words through clenched teeth. "As scared as I was, do you think, DeYonna, when the authorities came into my room and took me away? I remember it like it was yesterday...July thirty-first, 1949...twenty-three years ago today."

"I told you, I know nothing about that time. I was just a little girl, only five years old," my mother repeated.

I moved toward my mother and wrapped my arms around her leg. She was trembling with fear. Was this how it would all end, then? Was one uncle's plot to destroy the family thwarted only so another uncle could finish the job? I closed my eyes and mentally summoned Quentin for help, but then I realized this turn of events wouldn't be something he'd have knowledge of, because it had never happened. By this time, my family would be dead and I would have been taken to the orphanage. Presley Grayson, if he'd come to the house, would have found it empty.

I opened my eyes, wishing to be back in my original form. If I were in my man's body, I could handle this situation. I had taken martial arts, and though I wasn't a black belt, I could take this guy on and save them all again, instead of crouching in fear behind my mother's leg.

Another solution struck me, and I rubbed the raven crest with the tip of my tongue. If I could strip off all my clothes and transport myself back to yesterday; I could warn my father of what would happen today.

Presley's anger rose, his sharp, grating voice pulling me from my thoughts.

"I was only ten, but they didn't care how they treated me." His left eye twitched. "They said I did something bad to the little girl our mother babysat for, little Valerie Taylor. She was six months old. I helped sometimes, played with her, held her while Mother made dinner, while she paid attention to you," he said, his tone begrudging. "You were her little darling, the little princess. When you came along, I became chopped liver."

"Presley, I'm so sorry. I never knew—"

"Let me finish," he screamed.

My mother cringed at his loud response.

"The men who took me away said I hurt Valerie. But I didn't mean to, and I told them so. I was trying to get her to stop crying, so I flung her in the air like father sometimes did to you, but I didn't catch her on time and she fell."

My mother raised a shaking hand to silence him. "Please, say no more...the children—"

"No one believed it was an accident," he interjected. "They said I wanted to hurt Valerie." His mouth twisted into a sneer. "Why would I want to hurt a baby?"

"They were wrong...they got it all wrong..."

"It was unfair," he added.

"Yes, it was very unfair and I can help you fix it, but you've got to let me take the children away from here. Then we can sit and talk," she bargained.

"I got away from them," Presley rattled on. "Escaped while they were taking me to the doctor for tests...the head pains keep coming no matter what the doctor does. It's a waste of time and I told Johnny that, but he made me go anyway." He licked his lips. "So, I pushed him down the stairs and took his pocket knife before I ran away from that place. I ran, and ran, and ran. That was many days ago, and they haven't found me yet. They won't find me now." He tightened his grip on the knife. "They can't ever find me."

"I won't let them find you," my mother promised. "Just give me my daughter and then I can help you."

Frightened out of my wits as I was, it didn't register immediately that I was hearing Luna's muffled barks. We had left her out back, lying in the hole she'd dug at the far end of the yard. Because we had all been outside, my mother must have locked the doggie door, and Luna was unable to get in.

While my mother negotiated with Presley, I made my way back into the kitchen and to the doggie door. The latch was down low, so I had no trouble reaching it, but it was old and rusted, impossible for a three-year-old to unbolt. I peered out the side window at Luna barking and scratching at the door.

What happened next, I'll never forget.

A bright green mist rose from the ground, enveloping Luna, and she vanished right before my eyes. The emerald-colored fog seeped beneath the bottom of the door, blanketing the kitchen floor. It swirled and twirled like a mini-tornado, leaving in its place the strangest thing I'd ever seen.

The creature had amber eyes, grayish-black fur, and the skin of a seal. The mane framing its dragon-like head was dripping with water. Turning to me, the extraordinary entity's reptile-like tongue emerged from its mouth and licked me...or tasted me, I wasn't quite sure which.

I frowned and mentally questioned it. *Did you eat Luna?*

The weird being answered in the same manner. *I am Luna.*

I walked toward it and reached out with a hand. It felt deathly cold to the touch.

My mother and sister need help.

Luna nodded. *I will help, but then I must go.*

Go...go where?

Then I remembered what Olena had told me about Luna...how the dog had run away from my grandmother's friend and was never found again. It became clear to me now, Luna had an agenda, her own schedule to follow. Obviously, I wasn't Luna's only boy, nor would I be her last.

I will go where I am needed. Her amber eyes grew tender. *You must go, too. Our work here is done.*

I nodded and stroked her once more on the bridge of her large snout. *Where will you go next?*

She inclined her head. *Wherever I am needed the most.*

Will I ever see you again?

She almost smiled. *I will have my eyes on you.*

The unbelievable occurrence that followed, I questioned for years.

Luna floated out of the kitchen and I followed, shielding myself behind the archway and peeking out into the foyer. She rose to the ceiling, hovering over my mother, sister and Presley Grayson. Then she blanketed them with her large form. Lightning exploded in the foyer; the room was ablaze in the bright, greenish illumination. The blast knocked me off my feet. I fell, hitting my head on the wall behind me. When I opened my eyes, my mother stood over me, Audra hanging onto her leg and crying.

Panic edged her voice. "Guylan, can you hear me?" She gathered me into her arms. "I think the house was struck by lightning, and may be on fire." She took Audra by the hand and the three of us went out the front door.

I looked around for Presley Grayson, but he was nowhere in sight. He had just vanished, along with Luna. Even more amazing... my mother and Audra didn't remember a thing.

We sat on the front lawn for a moment, stunned.

A neighbor from across the street ran over to help. Said she saw the flash from her living room window and called the fire department. The firefighters arrived and after a thorough search of the property, they assured my mother there was nothing burning.

She regained her composure and allowed the ambulance to take us all to the hospital for observation. We were all stripped and put in hospital gowns. I heard Audra crying behind the curtain next to the crib I occupied. She was upset because she had wet her sunsuit and feared her school friends would find out. It took numerous attempts, but finally my mother was able to quiet her, and the two of them fell asleep until my father arrived.

He entered the emergency room in a panic, his face stone white, eyes moist. This was the second time in three days he'd almost lost his family.

The doctor couldn't find any injuries, so we were finally released. Once home, my father combed the backyard and then the neighborhood for Luna.

Of course, his attempts failed. Luna was long gone and would never be found again. Near tears, he plopped wearily down on the living room sofa. I climbed up on his lap and hugged him, burying my cheek against his neck. He sighed and wrapped me in a warm embrace. "I'm sorry, sport. Luna is gone."

I pulled back to look at him. "Don't be sad, Daddy. She left to help someone else."

He searched my face. "You really know this, Guylan?"

"Yup, she's a *kelpie*."

He smiled. "My little man, you know about that, too?"

"Yup," I said again, returning his smile.

"Then we must wish her as much success with her new family as she had here."

There was no doubt in my mind Luna would have any trouble accomplishing whatever mission she tackled.

Thanks for everything, Luna...wherever you are.

~ * ~

That night it was my father who put me to bed. He gave me a sip of water, helped me brush my teeth and dressed me for the night. I knew what it all meant. Guylan the toddler was moving on to being a little boy, making room for the new baby. When he laid me in the crib to sleep, I glanced down at the braided rug where Luna always slept. My heart ached, I missed her so, but I knew she had to move on, as I did.

She was a hero—or should I say, heroine.

Because of Luna's bravery, my mother would never know she'd been a breath away from mortal danger at the hands of Mortimer MacRaven and Presley Grayson. She would never be told the part Luna and I had played to save her life, nor would she realize my father was a hero. The fact that he'd never tell her of his courageous deed proved to me his stellar character. In my eyes, Xavior Sincloud measured large.

Also, thanks to Luna, Audra was spared nightmares, post-traumatic stress disorder, adult issues, therapy and anti-depressants. All of them—my father, mother, the child my mother carried and my sister—were alive and well because of Luna. They'd all continue to laugh, cry, love and live their lives to their fullest potential.

And I wasn't an orphan.

The only thing bothering me about my time travel experience was I would never know or have a relationship with Sister Margaret or my best friend, Andy Beechum...unless.

Mentally I did a bit of arithmetic and decided to make a detour before I went back to my time. Next stop, April of 1985, when I was sixteen years old.

I slipped off my T-shirt and folded it neatly at the bottom of the crib. I removed the diaper and smiled to myself.

It isn't wet this time. I had a feeling, Guylan, my toddler counterpart, would never need to wear another diaper.

I lay on my back, hoping I wouldn't find myself transported to a busy mall. Arriving in my birthday suit was fine for a three-year-old, but at sixteen a boy was at the cusp of manhood. How would I explain popping up on a busy street stark naked?

I took a deep breath and pressed my tongue on the raven mark, closed my eyes and recited over and over in my mind...*April 10th, 1985...April 10th, 1985.*

Twenty-nine

I was falling, plunging further and further into an abyss I dared not open my eyes to see. Like a caterpillar's metamorphosis into a butterfly, my body changed from toddler to teenager. The transformation was acute, my bones and muscles altering as I fell freely through time. My torso stretched; arms, fingers, legs and toes lengthened. My genitals matured, pubic hairs prickling through hair follicles. Even stubbles sprouted along my upper lip and chin, chest, under my arms and legs.

My shoulders broadened, hips spread, neck, head and spine altering in proportion to the new body I'd occupy for a time. It was amazing and frightening all at once.

My mind was also being fed information as I transformed. Life, from the time I was three until sixteen, literally downloaded like software into the hard drive of my brain.

Important occasions: Family Thanksgivings, Christmases, Halloweens and birthday parties were stored in my thoughts. Sites I'd shared with my family, such as the Statue of Liberty, Valley Forge, the largest ball of twine and vacations to Disney World, Cape Cod, and the Grand Canyon, all loaded into my intelligence. The times

I'd played in Little League, joined the Cub Scouts and Boy Scouts—the badges I'd received and the camping trips I'd participated in, all the school plays I'd appeared in, fishing with my grandfather, karate class, swimming lessons, braces on my teeth, braces off my teeth, sleeping for years wearing a retainer and even the times I was grounded and disciplined for misbehaving...all of it compiled in my brain as if I had truly lived it.

Not only was I informed about what went on, but also who was around me.

My mother was blessed with the big family she'd always dreamed of having. The baby she was carrying when I left her last turned out to be twin girls. They are named Keira and Kendra. The two are twelve years old upon my landing in 1985, and they aren't the only additions. There is Egan, who will turn eight in September and Seth, my parents' final child, only three.

Audra is twenty and in her third year at Sacred Heart University in Fairfield, Connecticut, majoring in criminal justice and crime scene investigation. In another decade, computers and DNA will play a bigger part in solving crimes than they do in 1985, and I know Audra will just love the future technology.

I am a junior at St. Matthew's Academy for boys. My mother, a devout Catholic, has made sure all of us received a Christian education, as well as the Sacraments of Baptism, Holy Communion and Confirmation. I am, in fact, nearing the end of my religious instruction and scheduled to make my Confirmation within a month.

My Druid training is also underway. Quentin, now eighty-five and still mentally and physically sound, is currently instructing me in the soothsayer phase. I will receive my oracle commencement by summer.

Our cottage on Huckleberry Street, where Luna saved us all from death, was too small for our growing family and was sold after the twins were born. We now live across town, nearer to my grandparents, which makes it easier for Olena to run over and give a helping hand to my mother now and then. I suspect my grandmother is in her glory.

The house on Fernwood Boulevard is a spacious, split level in a modern complex complete with a cul-de-sac. It sits back from the road and has a large, fenced back yard with an in-ground pool. My father is the manager of several Sincloud bank branches and doing quite well.

Darby, the nine-year-old male Jack Russell is the family's dog, and Petunia, a three-year-old female calico, the pet cat. Egan's aquarium housing two goldfish called Fric and Frac and the twins' black, long-haired guinea pig named Albert, dwell in the family room.

I was given the complete file of my life before I materialized, in the shower, thankfully, where it was perfectly acceptable to be totally naked. I sighed, relieved, as the hot water cascaded down my back and touched myself all over, just to make sure everything was intact. When satisfied with what I'd discovered, I shut off the faucet and climbed from the tub.

I dried myself with a large, downy towel and heard my mother's voice.

"Guylan," she called down from the kitchen, "if you don't get a move on, you'll be late for school."

I dressed in my school uniform: gray pants, white shirt and black tie, and made my way upstairs, glancing at the family photos on the wall. Audra's senior school picture left me astonished. She is incredibly beautiful. Long, copper curls fall in graceful curves over her shoulders; little wisps of hair frame a perfect oval face. The ivory musk-rose flush on her high cheekbones gives her a pink-with-eagerness appearance. She has an exquisitely dainty nose, but a chin of iron determination and independent spirit. Full lips round over even teeth and large, blue eyes gleam with an intelligent brilliance. My own eyes moistened with the thought this serene, proud young woman had almost lost a chance at life.

Keira and Kendra have dark hair and my mother's green eyes. Keira's hair is cut short in a chin-length bob, whereas Kendra has straight, shiny tresses hanging past her shoulders. Better to tell them apart, as they have identical patrician features and pretty Grecian noses.

Egan and Seth's heads are capped with a wealth of dark hair, tumbling carelessly across their foreheads. They too, have my mother's eye color, but I could also see myself in them. They look well-fed, especially Seth. Egan smiles proudly to display his missing front tooth, a spray of freckles dotting his nose. The whimsical look on his face and mischievous gleam in his eyes made me laugh.

Closing my eyes, I breathed a prayer of thanks that all these precious children were alive and well, and were related to me.

I entered the kitchen and saw my mother standing at the sink, busy rinsing last night's cups and snack plates before stacking them in the dishwasher. "What good is it having a dishwasher if you have to rinse the dishes first?" she complained.

Mother, you will love the future dishwashers... a whole cake on a plate won't matter.

Keira, Kendra and Egan sat at the table eating their toaster breakfast treats, all wearing school uniforms. When I looked around for Seth, I found him sitting at the far end of the large kitchen. Wearing only a T-shirt, he sat on the potty chair munching on his breakfast from a small tray attached. Darby lay beside him, waiting for whatever dropped, reminding me of Luna.

With my own humiliation at being so widely observed coming to mind, I frowned and turned to my mother. "Wouldn't it be nicer for Seth if he could use the pot in privacy?"

My mother chuckled. "He knows nothing about shame at this age, Guylan."

"How do you know he doesn't?"

"Because he runs around naked whenever he can," Keira chimed in. "So I doubt he's all that shy."

"Maybe he feels different while on the pot," I said in Seth's defense.

Seth chose that moment to rip out a loud, lengthy fart.

I turned to look at him.

He giggled and popped a piece of the toaster treat in his mouth. "My tushy tooted."

"I rest my case," Keira said.

I turned my attention back to my mother. "But this is the kitchen, where we're trying to eat. He doesn't belong in here."

"It's true, Mom," Kendra agreed. "It's really gross trying to eat while he's taking a—"

"That's enough," my mother interrupted. Her dark hair was styled in the same bob as Keira's and it bounced around her chin when she abruptly turned to face her children. "I'm forty-four years old and I've spent half of my life nursing babies and changing diapers. Though I love you all, and wouldn't trade my life for anything, quite frankly, I'm tired."

I searched her face, and though still quite beautiful, I could see the years etched beneath her eyes.

"I can't be in two places at once," she went on. "If I'm with Seth in the bathroom, watching he doesn't unroll the toilet paper and shove it all down the toilet, I can't be in here making breakfast and cleaning up dishes from the night before that all of you so generously left for me." She sighed. "I've got to get Seth toilet trained by the summer. I *need* to do this, because I don't want to change another messy diaper again. And if it means he'll learn to use the toilet by sitting on the potty in the kitchen, then so be it."

I walked over to my mother and took her in my arms. I was taller than she was now, her head only coming to my shoulders. "I'm sorry, Mom."

She looked up at me. "Could you please help me on this, Guylan?"

"I tried," Keira said. "But when I put him on the pot, all he does is play with his wiener."

Egan shrugged. "Sometimes a wiener can itch."

"And you should know, since you can't leave your mitts off of your own," Keira said.

Egan's freckled nose curled in disdain. "I can too, just sometimes it itches and I have to scratch it."

"Keep it up and it will fall off," Keira teased.

"No, it won't...it can't fall off," Egan snapped, his face turning red. "It's attached to me, like my arm or leg, which doesn't fall off if you scratch it."

"Then we'll be calling you Eganetta," Keira continued to taunt. "And we'll put barrettes in your hair."

"No, you won't, 'cause that's not what's going to happen," Egan defended himself, tears welling in his eyes.

"Or Eganlena," Kendra added. "And you can wear a skirt to school."

Both girls giggled.

"Enough," I said sharply.

My mother smiled with satisfaction. "Thank you, Guylan."

"I'll see what I can do to help Seth," I promised.

She took an audible breath. "Anything will be appreciated, and since your father is out of town on business until Friday, I guess that makes you the man of the house for the next three days."

I cast a quick glance at the calendar. It was Wednesday, April 10th, 1985, my sixteenth birthday.

My mother followed my gaze. "I plan on having your favorite for dinner tonight...fried chicken, mashed potatoes with gravy and pecan pie for dessert. But come the weekend, when your father is home, we'll invite the family and you can have a few friends over, too, for pizza and cake."

I shrugged and put a toaster treat in the toaster. "You don't have to bother."

"It's not a bother, Guylan." She poured me a glass of juice and placed it on the table. "Don't you have a meeting with the guidance counselor today about college choices?"

I nodded. "I've decided I want to stay local for now." Anything I could do to keep the balance of my education, graduation and securing a place at the animal clinic the same as my first life, when I was an orphan, was essential if I were ever to meet Nela.

"That's surprising. Audra couldn't wait to get away from this crowd." She gestured with a wave of her hand to indicate my siblings gathered around the table.

I took a bite of my pastry. "I like being around family, and crowds don't bother me." I was used to fighting children at the orphanage... or had been in my other life...the one my mind had experienced still lingered on in spite of things changing in the flesh. I wondered if it would always be the case, or if I'd eventually forget.

"Well, they bother me," Kendra said, taking the last swig of her juice. "I need my privacy." She glared across the table at Keira. "And I'm sick of sharing a room with a slob."

"Look who's talking," Keira quipped, returning the banter with a scrunched-up face. "It's not my dirty underwear on the floor."

The two sat and glared at each other.

I thought back to when my mother first told my father she was pregnant. Had they known what daunting, feisty girls these two would be, would the moment have been so heartwarming?

I also remembered how loving and helpful Audra was toward me, her little brother. Time changes, generations differ. The twins acted nothing like Audra.

"Why can't I move into Audra's room, Mom?" Kendra begged. "She's not even coming home from college this summer."

I frowned. "Audra's staying in Fairfield?"

"I believe so, got a call from her late last night. She's renting an apartment with three other girls and working full time at the restaurant near the college." My mother sighed. "I guess working at your father's bank isn't as glamorous as standing on your feet all day, toting trays of food."

"She's at that age, Mom, where she's asserting her independence, needs to stretch her wings and not be under the watchful eyes of her parents all the time," I said in Audra's defense.

"Why, Guylan, you sound like someone all grown up and ready for your own family."

If you only knew.

"What about Audra's room, Mom?" Kendra nagged.

"Until your sister tells me she's permanently residing somewhere else, the room remains hers." My mother narrowed her eyes. "And if I catch you in there touching her stuff, you'll be sorry."

Kendra pouted. "That's just not fair."

"A lot of things in life aren't fair, Kendra," my mother said. "Now, all of you, out, or you'll miss the school bus." After all my siblings noisily left the room, my mother turned to me. "You'd better get a move on, too."

"I'm riding my bike today. I've got a stop to make before I come home." I took another bite of breakfast. "Mom, do you ever see the lady who taught Audra piano lessons?"

"You mean Sophia DelFino?"

"Yes," I said.

My mother smiled. "She was such a nice woman. Actually, the whole family was wonderful." She chuckled. "I remember one time I brought you with me to pick up Audra from her recital practice and Sophia's daughter, Gloria, was at the studio that day. The two of you got along famously. She was pregnant at the time and you wrapped your little arms around her belly, completely mortifying me, and you named her child."

"I remember that." I smiled. "I named the baby Nela."

My mother gasped. "Why, Guylan, what a memory you have! I mean, you were only Seth's age at the time."

"And did she name her baby Nela?" I purposely questioned, just to make sure things were staying on track.

"Yes, as a matter of fact, she did. Mrs. O'Riley gave birth to Nela a few months before I had the twins."

It was hard to picture Nela as a twelve-year-old girl, but right now, that's how old she was. "And why did Audra stop taking lessons?"

"Well, when we moved across town, it was just too inconvenient taking her back and forth over the bridge. I enrolled her with a woman closer by, a Greta Hanns, but Audra didn't like the woman's tactics, so she quit taking lessons entirely." My mother sighed. "Which was a shame. She was so good at it and loved it, too."

"And did you ever see Mrs. DelFino again?"

"I saw Sophia a few times at the new mall and Gloria once at the theater, just after I had Egan. She had just had another baby too, a girl she named Hannah, I think." She frowned. "Why all these questions about folks we haven't seen in years?"

"I just happened to think of them, that's all."

"I catch myself thinking of past people, too."

I frowned. "Like who?"

"My parents and..." she paused, "and sometimes my brother, Presley. He was taken away when I was only five and put in a mental institution. I don't remember exactly why because my parents kept everything quite hushed, but I suspect it had something to do with a little girl my mother babysat. I think Presley hurt the child in some way." My mother cleared the emotion from her throat. "It was 1949 and things were done differently than they are now." A troubled frown creased her brow. "Looking back, I wish I had taken steps to help my brother. He was all alone in the world, with no family to be his advocate."

I affectionately put my hand over hers. "It might not have done any good, Mom."

"I think it might have, Guylan. Had I established a relationship with him, he might not have been so angry." She searched my face. "Late one night, when you were only three, I received a phone call from the institution saying Presley had pushed an aide down a flight of stairs, robbed the man of his pocket knife and escaped. I'll never forget that day, because something strange had happened in the house."

I pretended to be curious. "Like what?"

"I can't rightly say. One minute I was in the kitchen with you in my arms, running after Audra for a reason I can't remember, and the next a flash of light exploded before my eyes. When I opened them again, I was lying on the floor with you and Audra by my side." She took an audible breath. "I think the house was struck by lightning, but when the firefighters arrived, they couldn't find anything burning." She shrugged. "Anyway, that night I got the call about Presley. Apparently, he'd been on his way to see me, but somehow never made it. They found him lying on Lake George's beach."

Where else would Luna the water horse journey to but to the water?

I wondered if that was how she regrouped for her next assignment.

Where did she go next?

"He was mumbling incoherently about sea monsters and dragons," my mother continued. "A few days later, he had a fight with another patient and was struck pretty hard in the head with a clock radio. He died two days later." Her lips thinned. "Your father paid for Presley's burial and I attended the funeral...too little too late. Later on, I felt guilty I hadn't tried to see him, get to know him, and I always regretted he didn't make it to see me." She sighed. "Who knows, maybe I could have helped him."

"I think that many years institutionalized, Presley was beyond help, and it was probably a very good thing he never got to see you. What if he'd tried to hurt one of us children?"

"You're probably right." She forced a smile. "How'd you get so wise? You're like an old soul."

"I have a wise mother." I stood, kissing her on the top of the head. "I'll take the garbage out before I go."

Her eyebrows rose in astonishment. "Well, what's come over you today?"

I pulled the bag from the trash can and wrapped a twisty around the top. "What do you mean?"

"I usually have to beg you to take out the garbage."

I shrugged, placing a clean bag in place. "Like you said, I'm the man of the house until Dad comes home."

She smiled, her jade eyes filling with pride. "Yes, yes you are."

An unwelcomed blush crept to my cheeks and I made my way over to Seth, sniffing the air. "Seth, did you go poop?"

He smiled wide and nodded proudly. "Two poops...I made two poops come out."

I reached down and ruffled his hair. "That's my buddy. You're a big boy now, like me, and you need to go poop in the potty all the time." I squared my shoulders. "No more diapers for guys like us, right?"

"Right," Seth agreed, throwing Darby a piece of food.

"Thank you for that, Guylan," my mother said softly.

I could hear the fatigue in her tone. "It's okay, Mom." I made my way, hauling the garbage, toward the garage. Hesitating, I turned back to look at her. "I should be thanking you...for all you do, for all you've done."

She smiled again. "I didn't think anyone noticed."

"Well, I do...I really, truly do." Then I added, "I love you," before leaving for school.

Thirty

The fact that Nela and I are bicyclists was a stroke of luck, and came in handy. My thirty-eight-year-old body was in shape to ride the three miles to school, although I did wonder whether it mattered, since I was in a sixteen-year-old body. In 1985, there were no helmet laws, and I was leery about biking those miles without head gear, but I remained cautious and didn't show off or speed as a typical teenager would.

I made it to school in time for the first bell to ring, put in my day and entered the guidance office after classes were dismissed. I sat next to another student, his blond hair spiked and dyed purple in places. Dipping deep into my memory, I came up with the name, Kevin Palmer.

Looking up from the punk-rocker magazine he was reading, Kevin wagged his pierced tongue at me. "You here to see dickhead?"

I frowned. "Who would that be?"

"You know, dickhead Dickson, the guidance counselor."

"Yes, I have an appointment at three-thirty."

Kevin looked up at the wall clock and I followed his gaze. It was 3:15. "My appointment was for two-thirty, but dickhead's running late." He stood. "Ah, who needs this bullshit?"

"You, I'd imagine, if you want to get anywhere in this world."

Kevin tucked his magazine beneath his arm. "For cripes' sake, you sound just like my father."

I frowned, annoyed. If anyone was a dickhead, it was Kevin Palmer. "Maybe your father is right."

He made his way to the door. "I'm going to be a rock star. You don't need colleg e for that."

"Well, good luck with that, then."

"Yeah, man, I'm going to be rich and everyone, including my father, can suck my cock."

Just as Kevin slammed the door behind him, the secretary entered the waiting area and called out his name.

"He left. He's going to be a rock star."

The secretary arched a brow. "You don't say?"

I nodded.

She glanced down at the paper attached to a clipboard. "And you're Guylan Sincloud?"

"That I am."

"Then I guess you're next." She gestured to a room on the far left of the waiting area. "Have a seat and Mr. Dickson will be in momentarily."

The large window in Mr. Dickson's office looked out onto the school's parking lot. Not exactly a monumental view. Various plants were placed on the window's ledge and pictures scattered here and there of Mr. Dickson and his family white-water rafting, climbing mountains, and riding horses, so I suspected he enjoyed what he saw in spite of the location. I also realized Mr. Dickson wasn't such a dickhead, but an active man who took pleasure in doing many of the things I enjoyed, and one day I hoped to do with my wife and children.

He held a folder in his hands when he entered the room, plopped it down on his desk, and without looking up, muttered, "Well, let's see what we've got here."

I remained silent, watching as he skimmed my file, the brows above his black-rimmed glasses rising with interest. He smelled like coffee and donuts, his cologne faded and mixing with the day's sweat.

He gazed over at me, pushing his glasses up on his nose with a thumb. "You've got an impressive academic history here, Mr. Sincloud." Smiling, he sat back in his seat. "What do you plan on doing with it?"

"I want to be a veterinarian...go to a local college in the beginning, then perhaps in-state for medical college. After I graduate, I plan on working my internship at a veterinary hospital, and then with an independent veterinarian in a private practice. By the time I'm thirty-five, I want to co-open an animal clinic."

Mr. Dickson chuckled. "God, where'd you come from?"

If you only knew.

He sighed. "I wish they were all like you, Mr. Sincloud. It's the reason I got into this field, to help others make their way in life."

"And I appreciate your help, sir."

He sat forward in his seat and reached for a pen and paper. "Then let's get started planning your senior year. After we're through with your schedule, we can take a look at colleges to apply to."

I smiled. "That sounds good to me, sir."

Mr. Dickson returned the smile. "You've made my day, Mr. Sincloud." He shook his head. "Yes, by God, you've certainly made my day."

~ * ~

After my appointment with Dickson, I hopped on my bike and rode to the orphanage. St. Bernard's Home for Boys was only a block away from St. Matthew's Boys Academy. When I had lived at the orphanage—in my original life—I passed the academy daily on my way to Park Elementary School.

Though the orphanage was a Catholic establishment, private school required tuition. If you were an orphan, there was no one around to pay the fee. I suspect, since Sister Margaret didn't want me to stand out among my peers, I was denied private school in spite of the fact there was ample money to send me.

Academy boys taunted orphan children. When I was in my early years at grade school, I was given wedgies about twice a week by a tenth grader named Lenny Jones and his sidekick, Bruce Hudson.

But I got off easier than Andy Beechum, my best friend. Actually, in those days, he was more like a brother. Not only did Andy receive the wedgies, but regularly had his pants pulled down to his ankles. And the taunts...I remember them well.

"Look at the skid marks on this kid's underwear," Lenny *pointed out to Bruce.*

They'd laugh and sneer, Andy's face turning red and his eyes welling with tears.

"Hey, kid, for Christmas you should ask for two ply toilet paper," Bruce added.

"Or have one of those nuns bend you over and wipe your crack," Lenny countered.

They'd both laugh again.

"Leave him alone...leave us alone...what'd we ever do to you?" I'd scream.

Lenny would grab me by the collar. "If you don't shut your mouth, we'll pull your pants down, too. In fact, we'll remove them completely and you two can walk bare-assed to school.

Then there were more humiliating jeers, followed by more laughter.

At any rate, the embarrassment was great, to the point that we actually protested going to school. The alternative, time spent over Mother Superior's desk, wasn't any better. So, Andy and I, to save our dignity, traveled the long way to Park Elementary. That meant we had to leave earlier each morning, missing breakfast. Our stomachs rumbled throughout the morning session and the other children laughed at us. Come afternoon, we arrived later at the orphanage, missing snack time and television privileges.

I wondered now, with my life changes, how Andy endured the walks to school. Going through a hard time alone is so much harder.

I glanced at my watch...it read 4:45 p.m. Sister Margaret would be in the homework room at this hour. Stopping before the large, brick building, I secured my bike and ran up the front steps. I hesitated at the door, remembering I was no longer a resident and walking in as I was wouldn't really be a polite thing to do.

I made my way to the receptionist's desk and glimpsed Andy sweeping the foyer's floor. I smiled and was just about to ask him how he had been, when I realized he didn't know me anymore. There was a void in the pit of my stomach as I realized I had literally lost my best friend. Hopefully, stopping by the orphanage today would correct the new outcome and I'd have Andy and Sister Margaret in my life again.

Andy and I had each other's back. When he had a wetting problem, the entire summer we were both nine, I helped him in the middle of the night, strip, wash and remake the bed so no one would be the wiser. And when I accidentally threw a ball through Mother Superior's hot-house window, Andy lied and said I was with him all day polishing the church pews.

Andy gave me a taut nod. "Hi, can I help you?"

I extended my hand. "I'm Guylan Sincloud, and I'm looking for Sister Margaret."

Andy looked down at my hand, his blond curls falling across his forehead, and kept his grip on the broom. "Sister Margaret isn't here anymore."

I stuck my hands in my pockets. "I don't understand."

He continued to sweep the floor. "She left, two years ago, after..." he paused, biting his lower lip.

My heart sank. "After what?"

"After the incident with Ronnie Fargus."

I frowned. "What incident was that?"

Andy stopped sweeping and raised a defiant chin, his gray-green eyes irate. "What business is it of yours? Who are you, anyway?"

I squared my shoulders. "I'm Sister Margaret's great-nephew and I need to see her."

"She's over at the St. Thomas Women's Shelter on Lansing Street now." Andy lowered his gaze to the broom and resumed sweeping. "Sometimes I stop in to see her, help with yard work and carrying out the garbage...stuff like that."

I remained silent, watching Andy as he swept the floor. He was so different. He was always a shy, quiet kid, a loner, but he had spirit.

What I was witnessing now was an Andy who looked like he'd had the stuffing knocked out of him.

Our friendship, obviously, had made the difference. With me out of the equation, Andy didn't really have anyone on his side. When my life changed for the better, Andy's changed for the worst.

I swallowed back the tears threatening to come and cleared my throat. "Would you like to go to a game at Yankee Stadium or the Glens Falls Civic Center to see a concert sometime with me?"

Andy's gaze shot up, his mouth agape. "What did you say?"

I repeated myself and smiled. "My father knows a lot of bigwigs and is always getting tickets to such events."

"Are you serious?"

I pulled from my shirt pocket the pen and pad kept there. "Here's my name, address and phone number." I wrote the information down and handed it to him.

Reluctantly he accepted the paper and put it in his pants pocket. "I should give you mine."

"I already..." I clipped my tongue. "Sure, go ahead." I wrote down his name and the office phone number as he dictated it to me.

"I have phone privileges on Thursday nights from seven to eight. Can I call you then?"

I smiled. "Sure, I'd like that. Maybe we could hang out. You could come over to my house for supper, stuff like that," I offered. "In fact, I'm having a birthday party on Saturday night. Just pizza and cake, but I'd like you to come."

Andy's face brightened. "Yeah, really?"

I laughed. "Yeah, really," I repeated. "My dad will square it with Mother Superior and we'll pick you up by three."

"That'll be great." Andy wiped the palm of his hand on his thigh and extended it to me. "Thanks, Guylan."

I shook his hand, my heart hopeful we'd again have the opportunity to be friends.

Before I walked out the door, I glanced back at Andy and thought he was sweeping the floor with a lot more vigor.

Lansing Street was another four blocks away, heading east from St. Bernard's. If I took the time to visit Sister Margaret now, I'd be traveling home in the dark and miss my birthday dinner. I decided to wait until Saturday afternoon to see my great-aunt, when I had more time to make it further across town.

For now, I was heading home, my mouth watering for my mother's fried chicken and pecan pie.

Thirty-one

On Thursday, I rode my bike to school again and skipped the last class so I could make it across the bridge to Nela's part of town. My curiosity got the best of me, and I just had to see how she looked as a twelve-year-old. Even though she'd shown me pictures, the real thing is so much better, and to be near her again was something I craved.

I pulled up to the O'Riley home, a large yellow and white Victorian with an apartment in the basement. Brian O'Riley, Nela's father, rented the bottom half to his brother and his wife while Nela and her sisters were young. Later, in my era, it was Nela's sister Hannah and her daughter Cara that lived in the apartment, while Hannah's husband Joe was fighting in Iraq.

I glanced at my watch and saw it was almost time for Nela to be arriving home from school. I positioned myself across the street behind two large oak trees. From this vantage point, I could see the corner where the bus dropped her off. Since Nela's house was only a few doors down, I'd also be able to watch her walk home.

When she stepped off the bus, my heart raced.

She walked with brisk, confident steps. Even as a young girl, her legs were long and shapely. She held her books in her arms, low against her belly. The shoulder bag was slung across her chest, the strap nestled between her small, perky breasts, accentuating the budding mounds.

I closed my eyes for a moment, picturing how they would one day bloom, full and lush, nipples hard and rosy. I remembered cupping their heaviness, drawing on the pink peaks, and nibbling them gently with my teeth.

She passed the oak trees shielding me from her view and I inhaled the light scent of musk she wore. How I yearned to stop her, talk to her, hear how her young voice sounded. But I feared I'd put a glitch in the scheme of things. Already my life's history had been drastically changed; I dared not tamper further. There wasn't anything I was willing to risk that would alter my meeting Nela in the future.

"Hey, O'Riley," a boy on a bike shouted from behind.

He was a red-haired, freckle-faced kid with a large nose. He wore his hair slicked back and a black leather jacket.

Nela turned, her eyes narrowing with displeasure. "Leave me alone, Greg. I told you this afternoon, I'm not doing your homework for you anymore."

Greg neared her, pulling his bike to an abrupt stop, road gravel spitting from the tires. "And I say you are, or I'm telling everyone you kissed Jamie Holloway."

Nela's chin rose in defiance. "That's an out-and-out lie, Gregory Oliver, and you know it."

Greg braced his feet on each side of the bike and reached out to touch a long, dark curl falling across her shoulder. "Yeah, well, you and I know that, but everyone else doesn't."

I frowned, not liking this little punk touching my girl, even though she wouldn't be mine for decades to come.

Nela slapped his hand away. "It's your word against mine."

"Wrong," Greg said, his lips turning up into a sneer. "My word and Jamie's against yours."

Nela gasped. "Jamie knows I didn't kiss him."

"Yeah, well, he's trying to make Holly Addison jealous, and if she thinks he's kissed you, she'll invite him to her big birthday bash next weekend."

"So that's what all this is about?"

Greg shrugged. "It is what it is."

It's blackmail in all its glory.

"Go to hell, you and Jamie," Nela shouted and continued to walk home.

I smiled at her tenacity.

Way to go, babe.

"Then I'm spreading the word," Greg yelled after her.

Nela turned. "Then spread the word...spread two words, and I'll tell everyone I saw you eat baby food."

Greg's face turned red. "But I didn't eat baby food."

Nela shrugged. "Oh, well."

"It's your word against mine," Greg countered.

"Mine and Holly Addison's, because when I tell her what scheming little freaks you and Jamie are, she'll side with me, especially since we're in Girl Scouts together and I'm helping her get her cooking badge." Nela smiled, braces covering her white teeth. "And Holly really wants that badge."

"You're a little douche bag," Greg snapped, nearing Nela again. Reaching out, he knocked the books from her arm. Papers went flying and Greg rolled over them. "Douche bag, douche bag," he taunted.

Nela punched him in the back. "Get away from me, creepo."

"Douche bag, douche bag," he chanted.

I'd seen enough.

Racing out from behind the trees, I blocked Greg's bike with my own.

He stared at me, stunned.

"Leave her alone, asshole, before I wipe the street with your face." A wave of excitement coursed through my veins. I hadn't had a good fight in years. I'd like nothing better than to knock a few of Greg Oliver's teeth down his throat. And I could do it, too. Living in an orphanage conditioned you to fend for yourself. That part of my life was still very real to me, not to mention I knew Karate.

"Who are you?" he said, standing.

I climbed off my bike, so he could see my height...a whole head taller than him. "I'm your worst nightmare."

He got back on his bike, readying himself to leave in case I did what I threatened. "This is none of your business."

"Oh, on the contrary, it's every man's business...every *real* man, that is, to stop a jerk from bothering a lady." I felt Nela's eyes on me and I glanced her way, giving her a polite nod before I turned my attention back on Greg. "Doesn't take much to bully a girl. Then again," I eyed him up and down, "you're not much of anything, except maybe a twerp." I moved closer, got my face right in his. "From here on out, I'll be watching you, and if I ever see you so much as talk to this girl again, I'll make sure you're taking your baby food through a feeding tube."

Greg's face turned red, but he remained silent. He gave Nela an evil glare and peddled away.

When I knew Greg was out of sight, I bent to pick up Nela's books.

She knelt down beside me. "Do I know you?"

I turned to look into her large, chocolate eyes, loving the tone of her little-girl voice. An emotional fire burned in my heart; the inner compulsion to reach over and stroke her face consumed me.

"No, you don't know me," I said.

Not yet, anyway...but when you do, I'm the guy that's going to ravage your entire body.

Her pink tongue moistened her full lips. "I haven't seen you around here before."

I handed her the papers I'd retrieved and our fingers brushed together. Heat rushed to my loins and every fiber of my being fought for control. "I'm not from around here."

I stood and politely helped her to her feet. Her tiny hand in mine felt warm and soft.

She smiled. "My name is Nela O'Riley."

I hesitated to give her my name. If I did, it could spoil everything for us in the future. "It's nice to meet you, Nela." I climbed back on my bike and gave her another nod of my head. "Have a nice day." I peddled ahead.

"Wait...wait, please," she called after me.

I stopped and twisted in my seat to look at her.

"Can I know your name?"

I smiled. "Someday, Nela O'Riley; you will someday," I promised and rode away.

~ * ~

When I arrived home, I headed straight for my room. I just wanted to be alone, turn on my stereo, lie back on the bed with my headset on and think of Nela. What a sweetheart: doe-like eyes, full pouting lips, cute little swing to her hips. When we'd met in my era— or should I say when we did meet—she was thirty-three. Why hadn't someone else snatched her up before me?

I glanced in the dresser mirror and smiled at my reflection. "Because she never forgot the way I rescued her from that little scrotum, Greg Oliver," I whispered.

Or else I'm just a lucky slob.

More the latter I decided, because in our first meeting, the encounter on the bikes had never taken place.

Egan peered into the room, smiling at me with a toothless grin. "Can I stay in here with you, Guy?"

I made a gesture with my hand for him to enter. "What are those girls doing to you now?"

"Hogging the television, calling me Eganetta, saying they took pictures of my bare butt while I was sleeping." He plopped down on the bed belly-first and gazed at the Kenny Loggins and U2 posters hanging on the wall.

My heart went out to Egan. The twins had each other to confide in. Seth, being a toddler, had my mother. I knew, as the oldest male sibling in the house, I tended to bond with my father. And when Audra was home from college, she hung with either my mother or the twins. Who did Egan have?

He fidgeted with the buttons at his collar. "Can an ant crawl in your ear and make a nest in your brain?"

I climbed on the bed and lay down beside him. "No, that can't happen."

"Keira said it could and that they'd eat away at my brain and then I'd turn into a giant ant."

"Keira's been watching too many science fiction movies."

"Can I ask you something personal, Guy?" he whispered.

"Anything you want, Egan."

"And you won't tell Mom or Dad or the twins?"

"It will be just between us brothers," I assured him.

"Well, sometimes, when I wake up in the morning my...my," he stammered.

"It's okay, Egan." I placed my hand on his shoulder.

"Sometimes my wiener is hard, poking straight up in my pajamas and when I touch it, it feels good," he blurted out, hiding his face in his hands.

Like father like son...like brother. I stifled a smile. "That happens to guys sometimes. It isn't anything weird or wrong."

He raised his gaze to mine. "Why does it happen?"

I cleared my throat. "Well, because blood flows through the penis and it becomes engorged...hard."

"But why does it need to be hard? All it's used for is to pee, and I can do that fine when it's soft."

How much do you tell an eight-year-old boy about himself? I decided to stick to the scientific angle, the body's reaction to nerves, muscle and blood flow and leave the sex talk to my father. Egan was an eager listener, hanging on my every word. When I finished my biology spiel, he smiled, gazing at me with adoring eyes.

"You know everything, Guylan."

"No one knows everything, Egan. And if someone thinks they do, they'll stop learning. When you stop learning, you stop growing as a person because there are new things to discover each and every day."

"Like I did today," he said.

I smiled. "That's right."

Egan gave me an affectionate pat on the back. "You're going to be a good father, Guy."

I sighed. "Oh, I hope so, Egan; I truly hope so."

~ * ~

I talked to Andy on the phone after supper. Several times I made an attempt to get out of him the reason Sister Margaret had left the orphanage, but he always changed the subject. We talked a while longer about school, the things we liked to do...which I already knew were similar...and then he asked me what it was like to have a family. I swallowed the lump in my throat. It really was all new to me as well.

"I always wanted a brother," Andy said.

"My brothers are only eight and three; not much in the way of companionship."

"Yeah, but they won't be that age forever. In time, they'll sort of grow even with you, like when you're say...thirty-eight and they're thirty and twenty-five. Then you'll have them to do things with. They'll be your best buds."

Andy was right. When I returned to my era, I'd have men brothers waiting for me.

I heard Mother Superior's twang in the background.

"I've gotta go now, Guylan. Make sure your father or mother talks to Mother Superior about me coming to your house on Saturday. Don't forget, okay?"

"You don't have to worry, Andy; I won't forget."

"Thanks, Guylan. Bye."

I held the phone to my ear a moment after Andy hung up, wishing his bed were beside mine so we could whisper and laugh a bit before falling asleep.

Who did Andy have to do that with now?

~ * ~

My father arrived home from his business trip on Friday afternoon and was waiting inside the house when we got off the school bus. My younger siblings, when they spotted his black Volkswagen minivan in the driveway, ran from the corner to greet him. I took my time, preparing myself for eye contact. Would he see the difference in me as he had when I was three?

He did, his face turning pale upon his scrutiny. At dinner, he avoided looking my way, keeping his eyes on his plate as he chewed his food. When we all sat around the television in the family room, he excluded me from the conversation.

His avoidance hurt, angered and disappointed me. I thought the two of us had a special bond. Unable to take this treatment further, I removed myself from his presence before I either broke down and cried or shouted things I'd later regret.

In my room, I lay upon the bed, eyes closed, listening to music, the headset blocking out the laughter and banter going on in the next room. I was an outcast in my own family, and as soon as I'd talked with Sister Margaret, I would be on my way to the future, where I belonged. This whole time-travel thing was getting tiring.

I jumped nearly out of my skin when a hand rested on my arm. My eyelids shot open, my gaze locked with my father's and I ripped the headset from my ears.

"I knocked, but I guess you didn't hear me."

I sat up and turned off the music. "I'm sorry."

"Is someone going to die, Guylan?"

I blinked, his bluntness catching me off guard. "Pardon?"

"The last time you came," he made a motion with his hand, "like this, like you are now, it was to save us from dying." He sat on the edge of the bed and searched my face. "Is that why you're back? Is someone else supposed to die?"

"No, no one is going to die. That's not why I'm here."

"Then why...why are you here?"

I hesitated, not sure of how much to divulge.

"I want to know why you change." He crossed his arms over his chest. "We get this, all of this, out in the open now."

"Okay," I agreed, swinging my legs off the bed and taking a seat in the desk chair opposite him. "I grew up in an orphanage before...

in my original life. I was too small to communicate this fact to you when I came the last time."

My father frowned. "Explain to me what you mean by that... your original life."

I sighed and unraveled the past I'd lived, the future I was living, and why I'd returned in 1972.

He nodded. "I knew something was different, felt it deep inside; I just didn't realize the extent."

"Who could?"

My father gave a sardonic chuckle and combed his fingers through his hair. "Incredible, effing incredible, and yet, what I experienced the night I dealt with Mortimer MacRaven should have conditioned me for almost anything."

"Luna helped, didn't she?"

He nodded. "Now, that's a name I haven't heard in years, but by no means have I forgotten."

I leaned forward in my chair. "How...how did she help, Dad?"

He went on to explain, his eyes growing distant as he relived that night for me.

"I had a similar experience with our little *kelpie*." I told him about Presley Grayson's visit.

"How are you doing all this?"

I opened my mouth, showed him the raven branded on the inside of my cheek. He compared it to the one on his ring, an identical match. I then explained how I stepped through the attic portal, how I moved from era to era and the way I collected information.

"Then you're living on fast forward," he said.

"Yes, exactly."

"Will you remember any of this when you return to your own time?"

I frowned. "I'm not sure, since I haven't been there yet, not since I walked through the portal."

He smiled. "Then I am anxious to meet you there."

"Me, too."

"Now, tell me why you're here."

"I've changed things a lot with my travels. Most of what happened to me while living at the orphanage I couldn't give a crap about, but for two people. I've returned to get to know them again, because I want them to still be a part of my life."

My father tilted his head sideways. "And who are these two people?"

I explained about Sister Margaret, who she was and the vital part she'd played in helping Olena save my life. Then I moved on to tell him about Andy, my best friend, the person I considered my brother.

"I met him on Wednesday—or should I say, met him again—and already I've started to build a friendship."

Lastly, I told him about Nela and how important it was I remain on the same course with my education. "It's essential if I'm to come out to the same point in time as when I met her."

"Big responsibility, this time travel stuff."

"You couldn't begin to imagine," I began. "With some of it, like persuading Sister Margaret to come back into the family realm, I might need your help."

He instantly agreed. "Whatever it takes, I'm willing to do."

"I appreciate that. In fact, could you call the orphanage?" I pulled the pad from my pocket and ripped off the piece of paper I'd written the St. Bernard's phone number on a few days earlier. "I need you to speak to Mother Superior about Andy coming to my birthday on Saturday."

"I'll get right on it." He took the number. "And I'll drive you on Saturday afternoon to see Sister Margaret?" He sighed. "Truth be told, I've been a bit curious about my mother's sister all these years myself."

"I think she'd like to meet you, too."

He stood. "I'll leave you, then, to plot your mission." He smiled down at me. "I'm proud of you, Guylan...of what you are now, of what you've become—or should I say, what you've already become and must get back to?"

I returned the smile. "I couldn't have done any of it without you and Great-grandpa."

He gave me an affectionate pat on the shoulder. "We're quite a team, then."

"Yes...yes we are, like those brothers on TV who hunt demons."

My father frowned. "Like who?"

I waved my hand, dismissing my words. "You'll see."

He nodded and made his way to the door.

"Oh, and Dad?"

He turned to look at me. "Yes, Guylan."

"Could you have the sex talk with Egan?"

His eyes widened. "Already?"

"Well, if not now, then real soon." I smiled and replaced the headset over my ears.

Thirty-two

I woke early on Saturday to sparrows chirping beneath the eaves of my bedroom window, and took a shower before anyone else could claim the bathroom. Then I helped my mother with Seth's potty training so she could start breakfast.

"You're really going to do this?" She handed me a naked toddler, fresh from his bath.

"I promised, didn't I?" I placed Seth on the potty chair and sat cross-legged on the floor in front of him.

Kendra peeked into the room. "Take it from me. You're wasting your time. All he's gonna do is play with his..."

"Yeah, yeah, I know," I interrupted, stretching out a leg and kicking the door shut with my foot.

Seth pointed to the door. "Stay out, Kendra."

I smiled. "That's right, no girls allowed. It's nice for a man to have privacy when he's doing his business."

"Tell me a story, Guy."

I nodded and told him the one about the three pigs.

Seth interrupted me with questions between grunts and farts. By the end of the story, he had accomplished his bathroom goal. I praised him and cleaned his bottom with a baby wipe. After emptying and washing the pot, as well as my own hands, I gathered Seth in my arms. He wrapped his soft, naked baby's body around my hips, his chubby arms around my neck. I kissed his ear and inhaled the scent of the baby shampoo in his hair, remembering my mother washing my hair with the same shampoo...No More Tears, the bottle said. Or was it Sister Margaret? I had the memories stored in my head of two women caring for me.

I carried Seth to the room he shared with Egan and laid him on the bed. He smiled and lifted his legs so he could touch his toes. I marveled over him, thinking about the children Nela and I would have. I couldn't wait to hold the child of my seed, look upon the face that was a combination of both Nela and me.

Egan watched as I slipped a T-shirt over Seth's head and helped him on with the pull-up pants and jeans my mother had left out for him to wear.

"We brothers have to stick together, don't we, Guy?" Egan sat the edge of his own bed, tying his sneaker.

"Most definitely," I agreed, thinking again on meeting these two boys as men when I returned to the future.

"You're the best big brother in the world. You don't tease us or pinch and hit us, or give us wedgies."

No, heaven forbid those wedgies.

"Best in the world," Seth repeated. "Good Guy Guy."

I smiled and hoisted Seth on my hip, giving his chubby cheek a big kiss. Then I reached down and ruffled Egan's hair. "You guys aren't so bad yourselves."

After breakfast, my father drove me to Lansing Street. We parked in the lot and stared for a moment at the tumbled down, three story building housing St. Thomas Women's Shelter.

"The place needs a coat of paint and the rain gutters repaired," my father observed. "Stairs need fixing, too. Probably wouldn't hurt to add railings."

"I can do those things."

He turned to look at me. "Would you want to?"

"Yeah, I would, as well as help out at the orphanage," I added.

He smiled. "Care for some company?"

I returned the smile. "Sure."

"Then you've got a partner."

I glanced again at the building. "What kind of man would make a woman need to seek shelter somewhere other than her own home?"

"A man who has low self-esteem, for one," my father reflected, "or who doesn't feel like a man until he can control his women with brute force."

"The whole thing sickens me." I thought about Gregory Oliver and his abuse toward Nela a few days ago. What kind of a man—husband or father—is he going to become, or, already is?

I was glad I was there to help Nela, but pleased to see her for another reason. She was a link to the future, and her energy would keep me grounded. Seeing Sister Margaret today would also help to balance my perspective.

"I agree, Guylan. I'd never lay an angry hand on your mother, no matter how we might argue. She's my life partner, the mother of my children, my heart. I would never want her to fear me, disrespect me, or hate me for using such tactics. I'd never do anything to harm any woman...it's just not proper. I don't think a man is much of a man when he bullies a woman."

Much like I'd said to Greg Oliver.

"The men who do this to women make all men look bad," I said.

He sighed. "In the eyes of these women, battered by a husband or a father, or some other man, that assumption is true. But a woman brought up in a healthy atmosphere, or married to a loving husband, can see the difference. Those women realize one man's actions don't represent them all. And in places like St. Thomas, a battered woman can get counseling, an education, all the tools she'll need so she can walk away from the violence and make a better life for herself and her children."

"Good thing for those places, then," I said.

"Yes, it's a very good thing."

I turned to look at my father. "Sister Margaret is a good woman, Dad. When she cared for me at the orphanage, though she couldn't blatantly show favoritism, I have to say she attended to all my needs. And in her roundabout way, she loved me, too. I knew it and felt it. She loved working with kids, period. And I don't know why she left the orphanage, but I'd like to find out."

He nodded and reached for the door handle. "Then let's get inside and ask her."

When my father and I opened the main door and walked into the lounge, all eyes turned our way. Women sitting at a table, playing cards and chatting seconds before, went silent. Young children playing games in another corner stopped and stared. A mother sitting in a rocking chair, lulling her infant to sleep, stopped rocking.

I could only imagine what was going through their minds... were we someone's irate male relatives here to drag a woman back to dysfunction? Maybe there should be an alarm on the door, a way to keep someone off the street from entering the building. But then again, in my experience working with donations and fundraisers, I'd learned places like this were lucky if they had enough food and beds for those they helped.

A woman who'd been sitting on the sofa knitting, put her work down and made her way to us. "I'm Lucy Gorman, child and family liaison." She extended her hand. "Can I help you?"

My father politely accepted her greeting. "I'm Xavior Sincloud and this is my son, Guylan," he said, gesturing to me. "We're here to see Sister Margaret."

"Do you have an appointment?" Lucy probed.

"No, no we don't. We were just in the neighborhood and thought we'd drop in to see her." He smiled. "I'm her nephew."

"Oh...oh, then please, follow me." Lucy led us to the kitchen.

I remembered the smell of pumpkin bread. The aroma had filled St. Bernard's kitchen every Saturday, along with pancakes. My mouth watered with the thought of hot, thick slices of the homemade bread smothered in creamy, melting butter. Sister Margaret would gather us all together and make hot chocolate, placing the steaming mugs topped with marshmallow fluff beside a plate of pumpkin bread. Andy and I used to stick around to clear and clean the kitchen, so we could gain an extra piece.

My stomach rumbled and I licked my lips as I leaned over and whispered to my father, "She makes the best pumpkin bread. Hope she'll give us a piece."

"And here I'm just hoping she'll talk to us."

My father was right. Sister Margaret didn't know either of us; she'd disowned the family, thinking us all pagan worshippers. If we were allowed to stay past the introductions, we'd be lucky.

"Sister Margaret, you have company," Lucy said.

Sister Margaret turned from the oven, where she'd just placed another pan of pumpkin bread to bake. Her blue eyes locked with mine. It was the same look Nela had given me...deep and long, searching for an answer as to why she was suddenly having a *déjà vu* moment. And she followed the look with the same question.

"Do I know you?"

You did...once...in another time, another life.

My father responded for me. "I'm Olena's son, and this is my son, Guylan."

She turned her attention to my father. "Olena's son..." A slow smile curved her lips. "Yes, yes, I see the resemblance." She removed the oven mitts covering her hands and dropped them on the table. "Xavior, you're Xavior?"

I was shocked she knew his name, and encouraged, too. It meant she'd been keeping track of the family, still held an interest. Perhaps this visit would be successful in reuniting everyone.

"That's right, Aunt Anya."

Tears glistened in her azure eyes. "Mercy, I haven't been called by that name in so long."

My father inclined his head respectfully. "I apologize...Sister Margaret."

"No, no, it's quite all right, really." She moved around the table and stood before me. Slowly she reached out and caressed the side of my face with a finger. "And this is your boy?"

"Yes, one of them. I have two other sons and three daughters."

She captured my chin between a thumb and forefinger, moving my head from side to side. I blushed under her scrutiny. "He's a fine young man. My sister must be so proud to have such a nice family."

"I'm your family, too," I blurted out, then bit my tongue for being so presumptuous.

The tears welling in her eyes slipped down her cheeks. "Yes, you are, aren't you?" She giggled. "Ironic, isn't it? I woke this morning with no one, and this afternoon I have a family."

My father took her hand and gave it an affectionate squeeze. "Can we go somewhere and talk?"

She nodded and called into the next room for a woman named Theresa. "The loaf in the oven must come out in thirty minutes," she instructed before she led the way to her office.

I sat in the corner of the room on an old, rose-colored, paisley upholstered arm chair. My father took a seat beside the desk. Sister Margaret sat in a chair between us.

"My father...is he still alive?" she asked.

"Yes, Grandpa Quentin is alive and as feisty as ever." Xavior smiled. "He just turned eighty-five and is as sharp as a whistle."

She sighed, relieved. "I thought for a moment, perhaps you came to tell me—"

"We came because we want you to be part of our lives," I interjected.

Her gaze shot my way.

My father cleared his throat. "My son sometimes has a way—"

It was her turn to interrupt. "Children say what they feel, something adults need to do more often," she said, still meeting my gaze.

"My grandmother misses her sister. She talks about you all the time. And my great-grandfather is getting older. He would love time with his daughter before he dies." My eyes filled with tears. "And I want to know you, be a part of your life and have you be a part of mine."

She swallowed hard. "Oh my, Guylan."

I didn't stop there. "I know you think we're all pagan devil worshippers, but we're not."

"Guylan, that's enough," my father scolded.

Sister Margaret put up a hand to silence my father, still keeping her eyes on me. "Let him speak."

"Great-grandfather is a good man, a loving man," I said in Quentin's defense.

"Who practices wizardry," she said. "He's a man who casts spells and bestows blessings, which isn't his place to do." She shook her head in disgust. "Psychics, mediums, those dabbling in the supernatural in the hopes of finding a quick answer for their future practices, are things forbidden by the scriptures. Consulting ungodly sources undermines faithfulness to God's covenant. Reliance on the words of soothsayers and evil practices indicates failure to trust God with our lives, Guylan." Sister Margaret sighed. "He's the only one who holds the answers to the questions we seek...only Almighty God, The Father, Son and Holy Spirit have that power."

"How do you know Quentin's not empowered by God?" I countered.

"He's empowered by the raven, an unclean bird, a scavenger, a forbidden food in the Bible. Noah sent a raven out after the flood and it never returned."

"The raven also fed Elijah, the prophet, when he hid from King Ahab," I said.

She gasped. "You've read the Bible?"

"Read it, memorized scripture, and practice it," I said.

Sister Margaret's eyes widened. "But how can that be?"

"My mother is a devout Catholic. All of us children attend Catholic school and will receive the sacraments of Baptism, Holy Communion and Confirmation. In fact, I am making my Confirmation next month and would love to have you present at the ceremony and the dinner that will follow."

She turned to look at my father, glancing down at his hand. "You wear the raven crest ring, yet you serve God?"

My father nodded. "I worship only Christ as my God, believe in His Resurrection and the Creation in Genesis. When I pray, I call upon the same God you do, but I also embrace the spiritual powers of a Druid, and uphold those blessings given to me by inheritance."

Sister Margaret's voice was cold and exact; it was the tone she'd used just before she washed my mouth out with soap for swearing. "You can't have it both ways."

My father quirked an eyebrow. "Why not?"

Sister Margaret leaned forward in her seat. "Because it's blasphemy."

I remembered something Olena had told me. "Did you know there are many variations of Christian denominations and groups belonging to the Druid heritage?"

She turned toward me, shaking her head disapprovingly. "Don't tell me you're a Druid, too?"

"Yes, I am," I said. "Though I'm still in training."

"Training to go to hell," she snapped.

I squared my shoulders. "And won't you also take the same trip because you can't forgive? Christ Himself forgave His executioners, and you can't turn the other cheek to make amends with your family? Hate the sin, if you feel there is one, but not the sinner, Sister...never the sinner."

"Well, you put my faith to shame." She forced a smile. "You've been taught well."

"I've been taught by the best." *If you only knew it was you who taught me.*

"I don't know what to say. I...I..." she stammered.

"Say *yes* to coming to dinner at our house next week, and meet my wife and children. See Quentin and Olena again," my father said. "Come back to us, Aunt Anya."

"Say *yes* to attend my Confirmation," I added. "And allow me to come with Andy Beechum to help around here, even fix up the place."

Her brows shot up in surprise. "You know Andy Beechum?"

I nodded.

"How do you know him?" she probed.

"I met him Wednesday when I stopped by St. Bernard's Home for Boys to find you, and we became fast friends."

"I'm glad you've befriended Andy. He's been through a lot, hasn't had an easy time in life ...picked on by others, humiliated and ridiculed. He needs a good friend." She smiled. "He's always wanted a brother. All my boys yearned for family of some sort, but Andy most of all." She sighed. "I miss him...I miss all of them."

"Then why did you leave, Aunt Anya?" my father said.

She bit her bottom lip. "I had to. Just couldn't stay there after the Ronnie Fargus incident."

"What happened?" my father said.

Sister Margaret shook her head. "I won't say with a child around."

"My son's a young man. I give my permission for him to stay and hear whatever you have to say."

"Very well, then." She sighed. "Ronnie Fargus came to the orphanage when he was eight years old."

I remembered the day, a busy one for the orphanage. Three older boys were finally adopted and Ronnie arrived. A scowl was etched on his face, and he peered at all of us through gray eyes narrowed and full of resentment. It was a cold, February day, and as the oldest out of the remaining ten, I greeted Ronnie with a plate of cookies and a glass of milk. He knocked the refreshments out of my hand and onto the floor. While I cleaned up the mess, I knew we were all in for trouble.

Sister Margaret broke through my thoughts. "His mother and father died in a car accident the summer of 1977. It was so many years ago I can't remember the exact date, but I do know it happened in front of Shirley's Ice Cream Emporium. They were sideswiped by a truck. The driver said he'd passed out at the wheel. Ronnie received massive head injuries and remained in the hospital for six months before he was able to be placed elsewhere. There were no surviving relatives, so Ronnie was brought to St. Barnard's." Sister Margaret sighed again. "Lord knows I tried my best to reach Ronnie, but he had such anger issues. Looking back, I often wished there were another boy his age living at the orphanage confident enough to embrace Ronnie as a friend. Or strong enough to show Ronnie he couldn't get away with bullying others."

I was that boy. I had kept Ronnie in his place, let him know I was watching him.

"Basically, Ronnie ran amok," she continued. "In spite of the punishment he received from Mother Superior and Father Samuel, he still acted out."

I knew of those punishments. They were humiliating. Not the proper treatment for any child, but certainly wrong for a child with anger problems. I'm sure Father Samuel's beatings only fueled Ronnie's fire.

"He tortured insects, harmed birds' nests and injured other small wild life," Sister Margaret said.

I remember those days like they happened yesterday.

Her voice trembled. "Are you sure you want Guylan to stay?"

"Yes," Xavior said.

She cast her eyes to the hands folded in her lap. "When he was twelve, Ronnie set the neighbor's cat's tail on fire."

I cringed. As a veterinarian trained to care for all God's creatures, I was sickened and offended at Ronnie's behavior, but also surprised. Ronnie tortured insects and birds, but he was afraid of cats and dogs. I remember the neighbor's cat, a large Main Coon with sharp claws, and Ronnie was petrified of him.

"Mother Superior's answer to this problem, and to keep the neighbor from calling the authorities, was to have Ronnie isolated for a month, locked away in an upstairs bedroom of Father Samuel's flat." She shivered. "I can only imagine the beatings he received nightly from that priest."

I knew exactly the beatings Ronnie had been subjected to.

She bit her bottom lip. "I tried to get Ronnie the help he needed, but ran up against a brick wall each time."

"How was Ronnie when he returned from isolation?" my father said.

"Quiet, withdrawn, and he stole food from the corner deli. I found candy bars and gum, chips and peanuts stashed in a box beneath his bed," Sister Margaret said.

This shocked me too, and I frowned. Ronnie, the boy I knew in my first youth, was severely allergic to peanuts. I remember him eating just one chocolate-covered peanut, and his throat swelled. He was rushed to the hospital.

"Then, when Ronnie turned fourteen, he molested one of the younger boys. Andy Beechum found little Michael Harmon curled up on the bathroom floor late one night, crying. He was naked and sitting in a pool of blood," Sister Margaret concluded.

I know now why Andy wouldn't talk of the incident to me.

My jaw clenched with rage for what Michael Harmon had endured, but again I was troubled by hearing of Ronnie's behavior. Aside from his antics with me, Ronnie was very shy about his body: wouldn't use the boys' room if there were other boys in it, waited till they were all in bed before he'd shower or pass his bowels. I frowned. Nothing was adding up.

"What happened next?" my father said.

Sister Margaret raised her eyes to meet his. "Michael, of course, was brought to the hospital for treatment, and because of the nature of his trauma, the authorities became involved. He wouldn't say who had violated him, no doubt being afraid of repercussion. Everyone was interrogated, but we never found out who had done that travesty to Michael." Sister Margaret's lips thinned. "I always thought Andy knew more than he let on, but by this time all the boys were so terrified, I couldn't be sure of anything. Then one night, I overheard Ronnie threatening another young boy, Ben White. Ronnie said he'd do the same to Ben as he'd done to Michael—going into graphic detail—if Ben didn't do everything Ronnie told him. I was appalled at Ronnie's language, the depth of such sinister tactics and went immediately to Mother Superior. She was forced to have Ronnie removed. He was taken away and placed at Urban Farms, a home for boys with severe behavioral problems. Three weeks later, he set off a fire alarm and when everyone evacuated the building, he broke into the staff's lounge, stole a total of five hundred dollars from the purses of the female counselors and ran away. No one has found him since. That was two years ago."

"And you felt it was your fault," my father said.

Sister Margaret gave a taut nod. "Ronnie was in my care and I missed the mark. Because of that, a cat was maimed, Michael was compromised, St. Bernard's ethics were scrutinized, Father Samuel was let go, and everyone was bitter and anxious. My negligence brought shame upon the orphanage as well as myself as a professional. All in all, my leaving was best for everyone concerned."

My father reached out and touched Sister Margaret's hand. "None of it was your fault. Ronnie was a troubled child and needed professional help."

"And it was up to me to get him that help," she said.

"It was up to Mother Superior," my father said. "She was the acting head of the orphanage and had a responsibility to her staff and the children to maintain a safe environment."

She forced a smile. "Thank you for that, Xavior."

There was a long, awkward silence.

"You never said *yes*," I blurted out.

She frowned. "To what?"

"Our invites," I reminded her.

"I never did, did I?" Her smile this time was genuine. "Well, then, yes to both."

I jumped up and hugged her.

Astonished and a little embarrassed, she returned the affection.

"Now, is there any chance I could get you two to say *yes* to a piece of pumpkin bread and butter?" she said.

I could already taste it melting in my mouth. "I thought you'd never ask."

She chuckled. "Do you know what's wonderful with pumpkin bread?"

"A cup of hot chocolate with marshmallow fluff," I said.

Her brows rose. "Why, yes...how did you know?"

I shrugged and glanced in my father's direction, catching the smirk on his face. "I'm just a lucky guesser."

Sister Margaret stood, took my arm and led me to the kitchen. "How are you at lotto?"

Thirty-three

We didn't leave St. Thomas Women's Shelter until nearly two. Sister Margaret, once she warmed up to the fact she had family again, made my father pull out his wallet and show her pictures of the twins, Egan, Seth, my mother, Quentin and my grandparents; then she had him tell her what was going on in all their lives.

"Your mother's going to skin my hide alive," my father remarked on the drive to get Andy. "I promised to help her clean the house for the party tonight."

"I'm the one who took you away from your duties, so I'll help with the chores."

My father chuckled. "Your hide's in danger, too."

"Well, it wouldn't be the first time."

He glanced my way. "Did Father Samuel ever beat you, Guylan?"

I nodded, turning my gaze out the window. "With a large wooden plank he called the *board of education*." I explained in detail what the punishments were like, how Father Samuel allowed Ronnie to watch and made me stand naked from the waist down until I apologized.

"Good Lord," my father gasped. "And he called himself a man of God. You boys were orphans, not prisoners."

"In my era, even prisoners have rights and are often treated better." I turned to look at him. "Did Grandpa and Grandma ever beat you?"

His brows shot up. "Beat me...gads, no. I got spanked now and then when I misbehaved, but with only a few smacks on the bottom with a hand." He frowned. "Only once, when I was nine, did I get an over-the-knee version, but looking back, I believe now I thoroughly had it coming."

"Why?"

"I threw a baseball through the living room window after I was repeatedly asked to play elsewhere. The glass shattered and hit my mother in the forehead, as she sat on the sofa sipping tea. She had to be rushed to the hospital and received fourteen stitches. I was sent to the neighbor's and the whole time I cried, thinking I had killed my mother. When my parents arrived home, my father came to the neighbor's house to fetch me, marched me in front of him all the way home and up to my bedroom. He shut the door. Not even my mother was allowed in the room, and he had it out with me. He never used a weapon of any sort, just the palm of his hand."

"What about you and Mom?"

"Your mother gave Audra a few whacks to her bottom; the twins as well." He turned to look at me. "I spanked you a few times, and have given a few spankings to Egan when needed, but to beat, humiliate and degrade...never. That kind of discipline is abuse."

"I wonder if Andy will talk about what Ronnie did to Michael Harmon," I said. "I remember Michael to be a thin, frail kid, timid and shy. It probably wasn't hard for Ronnie to strong-arm him."

"For Andy's sake, you must stay silent about the incident, Guylan. The quickest way to lose him as a friend is to bring up something he'd probably like to forget. Finding Michael as he did must have scared the piss out of him. Let him come to you about the situation. When and if he does, then you can let him know you're there for him. You can be a good friend by listening, not by giving him your opinions."

"The thing is...I'm responsible for Michael's tragedy, for what Andy saw, for Sister Margaret's leaving the home, and even for the way Ronnie turned out. If I were there at the orphanage, none of this would have happened."

"No, you're right, but we wouldn't be sitting here talking, either. Mom, Audra and Grandpa Zack would be dead, and the twins, Egan and Seth would have never been born. A lot of lives would have been lost—good lives too, Guylan—if you hadn't gone back and changed it all."

"But in changing things for the good, something changed for the bad," I reflected.

"Are you willing, for Michael, Andy and Ronnie's sake, to reverse what you did?"

"No," I said, gazing out the window again. "I guess that makes me selfish."

"I'd say it makes you human. You love your family, son. And we love you. Let go of this incident, help Andy the best you can, embrace Sister Margaret, pray God will watch over Ronnie and live a happy life."

"Ronnie wasn't like the way Sister Margaret described when I knew him. Grant you, the kid was difficult...but perverted, sinister..." I shook my head.

My father frowned. "What are you trying to say, Guylan?"

"I'm not quite sure, but the Ronnie in this time isn't the Ronnie I knew. The Ronnie I grew up with married a politician's daughter, became a dirty dealer but was not an abuser. He cheated on his wife and harmed animals, but he never abused anyone sexually that I know of." I shrugged. "It just doesn't add up, is all...not one bit of it."

My father took an audible breath. "It's what happens when we alter the original, Guylan."

I nodded, remembering what Quentin had said would happen to time when I went through the attic portal...but something inside nagged at me. There was more here wrong than the backlash from altered states...something was very wrong.

~ * ~

Andy wore a pair of clean, but worn jeans, and his pale blue plaid shirt, the one and only good shirt he owned. There were a few times cash donations aided Sister Margaret and Sister Catherine in buying the boys shoes, socks and underwear, but the outer garments, like jeans or dress trousers, shirts, sweaters, coats and hats, were hand-me-downs. The littler children always had the most to pick from, and because of this, the bigger boys didn't look as fashionable.

I remember wearing a pair of jeans with large holes in the knees, holes stitched and patched so many times, the material was completely gone. Now, in my future era, I've seen the stores sell jeans with ripped out knees...it's all the rage.

Andy's blond hair was slicked back; he even smelled like men's cologne.

I introduced him through the window to my father, then opened the car door and climbed in back with him so we could talk. "I saw Sister Margaret today," I said.

"Did she tell you about the Ronnie Fargus incident?"

"Yes, she explained things."

Andy's fists clenched in his lap. Then he took an audible breath and changed the subject. "Did she make pumpkin bread?"

"She sure did."

"Oh, man, she makes the best pumpkin bread," he said.

I agreed.

"Usually, I'm there to help with chores on Saturday, but since I was having time with you tonight, I switched with Ben White. I did his afternoon work so he could see a movie with a friend he met in school, and he's taking over for me tonight."

"That's nice you traded chores so both of you could enjoy time with friends," my father said from the front seat.

"Yeah. Ben's an okay guy, tries to be a good friend. It's just he's a few years younger than I am and sometimes our views are different."

I frowned. "Different how?"

"Ben likes to watch wrestling on television and listen to head-banging, heavy metal music. He's always getting yelled at for not doing his homework. He likes to socialize, and consequently doesn't do well in his studies."

"And what do you like to do?" my father said.

"I like to follow the stock market, as strange as it might sound, and I can really get into a good science fiction movie."

I chuckled. "You'd get along well with my sister Keira. She goes in for the science fiction stuff, too."

His face brightened. "Really?"

"No kidding."

"What else do you enjoy, Andy?" my father probed further.

"I like to be alone more than I do with a bunch of people. Most of the guys I know wanna hang out at the mall, play the arcade games. But I'd rather sit and read a book. I really get into the true-life stories of athletes and Revolutionary War heroes. The way some struggled to obtain their goals, against all odds, inspires me toward my own aspiration."

"And what might that be, Andy?" my father said.

"At first, I thought I'd like to go into the field of finance, insurance or investments, but after..." he refrained from finishing his sentence and sighed. "I think now I want to be a cop, get rid of all the bad people who hurt the good people, like the creeps who hurt the women at St. Thomas Women's Shelter. I see the way they look when they first arrive...blackened eyes, split lips, shaking and crying, afraid of their own shadows. No one should have to live in such terror or have their body abused like that. Their pride and dignity are robbed, they feel dirty and unworthy of anyone's love and respect." Andy's hands balled up into a fist again in his lap. "It makes me mad stuff like that is going on, and I just wanna catch those jerks and arrest them, make sure they can't hurt anyone ever again."

I was uneasy at the way Andy got so fired up in his crusade-like attitude to rid the world of criminals, and glanced at my father's eyes in the rearview mirror. It appeared like he felt the same. Andy's own experience finding Michael as he had was definitely at the core of his zeal for cleaning up the streets.

"My oldest sister is studying criminal justice at a Connecticut college," I shared. "She told me the first thing she learned is that to be fair-minded and effective as a law enforcement official, you have to dispel your anger. There is no room for vigilante-like behavior. A good law official must be ready to stay objective, focused and calm to nab the right law breaker, because in the end it's about justice for the victim. And you can't do that if you go off half-cocked and angry in your duties. As a lawman, your main responsibility is to perform your job with honor, no matter how disgusted you are with the criminal's actions. And always, always stay within the confines of the law."

"Your sister sounds real smart, like she's going to be good at her job," Andy said. "That's the way I want to be...fair and respected." His hands relaxed again beside him.

"Then remember to keep in perspective the main reason you decided to be a cop. If you do that, you'll accomplish a lot," I said.

"I'll remember...really, I will." He reached for something in his pants pocket. "I wanna give you this before I forget." He pulled out a piece of paper and handed it to me. "It's not much."

"Andy, that isn't necessary."

He shrugged.

I opened the paper to discover a gift certificate for a hamburger, an order of fries and a chocolate shake at Big Al's Hamburger Shop. "Oh, wow! I love Big Al's burgers."

Andy smiled. "Yeah, me too. That's why I got a job there on Tuesdays and Thursdays after school. I only make a dollar and a quarter an hour, but I've been there for two years now and I'm stashing my money away for college."

"Where are you stashing this money, Andy?" my father said.

Andy hesitated.

"He's not being nosy; he's the CEO of Sincloud Bank and Trust," I said.

Andy's eyes widened. "Really, that bank is yours?"

My father nodded. "And I tell all my clients their money is safer in an interest-bearing account, where it can grow, than stashed under the mattress where anyone could steal it. And in your case, that's a very real possibility, with so many hands milling about."

"Yeah, you're right," Andy agreed.

"Tell you what," my father said. "On Monday after school, come on over to the bank and I'll help you open an account."

"Really? I mean, that would be perfect. Your bank is only down the street from Big Al's and on payday, I can run over and deposit my check on my supper break." Then he frowned. "But, I'm under age. I mean, it was hard enough getting working papers so I could work at Big Al's. Won't I need an adult to vouch for me to open an account?"

"I'll vouch for you, Andy," my father offered.

"Sounds good to me," Andy said.

"Me too," my father chimed in.

"Me three," I added and we all laughed.

~ * ~

I thought Andy, as the shy and not very sociable type guy that he is, would feel overwhelmed in the presence of my family. Instead, like a sponge, he soaked up the chaos and banter, fitting right in.

His face brightened when I introduced him to Keira. "You're the sister who enjoys sci/fi flicks?"

She smiled, transforming from the teasing, bratty sister into a demure, flirtatious girl. "What movies are your favorites?"

Andy told her the films he liked, and from there they shared the most memorable scenes. Surprisingly enough, their tastes were similar.

Keira flashed Andy a warm smile and headed for the stairs. "I've gotta clean the guinea pig's cage now, Andy."

"I love guinea pigs; can I help?"

Keira shot a look my way. "It's okay with me, but..."

I shrugged, a bit disappointed Andy preferred Keira's company to mine, but he was so happy, I didn't want to spoil his mood. "It's okay with me, too. I promised to help Dad anyway."

The two made their way down the stairs, chatting and laughing like old friends.

Kendra, standing off to the side watching Andy and Keira, folded her arms across her chest. "Did you see the way she kept flipping her hair, so it would bounce around her face? She thinks she's such a *Miss Thing*."

"Do I detect a note of jealousy?"

She frowned. "No, why would I be jealous of *her*? I mean, who cares what the little jerk does?"

"Obviously, you do."

Her frown deepened. "Guylan, you're a real *dweeb*."

"Kendra, it's natural for you to feel threatened, left out. Keira's your twin and the two of you have shared everything till now."

Kendra blinked back tears and raised her chin defiantly. "I don't feel threatened or left out."

I walked over to her and put an arm around her shoulder. "One day, you and Keira will meet friends, both female and male, you won't care to share with one another. You'll have different ideas about life and the things you enjoy. There's nothing wrong with that, and you two still can be close. It will just mean your perspectives have grown in different directions."

She sniffed and wiped her nose on the back of a hand. "We always clean the guinea pig cage together."

"And when you were little, you wore matching outfits, but that's changed."

She sighed. "That's true. I wouldn't be caught dead in the clothes she wears."

I smiled. "There, you see?"

She nodded and rested her head on my shoulder. "But why do you suppose Andy liked Keira instead of me?"

"She just had something that attracted him."

Kendra pulled back to look up at me. "But we look exactly alike, except for the length of our hair, and I always thought boys liked long hair."

I wiped a tear trickling down her cheek. "You're a very beautiful young woman, Kendra."

She blushed and cast a glance down at her feet.

I lifted her chin. "Look at me."

She raised her gaze to mine.

"Andy wasn't drawn to Keira because she was prettier, smarter or better than you. He was attracted to her because they had something in common."

"So, what a boy likes about a girl is common ground?"

I smiled. "It helps."

"But the boys in school always want the pretty girls, the cheerleaders, the ones with big boobs." She blushed again and looked down at her flat chest. "You know what I mean."

"Yeah, I do Kendra, but when you get older, you'll see the real nice guys, the ones you'd want to have a meaningful relationship with, want someone they can talk to, laugh with, and enjoy their company. Those are the things that foster love."

"Is that what you want, Guy?"

It's what I already have.

"Yes, with all my heart. I think Andy's like me in that way, too." I chuckled and added, "Although big boobs are nice, too."

She gave me an affectionate slap on the arm and smiled. "Thanks."

"Don't mention it."

She wrinkled her nose. "Don't you *mention* this conversation to anyone or I'll spit in your food when you're not looking."

I laughed; the old Kendra had returned. "And I'll take pictures of your bare butt when you're asleep."

She gasped, covering her backside with her hands. "You wouldn't dare."

"Hey, I got the idea from you. Isn't that what you said you'd do to Egan?"

She narrowed her eyes. "Keira said it...all I did was laugh." She flipped her long hair over a shoulder, shouting as she ran up the stairs, "You're a *dweeb*, Guy, a real *dweeb*."

~ * ~

My grandparents and Quentin arrived around six along with the pizza delivery man. Andy and I sat at the end of the table, joking and teasing each other as we gobbled down slices of pizza covered with cheese, black olives and pepperoni, as well as chicken wings in hot sauce, and washed it all down with orange soda. Then Andy and I went down to my room while my father told Olena and Quentin about our visit to see Sister Margaret.

Standing by my boom-box, looking through my cassettes, Andy chose one by Huey Louis. "I take it Sister Margaret doesn't get along with your family?" He slipped it into the player and plopped down at the edge of the bed.

I joined him. "That's very perceptive of you."

"Yeah, well, when you live with a bunch of boys that aren't your family, you keep an ear and a close eye out to everything going on. Otherwise, you might wake up with someone standing over you, watching you sleep."

"Has anyone watched you sleep?"

"A few times." He turned to look at me. "Ronnie Fargus did stupid stuff like that all the time. He was forever walking around at night, running the water in the bathroom and gawking down on everyone while they slept."

"Why do you think he did things like that?"

Andy shrugged. "I have no clue as to why Ronnie does anything he does."

"He sounds like he's got lots of problems."

Andy hissed. "He's a pig who likes doing piggish things."

I did as my father suggested and let Andy do the talking.

Andy cleared his throat. "The night Michael was...was...hurt, I saw Ronnie standing over his bed, watching him sleep. Michael must have felt Ronnie, heard him breathing or something, because he woke, sat up and asked Ronnie what was going on." Andy paused, taking a deep breath.

I remained silent.

"Ronnie motioned to the bathroom...that's all he did...and Michael pulled back his blanket, got out of bed, and walked ahead of Ronnie. I remember thinking Michael looked like a captive from a war, marching to his doom at the hands of the enemy."

"Do you think Michael was intimidated by Ronnie before?"

"Not in the way he was that night," Andy said.

I frowned. "What do you mean?"

"I think Ronnie made Michael take off his pants so he could look at him. Ronnie might have even touched Michael, but the night

I found Michael, Ronnie had *done it* to him." Andy looked down at his shoes. "There was blood all over the bathroom floor and it was coming from Michael's..." his voice trailed off.

A chill ran down my spine. "I can't imagine—"

"Me neither," Andy interrupted, meeting my gaze.

I searched his face, wondering if Ronnie had also done something to Andy.

Andy stood and filed through my cassettes again, this time choosing Billy Ocean. "You never said why Sister Margaret and your family were not speaking to each other."

I wasn't about to tell Andy the family secrets. "I think Olena and Sister Margaret had a falling out when they were young," I lied.

He turned to look at me. "Do you think, after all these years, they can patch things up?"

"Yeah, I do, if they want it bad enough."

He moved to sit on the desk chair and examined the central processing unit. "These word processors are something, better than typewriters. It's much easier to fix mistakes."

"Someday I believe there'll be units a lot more innovative than this one. In the future, we'll be able to link ourselves to anyone and anyplace all over the world. Research and communication will be on a phenomenal level...instant messaging, electronic mail, even downloading music and movies."

His eyes widened. "You mean, like transmitting through air waves or something?"

I nodded and quoted Webster's dictionary: "An electronic system of linked computers for information and interaction... cyberspace."

"Cyberspace," Andy mused.

"Hey, you guys," Keira knocked at the door. "Can I come in?"

I rolled my eyes. "No."

Andy ignored me and went to the door, opening it.

Keira smiled up at him. "Cake and ice cream is ready to be served."

He returned her smile. "Thanks, we'll be right up."

"I've saved you a seat beside me, if that's okay?"

His smile broadened. "Yeah, thanks."

I waited until Keira left to tease him. "Got the hots for my sister, hey?"

He chuckled. "Is it that obvious?"

"Oh, yeah."

His face turned red. "I don't get out much, between working at Big Al's and my duties at the orphanage, homework and helping out at the women's shelter. Guess I need to work on not looking so eager, huh?"

I smiled. "I think you should be just who you are. Anyway, girls love it when a guy's attentive." Something I'd learned at the age of thirty. Why not help Andy get it right now? I frowned. "But don't you think Keira's a bit young for you? She only just turned twelve." This coming from someone who only two days ago melted for another twelve-year-old girl. In my defense, I'd met her at thirty-four.

"Well, I'm not even going to be fifteen until October," he said.

Ah, yes, now I remember...you're a year and a half younger than me.

"Anyway, one day we'll be closer in age, like when she's twenty and I'm twenty-two going on twenty-three."

I laughed. "You plan ahead a lot."

He nodded. "I don't have a father I can count on or a mother who cares, Guylan. If I don't look out for my future, no one else will."

"I know you're not going to believe this, Andy, but I understand that mindset more than you'll ever know." I opened the door. "Now, let's get dessert."

~ * ~

I watched Andy talk and relate to each member of my family. He had a charisma with both young and old. He looked like he'd won a prize when my mother asked if he'd help clear the table. Standing beside her, admiration gleaming in his eyes, he rinsed each plate while my mother stacked the dishwasher.

I remembered the first time I'd gotten her undivided attention. The warmth and contentment I felt was paramount. I knew Andy was experiencing the same now, falling for her charm and basking in the rays of her praises and gratitude for his help. DeYonna Sincloud had a way of making each of her children feel they were her favorite, and Andy was receiving some of that magic tonight.

Quentin came up from behind me. "Now ye know why yer da is such a pushover for the lass." He chuckled. "She has a way o' makin' a lad a *doiter,* blunderin' fool.'"

I turned to face him. "That power she has, for sure."

"Aye, and one a lad can't resist, and she is genuine as well. I think 'tis that feelin' o' trust that makes her even more irresistible. *A beannachd,* me blessin' she still lives, is still a part o' my life." He searched my face and drew me aside, away from the others. "Decided to take a detour before findin' yer way to yer own time, laddie?"

"You know?"

"Aye," he whispered.

My mother interrupted our conversation. "Another piece of cake, Grandpa?" she inquired before wrapping what little remained.

Quentin held up a hand to decline the offer. "*Cha ghabh mi'n corr, tapa leibh,* I will have no more, thank ye, DeYonna." He pulled me aside. "Let us get away from this *kebbie-lebbie,* commotion."

I followed him to my father's den before speaking again. "I needed to see Sister Margaret and Andy. I couldn't let them go out of my life."

He sighed. "Ye are takin' a chance bein' so long away from where ye belong. *Cuimhnich,* remember what I warned ye about."

"I have Olena and Andy here to keep me grounded. I've seen Sister Margaret, even Nela, so I'm doing okay."

He nodded. "Well, then, in that case, if ye stay one more day, 'twon't matter."

I frowned. "What have you got in mind?"

"How about a wee family reunion?" He sighed. "Come with yer da, Olena and me tomorrow afternoon to see Anya."

I smiled. "I'd love to."

"Then, after ye must be on yer way to where ye came. My energy will not sustain much more."

I reached over and squeezed his arm. "I'll miss you."

"I feel the same, lad, but we have many years from this point to know each other."

"But it will be something I'll only have a memory of and not really live."

"Aye, 'tis true, but before ye had no memory o' a thing, so count yer good fortune and rare opportunity, *mo ghile*."

I frowned. "Why do you and my father sense I'm different, and not Olena?"

"She is not a Druid...her energy is not part o' yers."

"Will she remember my journey through the attic portal when I return?"

He nodded. "From that point, aye."

"Why?"

"Because she already knows what really transpired and will know how it all changed." He smiled. "Miraculous, is it not?"

I repeated my father's favorite phrase: "Incredible...effing, incredible."

We both laughed.

Andy interrupted us with a knock on the door frame. "Guylan, I really wish I could stay longer. I'm having so much fun, but curfew is ten o'clock." He glanced at his watch. "And it's nearing nine-forty-five now."

"I have had *gu leòir*, plenty enough partyin' for tonight meself," Quentin said. "Can we be givin' ye a lift home, lad?"

Andy shrugged. "It's okay by me."

Quentin smiled. "Then let us each get the last pieces o' that cake to take home and be on our way."

~ * ~

I tossed and turned all night. I knew I'd be heading back to my time in another day and I had some mixed feelings. I hated leaving the family unit, the everyday happenings with my parents and siblings. I'd retain all these years, but on fast forward. It was so much nicer to actually live them and I was sad to say goodbye. Then I was apprehensive. There were a lot of folk's lives altered by my time travel, and I was a bit worried as to how well things turned out, what damage I'd find when I arrived home.

Sunday morning came too soon. I'd just fallen asleep when Egan burst into the room and jumped on the bed. "Mom said to get up...you're coming to church with just us."

I groaned. "Define *just us*."

He smiled down at me. "Just me and Mom...and you."

I groaned again and hurried to get dressed.

"The twins are sleeping in and I've volunteered to watch Seth so your mother could peacefully enjoy the service with her two elder sons," my father informed me when I entered the kitchen. "I didn't have to tell her twice."

I chuckled. "Yeah, well, Mom needs her children to grow up, have all of them use the toilet and drink from a cup."

He sighed. "That will happen soon enough, Guylan. In no time, Seth, our last baby, will be an adult and your mother and I will be empty nesters."

I believed my mother would relish the thought.

Having a driver's permit allowed me to drive with an adult on board. I was surprised when my mother said I could drive to church. Then she was stunned I did so well.

Ah, Mom, if you only knew I've been driving for years.

Egan sat between us in church, leaning in to ask me a question now and then. "Does God watch over us all the time?"

"Yes," I whispered.

His eyes widened. "He sees me even when I'm picking my nose or going to the toilet?"

I stifled a smile. "Yes, all the time, even then."

Even when I'm making love to Nela.

I blushed at the thought.

"Does God watch girls while they undress?" he said.

I think my father needed to have the sex talk with Egan sooner than later. "He's God, He wouldn't do that."

Egan frowned. "Then He only watches the boys?"

My mother turned and put a finger to her lips. "Shush now, enough with the talking."

Thanks, Mom.

The afternoon flew by...eating grilled cheese sandwiches for lunch, reading the Sunday comics and taking a cat nap on the sofa. Around three, I went with my father to pick up Olena and Quentin, and the four of us headed over to visit Sister Margaret.

Olena fretted all the way. "What if she won't see us?"

My father looked through the rearview mirror at his mother sitting beside me in the back seat. "I've already called and talked with her earlier today. She's very excited to see you and Grandfather."

Quentin, sitting next to my father, glanced back. "I told ye everythin' will be fine, daughter." His eyes met mine and he winked.

Fine ended up being an understatement.

"*Ciamar a tha tu, mo chridhe,* how are ye, my heart?" Quentin said in Gaelic, opening his arms to his long-lost daughter.

Sister Margaret ran into his embrace and answered with, "*The mi gle mhath, asthair,* I am well, Father."

"That's how they always greeted each other when Anya was small," Olena explained.

After that reception, there wasn't a dry eye in the house. Sister Margaret hugged and kissed Olena and there were heartfelt confessions and teary regrets, and then more hugs.

When things settled, Quentin pulled from his jacket pocket an envelope and handed it to Sister Margaret. "This is to let ye see, daughter, ye were never far from me thoughts."

Sister Margaret read the reports sent to her father on her whereabouts and accomplishments. A sob caught at her throat. "All this time you knew where I was, what I was doing?"

"Aye, 'tis the way o' it, *mo maise,* me beauty. Ye were born a part o' me and ye shall always be a part o' me, even if 'tis somethin' ye did not want."

She went to her father again and gathered him in another warm embrace. "All the years I wasted...all the holidays I spent alone, when I didn't have to."

Quentin smiled through his own tears. "Well, there are many more ahead o' ye, and me. Let us enjoy those to come."

"There is something I need your help with, Anya," Olena said softly.

Sister Margaret turned to her sister and smiled. "If I can, I will."

"Can you help Zackery and me adopt Andy Beechum?"

I almost fell off my chair. "Grandmother, when did you decide this?"

Olena looked over at me. "The moment I set eyes on him, Guylan, I knew he needed—deserved—a home and family."

"We all talked about it when we arrived home from yer party last night, and agreed 'twas the right thing to do," Quentin said, giving me another wink. "Is he not yer *anam cara*, soul friend?"

I nodded and swallowed my emotions. I made my way to Olena and knelt down beside her chair, taking her hand in mine. "Thank you, Grandmother."

Sister Margaret's eyes glistened with fresh tears. "I don't see any of this being a problem, Olena. Andy is nearing fifteen and a court will ask him if he's open to the arrangement, which I'm sure he will be, and he'll probably be able to live with you while the final paperwork is being legalized." She smiled. "Saint Andrew is the patron saint of Scotland, so it's only right Andy be in a Scottish family."

Olena returned her sister's smile. "Then you have no objections, because of—"

"Absolutely none whatsoever," Sister Margaret interrupted.

"You'll get on it for us, then?" Olena said.

Sister Margaret nodded. "Immediately. But first," she smiled at me, "how about some pumpkin bread?"

Later, when my father dropped Olena and Quentin off at the mansion, I escorted my great-grandfather inside. He held on to my arm and we took our time getting to the front door.

"'Twill, no doubt, be the last time I will be seein' ye in this way, laddie."

My heart saddened. "I know."

He stopped walking and turned to look at me, tears glistening in his eyes. "Ye have made me a proud man. To think me great-grandson is so *braw*, brave, such a hero."

"I couldn't have done any of it without you and my father."

He patted my arm. "Ye held yer own just fine." He smiled. "*Cuimhnich*, remember lad, *gra anois agus go deo*, love, now and forever. And I will leave ye with that thought."

I hugged him. "I'll remember."

~ * ~

I walked around my room, hung up the clothes tossed on the desk chair and straightened the dresser top. Guylan, my sixteen-year-old counterpart, would be surprised to find his room tidy.

I smiled to myself and gazed out the window at two large oak trees standing opposite each other on the side lawn of the property. I remembered climbing them, saw Seth climb one just yesterday, and I couldn't help but think of them as sentinels of time. They would be the same when I returned as a man, when my own son and his son were men, and for years thereafter. They are steadfast, ancient sentries guarding the grounds, their large limbs offering Sincloud children a wonderful climbing experience.

Again, my decision to leave was bittersweet. Though I was anxious to return to my own state of being, a small part of me wished I could stay and grow up all over again, only this time with my actual family instead of just memories.

I began to remove all my clothes, when a knock sounded at the bedroom door.

My father opened it a crack and peered in. "Quite a day, huh?"

"To say the least."

He shut the door behind him. "Are you leaving now?"

I nodded.

He embraced me. "You're amazing, Guylan." He pulled back and looked deep into my eyes. "Would you mind if I watched?"

"No, not at all." I finished stripping off the rest of my clothes and lay down naked on the bed.

My father sat on the desk chair. "Safe travels."

I reached to turn off the lamp. "I'll see you when I see you."

"That you will, son."

I closed my eyes and pressed my tongue hard against the raven brand etched in my inner cheek, mentally reciting over and over... *midnight, Saturday, May 5th, 2007.*

Just before the whirling sound rushed to my ears, I heard my father exclaim, "Incredible...effing incredible!"

Thirty-four

My life passed before me—or should I say, through me. My anatomy changed: arms and legs grew a bit longer, my torso more muscular. Data downloaded...my Confirmation, Druid ceremony, high school graduation and college...no more holidays spent alone in a dorm now that I had a family.

Then came Quentin's death when I was twenty, Grandpa Zack's passing when I was twenty-five. The grief and emptiness of missing them was as sorrowful to me as if I'd been there to witness it.

There was my graduation from college and my work as a veterinarian—I had comprehended and stored—plus the things happening to those I loved. Audra stayed the summer of 1985 in a Connecticut apartment with a few college girls, but by the fall of that year the female roommates were replaced by Ken Drake, who married Audra in 1987. The two have permanently made their home there, each working in the criminal justice field. They have three children: Liam is twelve, Brock is nine, and Kayla is seven.

Andy is a cop, and after years on the force, he's moved to narcotics. He has a canine partner, a German Shepherd that reminds me of Luna. Her name is Callie, and Andy brings her to my animal clinic for all her medical needs. He is married to my sister, Keira. They were wed the year she turned nineteen. She's a nurse in the ER at Shire Downs Medical Center and they have two children: Justin is five and Marla is three. They live with Olena in the mansion. The standing joke, since my grandparents adopted Andy, is that by law he's my uncle and brother-in-law, thus making my sister also my aunt, their children my nephew, niece and cousins. To my father, Andy is a brother and son-in-law, making Keira my father's sister-in-law and daughter, their children his nephew, niece and grandchildren. It's something we all have fun with.

Kendra married Wexley Hume when she was twenty-one. He was a foreign exchange student from England whom she met in college. They moved to London a few years ago. Both are lawyers and they have twin daughters, Anya and Olena. They're three, the same age as Keira and Andy's little girl, Marla.

Egan is a firefighter and paramedic. Two years ago, he married his high school sweetheart, Stella Killman, and they live in a quaint town in Vermont. She co-owns a used bookstore and they are expecting their first baby in September...the ultrasound says they're having a boy. Egan and Stella like the name Quentin.

And Seth just joined the police force, hoping to work his way up the ladder like Andy did. He dates lots of girls and has no intention at this point of getting serious with any of them. He still lives at home—the basement has been fixed into a private apartment—and is still the spoiled baby of the family. My mother loves to dote on him.

My father retired from the bank five years ago and goes fishing a lot. He and my mother travel each year to a new destination—Scotland, Ireland, Australia, France, Italy, as well as taking a few Caribbean cruises—and to England to see their little British granddaughters. He is now the Archdruid of the Sincloud clan.

Sister Margaret lives in a community for retired nuns. She remains very close to the family. She and Olena see each other twice a week for lunch and go to church together on Sunday mornings. Sometimes she even stays overnight at the mansion. Both Olena and Sister Margaret are very involved with Andy's children.

When all the life information finished installing in my brain, I emerged from the attic portal and landed face down on the Oriental carpet of Quentin's chamber. Naked and tired, feeling a bit jet-lagged, I shot a quick glance around the dimly lit room.

It saddened me to see Quentin's glass encasement gone. I wished I could see him one more time. I sighed and looked around for my clothes.

"Trying to find these?" a voice said. I turned to see Xavior Sincloud sitting at Quentin's desk, holding out the garments I'd discarded before entering the portal. He smiled. "I see you've made it."

I returned the smile. "You have, too." He sat back and looked through the photo album lying on the desk while I dressed. In his sixties now, with gray hairs at his temples, he was still an arresting looking man. "You've aged well."

He looked up from the album. "You're not bad yourself." He narrowed his eyes. "You look a lot like I did when I last saw you... handsome devil."

I laughed. "Not one for modesty, are you?"

"Hell, no. I say it like it is." He placed the album aside. "And for your information, you've still got one hot mother."

"I knew she'd age well, too."

He stood and extended a hand.

I laughed and embraced him instead. "Welcome back, Dad."

"Welcome home, son."

I pulled back to look at him; I was slightly taller. "I've got to call Nela. There's a lot of explaining to do." I went on about Nela's grandmother and how her family came to receive a blessing from Quentin.

I searched my jeans pockets for my cell phone and he stilled my hand. "It's late, Guylan. Wait until tomorrow. Better still, make a trip to see her and bring Olena with you. She'd like to meet Nela's grandmother. Your mother and I would, too."

I hesitated.

"Nela deserves to know you're a Druid and that Quentin was the one who blessed her family. But waking her and telling her all this over the phone isn't my idea of a quality explanation."

I sighed. "You're right, of course. I'm just anxious to set things right between us. We've never gone to sleep mad at each other."

"Admirable, a policy your mother and I also believe in, but tomorrow is soon enough to make amends." He motioned to the door. "Now you need to go downstairs and see your mother. We were having dinner with Olena, Andy and his family when you marched in here all upset over something that transpired at Nela's. Then you ran upstairs to Quentin's chamber."

I frowned. "Is that how things played out here?"

"Yes," he said. "I excused myself and came upstairs to see if you wanted to talk."

I sighed. "I guess I owe them the same explanation I gave you, about Nela's blessing."

"But leave the time travel part out, Guylan. There is no need for your mother to know she was once murdered by Mortimer MacRaven."

"Or Nela to know she was almost de-souled," I added.

Xavior sighed. "I think Nela should know everything, since she's been upfront with you about her family secrets. Besides, with her grandmother returning each year as she does, Nela can handle the truth much better than your mother."

"Quentin told me Olena would know."

"If she does, she isn't letting on. And if the others aren't any the wiser, it's best to keep it that way."

"You're right, of course," I agree. "What's the rest of the damage?"

He shrugged. "You could see the negative effects in moments and then maybe not for years to come."

"Great," I muttered. "There's nothing like waiting for the other shoe to drop."

Xavior reached for my hand. "I'd say you earned the right to wear this."

I looked down at the raven ring he'd placed in my palm. "Dad, are you sure?"

"I've never been surer about anything." He squeezed my fingers shut around the ring. "And I put the book of secrets on the desk in your apartment." He smiled. "Now, let's go see your mother."

~ * ~

I was glad to be home, to enter my apartment in my own time. But things had changed. Along with the photos of me and Nela, family pictures graced table tops and shelves. My parents, grandparents, siblings, nieces and nephews smiled at me from pictures taken at the park, during the holidays and at birthday parties. I now had a history, a past chock full of people I loved and who loved me.

On the desk in my den the book of secrets sat, right where I'd left it before I went to Nela's for dinner...correction, where my father had placed it. Curious, I wondered if it were indeed last night that I'd been to Nela's house. I sighed, realizing I'd probably never really know just how much time *had* actually elapsed, only how many times I had thought of Nela.

I undressed and lay on the bed, my fatigue mind-numbing, yet I couldn't fall asleep. Scenes from my time travels played over and over in my thoughts. Did I really nurse from my mother, open Christmas presents with my siblings, go on summer vacations? Did my father really teach me how to ride a bike, fish, play basketball? Had I really known Quentin and Zackery? Stretching, I yawned and forced myself to delve deep into the quiet of my spirit. Tomorrow I'd see Nela and atone for my actions. If I wanted that time to come quickly, I needed to sleep away tonight.

My final thought was of the last time Nela's lips fused with mine. I closed my eyes and tasted their sweetness, felt their warmth, and fell asleep.

~ * ~

"How much do you know?" I asked Olena on our way to Nela's the next day.

She gazed out the passenger's side window. "I am aware of everything...every horrible thing that once happened." She turned to look at me. "And now I know of every wonderful replacement."

"My father believes it's best we keep the time travel quiet from Mom, but that I should tell Nela."

"I agree," she said.

"Thank you again for adopting Andy."

She smiled. "I should be thanking you, Guylan. Andy's been like a son to me, and his children are more grandchildren for me to love and spoil." She laughed. "I guess in Andy's case his children are also my great-grandchildren."

I laughed. "Like you don't have enough of both?"

Her smile deepened. "No, I'll never have enough. In fact, my hope is to live long enough to see your children." She narrowed her eyes. "So, you'd better make your apology to Nela really count."

I sighed. "That's my intention."

Nela opened the door, and for a moment I stood and stared, savoring every inch of her—the wealth of ebony curls falling to her shoulders, large, chocolate eyes, pouting lips, defiant chin, long, swan like neck—down to full, round breasts. She left me hungry.

"I'm so glad, so very glad, Guylan, you're here."

I pulled her into my embrace and covered her mouth with mine.

She deepened the kiss, and my heart soared. I whispered against her mouth. "Babe, I'm so sorry."

"What matters most is you're here." She gave me another kiss, quicker this time, before turning her attention to Olena.

Olena took Nela in her arms. "I wanted to meet your grandmother while she was here."

Their familiarity to each other took me back for a moment, and I found myself putting their relationship into the proper prospective. Because I had gone back in time and changed my orphan status to a family affair, Nela knew my grandmother, as well as the rest of my family.

Nela smiled. "She's in the kitchen, preparing lunch for us all."

"Oh, she needn't go to such trouble," Olena said, taking Nela's arm.

"It's no trouble at all." Nela glanced back at me. "Your parents called and said they'd be by to meet Gram later."

Nela's grandmother turned from the kitchen sink, where she was washing vegetables, and smiled at Olena. "I am so glad to finally meet you." She placed the wet peppers in a bowl and wiped her hands on the apron tied around her waist.

Olena returned the smile. "But you've known me for years, Sophia."

Sophia hesitated, searching Olena's face. "I do know you...but from where?"

"Your father's bakery, many years ago...the little girl who—"

"Choked on a peppermint stick," Sophia interjected.

"One and the same."

Sophia neared Olena and the two embraced.

Nela's eyes widened and she reached for my hand, leading me downstairs to the salon. "Your grandmother's the one...the one who choked...the one my great-grandfather saved?"

"Yes, Nela, it was.".

"So that would make your great-grandfather the wizard who bestowed the blessing?"

I drew her close. "Yes."

She looked deep into my eyes. "And are you...are you a wizard, too?"

I chuckled. "I prefer to be called a Druid, but yes, I'm a wizard, too, as well as my father."

She swallowed hard. "And when...when were you going to tell me?"

"It was something I just discovered myself."

She frowned. "I don't understand."

I took an audible breath and went on to explain about the book of secrets and how I'd seen her family name listed among others who'd received the blessing.

"Was that what you had to tell me last night?"

I nodded.

"Then, after I told you about my family's blessing, why did you leave without explaining yourself in return?"

"Because I didn't know then what I do now."

She frowned. "I don't understand."

I sighed. "The book of secrets, used for special rituals, occasional ceremonies, spells and such things as that, was stashed away, kept in a safe and sacred place. Until last night, I never knew it existed, or that I had a family."

Her eyes widened. "Again, I don't understand."

I combed my fingers through my hair. "There's something I need to tell you, Nela." I led her to a drier chair and made her sit, and then I explained everything to her: the orphanage life and being called by the last name of Quinn, right down to the attic portal and my time travel experiences. I held up my hand when she opened her mouth to talk. "When I returned, everything from before was changed. My family was alive, and I received the Druid ring and the family powers."

"Then Mortimer kidnapping me and Gram wasn't a dream?"

"No, it all really happened."

She shivered. "Guylan, I'm scared. What if—"

I took her hand. "There's nothing to be frightened over now. He's gone, you're safe...we're all safe." I sighed. "I feared you wouldn't believe me. I certainly wouldn't believe any of it if it hadn't happened to me."

She chuckled. "Well, I guess that's part of the very reason why I do believe you. Given my own family secrets and circumstances, how can I *not*? Look what I'm bringing to this marriage." She narrowed her eyes. "Assuming that's what you still want for us."

"More than anything, babe." I pulled her to her feet, drawing her close. "After I left here, I had much to sort out, Nela. You can't imagine the journey I took before I was able to return here this afternoon. But if we can put all this into perspective, I think you'll agree with me, we've been destined to meet and belong together."

"How do you know this?"

"Do you remember when you were twelve, walking home from school and being harassed by a boy named Gregory?"

She nodded, then she gasped. "You were the boy who rode your bike from behind the trees and stopped Gregory from destroying my books?"

I smiled. "And I kept my word to you, too."

She frowned. "Your word...what word?"

"I promised you then that one day you'd know my name." My smile deepened. "I wrapped my arms around you while you were still in your mother's womb, too."

"Guylan, my God."

"Now I'm hoping you still want to share the Sincloud name with me."

She looked deep into my eyes. "I do, Guylan. That's all I've ever wanted."

"I feel the same, *mo nighean dubh*."

"What does that mean?"

"My black-haired lass," I translated.

"Do you realize, after we're married, you'll have the chance to return from the afterlife?"

I took a deep breath. "Pretty amazing, huh?"

"Do you think that's what your great-grandfather wanted?"

"In the grand scheme of things, with how powerful he was and all, it's a possibility, but we'll never know for sure." I kissed the tip of her nose. "Does it really matter now, Nela?"

"No," she said softly and laid her head against my chest. "All that matters is we're together."

"I agree."

Her body melted against mine. "Love me, Guylan."

"Now...here?"

"Yes, right now. Fill me."

"Where?" I choked out.

She led me to a room at the back of the salon. A set of large, metal shelves stood in the corner, where several mats were rolled up and stored. "This is the yoga room. I offer classes here on Tuesday afternoon." She pulled down a mat and spread it out on the floor, then turned to me and smiled mischievously. "Now, love me."

She didn't need to ask me a third time. I didn't just undress Nela. Instead, I unwrapped her, like a priceless, breakable gift, slowly and gently. Over her head I pulled the bright yellow T-shirt and threw it aside. Then I unfastened the bra, slipping each strap off her shoulders. I caressed her breasts, tweaking and teasing each rosy peak until it hardened between the tips of my fingers. My pulse quickened, my loins swelled. I lowered her down on the mat and unbuttoned her jeans, pulling them and her pink silk panties down to her ankles. I sat back on my haunches and savored her, my eyes roaming the length of her perfect body...slim waist, rounded hips, dark curls at the juncture of her thighs covering her womanhood. "Good God, you're magnificent."

She sat up, removed her shoes and slipped the pants off her feet. Then she knelt before me and unbuttoned my shirt. I shrugged it off my arms and stood to unfasten my jeans. She yanked them down to my ankles and raised her face to my groin, taking my phallus into her mouth.

Her hot, moist lips sucked and drew on my flesh. My posterior muscles clenched, knees weakened. "Nela, wait."

She raised her face and moistened her full lips with a slow flick of her tongue. "Why?"

"Because...because I'll lose it right here, and I don't want to do that."

She curled her lips into a slow, seductive smile. "Why?"

I swallowed hard, every fiber of my being straining to hold myself at bay. "Because I want to be inside of you, feel your warmth tight around me."

She lay back on the mat, staring at me with longing as I removed the rest of my clothes.

I lay beside her, my gaze first riveted on her face; heart jolting, pulse pounding as I looked deep into her eyes. "Nela, I love you."

She wrapped her arms around my neck and drew me closer, bare breasts against bare chest. "I love you, too."

I buried my face against her throat and kissed the expanse of her neck. She threw her head back, widening the gap between us. I moved to capture a swollen nipple, teasing the taut, dusky peak with flicks of my tongue.

She moaned with pleasure and draped a leg over my hip.

I suckled and nibbled, drawing a mound fully into my mouth.

Her nails dug at my back, her touch sending currents of desire through me.

I caressed her smooth belly with the tip of my tongue, playing with her navel. Then I kissed a path down to her pleasure point.

She opened her thighs and I teased the slippery bud hidden in the folds.

"Do that faster," she said in a breathless gasp.

I happily complied, bringing forth a climax that shattered through her body and trembled against mine.

Nela was on the pill, which allowed us the freedom to have spontaneous sex. Once we'd made love in the car, another time at midnight on the beach. Each time we worried someone would catch us. Strangely enough, that added to the thrill. But this afternoon, lying on a mat on the floor of her salon, making love while both our grandmothers were upstairs, I was very excited.

Eye level with a shelf holding hair dye and bleach, rubber gloves and spritzer bottles, I realized this was where women came to get glamourous, to achieve a youthful glow. I looked up at Nela's face, flushed and glistening with perspiration, and thought there was no more beautiful glow than hers. "Will you remember this moment when you sit on this mat again to conduct your next yoga class?"

She giggled and sat up. "I most definitely will." Rolling onto her stomach, she arched her back, affording me the most decadent view of her round buttocks. She glanced over a shoulder and smiled. "But will you?"

I returned the smile, tingling with desire and moved to pull her against me. "You know it." Entering her sheath from behind, I closed my eyes and rocked within her. She pushed against me like a wild stallion, and I rode her hard and fast...and long.

"Go, Guylan," she encouraged, her eager response matching mine.

My breath came in long, surrendering moans as I burst deep within her. The release drained me and I fell down, limp beside her. "I've yielded completely to your masterful seduction."

She rolled into my arms and laid her head on my shoulder. "Then, would you say your imagination has been tickled?"

I wrapped my arms around her. "Oh, baby..." Purposely I didn't finish that sentence and let my voice trail off, capturing her mouth with a most compliant kiss.

~ * ~

When Nela and I finally rejoined our grandmothers, we were pleased to see how well they were getting along.

"There you two are." Sophia placed a plate down for each of us. "I didn't want to disturb you, knowing you had much to discuss, but I'm afraid the mincemeat and vegetable quiche is growing cold."

I glanced over at Nela and she stifled a smile. What would we have done if Sophia had come looking for us?

"I'll just nuke it, Gram." Nela put the quiche in the microwave and set the dial.

Sophia reached out and gave Olena's arm an affectionate pat. "It's been so wonderful to learn about the man who gave our family the blessing."

Olena smiled. "I'm glad I could finally help you put the pieces together."

My parents arrived at dinnertime, along with Nela's parents, her two sisters, niece and Sophia's two brothers and their wives. There were fifteen of us all together. Some sat at the table, others on lawn chairs or the sofa, eating on trays. Sophia put on another wonderful meal, Nela and I helping out in the kitchen...and I finally got to taste the pecan pie.

My parents drove Olena home and Nela's family left after numerous hugs and tearful goodbyes. I waited with Nela while Sophia changed into the rose brocade dress and worn hat she'd arrived in, and then accompanied the two ladies to the train station.

On the ride there, I remained quiet. Nela and her grandmother sat in the back seat, and from the rearview mirror I saw Sophia's color wane. She also looked anxious to leave.

Nela picked up on this, too, because she gave her grandmother a reassuring pat on the arm. "You miss Gramps, don't you?"

Sophia smiled. "I truly do."

There were a few moments to spare before *The Blessing Train* arrived. Nela hugged her grandmother, tears welling in her eyes. "There's a gnawing, a loneliness that rises each and every year when I have to say my farewells to you."

"Let thoughts of the coming year keep you going," Sophia said. "And Gramps will be along next year, too."

Nela sighed. "I haven't seen Gramps in five years. I miss him so much."

Sophia patted Nela's hand. "He misses you too, honey."

The quiet of the night was assaulted by the sound of the large clock in the park across the way striking midnight. The train appeared out of nowhere and my eyes grew wide, my mouth agape.

"Pretty impressive, don't you think?" Sophia said.

I simply nodded, my gaze still fixed on the massive white train.

"Now, sweetie," Sophia said to Nela as she walked to the steps. "Have your dad get Gramps a gray suit, gray's universal...goes with everything. And you pick me out a nice beige dress and black shoes, so I'll complement your color scheme, too."

Tears again welled in Nela's eyes. "I will, Gram."

"And make sure the menu has pasta," Sophia called out. "Gramps loves his pasta."

Nela nodded. "I love you, see you next year."

Sophia waved and boarded the train. "Love you too, Nela, and you as well, Guylan. Take care of my girl."

"Not to worry," I reassured her.

As soon as Sophia stepped a foot on the train, it dissolved into thin air.

I gasped. "Holy shit."

"Yeah, pretty incredible, huh?" Nela said.

"And that's going to happen to me, too?"

"Only if you're married to me when I die," she reminded me.

I pulled her close. "That's the only way I'd get married to you, Nela...for the rest of my life."

She stood on tiptoe and kissed me. "Me too, Guylan."

I frowned. "Oh, damn!"

"What?" she said.

"I wanted to ask Sophia what it was like to be dead."

She smiled. "You can ask her next year."

I chuckled. "I guess in some families, not even death is final."

"Nor are there only skeletons in their closets," she added.

I arched a brow. "That was exactly what Quentin said."

Part Three – Nela

The Cedar Wood Box

Thirty-five

One Year Later
April, 2008, Anglewood, New York

"Fornication…this is fornication," I muttered against his throat.

Guylan chuckled. "We've been fornicating for the last year, and it's just hitting you now?"

I pulled back to look at him. "With only a month to go till we're married, I'm thinking more and more about my wedding gown and what the *white* of it is supposed to imply."

"Well, since your soul is completely tarnished, I guess white just isn't your color anymore. Better return it for black," he teased.

I gave him a playful slap and rolled onto my back, looking up at the ceiling, which was in need of a paint job. "Do you think when I return after death, it will be from hell?"

He turned onto his side and propped his head upon a hand. "That last sentence of yours, you realize, would have had you committed under normal circumstances."

I gazed into his azure eyes and made a quirky face.

Guylan was absolutely correct. Any other man would think me crazy and go running from my room to call the men with the straitjackets.

"If anyone's going to hell, it's me," he said, caressing my shoulder. "I've just about played God, with going back in time and changing history." He sighed. "And I'm worried for the repercussions to come."

I reached out and traced the outline of his full lips with the tip of a finger. "I know you are, but it's been a year since you went through the attic portal and nothing's happened yet."

"Ah, *yet* is the key word here, Nela."

I rolled onto my side and embraced him. "Whatever happens, Guylan, we'll deal with it as a team...Hades and all."

He chuckled again. "With you by my side, babe, even hell won't be so bad."

~ * ~

There was only a month left until my wedding. Both my grandparents would be arriving this year, and I still had tons of things to do. My sister, Hannah, and I sat on the sofa in my mother's living room, putting together little candy baskets to place at each guest's seat. I wondered if she realized, when she accepted being my matron of honor, I'd run her ragged for an entire year.

Hannah finished tying a pale pink ribbon around the veiling of another basket. "I truly hoped Joe could be home for the wedding, but it doesn't look like that's going to happen." She sighed. "I'm so tired of my husband being in Iraq, Nela. There's not a day that goes by without my worrying for his safety."

My heart went out to my sister. I couldn't imagine being away so long from Guylan. With each news broadcast, all of us held our breaths. I remember one night in late March, the *Nightly News* anchorman announced the death toll for American soldiers serving in Iraq had hit four thousand.

In moments, the phone rang and Hannah was on the other end, hysterical. "Are you watching the Nightly News?*"*

"Yes," I said.

"What if Joe is four thousand and one?"

"He won't be...he can't be. Why are you watching this stuff?"

Hannah sighed. "Why are you?"

The truth is we all watched and worried, obsessed, prayed, and prayed some more.

"If I have to make one more basket, I'll scream." Hannah's voice interrupted my thoughts. "Why have you waited until the last minute to do this?"

I scrunched my face up at her. "Baskets filled with stale candy aren't posh."

"Oh, piss on posh, no one eats them anyway."

I frowned. "I do."

She finished tying another ribbon. "Well, you're weird."

"Always thought so myself," my mother teased as she entered the room.

Gloria O'Riley had scared the family with the lump she had found last year in her left breast. Thankfully it turned out to be a fibroid, but it woke her up to the realization she needed to take better care of herself.

It woke all of us up, too.

Hannah's new job with Dana Clair at the piano studio has flourished to her favor. With Dana opening another studio in Manhattan, Hannah is co-runner of the Anglewood branch and paid handsomely, enough to be able to contribute rent for the apartment she and my sixteen-year-old niece, Cara, occupy in the basement of my parents' home.

Alana also stepped up to the plate, this being her last year in college. She moved in with her significant other, Beth, and got a part-time job waiting tables to contribute toward her tuition. Although the move played some havoc with my father and Alana's relationship, it also eased my parents' financial burden, and my mother was able to cut her own work hours. In six months, she plans to retire.

Even my niece Cara's monstrous teenaged mannerisms took a turn for the better. She often helps my mother with meals and the cleaning, leaving her attitude out of the mix.

Looking rested and on the mend, Gloria looped a dark hair behind an ear and sat on a nearby stuffed chair. "Could you gals use another helping hand?"

"Always," I said, handing her the last of the lace. "Looks like I'm going to need more of this netting."

My mother placed the material aside. "I think I've some up in the attic. It's wrapped in plastic too, so it shouldn't have discolored."

I stood. "I'll get it."

My mother smiled. "Exercise is good for me, Nela."

I shrugged. "It is for me as well."

My mother sighed. "Very well, then. Look in the boxes near Gram's old trunk."

I both hated and loved the attic of my parents' Victorian home. Spooky, musty and full of spiders, the upstairs also held a romantic ambiance. I looked around at all the angled nooks and crannies, picturing past female residents stealing away from chaperoned eyes to hide with their beaus behind old trunks and large paintings, lifting their skirts to forbidden passion.

Anyone who tells you such things didn't happen way back then is either terribly naïve or downright stupid. The only reason such goings-on stayed hushed was because communication wasn't as convenient as it is today. There weren't talk shows or the local evening news to broadcast other people's business. But life was life, feelings and desires the same.

I smiled and picked out my own hiding place to make love to Guylan, then spotted Gram's old trunk. The plastic bag of netting was in a box right where my mother said it would be. Placing it aside, I pulled off the white sheet covering the trunk and ran my fingers over the smooth, wood grain. The lock, broken years ago, made it easy to open.

I spread wide each side and viewed the brightly colored garments neatly folded in various compartments. Gram's dresses and hats were wrinkled and crushed, but still in decent condition. I remembered Hannah playing dress-up, my grandmother laughing as my sister put on the *Miss Hannah Show*. The memory gave me a pang of sadness. I missed my grandmother walking among us.

Off to one side of the trunk, I spotted a tiny door, unlocked. I opened it and found a cedar wood box. Pulling the wooden container from the trunk, I examined it carefully. On the lid, etched in bold letters, was my great-great-grandmother's name, *Nelana Caralena.* It was my name, too.

I fiddled with the latch, but couldn't get it to open. Reaching for a jeweled-handle letter opener from another trunk compartment, I jiggled the catch until the lid of the cedar wood box flew open. Out popped a pair of rimless glasses, a black diary and a pencil.

A surge of excitement washed over me. I'd heard stories about my great-great-grandmother; she was an exotic beauty. I inherited her dark eyes and hair, as well as an olive complexion and long legs. She made soap, baked, drank a glass of hot water with every meal to stimulate good digestion and dabbled in the supernatural, although the latter information was always played down by my father, a man who's had a hard time accepting the family blessing.

I reached for the diary and held it a moment close to my heart. Would I read within these pages the heartfelt emotions and thoughts of a woman I wondered so much about? Would I, reading her words, finally know the answers to questions I'd never dared to ask?

With trembling fingers, I opened the diary, turned a blank page, then another blank page. To my disappointment they were all blank, except for the last one. Written in Italian, which I knew how to speak and read at my grandmother's insistence, were these words:

Look through the glasses and see what you see...if all is not well, then change what might be. Just right the wrong by writing it right, bring forth what you desire, what you wish, what you dream on this night. When all dissolves, what you request will come true, but take care what you ask for, when you ask and for whom.

I frowned. *When what dissolved...the words? But how can words, when written, dissolve?* I reached for the glasses, hooked them over each ear and looked around the attic. Everything was a blur. Glimpsing over at the window, the sun's light expanded, surrounding me in a burst of color and shapes.

Suddenly lightheaded, I was weightlessly drawn down a long corridor. I pulled back, but the force was too strong. My heart pounded in my ears, my lungs gasped for air as I was carried further and further along a dark tunnel.

I emerged onto desert sand, sounds of gunfire in the distance. I turned toward the noise and spotted my brother-in-law. Joe West was lying beside an overturned jeep, badly wounded. Blood streaked his face and covered his chest. I screamed his name and wanted to run to him, but my feet wouldn't move. Instead, I floated on air over to where he lay.

He opened his eyes, and I could swear he saw me...knew I was there. He coughed, gasped, and with his last breath called out, "Hannah, I love you."

I threw myself down upon him, shook him, called out his name, but he was still. I picked up his hand, bloodied and limp, and brought it to my face, my tears wetting his fingers. "Oh, God, no, don't take him now," I cried. "Not this man, not this man." *Not my sister's husband.*

Then Joe's hand vanished within my grasp; the scene before me closed like the end of a movie. I squeezed my eyes shut, and within seconds I was again sitting in the attic beside my grandmother's trunk.

I ripped off the glasses and looked down at my hands. There was no trace of Joe's blood. My stomach churned and I lay down on the floor, swallowing the nausea threatening to choke me. My insides trembled and I squeezed my eyes shut. Did I actually witness Joe's death right now, in Iraq; did Joe really take his last breath?

How can this be...how could I have...?

Then I remembered the words in the diary—*if all is not well, then change what you see.*

"Of course, *all is not well.* I just watched my brother-in-law die," I whispered.

Sitting up, I searched for the diary. *Could I change what happened?*

I opened the page and read the rest of the incantation. *Right the wrong by writing it right.*

I looked for the pencil, throwing everything I'd taken from the trunk aside. I found it beneath a hat. With a shaky hand, I turned to a page and wrote:

I wish for Joe West not to be dead. He did not die, will not die fighting this war. Instead, he will come home to live a long life with his wife, Hannah, and their daughter, Cara.

I looked at the words I'd just written, tears falling down my face and staining the page. To my amazement, one letter at a time, the sentence vanished before my very eyes, leaving the page blank. I wondered then how many wishes and desires had been written on the pages before mine.

I gathered the items and replaced them in the cedar wood box, but I didn't stash it away in the trunk with the rest of the things. Grabbing the plastic bag of veiling, I stood on wobbly legs and descended the stairs. Once into the foyer, I made my way to where I had left my coat and hid the cedar wood box in my tote bag.

I took a deep breath to calm myself, inhaling the aroma of zucchini cooking in the kitchen, before making my way back to Hannah and my mother.

My mother called out to me, "Nela, did you find the veiling?"

I cleared my throat and looked down at the plastic bag of material I held. "Yes, it was right where you said it would be." Squaring my shoulders, I entered the living room.

My mother searched my face and frowned. "Good heavens, you look like you've seen a ghost."

Hannah looked up from filling a basket and laughed. "Probably more like a spider."

My dear sister, you wouldn't be laughing if you really knew what I'd seen.

~ * ~

I was on pins and needles for the next few days, unable to sleep or eat. Everyone thought it was just pre-wedding jitters.

Guylan was at a medical conference for veterinarians in Philadelphia until Saturday, and I counted the days till he arrived home. He would, being a Druid and into the mystical realm, be able to explain to me how I was able to see what I saw. He had traveled through space and time to another dimension, and was able to read the oracle. I thought he could probably shed some light on what had happened, if it had really happened at all.

Then the call came.

Hannah was hysterical on the other end of the phone line. "He's coming home, Nela," she choked out, excited. "He's lost an arm, but he's alive and he's coming home in two weeks."

My head spun. I sat on the floor before I collapsed. "Are you flying out to be with him?"

"No, he doesn't want me to," she said.

"Then you've talked to him?" I wanted to make sure it was really Joe, alive and coming home.

"Yes, only for a few moments, but yes. I heard his voice. He said he thought he was going to die and called out my name, said, *I love you, Hannah*. He thought they would be his last words."

I swallowed hard. *They were his last words.*

"Then something strange happened," Hannah said.

"And what was that?"

She cleared her throat. "An angel...he thought he saw and heard an angel."

Hardly an angel.

"She had long dark hair and she said '*not this man,*' and the next time he opened his eyes, he was in a hospital."

"Mother of God," I whispered.

"It was a miracle, Nela," Hannah said, her voice shaking with new sobs. "Joe's been given a miracle."

"That he has," I muttered into the phone, not sure if it was of the heavenly kind.

Thirty-six

Sister Margaret sat at the edge of her bed, dabbing a cold, wet cloth to her flushed forehead. The pain around her eyes sliced clear through to the back of her head. Always, after one of her visions, her head ached in such a way. The images had begun when she was only six and nearly frightened her to death. She realized even then, she'd never get used to them, take them in stride and work with them as her father did.

Quentin spent hours helping her embrace his realm, hone the gifts she had inherited. But she wanted no part of what he was. Lately, she hadn't had a choice. The apparition of Ronnie Fargus came to her nightly, in spirit form, his shape wavering as he begged her to help him.

"Oh, Ronnie, when did you die...how did you die?" she whispered, lying back on the pillow and closing her eyes.

Ronnie's screams echoed in her thoughts.

"Help me, help me, Sister. You're the only one who can, the only one who will. Free me...free me."

Free him from what, hell? How could she help if he was already damned?

"I'll pray for you, poor boy," she mumbled, rolling onto her stomach and reaching for her rosaries in the night table drawer. Fingering each glass bead, she mouthed the prayers, asking for help in this matter.

She was guided to Guylan.

She lay in pain and torment till dawn, apprehensive, confused, and detesting the thought of any involvement with the family business. Then she rose from the bed, in spite of her throbbing head, and managed to wash and dress; she even sat through Sunday morning services before giving in to the silent command.

Guylan and Nela would be having brunch at Olena's, as they did every Sunday.

Sister Margaret rose from the church pew and made her way to the foyer. At the door, she dabbed holy water on her forehead. Standing out on the church steps, she breathed deeply the warmth of the spring day, the wind catching playfully at a salt and pepper strand of hair. The birds sang, the flowers prepared to bloom...and she reached into her purse for the cell phone to call a cab.

~ * ~

Guylan and I were up late talking about my experience with the cedar wood box, so we overslept. I reached over and shut off the alarm...now we would have to forgo Mass. This Sunday I needed to sleep in, since I hadn't gotten much rest in the last week. I yawned, closed my eyes and pulled my legs to my chest, curling into a fetal position.

Guylan spooned me, whispering in my ear. "You're a sinful child, missing church."

I smiled. "I'm sleeping with you before we're married. I'm already damned."

"True," he said, throwing a leg over my hip and nudging closer.

The tip of his phallus snooped around my backside. I curled my legs tighter to my chest and stuck out my bottom.

"Be damned, then, with being damned," he said, penetrating me with one quick glide and moving a hand between my thighs.

I groaned and pushed against him as his finger teased my passion spot, the spasms he created working to engulf me. He kissed the back of my neck and drove his thick shaft deeper, peaking the desire already mounting inside of me. I let him take me all the way, thrilling in the climb and shattering together in the ecstasy our bodies shared.

"I love wearing you," he mumbled. "You're always so warm and tight."

And wet.

We fell back to sleep entwined, the moistness cooling between my thighs. I didn't wake again until his limp member slipped from within me. He rolled onto his back when he felt me stir, his bones cracking as he stretched. Sitting up in bed, I glanced at the clock. "We can still make it to your grandmother's house for brunch, if we share a shower."

He pulled me atop him, kissing a nipple. "What if we skip the shower?"

~ * ~

Andy rolled over in bed, reaching for Keira, making sure she was still there, safe by his side. He'd looked in on Justin and Marla a few times throughout the night, too, just to make sure they were sleeping in their beds. Was he overprotective? Damn right! When you work as a cop, you become protective of the ones you love because you know firsthand what's out there. The things he had seen from years on the force sickened him, scared him, and made him realize the depth of humanity's depravity. He'd wished many times, especially after his children were born, he could hide them all somewhere to keep them away from the sickos of the world.

"Did you have the dream again?" Keira whispered, turning to face him.

He pulled her close and kissed her forehead. "Yeah, a few times during the night."

"Then you haven't had much sleep again?" she inquired, concerned.

Andy stifled a yawn. "No, not very much."

"It happened a long time ago, honey. Why are you still letting it take up space in your head?"

He shrugged.

Keira caressed his face. "You can't go on like this. You've got to talk with someone."

"I can't, Keira."

She sat up in the bed. "Why, Andy?"

He rolled onto his back, hands clasped beneath his head. "If I say anything to the shrink at work, I'll be grounded to desk duty until they think my head's clear. And I'm in the middle of a big drug bust, something I've been working on for over a year. I can't chance anything ruining this operation."

"Then talk to my father."

He shook his head. "As nice as he is, he intimidates me."

"Then talk to Guylan," she said, lying back against the pillow. "He's good at explaining dreams." She rolled into Andy's embrace. "He's been your best friend for years; certainly you feel comfortable with him."

"I do. Guylan's an okay guy."

"Well, you'll have your chance today. He and Nela will be here for brunch at noon." She glanced at the bedside clock. "Good heavens, I should shower and help Olena with the children's breakfast."

He stopped her from leaving the bed. "She likes having private time with them."

Keira snuggled against him, her hand moving to the juncture of his thighs. "And what do you like?"

He smiled, spreading his legs wider. "Keep going, honey. You're on the right track."

~ * ~

Brunch at Olena's was always quite an affair, with her cooking up all sorts of Scottish dishes for everyone. The oatmeal, grainy and honey-hued, I could handle. And the *cock-a-leekie* soup, made up of chicken, leeks and prunes, tolerable. I didn't mind the *bashed neeps* either, which were mashed turnips. But I drew the line at the *haggis*, chopped sheep innards mixed with oatmeal and spices and traditionally boiled in a sheep's stomach. Although Olena boiled it in a pan, I still couldn't muster putting it in my mouth.

Keira sat beside me at the table, holding Marla on her lap. "I'm with you," she agreed, following my gaze to the pot of *haggis*. "Just give me a bagel and cream cheese and I'm happy."

I laughed and reached over to push aside an auburn curl from Marla's forehead. "She's got coloring like my sisters, Alana and Hannah."

Keira rubbed her daughter's back. "With Olena being a redhead on Guylan's side, and your dad the same, you and my brother have a strong chance at having a child with auburn hair as well."

A little girl with copper curls...to carry on the family blessing.

"Will you try to get pregnant right after you're married?" Keira said, wiping jam from Marla's face and setting her down to follow her brother into the playroom.

I sighed. "Neither of us is getting any younger, so we've decided to start a family immediately." I reached for a slice of toast and smothered it with grape jam.

"And of course, you have the family tradition to uphold, so you'll want a girl first," Keira said.

"But Guylan needs a son to carry on your family's ways," I said, taking a bite of the bread.

Keira laughed. "Guess you'd better hope for twins."

"Guess so," I agreed.

Sister Margaret arrived around one, an anxious glimmer in the shadows of her eyes. "Guylan, could I talk with you, please?" she said, ignoring Olena's invitation to sit and eat before everything grew cold. "I need your...your Druid skills."

Sister Margaret didn't take to Guylan's abilities, so for her to ask of him such a request, it had to be something important and pressing. Immediately, Guylan rose from his chair, directing Sister Margaret to the den. Before he closed the door, he summoned me. I shot him an *are-you-sure* look, and he smiled in agreement. I took a seat beside Sister Margaret on the leather sofa.

Guylan sat at the desk. "I hope you don't mind Nela listening in. I want her to know and be comfortable with every aspect of my training."

Sister Margaret clasped her hands in her lap. "To this day I'm not comfortable with them."

Guylan frowned. "Then why seek my help?"

Sister Margaret chewed on her lower lip. "I haven't a choice this time. I'm having a vision, over and over, and I believe you are the one who can help me understand its meaning."

Guylan sat back in his seat. "I'm listening."

Sister Margaret took an audible breath. "Do you remember me mentioning Ronnie Fargus, the child I cared for in the orphanage with behavioral problems?"

Strong recognition touched my husband's face. "Yes, I remember the name."

Sister Margaret swallowed hard and paused to choose her words carefully. "I am haunted by him, by his spirit. The entity wavers and cries out for help, asks me to set him free." She looked down at her hands and shook her head in regret. "How can I help a dead man?"

"He might not be dead," Guylan said.

Sister Margaret's eyes met Guylan's...mine did too. "But he came to me in spirit form."

"You said the entity wavered, didn't you?" Guylan sat forward in his seat, leaning his elbows on the desk.

"Yes," Sister Margaret confirmed.

"Then he's not a dead soul, but a displaced one," Guylan said.

I frowned. "What are you saying?"

"What Sister Margaret is seeing is a displaced spirit." Guylan's eyes chilled. "Ronnie Fargus is still alive, but is not allowed to be in control of his own body."

Sister Margaret's hand went to her throat. "You mean he's possessed?"

Guylan turned his attention back to the elder nun. "Yes, by either another spirit or a demon needing a host."

Sister Margaret gasped. "The devil?"

"Something very evil," Guylan concluded.

My heart raced. "And this thing...this other spirit can just enter Ronnie, take over his body and use it to its advantage?"

"That's how it's done," Guylan said.

Terror filled Sister Margaret's eyes. "What can be done to help him?"

Guylan stood and made his way to the sofa, taking Sister Margaret by the hands and helping her stand. "I will consult my father. Together we will work on a way to free Ronnie." He gave her a reassuring smile. "You've done all you can."

Sister Margaret's voice shook. "How can you help him when you don't even know where he is?"

"It won't be easy, but I'll find a way." He searched Sister Margaret's face. "Tell me, why did you come to me for help and not my father?"

"Your name came to mind. I was guided to you," she said.

"Then give me the chance to do my best to help Ronnie." He gave her a reassuring smile. Now, go eat Olena's brunch and leave the rest to me."

Reluctantly Sister Margaret nodded in agreement and left the den.

Guylan looked down at me. "Well, Nela, quite a task has been set before me." He took a seat beside me and combed a hand through his hair. "Sister Margaret's right about one thing. I can't help him if I can't find him."

I placed a hand on his knee. "Won't your oracle reading lead you to him?"

"Not necessarily." He turned to look at me. "Oracles show you things that *have* happened, that *will* happen. Many times they are unclear on the *where* part. That is up to the Druid doing the asking to decipher."

"And can you?"

"Sometimes, if I'm close enough to the subject," he said.

"And were you close to Ronnie Fargus?"

Guylan stood and made his way to the window, looking out at the front lawn. "In my first life, the one I had before I went through the attic portal." He sighed. "He's someone I wish to forget."

"Why?"

He turned to look at me. "When you change the course of time, Nela, ripple effects happen. Your life isn't the only one that changes. When I saved my family, I changed the course of time for those I knew before."

"Like Andy, and now Ronnie," I concluded.

"Exactly, and Ronnie's fate turned out worse than ever." He rubbed his hands over his face. "And I'm to blame for it all."

"You can't punish yourself over this, Guylan. You did what you had to do to keep your family alive."

"But now, Ronnie's in trouble and I'm the one who has to help him out of it. Deep inside I think his possession has something to do with the evil I battled before."

"Let me help you find Ronnie Fargus, Guylan."

He shook his head. "It would be too dangerous."

"I have a feeling...if all this *is* connected to what you did before, it will be too dangerous not to."

His tone was firm. "I can't allow you to be a part of this, Nela. I'm not sure right now what I'm dealing with."

"Let me at least see if I can help you find Ronnie Fargus with the glasses," I begged. "With you reading the oracle, we just might pinpoint the exact location where he's being held in possession," I added.

Guylan arched a brow. "It just might work."

A knock at the door interrupted further discussion of the matter. "Can I have a word with you, Guylan?" Andy called from the other side of the portal.

"You're like a mob boss, granting requests to family members at a gathering."

He sighed and reached for the knob. "Let's see what this is about now."

Andy looked from Guylan to me and back to Guylan, his face flushed. "Sorry to interrupt you two, but I really need to speak to Guylan privately."

I held up a hand. "Say no more. I should help Keira and Olena with the cleanup anyway."

Andy smiled, relieved. "Thanks, Nela."

I gave Guylan a light kiss on the cheek and whispered, "Good luck, boss," before I shut the door behind me.

~ * ~

Andy moved to the window and glanced out. "You don't think I hurt her feelings, do you?"

Guylan took a seat on the sofa, crossing his foot over his knee. "No, Nela knows the history you and I share."

More than even you know.

Andy turned around, his face strained and weary. "I've been having these dreams lately and Keira believes you might be able to help me decipher them."

"I'll do my best to try."

Andy made his way to the desk and sat on the edge. "They're of a personal nature, about something that happened long ago." He looked down at the foot he was swinging back and forth. "The dreams went away right after I married Keira, but for some reason they've begun again."

Guylan sat forward, his arms on his knees. "Did something happen in your daily life that might have triggered the old memories?"

Andy picked up a paperweight shaped like a cat. "I think so. About six months ago, I busted a small drug ring." He rolled the weight in his hands. "After my men took away those involved, Callie and I searched the premises for the goods." He set the paperweight down. "She's a good dog, my Callie. She never leaves my side when we're on a call, real loyal and devoted." He glanced at Guylan. "Did you ever have a dog like that, Guylan?"

"Yes, years ago. Luna was her name. Callie, in fact, reminds me a lot of her."

"Well, Callie sniffed out the drugs hidden in all the usual places, but then she stopped short at the basement door." Andy moved to the window again. "I don't know how to explain this, Guylan, without sounding nuts."

Guylan stood, making his way to stand beside Andy. "I don't think there's much you could say that sounds nutty to me."

"Callie began to growl, that slow, deep rumble dogs make when they sense extreme danger. I literally saw the hairs along her spine spike. I pulled out my revolver and the small flashlight I always carry, then opened the door. Callie made her way down the stairs, looking from side to side, nose in the air, sniffing. I followed, my gun drawn."

"What happened then?"

Andy turned to face him. "Callie spotted something at the far right-hand corner of the cellar, but instead of taking off for the attack, she turned back to look at me." He shook his head. "I swear her eyes were an amber shade."

Guylan's heart raced. "Maybe from the angle where you stood, coupled with the light, it appeared that way."

"No...no, her eyes were amber, and then the place filled with a green mist. It was so thick I couldn't see and missed my footing. I fell down the stairs, hitting my head on the concrete floor. Before I blacked out, I smelled something I had smelled before, but never since."

Guylan wiped sweaty palms on his jeans. "What was that, Andy?"

"It was the same scent lingering on Michael Harmon's skin the night I found him on the floor in the orphanage bathroom after Ronnie Fargus abused him, a mixture of rotten eggs and vinegar." Andy's lips thinned. "The same smell remained in the bathroom after Ronnie used the toilet or showered. I actually thought he had stolen vinegar from the kitchen and poured it down the toilet. One night I snuck out of bed and spied on him. What I saw, Guylan, what I saw, I shouldn't even repeat."

He placed a hand on Andy's shoulder. "Whatever you say goes no further than these walls."

Andy swallowed hard. "Ronnie was standing naked in front of the sink with the water running, scooping it up in his hands and dousing his head. His back was to me, and at the base of his spine there was a growth. It looked like the beginnings of...of a tail. Ronnie Fargus was growing a freaking tail."

Guylan's knees trembled. "Is that why you never told anyone it was Ronnie who molested Michael Harmon?"

Andy inhaled sharply. "It was just so freaky and frightening. I mean, what was he?"

"After you smelled the odor, what happened in the basement at the drug house?"

"I don't know. I blacked out; and when I came around, I found myself in an ambulance on the way to the hospital," Andy said.

"Did Callie or your men find anyone in the basement?"

"No, no one," Andy said. He ran a hand through his hair. "What do you think it all means, Guylan?"

"Maybe whatever drugs lingered in the atmosphere caused you to see things you wouldn't otherwise see," he lied. "And maybe Ronnie was doing drugs, too, filling the bathroom with the aftermath, causing you to go on a very bad trip. That's why the same smell in the basement triggered the bathroom scene."

Andy reluctantly agreed. "That could be the answer, but..." his voice trailed off.

"You're not convinced?"

Andy shrugged. "It has to be. I mean it's the only logical explanation, right?"

Logical, yes, but the truth...no.

"Right," Guylan agreed.

Andy gave Guylan's arm a pat. "Thanks, buddy, this talk has helped a lot." He frowned. "But you'd think, with all my experience in this field and all the scumbags I've busted, I would have realized this for myself. I guess sometimes the obvious isn't obvious." Andy chuckled and shook his head. "Imagine, Ronnie Fargus having a tail."

Guylan forced a smile. "Imagine."

Thirty-seven

I have to admit, as much as I was scared out of my wits, I was also extremely intrigued. Guylan and I are going to experience time travel...leave our present state of being and manifest ourselves into another era or a dimension of this one. We will defy the laws of gravity, sound, and all those things I learned in science class. Awed by our accomplishment, I was having a sci/fi moment when Guylan's voice interrupted my thoughts.

"How do I look in these, Nela?"

I turned to see him wearing the rimless glasses I had found in the cedar wood box. "Like a handsome science professor." I frowned. "Aren't you seeing anything, other than me I mean, through them?"

"No...everything's wavy because they're prescription lenses, but I see nothing more than you."

"Hmm, the minute I put them on I was transported into the realm of my vision."

He removed the glasses and handed them to me. "You're the only one, then, with the power to activate them."

My frown deepened. "But you're a Druid...your powers way exceed mine."

He shrugged. "In this instance, they don't." He searched my face. "Didn't you say you're named after the great-great-grandmother the box belonged to?"

"Yes, but what would that have to do with anything?"

"Perhaps your name connects you to her, giving you two a common bond," Guylan explained. "She's able to transmit her powers to you because of that link."

I shivered. "A broadcast from the grave."

"No, from the afterlife. You of all people should understand that."

I glanced for a moment at the glasses in my hand. "Then I'm the only one who can get these to work?"

"It looks that way to me, but it doesn't hamper our plans. We agreed you'd work the lens end and I'd work the water bowl."

He set the oracle instruments out on the coffee table in front of my living room sofa, and after closing all the blinds, he lit white candles and placed them in various places around the room. Then he went to the kitchen for bottled water. The candlelight cast a warm glow on my ecru painted walls, the flames dancing like puppet shadows. When Guylan returned, he poured the water into the oracle bowl, and then stripped himself naked of the clothes and jewelry he wore.

I arched a brow. "Is that a requirement?"

"Wearing clothes can hamper the flow of time travel, and if I should suddenly get sucked up into your flight, I want to be prepared."

I smiled mischievously and stared at his manhood dangling between his thighs.

He covered himself with a hand. "I never thought I'd say this, but don't look at me in *that way*. It will break my concentration."

I cleared my throat, adopting a somber expression, and changed the subject. "You think that can happen?"

"What's that?" he said, taking a seat on the floor in front of the coffee table. Leaning his back against the sofa, he crossed his legs.

"Do you think you could get sucked up into my flight?"

"I'm not sure of anything, Nela. This is all new to me and my training."

My stomach tightened. "Then we're pioneers in this?"

"Like the forefathers who went forth to build a new nation," he said.

"Let's hope it's not like those of the Donner Party," I muttered, removing my clothes and jewelry and sitting on the floor beside him.

He glanced at my breasts and smiled.

I slapped his arm and quoted my grandmother. "Conduct yourself in accordance." Then I narrowed my eyes. "Remember your concentration."

He cleared his throat. "Touché, my love."

I placed the glasses in front of me on the table. "Now what?"

"I'm hoping what you see through the glasses, I can duplicate in the water."

I smiled. "So, it will be like you're following me?"

He cupped the bowl and glanced into the water. "That's my idea."

I put on the glasses and clenched my fists to my side.

"Relax, Nela. Take deep breaths and calm your spirit."

I nodded and did my yoga inhaling and exhaling exercise. With shoulders relaxed and fingers uncurled, I allowed a warm calmness to enter and wash over my entire body.

"How did you launch yourself before?"

"I looked at the sun's rays streaming in from the attic window," I whispered, not to break the mood. "For some reason, the light fueled the transport."

"Then look into the flame of the candle placed before you," Guylan instructed. "Block from your focus everything around you and only concentrate on the light of the fire."

I zeroed in on the flame, and within seconds, the walls of my living room evaporated. I was standing in a dark alley. I glanced around at my surroundings, ready to give an account to Guylan, when I heard him speaking in my head.

You've done it, honey. You're out of your dimension.

I frowned and opened my mouth to answer, but he interrupted to prevent me from speaking.

Don't use your voice to communicate with me. Talk with your mind.

I can do that and you'll hear me?

Guylan chuckled. *You just did and I heard you fine. Now, tell me what you see.*

I'm in an alley. There are old tires propped against the side of the building wall to my left. Broken glass is everywhere.

I gasped.

And I have bare feet...I'm walking around naked!

You need to calm down, Nela. You're not really there in the flesh. The glass won't hurt you and no one can see you.

You're wrong, Guylan. Joe saw me, remember? He said he saw a dark-haired angel.

He was dying, Nela, heading for another plane and caught a glimpse of you on his way out.

I took a deep breath.

Okay, okay...sorry. Let me try this again.

I walked a few feet to the rear of the alley.

The further I walk, the darker it gets, but I can make out a door to my right.

Guylan's thoughts burst through mine. *And from this angle, your ass is even sexier.*

The compliment thrilled me and I smiled to myself.

You can concentrate on my ass later, Sincloud.

He cleared his throat. *Sorry, babe.*

I'm going through the door.

I heard his voice deepen. *I'm going to shed some light your way so you can see where you're going.*

Roger that. I thought of myself as a space commando. In truth, I was traveling through the space of time.

Okay, move it, my little space commando.

I gasped. *You heard that?*

I can hear everything you're thinking. He chuckled again. *This would come in handy when we're making love. I'd always know if you were really having an—*

It was my turn to interrupt him. *Where's that light you promised me?*

How's this?

The way before me brightened. *How'd you do that?*

I moved the candle closer to the oracle bowl.

I opened the door and walked down three flights of steps before I came to a room. The walls were gray, oppressive, in spite of the light Guylan had afforded me. A dilapidated mattress was pushed to one side; empty cans of food littered the floor. I heard scampering in the corner.

Rats, Guylan...there are rats down here.

They can't hurt you, honey. You're not really there, remember?

I allowed myself a moment to take a few calming breaths before I walked on.

Are you getting all this?

Yes, just as if I were walking right behind you.

A foul odor penetrated my senses.

Can you smell what I smell?

His thought-voice cracked. *Yes.*

It smells like rotten eggs and vinegar. The silence of his thoughts disturbed me. He was doing something to block me from reading his mind. *What is it, Guylan?*

Honey, I want you to go back up the stairs and into the street.

I frowned. *But we haven't found Ronnie yet.*

I think we have...that odor is his.

A disturbing thought struck me.

How am I able to smell him if I'm not really here?

Ronnie Fargus is possessed, remember? He has demon powers.

My heart raced.

Then he could see me, hurt me?

Yes, Nela, I believe he could.

I ran for the stairs and took them two at a time, reaching the alley in record speed.

Walk out to the street, Nela. I need a location.

I hurried to the sidewalk and glanced around for a street sign, spotting one a few feet away.

I see it, but can't make out the writing, Guylan conveyed.

Brierwater and Colburn. I'm on the corner of Brierwater Road and Colburn Drive.

You need to get out of there now, Nela. How did you exit from the glasses before?

I just closed my eyes.

I see Ronnie Fargus running down the alley, honey. Close your eyes, now...get the hell out of there.

I squeezed my eyes shut and within seconds I was back in my own element. Ripping the glasses from my eyes, I turned to look into Guylan's terror-stricken face.

He pulled me into his embrace. "That was too close for comfort."

"I've got to get the carpet cleaner," I muttered against his neck.

He pulled back to look at me, quirking an eyebrow. "This is a hell of a time to worry about cleaning."

I glanced down at my thighs, separating them to reveal a large, wet stain soaking the rug beneath me.

He followed my gaze.

An unwanted blush heated my cheeks as I caught the smile he stifled. "Don't you dare think this is funny, Guylan Sincloud." I pointed a finger at him. "And never, ever tell anyone I peed on my carpet."

There was a trace of laughter in his voice. "Not to worry, babe; no one would believe the reason why anyway."

~ * ~

Guylan turned to look at Nela, lying in bed beside him, and stared with longing at the heart-rending tenderness of her face. His gaze moved to her arms that stretched above her head, then slid downward. Lazily he appraised her, his eyes roving to the creamy expanse of her neck, to the swell of her breasts and the nipples peeking out from beneath the blanket.

His intense love for her jolted through his body. Every day, his love deepened and he was powerless to resist her, knew he couldn't live without her. For that reason, he couldn't ever put her in a compromising situation again.

Earlier in the evening, during the vision quest, Ronnie Fargus had been only a few feet behind Nela. Although there still remained a question in his mind as to whether she was in harm's way, he wasn't taking a second chance to find out. Demons were unpredictable, evil creatures, and to underestimate their power was the most unwise thing a Druid could do.

To say Nela was miffed when he told her he would handle the rest of the situation alone, was putting it mildly.

"We made a deal you'd only help locate Ronnie with the glasses, and you've already done your part," he reminded her.

"But I want to do more to help," she protested, pacing the room. *"I can kill the demon within him by writing 'kill demon' in the diary."*

"Demons can't be dealt with like that...there are words to chant, a ritual to perform before dissolving them," he said. *"You'll only make matters worse."*

In spite of her bravado, he wasn't about to put her in any further danger. The only way to keep her from following him was to make sure he left her in a deep sleep. He hated deceiving her, but things had gotten a little too close for comfort. He was left no other choice but to sneak sleeping herbs into her tea. It was a good thing he had remembered to pack them along with his oracle tools...thinking ahead is always a plus.

Her breathing, easy and relaxed, left him satisfied. Rising from the bed, he dressed quietly in the dark, kissed her warm, full lips and left to finish the job they had started...on his own.

Once he was at his own apartment, he opened the book of secrets and found the passage his father had used to dissolve

Mortimer MacRaven thirty-six years earlier. He committed the words to memory:

The unfruitful works of darkness have no domain amongst the good. So, I banish thee to hell, where thee rightly should burn away to ashes, blown aside by gale and gust, bones and flesh, mind and spirit, now nothing more than dust.

He twirled the raven signet ring around his finger as he read the incantation over and over. When he had every word etched into his brain, he closed the book, squared his shoulders and reached for his keys. He made his way to the car, driving to where Ronnie Fargus dwelled, the building on the corner of Brierwater and Colburn.

Thirty-eight

I woke with a start and knew before I glanced over to where Guylan slept, his side of the bed was empty. I stroked the indentation his head had made upon the pillow. The linen was cool, which meant he'd left hours ago. And I knew where he'd gone...to see Ronnie Fargus. I could dress and follow him, but I had promised I wouldn't. Anyway, I had a much more effective way in mind to help Guylan with this demonic situation. If I tagged along in the flesh, there would only be another aspect for him to worry over. I knew he needed complete concentration and no distractions to fight this foe.

I reached for the silk kimono draped over the bedroom chaise, purchased last summer at a downtown Asian apparel shop, and slipped it on before I made my way to the living room. The oracle equipment was gone, but the rimless glasses remained where I'd left them, on the coffee table. Now, they beckoned to me. I scooped them up, along with the diary and pencil, and hurried back to my bed. I added Guylan's pillow to mine, propping both behind my back, and a whiff of his cologne filled my senses, reminding me of his heated flesh. He dripped with passion, taking me with tender, sensuous caresses. Would we ever cool each other's desire with our lovemaking? I sincerely hope not.

I shook my head to clear it. Though I absolutely loved remembering the look of him naked, his arousal deep inside of me, this was not the time. Guylan, even now, might need my help. I shivered to think of him coming against something as sinister and evil as a possessed Ronnie Fargus. I also knew he held a certain amount of guilt and responsibility for the way Ronnie's life had turned out. Guylan, the good man that he is, wouldn't rest until he'd made things right again...but could he? He had changed the course of time, something I was sure had never been done before. And if he could somehow reverse Ronnie's fate, could he do it alone? I had my doubts, simply because I knew that before, Quentin and Xavior, even the dog Luna, had helped to fight Mortimer. I remembered the look in Mortimer's eyes when he went after my soul. Was this demon as bad or worse?

Flicking on the bedside lamp, I removed the decorative shade and angled the light in such a way that I could stare easily at the bulb before I slipped the rimless glasses over my eyes. Again, I was back in the alley I had visited earlier. I crept along the wall, feeling for the door. Without Guylan's light, I fumbled, tripped, stubbed my toe, hit my shins and bumped into debris. It was fortunate I couldn't feel the pain.

I knew from my first trip, the demon could hear and see me, so I took each step down the stairs with quiet caution. When I came to the last flight, I heard Guylan's voice and one other: a woman. She spoke in a deep, throaty tone. I made my way to the landing, stayed hidden by a large crate, and peered down into the basement room. A lit torch burned in a wall sconce, adding to the eeriness of the chamber. Guylan and the woman stood about ten feet apart. The air was charged with electricity. If they sensed I was there, neither of them responded.

"I command you to tell me who you are," Guylan demanded.

The woman was dressed in a long, white cloak, wavy dark hair falling to her shoulders. "You are in no position to command me to do anything, Druid."

Guylan stood his ground, speaking with a calm, exact tone. "I will not leave here until I have answers to all my questions."

I admired his bravery, thankful I was viewing the creature while standing on another level.

"You may not like what you hear," she said. Her voice echoed throughout the tunnel with such force, the hairs at the nape of my neck rose.

"Who are you?" Guylan demanded again.

What's the difference who or what it is... just zap the thing with your ring!

"I am *The Morrigan*, Celtic goddess of war and death."

"Ah, I've heard of you," Guylan hissed.

The woman laughed a sardonic chuckle. "I am flattered, Druid."

"Don't be. My knowledge of you doesn't inspire awe. I've been warned of you, shape-shifter, and the way you change your appearance to terrify and confuse your enemies—both beautiful and horrible in your seduction. Now, why are you here and what do you want?

"I...I want nothing. I am merely a messenger," *The Morrigan* snapped.

He frowned. "Who do you carry a message from?"

"I bring you word from your great-grandfather, Quentin MacRaven. He wishes to warn you of approaching vengeance."

Guylan squared his broad shoulders. "I am already aware danger lurks. Ronnie Fargus's spirit showed itself to Anya MacRaven, Quentin's daughter."

"Ah, the woman who has taken vows to serve the Christ," the goddess acknowledged.

"She is known as Sister Margaret to her order," he explained. "Ronnie's spirit pled to her for help. I have reason to believe his soul is displaced and his body possessed."

"And so you have come to exorcise him," *The Morrigan* concluded.

"Yes, it's the least I can do for...for—"

"For the way you changed the course of time," the being interjected.

He gave her a taut nod.

The Morrigan threw her head back and laughed. "I am amused by the way you humans simplify things." She moved closer to Guylan. "Ronnie Fargus is just a pawn, a soul easy to control after an accident left him mindless." She inclined her head. "Think, Guylan, great-grandson of Archdruid Quentin, who would use Ronnie Fargus to gain your attention?"

Both Guylan and I breathed the name...*Mortimer*.

"You said you want answers, well brace yourself. You stole Mortimer MacRaven's assets and he has been watching, waiting. Now he will steal yours," *The Morrigan* explained.

"My soul, my powers, is that what he wants from me?" he shouted.

"Ah, there is something much more precious to you now, Druid. Mortimer has found your vulnerable point." With a wave of *The Morrigan's* hand, a vision appeared. "Look for yourself at what he will do."

I gasped at the sight of me, chained to a bed, wearing nothing but a backless hospital gown. My stomach lurched as the memories surfaced to choke me. But instead of Mortimer, Ronnie Fargus stood over me, ready to end my life with the dagger he held in his hand.

"She won't be the first, Druid," she roared. "Mortimer's legions of dark fae have been cultivating the human you call Ronnie Fargus for years."

"How...how could anything evil enter holy ground?" Guylan asked.

"It wasn't the orphanage grounds that kept evil away," the war goddess challenged.

He frowned. "What did, then?"

"The one with a pure heart that loved you, something Ronnie didn't have."

Sister Margaret. Her love, her faith in God, had silently and invisibly worked behind the scenes to keep Guylan safe, helping him to pass through each crisis.

Guylan swallowed hard. I knew it was a mixture of fear and anger rising to his throat. "What has Mortimer's legions made this man do?"

"The many young men gone missing throughout the years were Ronnie's victims. They lie buried in this tunnel."

"No...no!" he screamed.

"Oh, yes, Druid. When you robbed the dark fae queen of your father's soul, you started a war."

Guylan's voice cracked with emotion. "No more. This must end here and now."

"It is Mortimer's claim as well." The scent of rotten eggs and vinegar filled the underground chamber. "You've been warned."

The Morrigan turned to look in my direction, her dark and probing eyes meeting mine. The milk white complexion was flawless, beautiful. I understood now why she could seduce her victims.

She cast a crooked smile and let her thoughts speak her words. *I am also known as the goddess of fertility. At this very moment, beneath your heart you carry twins, a boy child and a girl child.*

I placed a hand over my belly and responded in the same manner. *How can that be?*

Your prevention pills are of no match to the powers at hand. It is your destiny to give life to his seed, and if you love him, you must save him so his eyes will also look upon your offspring.

With that said, *The Morrigan* vanished. The horrible stench increased as Ronnie Fargus made his way, walking like a zombie, into the light. From my angle, I caught a glimpse of his eyes, staring ahead with milky blankness. Then he threw back his head and opened his mouth, wide. Out came a black, billowing cloud. Ronnie's body fell limp to the floor, and the darkness took the form of a man.

There, after the smoke cleared, stood Mortimer MacRaven.

Guylan's eyes widened.

My own heart stuttered, freezing the blood beneath my flesh.

"I will show meself to ye, lad, one last time before I take yer soul, and yer little lassie's life," Mortimer said, taking a step toward Guylan.

"My father dissolved you...how have you returned?"

"Through the mindless, empty soul o' the lad lyin' at me feet and the will o' the dark fae queen, I've been resurrected." Mortimer laughed with wild and wicked delight. "I've been here, walkin' the earth all these years, lad, bidin' me time. When ye changed the course o' things, ye changed me destination. Ye angered the dark forces. Their queen has a real taste for yer da's soul. With such power, she can destroy humankind forever."

Guylan aimed the ring at Mortimer, reciting an incantation. "The unfruitful works of darkness have no domain amongst the good."

"And there is where the problem lies, me lad. Are there any good amongst the darkness? I could tell ye stories, had I the time, o' how corrupt and evil mankind is. 'Tis easy to control yer kind, lad, and bring them over to the dark side."

Guylan ignored Mortimer's words and spoke louder, from the depths of his heart and spirit. "So, I banish thee to hell—"

"Hell could not hold me, Druid," Mortimer interjected.

Guylan continued even more strongly. "Where thee rightly should burn away to ashes, blown aside by gale and gust..."

"And 'tis where ye will falter, me great-nephew. Yer gale and gust are missin'." Mortimer laughed again bitterly.

Gale and gust...gale and gust...what are the gale and gust?

Then I realized Mortimer meant Luna, the *kelpie* Guylan had told me about. I believed she'd come to Guylan's aid if she knew he was in trouble. If only there was some way she could be summoned.

I can make her come!

I closed my eyes, leaving Guylan to battle Mortimer. His strength, his bravery overwhelmed me. After seeing the vision of my demise, I knew he fought for me. Now I had to fight for him, for our love and the right for our babies to have a father.

Transported back to my own element, I found myself sitting in bed, the diary in my lap. I pulled off the glasses and opened the book to a blank page, writing with the pencil:

Luna will come to help Guylan. Together they will defeat Mortimer MacRaven for all time. I added for good measure: *Quentin MacRaven, thank you for the warning, but your great-grandson needs more of your help!*

Then I leaned back against the pillows, watched the script dissolve and prayed.

Thirty-nine

Guylan couldn't fight his fiendish great-uncle in full concentration while he worried Nela was in the path of danger, so he sighed, relieved when he felt her leave, and blocked her re-entry into the chamber. When he saw her again, there'd be the devil to pay for keeping her at bay, but he couldn't stress over that now, not while he still battled a more dangerous demon. He repeated the incantation, aiming the crimson ray of the raven signet at Mortimer's heart, and gained confidence when the evil being faltered.

Mortimer fell back, gasping, but his lack of strength only lasted a few seconds before he rallied. Closer he crept, the stench overpowering. Guylan reached inside his pocket and pulled out a vial of holy water, something Sister Margaret would approve of, and pulled the cork with his teeth. Taking a swig of the water, he rolled it around in his mouth and when Mortimer neared him, he spat the blessed liquid, shooting out a spray of it through puckered lips, into Mortimer's face.

Mortimer fell back again, wiping his face with the end of his cape. It was then the chamber filled with a green mist. "Begone, begone, ye menacing *kelpie*. Ye will not mar me plans again," Mortimer roared.

Guylan's confidence rebounded when he glimpsed Luna, amber eyes large and round, long neck posed, ready to attack. His heart swelled with hope, tears of relief filled his eyes. Through his watery vision, he kept the ring's ray on Mortimer and continued to speak the words of the spell.

An earth-shattering screech escaped Luna's throat as she plunged at Mortimer, snaring him by the neck with her dragon-like mouth. Tossing her head side to side, she whipped him against the stone wall, then the floor, and the wall again. His body resembled a rag doll being tossed about.

Mortimer's screams were that of all the souls in hell combined. It was a torturous melody of pain and anguish. The gruesome sound made Guylan's ears throb. Bile rose to the back of his throat and he swallowed hard to control the nausea. Still he spoke the words. The room spun and he closed his eyes to keep from fainting. But as the queasiness overcame him, still he spoke the words. His knees buckled, his arms fell limp at his sides, but still he spoke the words, always the words...soft, then loud, then louder... lying now on his back, he screamed them.

Fingers circled his wrist and pulled him to his feet. A newfound strength coursed through every fiber of his being. He opened his eyes to meet those of Quentin MacRaven.

"Och, ye can do this, me laddie," he whispered. "Level the ring at me brother's heart and together we will say the words to send him back to hell. Forever, this time."

Luna's large mouth clamped down hard on Mortimer's torso, her head still and firm for Guylan to meet his mark. With his great-grandfather whispering the words along with him, power took over. His lungs filled with air; his chest was on fire. The red glow from the ring was hot on his finger.

"Now gale and gust, me lad, burn his flesh, mind and spirit, now nothin' more than dust," Quentin instructed.

When Guylan exhaled all the air filling his lungs, it blew forth like a torch. Flames shot from his mouth, burning to ashes Mortimer MacRaven.

"Not one chance will there be this time," Quentin said, moving to stand over the ashes falling from Luna's mouth. With a wave of his hand, he gathered the remains and dropped them into the urn materializing in his other hand. He sealed the top with another swoop of magic. "I will be takin' his ashes with me, where I can keep an eye on him." He smiled at Guylan. "I am me brother's keeper."

"Quentin," he choked, his throat raw and soar.

"No need to say a word, Guylan. I know what is in yer heart and 'tis all that matters," his great-grandfather said, then vanished.

Luna inclined her monstrous head.

I am watching out for you always, my boy.

She vanished, too, leaving in her place Andy's German Shepherd, Callie, who was barking over Ronnie Fargus's body.

Andy came running down the stairs, weapon drawn, and rushed over to Fargus. "On your feet, dill weed."

Guylan smiled to himself. It was exactly the same name he'd had for Ronnie. "He's out cold, Andy."

Andy spun around, gun aimed.

Guylan raised his hands in a surrendering gesture. "Whoa, man, I come in peace."

Andy frowned. "What the hell are you doing here?"

He coughed to clear his throat. "I could ask the same thing of you."

"Callie and I were on duty, just winding up a drug bust about two blocks north from here. My men were getting the dealers into the squad car when Callie broke away. I took off after her." He shook his head. "Good thing I joined a gym six months ago and cut down on the donuts."

Guylan glanced at his watch. "It's three o'clock."

"Yeah, well, these degenerates don't exactly keep normal business hours." Andy narrowed his eyes. "Now, what's your story?"

He shrugged. "You know me and my premonitions."

Andy rolled his eyes. "I'm fully aware of the family's forewarning. I'm married to your sister, remember?" He chuckled. "Keira puts a whole new spin on a man asking his wife what she's thinking."

"Then I trust you'll have no need to question me twice if I tell you to do some digging around here. You might just close a lot of missing persons cases."

Andy looked over at Ronnie, lying unconscious. "All his doing?"

Guylan nodded. "But in the flesh only."

"That won't wash downtown, Guylan."

He took an audible breath and cringed. He had the worst case of heartburn. "I know."

"He's going to take the rap for it all," Andy said, nudging Ronnie's leg with the toe of his shoe.

Guylan sat on a nearby crate. "I figured as much." He was sorry for all Ronnie had endured.

Andy knelt beside Ronnie and sniffed the air. "The sulfur smell is gone." He reached over and unbuttoned Ronnie's pants.

He frowned. "What are you doing?"

"I just have to know. I need to know." Andy yanked Ronnie's pants down to his ankles and rolled him onto his stomach, scanning the base of his spine. "No tail...there's no tail."

Guylan shook his head and laughed. "Well, of course there's not." *Not anymore.*

Andy turned and smiled, satisfied. "I just had to make sure." He stood and pulled a cell phone from his pocket. "I'm calling for backup, but I suggest you leave before they get here. No need for you to be involved in this further."

But I am involved, responsible for Ronnie's plight and the deaths of all his victims.

"Go home. Go to Nela," Andy said.

He stood, every bone in his body aching, and made his way to the stairs.

"Do you want me to phone you when he regains consciousness?" Andy called after him.

He turned to look at Andy, their eyes meeting across the distance. "If you don't mind. I'm curious about what he has to say.

"It's the least I can do after you hunted the beast down." Andy glared over at Ronnie. "I've been waiting to get this one for a long time."

Forty

I paced the living room floor, wringing my hands, my heart in my throat. I had no way of knowing if my calls for help to Luna and Quentin had worked, since I was unable to re-enter the basement scene. Either Guylan had blocked me or he was dead and Mortimer was on his way to end my life, too. The latter was bad enough to think about, but Guylan's death would be something I couldn't endure.

It was the sound of a man's footsteps climbing the stairs that halted me in my tracks. I ran to the kitchen for a knife, gripping it in my hand like a dagger. I was sure it wouldn't do much to Mortimer, but I wasn't going down without one hell of a fight.

"Nela, open the door," Guylan called through the locked portal.

I raised the knife. "How do I know it's really you?"

"You quiver when I make you come, a little shiver starting from your hips and ending with your toes curling," he said.

I smiled and reached for the knob, but then hesitated. Mortimer was a demon with powers beyond my wildest dreams. What if he had entered Guylan's body and knew his thoughts? "I still can't be sure."

I heard Guylan's exasperated gasp. "For Pete's sake, Nela, it's me...it's really me. Mortimer is gone, turned to ash, thanks to the combined efforts of Quentin, Luna and me."

I sighed, relieved. "Then they came...they really came?"

"Yes, all is well." He jiggled the knob. "Now, open the door."

I placed the knife on a nearby table, reached for the door, and swung it open. "Why did you block me?"

He took me in his embrace and held me close. "It was necessary." His heart beat against my chest. "I'm sorry," he whispered against the lobe of my ear. "I know how much you wanted to help, see this through with me, but I couldn't take the chance he'd hurt you."

"Oh, but I did see it through." I pulled back to look up into his weary, blue eyes, silently thanking the heavens he was alive and well, and not possessed. "I was the one who summoned Quentin and Luna, using the diary."

He frowned. "I thought we agreed you wouldn't write in the diary."

"No, we agreed writing in the diary wouldn't kill Mortimer. There was nothing said about using it to call for help."

A slow smile curved his lips. "Nela, Nela, what am I going to do with you?"

"Love me, Guylan," I whispered. "Forever and ever."

He drew me close. "I plan on it, babe."

"And our twins, too," I mumbled against his neck.

He pulled back to search my face. "What twins?"

"The ones *The Morrigan* said I was carrying. A boy and a girl."

His gaze dropped to my belly for a moment. "But you're on the pill?"

I shrugged. "It isn't foolproof, especially when it comes up against supernatural powers."

His eyes misted. "How can I tell you how happy I am, Nela, to hear this?"

I bit my bottom lip. "Yeah, well my dad's going to have a hissy fit, him being Irish and Catholic and all."

Guylan chuckled. "The man's not stupid, Nela. He knows we're...that we've been—"

"Occasionally cohabitating," I interjected.

He nodded. "Good way of putting it."

"Well, having an idea we're *lusting* after each other's bones before marriage, and the proof announcing it loud and clear are two entirely different things," I explained.

He lowered his head, angling his mouth near mine. "Then it's a good thing we've only a few weeks till the wedding," he said, sealing any further words and worries with a searing kiss.

~ * ~

Andy's voice was rough with fatigue when he phoned Guylan on Monday afternoon. "Well, the dill weed's come around, but we haven't gotten anything out of him amounting to much."

"You sound like you're ready to drop," Guylan said.

"I am, at least pretty close." Andy gave a sardonic chuckle. "I don't know if Ronnie Fargus really believes he's a little kid, or he's putting on the best damn mentally insane act there ever was."

He frowned. "Why, what's he doing?"

"Other than crying for his mother and soiling his pants, not a whole hell of a lot," Andy quipped. "They've got him in the infirmary, handcuffed to the bed and wearing diapers."

He remembered Sister Margaret saying Ronnie was only eight when his parents were killed in a car crash. Ronnie had suffered brain damage. With Mortimer no longer in possession of Ronnie's brain, he would go back to his original condition. An eight-year-old with brain damage would logically cry for his mother and mess himself. "I have a strong feeling he's not faking."

"There's something else, Guylan."

"I'm listening."

"The drug house—the one where I freaked out in the basement— it's connected to the tunnel where Ronnie buried his victims. So far three have been found."

Guylan closed his eyes in agony. All the lives lost, all the hurt endured, all because of him. Then a horrible and frightening thought struck him like a hard slap across the face. "The guys you arrested in that raid...they might be just like Ronnie."

"I thought of that, too. So far, they haven't displayed any supernatural tendencies, and they've been incarcerated for six months now."

"That means diddly, Andy. We're dealing with cunning evil, sly and clever creatures biding their time and waiting for a convenient opening. These degenerates are on a mission and won't stop until they've succeeded."

Andy sighed. "Yeah, I guess you're right. I'll give the word to have them heavily tranquilized until I can figure out what to do."

There's nothing you can do, Andy, but there's something I can do.

Guylan hung up, reached for his keys and made his way to the car.

It was time he paid a visit to his father.

~ * ~

"Your father is in the basement, the storage area on the other side of Seth's apartment, gathering the screens," his mother said as she welcomed Guylan into the split-level home with a kiss upon the cheek. "The spring weather came earlier than expected, before we had a chance to take down the storm windows. Now we're stifled at night." She smiled. "You know how warm your father gets when he's in bed."

He returned the smile. He had an idea how hot she made him... witnessed it when he was only three and slept in a playpen in their room. "Maybe I could lend a hand."

"Oh, sweetie, that would be so nice...get the job done much faster." She frowned. "There are so many windows in this house and Seth's always too busy to help."

Guylan found his father among a pile of screens. "I hear you're hot in bed."

Xavior arched a brow. "You should be so lucky."

He laughed. "How do you know I'm not?" He picked up a screen. "Thought I'd help you get this done so you could help me with something."

Xavior crossed his arms over his chest and leaned back against an old cabinet. "And just what would that *something* be?"

He told him about Sister Margaret's vision, Andy's strange drug raid incident and how it tied in with Mortimer's return. Lastly, he explained about Nela's cedar wood box and how the two of them teamed up to find Ronnie Fargus.

Xavior moved to sit in a nearby chair, running a hand through his hair. "Well, you certainly met your match in Nela."

"I know. It's all so surreal." He searched his father's face. "How could Mortimer come back, Dad, if you dissolved him when I was three?"

Xavior shook his head. "I'm not entirely sure, Guylan. Mortimer shape-shifted into a raven, Luna captured the bird in her mouth, and when I aimed the ring at its chest and chanted the spell, it turned to dust."

"Wait...back up there for a minute. Mortimer turned into a raven. A real, feathers and all black bird-type of raven?"

Xavior arched a brow, and then frowned. "Didn't he for you?"

"No, he remained human, if you can call what he was human," Guylan added.

Xavior's frown deepened. "Then what I can calculate from the training I now know is that Mortimer shape-shifted into the raven so he could reserve his body for a time when he needed it again, after he possessed another's soul."

"Which turned out to be poor little Ronnie Fargus. With his brain damaged and his parents dead, he was a prime choice."

Xavior added, "Oh, he was a major prime choice. Staying in Ronnie's body helped Mortimer to move about, be inconspicuous, and he was able to get closer to you without being detected."

"So, when he saw how perfectly the situation suited him, he stayed."

"That's the way it looks, Guylan."

"But what confuses me, is by that point I'd changed things, and was no longer an orphan. Ronnie meant nothing to me. Why did Mortimer think he could infiltrate my life by possessing him?"

Xavior stroked his chin in thought. "I suspect he realized if he affected Andy and Sister Margaret's life, with what he did to Ronnie, he'd eventually get to you."

"Ah, it's all becoming clear now. Ronnie's displaced spirit isn't what cried out to Sister Margaret. It was Mortimer who set the stage in order to trap me."

"I'm sure that's all true," Xavior agreed.

"Thinking back, the signs were all there; I just didn't pick up on them."

Xavior frowned. "I'm not following you, son."

"Do you remember the time you and I went to see Sister Margaret at the women's shelter?"

"I remember," Xavior said.

"Remember she told us then Ronnie had sexually abused another orphan by the name of Michael Harmon?"

Xavior nodded. "And if my memory serves me correctly, on our way to pick up Andy, you expressed doubts about Ronnie's behavior, said he wasn't the Ronnie you'd known."

"I had a feeling then something was wrong. If I had just acted on my instincts."

"It's useless to berate yourself, Guylan. You'd never have figured it out because we all thought Mortimer was gone for good."

Guylan sighed. "With Quentin's intervention from the afterlife, he is now. I saw with my own eyes Mortimer's body dissolve to ashes and be placed under lock, key and the watchful eyes of a Druid."

"And that's good news. Mortimer can never return."

"But the bad news is Andy might have his buddies locked up in jail." He sighed. "At this point Andy's keeping them drugged, but that's not going to keep a demon down forever."

"No, that's not likely." Xavior's eyes met his. "You know what needs to be done, son."

Guylan swiped the tip of his tongue over the raven mark branded on the inside of his cheek. "I guess the only way to fix this is if I time travel again to stop the car accident. If Ronnie's brain was never damaged, he couldn't be a target for Mortimer."

"That would save Ronnie, but the fact still remains Mortimer wasn't entirely dissolved by my efforts and could still resurface at another time."

"Like he did now," Guylan said.

Xavior nodded. "And what Quentin did in that basement last night would be undone...things changed again."

"Then I need to stop Mortimer, as well as the accident." He frowned. "How am I ever going to manage that?"

"When you return to the time when you're an eight-year-old, talk with Quentin. He'll know what to do," Xavior advised.

"Will you come with me to Olena's, be the energy I need on this end of the attic portal?"

"Of course," Xavior agreed, standing. He looked at the pile of screens. "I should have marked which went where. Would have saved a lot of time."

"Time. It's always about time, how it's saved, how it plays out, how it's changed."

Xavior handed him three screens and he took three. "We'll start with these." He made his way to the stairs and then turned to face Guylan. "You can't blame yourself for what's happened."

Guylan frowned, annoyed. "Well, who else is there to blame, Dad? I was the one who changed everything around."

"All this is Mortimer's fault, son—his greed, his bad choices are the reasons for the entire mess."

"But if I had done the job right the first time—"

"If I remember correctly, I'm the one who fought Mortimer," Xavior interjected. "Any blame, if there is any, falls on my head."

"You did what you thought had to be done."

"Exactly," Xavior said. "And now, you'll go in and do what has to be done again."

"And down the road, screw up something else, right?"

"All any of us can do is our best as each circumstance arises, Guylan. Anything more would be speculation."

"Are you two going to get moving sometime today?" DeYonna called from the top of the stairs.

Xavior arched a brow. "And right now, all we can do is put up the screens."

Forty-one

Guylan kept his mother occupied in the kitchen while Xavior called Olena. He wasn't privileged to hear the conversation, or what his father divulged, having to eat a plate of apple cobbler his mother insisted on rewarding him with for his help. It didn't matter much, anyway, how Xavior gained access for him to step through the frame of the attic portal, as long as he could get the job done.

The plan was to meet his father at Olena's around six o'clock, when Andy, Keira and the children would be at a friend's home for dinner. He decided he wanted Nela to be the co-energy force with his father, and arrived at her house around three to explain what he planned to do.

"Then you're going back...you're really going back in time," she said, her voice trembling as she spoke.

"It's the only way, babe, to fix this. And by no means is it over, especially if a few of Mortimer's demons are locked up in jail." He glanced at his watch. "We've enough time for me to do the research I need in order to land in the right decade." He pointed to her laptop. "I'd like to get online and search the Anglewood, New York archive site so I can pinpoint the exact time and date of Ronnie's accident."

Nela sat at the desk and booted up the computer.

Guylan swiped a chair from the kitchen and joined her. "Sister Margaret once told me Ronnie's accident happened during the summer of 1977, in front of Shirley's Ice Cream Emporium."

Nela typed in her password and turned the screen toward Guylan. "There you go, she's all yours."

He smiled. "Funny you should use the female persona for your laptop."

"Women get the job done, and this little unit," she gave the computer a loving pat, "never lets me down."

He laughed. "And what gender is the printer?"

"Why, a male of course. It only works when the laptop tells it what to do," Nela teased.

He reached out and tickled her side, happy to momentarily think of something other than the difficult and serious task lying ahead of him. "You're just asking for it, lady."

She giggled and kissed the tip of his nose. "Any way I can, sir."

Oh, how he wished he'd had the time to deepen that kiss, take her into the bedroom and shower her with them all over her pregnant body. He loved the passion they shared, as well as the playful banter. Nela was so versatile, stepping into each situation with a strength and gusto he admired.

She directed his attention back to the laptop. "But first things first."

Having her by his side boosted his confidence, meant the world to him. "Thanks for going through this with me, babe."

"I wouldn't have it any other way, Guylan."

He typed in the words *Anglewood, New York fatal car accidents for 1977* and a list of articles appeared. Narrowing it down to the summer months, his search brought up a newspaper clipping for August 27th. "It had been a warm Saturday, according to this article, and the victims, Phyllis and Stanley Fargus, and their eight-year-old son, Ronald, were just exiting Shirley's Ice Cream Emporium on Kelton Avenue at 5:00 p.m.," he read aloud.

"Go on," Nela urged.

"The Fargus family entered their parked car by 5:06 p.m., but never had a chance, according to witnesses, to drive off. Just as they started the ignition, a truck came barreling around a corner and sideswiped them, killing both Phyllis and Stanley in the front seat. Ronald, seated in the back seat, was injured on impact. He was rushed to Shire Downs Medical Center and for several days listed in critical condition, after having received a severe head injury."

"That's pretty much what you already knew, except for the exact time and date," Nela said.

"Yeah, you're right. The rest of the article goes on about the truck driver, Jerome Bates, who resided at Sixty-three Easthouse Road. He passed out at the wheel and didn't remember a thing. He woke up in the hospital two days later to discover both legs broken, along with a few ribs and his jaw."

Nela moved closer to the screen. "Does the article say he was living with an illness of some sort, or under the influence of anything that would cause him to faint?"

Guylan scanned the article further. "As a matter of fact, he had an impeccable driving record, wasn't a drug or alcohol user. His unconsciousness was something that shocked everyone. Just three days prior to the accident, Jerome Bates had had a complete and thorough medical examination, as required by Hanson and Hanson Trucking Firm, his employers. He was found to be in perfect health at the age of thirty-five and had just celebrated twelve years of service with the company."

"Hmm, not someone who would lose control of himself or the vehicle he was driving," Nela concluded.

"No, it doesn't seem likely."

"Then what does it seem, Guylan?"

He sighed. "What's racing through my mind right now, Nela, is that Jerome Bates was compromised somehow by an outside source."

"Like Mortimer?"

He nodded, dragging his eyes from the screen to gaze deep into hers.

She chewed on her bottom lip. "This just gets worse and worse."

Guylan leaned back in his seat and crossed his arms over his chest. "The plot does thicken."

Nela searched his face. "So, you not only have to stop the accident, but deal with whatever possessed Jerome Bates."

"I'm afraid that's what needs to be done."

"And can you do that, Guylan?"

He sighed again. "I'm going to give it my best shot. There are too many lives at stake not to."

Her face paled. "What about your life?"

He pulled her close. "I'll be fine, babe. I've got Quentin and my father in my corner."

"And me," she whispered against his throat.

He chuckled. "Especially you." She pulled back to look at him and he cast a brave smile. "Let's go now to meet my father."

~ * ~

Olena was a bit taken aback to see I was accompanying Guylan. "You know everything, too?" she said, opening the door to welcome me. I remained silent, just gave her a nod and a smile. She led the three of us to the attic. Before Olena left the room, she looked deep into my eyes. "You are truly an anchor, Nela."

I squeezed her hand. "You're all my family now, too." My answer pleased her, and she smiled, satisfied.

Xavior made his way over to a velvet curtain hanging from the ceiling and slipped behind it to change. When he returned, he wore a stole of pure white over another virgin white gown. It was the whitest white I'd ever seen. So bright and pure was the material, it shocked my eyes, and I blinked a few times to get them to focus. The gown was fastened by a girdle and at the center of the wide waist adornment sat a crystal encased in gold. Around his neck he wore a breastplate, below the plate a jewel suspended in the shape of a serpent. Upon his head he wore a gold tiara, and on his fingers, he wore a plain gold ring and a chain ring. I was quite impressed.

"Now, what other girl can say her future father-in-law is so dynamic?"

His cheeks blushed a bit and he chuckled. "I could say the same about my daughter-in-law to be."

My own face warmed and I smiled.

Xavior got comfortable on the chair at the large desk, setting out a candle and several large quartz crystals. I guessed this was how he'd connect his energy to Guylan's.

I sat cross-legged on the floor. I hadn't brought the cedar wood box. There'd be no way I could get reception on Guylan's travels to the past anyway, since the rimless glasses dealt with those events happening in the here and now, or the things to come. My ability was on a different frequency, but to be in the room with Xavior while Guylan traveled meant a lot to Guylan...as it did to me.

I watched Guylan strip to the bone. Even in the buff he stood with a commanding air of self-confidence. I hoped he held the same assurance within as he did without. I certainly wasn't as brave. My pulse quickened and my stomach clenched with uncertainty. I worried for his safety, and for the outcome of what he was about to do. Not only could things change for Ronnie Fargus, but for the rest of us as well. If Guylan wasn't absolutely precise in his dealings, I could wake tomorrow to discover him gone from my life. Even though I wouldn't realize he was missing, I'm sure I'd feel some sort of loss. I caressed my belly, where my babies slept. They'd be gone, too.

Guylan made his way to the desk, chest broad and muscular, his body beautifully proportioned. He removed the raven ring from his finger and handed it to his father, who in turn placed it in the center of the crystal circle. For a moment, he glanced down at the stones, the clear-cut line of his profile dark against the candlelight of the room. All of him kindled with a sort of passionate beauty as he moved to position himself in front of a large bookshelf.

His long, sinewy legs spread wide, bracing his male physique as he made himself ready for departure. Pointing to a wall sconce beside the bookcase he said, "Give it a pull, Nela."

Acutely aware of him, of every fiber and muscle in his body, I stood and did as I was asked. To my surprise, the shelves slid aside to reveal a portal. I glanced inside the dark tunnel, which reminded me of a haunted house carnival ride. I shivered and stepped away.

Guylan took a calming breath, relaxed his arms to his sides and spread his long, lean fingers.

"Are you ready, son?" Xavior inquired.

He neared the portal. "I'm ready."

My heart raced as Xavior chanted words I didn't understand.

Guylan walked through the frame and a burst of light shot out of the tunnel. So intense was the glare, it knocked me to the floor. When I sat up, he was gone; the portal had swallowed him up and closed behind him. I got to my feet and turned toward Xavior, needing reassurance Guylan would be able to return through the closed portal once the mission was completed. But my father-in-law to be's garments were aglow; the stones hummed and the candle's flame danced from side to side, growing in length. He was connected to Guylan, and I dared not speak to him for fear I'd break the link.

My stomach lurched and the room spun. I knelt on the Oriental carpet, placing my head between my knees to keep from fainting. Xavior needed his attention on guiding Guylan, not on reviving me. I swallowed hard and set my mind on the journey taking place. Time travel, imagine such a thing! I straightened my posture and glanced at the wall where the portal had opened, awed by the fact this very room housed a time machine.

My energy returned with anticipation for the adventure I was privileged to be a part of and I whispered to myself, "H.G. Wells, eat your heart out."

Forty-two

Guylan's anatomy shrank to the size of an eight-year-old boy. The pain, the strange sensations, weren't as frightening as the first time he had stepped through the portal, but he still remained cautious, keeping his tongue pressed on the raven brand in his cheek and his eyes tightly shut until he landed.

He set his arrival at August 25th, 1977...a Thursday, two days before Ronnie Fargus's accident. In this way, he would have the opportunity to become acquainted with his surroundings and the time to seek help from Xavior and Quentin.

His passage came to a halt before he'd expected, his body landing on something hard. The sound of a little girl's giggling met his ears. He opened his eyes to find himself sitting naked on a bench beside the family's first pool, the old above-ground only three feet deep. His sister Audra, at that time twelve, and four-year-old twins, Keira and Kendra, we're pointing at him and giggling.

"Mom, Guylan's decided to skinny-dip and took off his swim trunks," Audra called out from the lounge chair she occupied.

Totally humiliated, Guylan looked around for a means to cover his body. Spotting a towel nearby, he quickly wrapped it around his waist.

His mother, stomach bulging with another pregnancy—he mentally calculated it would be Egan she carried this time—stepped from the concrete patio and made her way toward him. Grabbing him by the arm, she gave him a quick, hard slap on his bottom, which caused his sisters to giggle again, and led him into the house. Darby, the family's Jack Russell, only a year old, danced behind them and barked.

"What in heaven's name possessed you to remove your clothes?" She didn't wait for an answer, but pointed to the stairs with her full lips pinched. "Whatever the reason, you can tell me when your father gets home. We'll have a discussion then about this rude behavior. Now, get to your room and stay there until dinner."

He hesitated, taking in his mother's form: rounded belly, breasts full and heavy. He'd only known of each sibling's birth, the event recorded in his mind as he traveled through time. Never had he actually seen his mother in full-blown, pregnant mode. She was absolutely radiant, complexion pink and vibrant, hair thick and shining, her eyes glowing...although that could be due to her outrage with his actions. He wanted to tell her how beautiful she was, standing in her bare feet, toes painted orange, the cotton sundress delicately draping over the magnificent changes of her body.

Would Nela look like this as her pregnancy progresse...soft, supple, and sexy?

DeYonna placed her hands on her hips. "What on earth are you staring at?"

"You," he said, his voice a mere whisper.

She caressed her belly. "Yes, well, I know. I'm a bit of a whale right now."

"I think you're beautiful."

She stifled a smile. "Flattery will not win you a reprieve, young man."

He neared her, wrapping his arms around her large middle and placing his head on her belly. Egan kicked, socking him in the ear.

DeYonna chuckled. "Even the baby is upset with you today."

He raised his gaze to his mother's and smiled. "When will he come?"

"*He*, you say?" She shook her head. "Just like your father. He keeps hoping for a boy, too," she mused. "I guess I can't blame you two...you're outnumbered by females." She pushed a strand of hair from his eyes. "In three weeks, this baby arrives." She sighed. "And I have so much to do beforehand...get the crib set up in your room, make sure you and Audra go shopping for school clothes, the twins set for preschool." She shook her head again. "I'm exhausted just thinking about it all."

He frowned. "The baby's sleeping in my room?"

"We've gone through this before, Guylan."

"Why can't I have the room off the family room?" he suggested. "It's just used for storage now."

She rubbed his shoulders. "You're too little to be so far away from your parents at night."

"I am not," he argued.

DeYonna's eyes narrowed. "A boy who takes off his swimsuit in front of his sisters is a boy who cannot be trusted to sleep two flights of stairs away from his mother and father."

"I promise that will never happen again," he vowed.

"You promised if you got a library card like Audra, you'd remember to return the books on time." She frowned down at him. "I had to pay the late fee."

"This time I mean it."

Her eyes widened. "So do I."

He knew when to cut his losses. "Okay, the baby can sleep in my room."

His mother kissed the top of his head. "It was never your decision, love." She then reached down and yanked away the towel from around his waist. "This is full of sand and not allowed in the bedroom. Next, I'll have ants."

He gasped, covering his tiny male member with his hands. "Mom!"

She put her hands on her hips. "Oh, now you're modest?" She pointed to the stairs. "Go put your clothes on, and if I ever catch that butt of yours bare again, other than to be in the tub or on the toilet, I'm reddening it so you can't sit down."

He took the stairs two at a time with Darby at his heels, ran to his room and shut the door behind him. Darby jumped on the bed and barked.

"See the risks of time travel," he mumbled. "You never know where you'll land without your clothes."

~ * ~

True to her word, his mother set a time aside, after the twins were in bed and Audra was engrossed in a television show, to gather Guylan and his father for the discussion of pool lewdness.

Closing the den door, DeYonna turned to her husband. "Guylan's behavior today at the pool can't continue, Xavior. The girls shouldn't see their brother naked. None of them are babies anymore." She narrowed her eyes at Guylan. "He needs to be a gentleman. Skinny-dipping is not an option in this house."

Xavior stifled the smile threatening to come. "Your mother's right, of course, Guylan. You aren't allowed in the pool without swim trunks."

"I think his punishment should be no more pool privileges for the rest of the summer," DeYonna decided.

Xavior crossed his arms over his broad chest. "I agree with your mother."

Guylan gave a taut nod, not really upset over their decision. He'd be leaving this era as soon as his mission was accomplished, anyway. And he wasn't concerned for his child counterpart's feelings on the matter, since there were only a few weeks of good swim weather left in the season.

DeYonna stood, extending a hand to Guylan. "It's time for your bath and then bed."

"Could I have a moment alone with Dad?"

She nodded and held up a finger. "Not too long, though."

"I understand," he said, watching her leave the room.

"Come here, Guylan." Xavior gestured for him to hop up on his knee.

Guylan obeyed.

His father braced his face between the large palms of his hands and searched his eyes. "Why have you come again?"

"It's not what you think. Our family isn't involved this time... well, not directly."

"Then who is, Guylan?"

He went on to explain the situation to his father.

Xavior took an audible breath. "So, I didn't vanquish the scoundrel correctly the first time."

Guylan placed a small hand on his father's shoulder. "It couldn't be helped. None of us knew Mortimer could resurface after his shape-shifting form was destroyed."

Xavior studied his son. "How do you get here each time you've come?"

He had explained to his father the attic portal's time travel process before, when he stepped into 1985, but since Xavior hadn't experienced that visit yet, Guylan gave him a recap. First, he explained about his orphanage days, divulged his true age and present occupation. He told Xavior about Nela and her family's tie to Quentin. Then he showed Xavior the raven brand and explained how the attic portal worked.

"And you can't travel wearing clothes. Threads from the material can slow you down or keep you trapped in limbo. That's why I popped up naked on the backyard bench," Guylan concluded.

"Ah, so you're taking a hit for the cause," Xavior mused.

"I guess you could say that."

"Amazing...effing amazing," Xavior mumbled.

It was how his father had reacted in 1985. "To experience it is even more so," Guylan added.

"I can only imagine." Xavior shook his head to clear it. "Well, we'd better work fast, then. I think you need to talk to Quentin next."

He nodded in agreement.

"I've taken tomorrow off from work, planned to take Quentin out for breakfast." Xavior smiled. "As my mentor, it's something I like to do for him every last Friday of the month."

"That's real nice, Dad."

"I guess this Friday you'll be joining us, Guylan."

He nodded again.

"Quentin likes an early breakfast; I usually leave the house at six."

"I'll be ready," Guylan promised.

"Not if you don't go now and get bathed, then hop right into bed. I need you to be awake, alert and ready to leave with me."

"Bathed...I still get bathed...by whom?" Though his life had downloaded in his brain as he traveled through time, snippets of things, here and there, seemed to get lost.

Xavior's brow rose higher. "Who do you think?"

His eyes widened. "Mom?"

"I'm afraid so." Xavior threw his head back and laughed. "I imagine it's going to be quite embarrassing for you now."

He frowned. "Could you, maybe, ask her to let me bathe myself, for just tonight?"

"You don't mess with a woman's routine, especially a hormonal woman, son. Anyway, she has a valid reason," Xavior said.

"What's that?"

"She does the laundry and your underwear is constantly stained with skid-marks. She wants to make sure you're at least scrubbed clean at bath time." He set Guylan on his feet. "But here's a simple solution, and a bit of advice."

"I can hardly wait to hear."

Xavior gave Guylan's backside a playful slap. "In the future, learn to wipe your arse better and your mother won't have to wash it."

~ * ~

The next morning, Guylan sat silent in his father's car on the way to pick up Quentin. Granted, having Xavior and Quentin in his corner was a definite plus, but Mortimer was evil, diabolical, a worthy and fearsome opponent. The idea of dealing with him again was anything but appealing. In fact, it sickened him throughout every fiber of his being.

Xavior cast him a glance. "Have courage, son. You're not alone in this."

"I know. It's just I'm not looking forward to facing Mortimer again on any plane," he stated flatly.

Xavior sighed. "Me either, but you've come all this way to do the job right this time, so you might as well buckle up, grin and bear it." He chuckled. "Anyway, you've probably endured the worst of your trip already."

He frowned. "I'm not following you, Dad."

"Your bath adventure," Xavior teased, his lips spreading into a smirk. "I've watched your mother clean her children and know what you were subjected to."

His face heated with the memory of his mother washing every private part he owned. "She wields a washcloth well, knows how to thoroughly scrub a child. I'll give her that," he mumbled.

Xavior threw his head back and laughed. "Thanks to her, you now sparkle where the sun doesn't shine."

He frowned. "I'm glad my predicament amuses you."

His father chuckled again. "I'd have thought the first time you traveled back would have been more humiliating for you. You weren't quite toilet trained then, at least by your mother's version."

"It was very humiliating at first, but then I sort of fell into the plan."

"What's the reason you're having more of a problem fitting in now?" Xavior said.

"I think two things might be the answer to that question." Guylan paused a moment to collect the right words. "First, a time traveler has to be very careful not to get too caught up in the era he's visiting. If that happens…if he really begins to believe he belongs, he can never return to his own time."

"And that would alter his life and those around him to a crucial degree," Xavior concluded.

"Exactly," he agreed.

Xavior's interest mounted. "So what precautions are taken?"

"The time traveler must draw energy from his own time in order to stay grounded. When I traveled to 1972, Quentin was my wingman, in a sense. He joined forces with my energy so I'd have a path to the future to follow when I was ready to leave the past. Another energy booster is being in the presence of someone you knew both in the past and future. Since I didn't know you and Mom, or Audra, my only anchor was Olena. But her presence wasn't constant, so my awareness of my own time wasn't as sharp. I was able to tolerate being in a three-year-old's body. But now, in the future, I know you, Mom, and my sisters, so on this trip I'm crystal clear as to who I am, my real age and where I belong."

"And what's the second part to your answer?"

Guylan sighed. "The first time back, I was enamored with the love and security of family life. Growing up in an orphanage, void of parents and a home to call your own, isn't an ideal childhood. I found myself actually enjoying the closeness and the opportunity to fall in love with all of you." He smiled. "Mom's care, her love and attention, her tenderness...it all moved me. Having you around, someone smart and strong to count on, being held in your protective arms, was wonderful."

"So, because you were so content, whatever came with the territory, you readily accepted," Xavior acknowledged.

"Yes," Guylan said. "I actually relished the time and took the memories with me into the future to help mold my new existence."

"Who is your wingman now?"

"You are, Dad."

Xavior smiled. "Tell me, how do I look in my later years?"

He chuckled. "You're dashing, distinguished, and Mom's still completely in love with you."

Xavior's smile deepened. "Well now, a guy can't ask for anything better than that, now can he?"

For the rest of the drive to Quentin's house, Xavior remained silent. Guylan knew his father was lost in quiet contemplation. But his own thoughts weren't as comforting, as they returned to Ronnie Fargus, Mortimer and the job he had ahead of him.

Forty-three

It was always good to set eyes on his great-grandfather. He thought the years when Quentin had trained him, bestowed upon him the family gift, were some of the best that he had lived...or remembered he had lived.

Quentin took Guylan's seat beside Xavior, and Guylan took a seat behind him, the elderly man turning to cast him a wide smile. "'Tis good to see ye, lad, even better to have ye along this mornin'." Quentin searched his face. "But I'm seein' a change in ye, and for sure I will be wantin' an explanation while I sip me first cup of coffee."

"It's why I brought Guylan today, Grandfather. There is a lot to tell you," Xavior said, putting the car in drive and heading for the diner.

Bebe's Diner on Larken Street wasn't much to look at from the outside. Resembling a large silver bullet, Bebe's sat at the edge of town in the factory and warehouse district. A different sort of clientele patronized Bebe's—truck drivers, graveyard shift workers and traveling salesmen. You wouldn't find white-haired ladies on a luncheon or mothers and their babies at Bebe's. They went to Gretchen's Dinette, an upscale eatery on Swallow Street. But in spite of Bebe's uncovered, red Formica tables, shabbily upholstered booths, juke box, and plain white china, the strawberry pancakes smothered in maple syrup were to die for.

Quentin rolled his eyes heavenward after taking a sip of his coffee. "Such a jolt this brew gives a body." He smiled. "The blacker the better, I always say." His eyes rested on Xavior's cup. "Let the *wean* try a wee bit o' yers, Xavior. 'Twill put hair on his chest, for sure."

"That's just what his mother needs to see, her son's lily-white torso covered in hair," Xavior said, pointing to the orange juice for Guylan to drink instead.

"Och, 'tis time yer dear wife let the lad stand on his own two feet." Quentin narrowed his eyes at him. "Tell me, Guylan, are ye washin' yer own arse yet?"

Guylan's face heated. "What, the whole family knows about that?" He turned an accusing eye on his father.

Xavior raised his hands in surrender. "Don't blame me. I haven't said a word."

"'Tis the females in the family doin' the talkin', yer mother and Olena," Quentin said with a chuckle. "But *dinna fash*, do not trouble yerself, *mo ghile*, me lad. Yer predicament is safe with me."

He sighed and drank the rest of his orange juice.

At that moment, the waitress, a thin woman wearing too much bright pink lipstick, brought their order.

Quentin pushed aside the strawberries long enough to spread butter on his pancakes, and then smother them with maple syrup. "Now, suppose ye tell me what goes on here?"

Guylan took a mouthful of his own breakfast before he explained his mission.

Quentin chewed his food slowly, eyes narrowing as he pondered the situation. "'T'would seem to me we have got to address this from two sides, that o' the lad Ronnie, and the truck driver. First, I will be buyin' ye a kite today and come tomorrow noon ye and yer grandfather Zack will be flyin' it in the park across from Shirley's Ice Cream Emporium. He and I have talked o' this before, flyin' kites with ye. So 'twill be a grand time for it to happen, not causin' a drop of suspicion as to why it need be tomorrow. Near to the given time of the accident, Guylan, ye will somehow keep the lad Ronnie and his parents from enterin' their car."

"That sounds like a good plan," he agreed.

"Do ye have the driver's home address, Guylan?" Quentin said, popping another piece of pancake in his mouth.

"Sixty-three Easthouse Road," he supplied, also revealing Jerome Bates' place of employment.

"Yer da and I will take care o' things from that end," Quentin concluded with a smile. "Now, eat up before yer meal grows cold."

~ * ~

On the drive home, a weight had been lifted from Guylan's heart. With his father and Quentin at the helm, the job ahead would be a lot easier.

His mother and sisters were in the pool when he returned, laughing and splashing. It was like soup outside, steam radiating off the asphalt, and the cool water looked appetizing. He wished he could jump in and be refreshed along with the rest of them, but his punishment for skinny-dipping was no more pool privileges.

DeYonna, catching the dejected look on his face, stood. The water dripped from her round belly, as she made her way to a towel draped over a lawn chair. Patting herself dry, she sympathized with him. "I'm sorry you can't join in, but we agreed there would be no more swimming."

"I know," he said, sitting on the bench.

"But there was nothing said about running through the sprinkler," his mother added.

He smiled.

DeYonna laughed. "Run upstairs and get your swimsuit on and Daddy will set it up for you."

He didn't have to be asked twice. Racing up to his room to change, his heart skipped a beat with joy and love for his family. If he'd ever had any doubts his time traveling should have never occurred, it had all vanished within the last few moments. He was very glad—electrified with happiness to be exact—he was able to change the past.

While running through the sprinkler with his sisters, eating Sloppy Joes at the picnic table and even having his mother bathe him, he marveled over having another opportunity to be a kid again. When his mother tucked him into bed, he reached out to hug her around the neck.

"Thanks for finding another way to let me cool off. It made me very happy."

She kissed the tip of his nose. "All any parent wants is their children's happiness." She smiled. "One day, you'll find that out for yourself."

He knew it would be sooner than his mother believed.

~ * ~

Grandpa Zack showed up around noon dressed in a dark blue shirt and knee-length shorts. His tanned face was all smiles as he led Guylan by the hand to the car.

"I've wanted to have time with you, Guylan. My grandfather took me kite flying when I was a boy, and I relish the memory." He looked up at the blue sky, licked his pointer finger and held it in the air. "There's a good wind brewing, should be a great day to fly a kite." He laughed. "And when someone tells you to *go fly a kite*, instead of getting mad, you'll recall today."

The hellish heat broke and the summer afternoon proved it couldn't be better for such an activity. The park wasn't crowded, just a few mothers with their children sitting on blankets playing or pushing them on the swings. Guylan and Zack moved to an open space away from the trees and jungle gym. The kite swooped into the air, and Guylan ran with the ball of string while his grandfather urged him on. He was exhilarated, the wind whipping at his face and playing with his hair. His little legs, strong and well formed, carried him with ease past the rose garden, around the fountain, and back to where Zack sat on a bench watching.

But in the midst of all his fun, he kept an eye on the large clock above the Cromwell Insurance Company building across the street, adjacent to Shirley's Ice Cream Emporium. When the large timepiece read four-thirty, he reeled in his kite and sat beside his grandfather.

"All tired out, are you?" Zack said, gathering the kite and string together.

"I'm kind of thirsty." Guylan gazed over at the ice cream store. "How about we go for an ice cream soda?"

"Well now, that sounds really good to me," Zack agreed.

They made their way together to the edge of the park, and as they waited at the crosswalk for the light to change, a large, black Cadillac Coupe deVille pulled up and parked on the corner. A tall man with red hair and glasses stepped out, and then ran around to the passenger side of the car and opened the door for his wife. She also was quite tall, with frizzy brown hair, cut short to her ears and a sharp, Roman-type nose. While she slipped the strap of her purse over her shoulder, the man pushed forward the passenger seat, allowing the boy sitting in the back to climb out.

Guylan recognized Ronnie Fargus the second the child emerged from the car. Searching Ronnie's face, he was surprised to see a beautiful calm upon it. The snarling, hard to handle, always frowning Ronnie was nowhere to be found in this boy's features.

The three walked over to where he and Zack stood, waiting to cross with them. Ronnie stood between his parents, holding onto each of their hands, and cast a quick glance at Guylan. "We're going for an ice cream."

"We are too," Guylan responded.

Ronnie looked up at his father with adoration. "And I'm getting a big cone this time, like my father has, right, Daddy?"

Mr. Fargus chuckled. "That's right, Ronald." He frowned playfully. "Do you think you'll be able to eat it all?"

"If he can't, he can't, Stanley," Mrs. Fargus said, releasing Ronnie's hand long enough to push an auburn, wayward curl from his forehead. "I don't want him getting a stomach ache."

"But I can, Mama, honest I can," Ronnie argued, taking her hand again.

Guylan's heart went out to Ronnie. Never had he seen him so happy, so at ease and content. Losing his parents, suffering a head trauma, then being possessed by Mortimer had been too intense to happen to one small boy in one beautiful summer afternoon.

The signal changed, permitting them all to cross. Guylan and Zack followed Ronnie and his parents into the shop. The line moved quickly, so Ronnie and his folks were headed with their ice cream order back to their car at exactly ten minutes to five. Guylan knew unless Xavior and Quentin had in some way detained Jerome Bates, at 5:06, he'd be driving an out-of-control truck around the corner and barreling it into the Farguses' car.

Guylan broke from the line and headed for the street, in spite of his grandfather's shouts for him to return. At the crosswalk, he slammed into Ronnie, knocking him to the ground. A shocked Ronnie landed on his large, strawberry-filled cone, smashing it into his chest.

Mrs. Fargus screamed and reached for Ronnie, who was crying and dripping with ice cream.

Mr. Fargus grabbed Guylan by the arm and set him on his feet. "What on earth possessed you, boy, to do such a thing?"

If you only knew what would have possessed your son, you'd be kissing me right now instead of being angry.

From that point on, everything happened fast.

Zack joined them, kite and string twisted in his hands. Mr. Fargus insisted Guylan was out of control and something should be done about it before he grew into an insolent teenager. Zack apologized for his grandson's behavior, took him by the arm and led him over to the large trash container, where he angrily discarded the kite and string.

Ronnie was hysterical by this time, crying over his ruined ice cream cone. Mrs. Fargus soothed her son, leading him back into the shop to clean Ronnie's shirt and buy him another cone. Mr. Fargus followed his wife and son, but his angry glare was still on Guylan. Zack then led his grandson to the crosswalk.

Guylan glanced up at the big clock. It read 5:06, and Jerome Bates' truck was nowhere in sight. He sighed, relieved his father and Quentin had been successful in stopping the accident from their end. But his relief grew short lived when he glanced up at his grandfather.

Zack's face looked like a red balloon, ready to pop. Blue veins stood out on his neck like street lines on a road map. His grip on Guylan's arm increased as he marched him to the car. He started the ignition and they drove away in silence.

Guylan was sorry for the way his day with his grandfather had to end. He would have loved to explain things, but that wasn't possible.

"I'm sorry, Grandpa," he mumbled.

Zack kept his eyes on the road, while the muscles in his jaw throbbed.

Guylan was surprised to see his grandfather had brought him to the mansion instead of back to his own home. When the car stopped in the circular driveway, Zack leaned over the front of him and opened the door. "Wait for me in my den."

He didn't dare protest. On his way into the house, he scanned the length of the driveway for Xavior and Olena's cars. Neither was in site. Making his way through the double doors and to Zack's den, he was suddenly tired and resentful. Now he'd hear a lecture from his grandfather about his bad behavior. Coupled with his naked stunt on the bench, his mother was really going to hit the ceiling. And none of what had happened was because he was out of control. His father and Quentin would understand perfectly his reasons, except they couldn't say anything on his behalf without explaining the whole situation—something they couldn't do either. In the end, Guylan's mother and grandfather would be left thinking wrong of him, and that hurt.

Looks like I take another one for the cause.

Zack entered the den, took a seat on the large stuffed chair and motioned for Guylan to sit on the matching sofa. He obeyed, looking down at the hands he had clasped in his lap.

Zack cleared his throat. "Did your father ever tell you of the time he threw a ball through the window after I warned him not to play so close to the house?"

He nodded without looking up.

"The glass completely shattered, hitting your grandmother, who was sitting nearby, in the forehead. The wound needed stitches."

Guylan remembered Xavior explaining the incident.

"Do you know how I addressed the situation when Grandma and I returned from the hospital?"

He raised his gaze to meet Zack's. "Yes, my father told me."

"He never disobeyed me again, Guylan. And now he's a fine man, a pillar of the community, a good father and husband."

Guyan swallowed hard. "I agree."

"But he might not have turned out so well if I had allowed him to run amok, not suffer the consequences for his actions." His grandfather sighed. "It is because I love him dearly that I did what I did." Zack searched his face. "And I love you just as much."

Guylan shifted in his seat, not liking the way the conversation was headed.

Zack stood, moving to stand in front of the desk, and raised his foot to rest on a nearby ottoman. "Come here, Guylan."

He stood, hesitating.

Zack pointed to the floor beside him, his tone calm but sharp. "Stand here, now."

His heart raced as he stepped closer.

In one fluid motion, Zack bent him over a bony knee and punished his lower posterior with the palm of his hand. Guylan choked back the sobs as his bottom grew raw and hot with the discipline being dealt. When his grandfather was done, he was ordered to walk to the car. He did as he was told in silence, grimacing with pain as his bottom met the car seat.

"I see no need to bother your mother with this. I want nothing to upset her at this stage of her pregnancy. But I will be talking with your father." Zack glanced over at him. "Are we in agreement over this decision?"

"Yes," Guylan choked out, humiliated beyond all measure.

"And am I right in assuming neither your father nor I will ever have to use such tactics to keep you in line again?"

He nodded once more.

"Good," Zack said and started the car.

Again, silence as Zack drove him home. He kept his gaze out the window, realizing history really did repeat itself, even when it had been changed. This was the second time in his life he'd had his ass reddened because of Ronnie Fargus.

Forty-four

Guylan was quiet during dinner, his spirits at an all-time low. He was pleased the Ronnie Fargus mission was a success, but was not happy over the way he had appeared to his grandfather. It broke his heart to think Zack thought less of him. And sitting on the hard kitchen chair with a throbbing backside wasn't pleasant either. He went up to his room early, forfeiting family game night.

His mother felt his forehead with her lips. "You're not running a temperature, are you?"

He shook his head.

She searched his face. "But you always love game night, and we're playing your favorite, Monopoly."

Guylan shrugged. "I'm just tired is all." He forced a smile. "I think I'll read a few comics and then get to sleep." In truth, it was time for him to move on.

His mother kissed him on the cheek. "I'll send Daddy up in a while to see how you're doing."

He nodded. "I'll wait for him, then."

She ruffled his hair. "Where else would you go, honey?"

He shrugged again and made his way to his room.

Xavior came upstairs an hour later and took a seat on the edge of the bed. Guylan was lying on his belly. His father gave his bottom a gentle pat and he flinched.

"Still a bit tender?" Xavior probed.

He turned onto his side and glanced at his father. "Grandpa told you?"

Xavior's tone softened. "I'm so sorry, son, you had to go through that."

"It wasn't as bad as when Father Samuel did it," Guylan said, and explained to his father the beating he had endured by the orphanage's priest for fighting with Ronnie.

Xavior frowned. "You realize Grandpa did what he did out of love for you, not to humiliate or degrade you."

"I do, but still..." he let his voice trail off.

"In his time, Guylan, that's how parents dealt with a misbehaving child."

Guylan sighed. "In the time I left to come here, what Zack did to me would be considered child abuse."

Xavior arched a brow. "I'm not in favor of the way my father dealt with the situation, and I told him so when we talked. I also told him he should have left the discipline up to me. But I wouldn't go so far as to classify his actions as child abuse."

"Then you will have a rude awakening, Dad."

Xavior took an audible breath. "I guess I'll learn to handle things as they come, Guylan."

"How about letting me in on how Quentin and you handled Mortimer?"

Xavior climbed onto the bed and stuffed a pillow beneath his head. "After we found where Jerome Bates lived, we followed him to the trucking company. While Mr. Bates went into the office to collect his daily schedule, Quentin and I hopped into the back of his truck, which wasn't all that easy for Quentin, and hid in the back of the cab."

Guylan snuggled closer to his father. "Then what happened?"

"We positioned ourselves near the front seat, and peered out from the curtain. Around four-forty-five, as Bates neared the scene of Ronnie's accident, thick, black smoke began to seep from the radiator vent. Jerome pulled the truck to a stop on a side street, and slumped forward in a dead sleep."

His eyes widened. "Did Mortimer appear?"

"Right before our eyes, and he didn't expect to see us emerging from the back of the cab."

"How'd you get him this time?"

"Quentin recited the incantation while I aimed the raven ring at his heart." Xavior shifted onto his back, staring up at the ceiling. "And then something inside of me exploded, and out of my mouth shot a ray of fire. The flame reduced Mortimer to nothing more than a heap of ashes." Xavior swallowed hard. "My throat's still raspy."

"It will be for quite a while," Guylan offered. "I vanquished him in the same way in my time." He frowned. "But he wasn't in bird form, was he?"

Xavior turned to look at him. "No, he was in human form this time, and never again will he harm another."

"How can you be so sure of that?"

"After I dissolved him, Quentin called upon the Keeper of Evil Souls, and within a matter of seconds, the truck cab filled with a glowing, white light. In its midst appeared a beautiful woman, with flaming red hair and piercing green eyes. She gathered Mortimer's ashes into an urn, sealed the top and took him away."

"And what happened to Jerome Bates?"

"He woke up and continued on his route, arriving back to the truck terminal at his usual time. When he left to punch his card, Quentin and I exited the back of the cab and came home."

Guylan sighed, relieved. "Then it's over. We did it."

Xavior chuckled. "That we did."

He hugged his father. "Thanks, Dad, for all your help."

Xavior's strong arms embraced him. "Will you be off now?"

"I've a stop to make first, to when I was sixteen. Ronnie's life change also alters a few other people's I know. So, I need to smooth some things over." He pulled back to meet his father's gaze. "And I'll need your help again."

Xavior released his hold and climbed off the bed. "Then I'll meet you there."

"Dad!" he called out.

Xavior turned to look at him.

"The baby Mom's carrying is a boy. His name is...or will be, Egan."

Xavior smiled. "I knew it was a boy this time. I guess we're not outnumbered after all, Guylan."

"Not at all, and in four years, Mom gives birth again, to another boy. He's named Seth."

Xavior raised a brow. "Six children...we have six?"

He smiled. "It's what Mom always wanted."

Xavior returned the smile. "Me, too."

He'd turned to leave when Guylan called him back one last time. "Oh, and Dad, buy lots of stock in Microsoft."

"Microsoft," Xavior repeated, and then nodded. "I'll remember."

Guylan waited until he heard his father's footsteps descend the stairs before he stripped and traveled on...eyes closed, tongue pressed against the raven brand, his body changing again into adolescence.

He made sure the events of 1985 took place as they had on his first trip; the only exception being, the visit this time to the orphanage would find him just missing Sister Margaret, who had gone sneaker shopping with some of the other boys.

Andy was sweeping the floor, as he had been doing before. But this time around, he didn't look like someone had ripped a carpet out from beneath his feet. With a cheery smile and a friendly greeting, Andy eagerly made conversation with him, accepting the invitation to dinner without hesitation. Guylan even got to see Nela again when she was twelve.

The next day, he returned to St. Bernard's with his father and everything fell into place accordingly. There was only one thing disturbing him. Sister Margaret was no longer in service to the women in the shelter. He knew how much they needed and depended on her; her absence from their lives could mean so many changes for them.

On the day he and his father accompanied Olena and Quentin to the orphanage for the family reunion, he bided his time. He waited for all the tears and hugs to subside, for the explanations and apologies to be made, and for the plans for Olena and Zack to adopt Andy to happen, since this was a very important moment. He wouldn't want to deprive Keira of a husband. Then he took Sister Margaret aside.

"I'd like to volunteer to help out here at the orphanage, but I also feel I'm needed somewhere else," he said.

Sister Margaret smiled. "May I make a suggestion?"

"I'm all ears."

"For a while now, I've been involved with helping out at the women's shelter. In fact, Andy comes with me now and then to do yard work and remove the trash. Would you like to join us?"

Guylan smiled. "I'd love to, and I think my father would lend a hand, too."

Sister Margaret winked at him. "Somehow, I had a feeling he would."

Her words left him wondering if he'd ever truly get a grasp on or unravel all of the family secret.

Forty-five

I can honestly say, if a great amount of time had passed while Guylan was gone, I didn't feel it. That might be attributed to the fact that he'd planned his arrival to be only two hours after his departure. It was exactly 8:00 p.m. when he emerged from the attic portal, head first and naked, like a baby exiting his mother's womb. I waited until the energy light of Xavior's crystals died before I made my way to him, wrapping a blanket around his shoulders and pulling him into my embrace. "You did it," I whispered.

He smiled and kissed me hard and long, stopping only when Xavior cleared his throat. "Let's get the damage straight, son," Xavior said, packing up his stones and handing Guylan the raven ring.

"Andy's not a cop, but an investment broker who owns his own firm. He got involved with finance after he opened up an account in your bank and then worked there during his college years. Recently he opened an insurance company and tax-preparing business," Guylan reported.

"That's the word we've got, right, Nela," Xavior said.

I agreed and added, "And Sister Margaret isn't living in a retirement home for nuns, but is still at the orphanage. In fact, she's

St. Bernard's Mother Superior now and has been for the last fifteen years."

"And Andy found a stray dog, a German Shepherd. He's tried for several weeks to find the owner, but no luck. He's decided to keep her and named her Callie. She's a sweet dog, nothing out of the ordinary...well, not now, anyway. Actually, she's kind of scrawny and lethargic. Andy's hoping you'll take a look at her," Xavior concluded.

"Is that the information you've gotten, Guylan?" I said, watching him get dressed.

He bent to tie his shoes. "That's it all in a nutshell, babe."

"Then let's get downstairs and get this show on the road," Xavior suggested.

Making our way to the first floor, we met Andy, Keira and family coming home from their dinner out. Andy's face brightened at seeing Guylan. "Did you come to check out Callie?"

"That and visit with my grandmother," Guylan lied.

While Olena and Keira went upstairs to put the children to bed, Guylan raised Callie's lips and examined her gums. "She appears to be a little dehydrated. Administering water beneath the skin will help that problem. I'll put an IV drip on her, check for ticks, give rabies and distemper shots, the whole works. I'll have her groomed, too: a bath and nails clipped," Guylan said. "I'm also going to prescribe a vitamin supplement to add to her food." He gave Callie a pat on the head. "After that, I think she'll be all set."

Andy nodded in agreement. "I'll bring her by the clinic tomorrow morning on my way to work."

The thought of having to work tomorrow exhausted me. Guylan and I hadn't had much sleep in the last two days. I glanced at my watch; it read a quarter to nine. Suddenly my entire body was heavy with fatigue. I stifled a yawn and reached in my pocket for my cell phone. I had turned it off while in the attic, so as not to disrupt or interfere with the energy waves of Xavior's crystals. Now, I checked my messages and saw I had one from Hannah.

Her tone, thick with panic, came across on my voice mail. "Nela, for God's sake, where the hell are you? I've got a real situation here and I need your help." Hannah cleared her throat, something she often did when she was nervous or anxious. "It's about seven-fifty on Monday night. If you could call me as soon as you get this message, I'd really"—she stressed the word *really*—"appreciate it."

I moved to the sitting room and dialed Hannah's number.

Her voice cracked. "Nela, thank God."

"What's going on, Hannah?"

"It's Joe. He's been drinking most of the day, ranting about how useless he is without an arm; he's worried he can't support his family now he's half of a man, and stuff like that. Around seven-thirty, he grabbed the keys and took off in the car."

My heart raced. "Do you have an idea where he's gone?"

Hannah's voice trembled. "I think he might be at the site of a building on Louis Boulevard he bid on to restore and lost," she added. "I found him there last week, just sitting on a pile of lumber. He did the same thing, had too much to drink, shouted about his uselessness and then took off with the car. Dad and Mom were home that night and took me out to find him. But they're away, left for Maine two days ago. I haven't been able to get a hold of anyone... Alana, you..." her voice trailed off.

"I'm at Guylan's grandmother's house now," I said. "I'm on my way."

"We're on our way where?" Guylan said.

I turned to face him and Andy standing behind me. I replaced the cell phone in my pocket. "There's some trouble with Joe, and I've got to help Hannah."

"Then let's go," he said, heading for the door.

Andy followed us. "You might need some help. Let me run up and tell Keira I'm going with you two, and I'll meet you in the car."

I thanked him as I ran out the door.

On the drive to Hannah's, I thought of the night I'd been transported to Iraq and saw Joe dying. I intervened in the natural flow of things, wanting him to live for Hannah and Cara's sake, but did I create more problems for them all in the long run?

"You can't think like that," Guylan said softly.

I turned to look at him. "You can read minds now?"

"I just know what my own thoughts would be in this situation, and I don't want you to beat yourself up over what's happened," he said.

Because Andy was sitting in the back seat, there really wasn't a way for us to get into any more detail. I patted his hand and forced a smile. "Thanks for understanding."

Hannah looked a wreck. Her mane of auburn hair was pulled back into a careless ponytail, eyes red-rimmed, and hands wringing in front of her. "Thank God you're finally here."

"Where's Cara?" I said, waiting for her to grab her pocketbook and lock the door.

"She's staying overnight at her friend Lydia's, and going to school in the morning from there." Hannah sighed. "I'm glad she wasn't here to see this. Last time it really upset her. I heard her crying in her sleep."

I reached out to take Hannah's hand. "I'm so sorry for all of this."

"It's no one's fault, Nela. It's something many of the guys returning from Iraq are going through." She sighed again. "I just hope Joe's open to getting help."

No one spoke on the way to Louis Boulevard. When Hannah spotted Joe sitting on a pile of lumber, she exited the car as soon as it came to a stop and ran to her husband.

Andy, Guylan and I followed, my heart going out to my sister as she got down on her knees and buried her head in Joe's lap. His one arm embraced her, and I choked back the tears burning the back of my throat.

Joe chuckled sardonically. "I see you brought the troops this time."

I swallowed the emotion threatening to choke me, and moved nearer. "Joe, we all love you. We were worried you'd—"

"What, Nela?" he interjected. "What were you worried I'd do?"

"You've been drinking, Joe. You know drinking and driving is a dangerous combination," I said.

His top lip curled. "Dangerous...you've no idea what dangerous is."

The scene returned in my mind's eye of the way I had found him, lying near death, bleeding profusely, the sound of guns firing in the distance. "What I do know is that you could have killed yourself, someone else as well."

"I should be dead, ya know? Dead like the rest of the soldiers I was with."

Hannah lifted her gaze to meet his. "Don't say that...don't ever say that."

He shook his head and tears welled in his eyes. "Why the hell was I the only one who got to live, Hannah?"

My heart, gripped with sorrow and guilt, sickened. It was then Guylan's hand went around my shoulders. "I heard you believe you saw an angel," he said, pulling me close.

Joe nodded. "I heard her say *not this man*, and when I opened my eyes, I was in a hospital."

"Then it's obvious it wasn't your time, Joe," Guylan rationalized. "You've something yet left to do."

Joe glanced at the stump of his arm. "What would that be... being a burden on my wife?"

"You're not a burden," Hannah said, wrapping her arms around his waist and laying her head on his chest.

He stroked her hair. "I am if I can't work, take care of you and Cara."

"But you can work, Joe," Andy broke in.

I'd forgotten he was along until now.

"Yeah, there's a real demand for one-armed construction workers," Joe retorted.

"Maybe not in the actual constructing, but there is in knowing construction," Andy countered.

Joe frowned. "What the hell are you getting at?"

Andy reached into his pocket and pulled out a business card. Moving closer to Joe, he handed it to him. "You're just the kind of guy I need, someone who knows if a home is structurally sound and free of rodents or pests, before I insure it for a homeowner or advise someone to invest in it."

Joe's eyes struggled to focus on the card Andy had given him. "I don't know diddly about the insurance business."

"I pay for all the training my agents need," Andy said.

Joe met Andy's gaze. "Does this kind of work pay well?"

Andy chuckled. "Oh yeah...very well."

Joe stuck the card in his shirt pocket and extended his hand to Andy. "You've got yourself a deal."

Andy shook Joe's hand. "Be at my office at noon tomorrow and we'll discuss it further then."

After we dropped Andy at Olena's and headed to my house, I laid my head back on the seat and gazed wearily out the window.

"You look exhausted," Guylan said.

I turned to look his way. "I am; it's been a long day...a long, unusual day."

He stifled a yawn. "I'm feeling it myself."

"Do you realize if you hadn't gone back to change things for Ronnie Fargus, Andy would still be a cop and wouldn't have been able to offer Joe a job tonight?" I sighed. "Who knows what would have happened to Joe then."

"It's the way things work. One situation feeds or builds off another. That's why it's very important to be careful about the changes made," he said. "There are always consequences."

"How do you pick and choose?" I reflected aloud.

"You don't, Nela. You just do what you have to at the time, as you did when you saved Joe, and hope, like tonight, it all works out."

"What do we do with this power, with the gifts we've been given, Guylan?"

"The best we can, babe. The very best we can."

Forty-six

The first weekend in May arrived sooner than I'd expected. I picked Gram and Gramps up at midnight from The Blessing Train and we talked until 3:00 a.m. I had lots to ask Gramps, since I hadn't seen him in five years. He was completely awed by his first visit back, savoring the bacon Gram made for breakfast that morning and marveling over the oldie songs playing on the radio. I had a heart-to-heart chat with him on the pros and cons of being the eldest in the family and the burden of being relied upon.

"Never figured it to be a burden, sweetie," he said, sipping at his third cup of coffee. "Just did what I had to so we all could get by."

His philosophy was simple: do what's needed to be done at the time and do it the best you can while you're doing it.

We had our usual family reunion dinner and by eight, I dropped into bed.

~ * ~

May 4th, 2008. My wedding day dawned bright and beautiful. Around eleven, my mother; grandmother; Hannah, my matron-of-honor; Alana, my bridesmaid; and Cara, my junior bridesmaid, accompanied me to the back room of St. Michael's church to help me dress in my gown.

I had opted for a simple, A-line style, strapless brocade in champagne. At my neck I wore a choker strand of pearls and pearl drops on my ears. The shoulder-length veil was held on my head by a pearled tiara, my dark hair pulled back in a cascade of curls falling to the middle of my back. I carried a bouquet of white roses and wore semi-heeled shoes dyed to match the gown, and sheer, white stockings. Just as I was putting the finishing touches on my make-up, a knock came at the door.

Hannah opened it and smiled. "Good afternoon, Father."

"And a good day to you as well," was his response, with a bit of a British accent.

I frowned. Father Malcom Dunstin was from Brooklyn. He had an accent but it was far from British. I made my way from the dressing area to the sitting room, wondering why it wasn't Father Dunstin at the door.

The new priest extended a hand to me when I entered the room. "Sorry for any inconvenience my presence must make."

I searched the younger priest's face.

Where have I seen him before?

"What's happened to Father Dunstin?" my mother inquired.

He glanced over to where she sat on the sofa. "I rushed him to Shire Downs with an appendix problem. He had surgery to remove the troublesome thing early this morning." He smiled and met my gaze, which, no doubt, was a mixture of panic and confusion. "Not to worry, Nela...if I might call you by your first name?"

I nodded, still trying to figure out why his face was so familiar.

"Not to worry a tad," he said, his smile deepening. "I have all of Father Dunstin's notes, the vows you and Guylan have chosen, and I'm confident this will all go as planned."

"And you've come all the way from England to take over for Father Dunstin?" Cara questioned.

The priest chuckled. "Well, no, not exactly. I arrived the beginning of the week to visit Malcom...Father Dunstin," he corrected. "When he took ill, he asked me to take over for him."

"What part of England are you from, Father?" Hannah asked.

"Actually, I'm from this area originally. When I was eight, my father was transferred to London, and that's where I grew up." He glanced at his watch. "I've yet to stop by and meet Guylan, so I'll take my leave and see you, Nela, promptly at noon at the altar." He made his way to the door and then turned toward me one last time. "I'm sorry, I don't believe I properly introduced myself."

"No," I said. "You didn't."

He inclined his head politely. "I'm Father Fargus...Ronald Fargus."

My mouth must have dropped open a mile. All I could think of was Guylan's reaction when he met the new priest.

Oh, Guylan, how I wish I could see your face.

~ * ~

At the ceremony, I heard Gram and Mom sniffling. Dad's eyes welled when he gave me away; Hannah and Alana grew misty, too. But it was Guylan's eyes I drowned in. They were beautiful orbs of blue adoring every ounce of me. I don't think he took his gaze off me once. He stood tall and looked so handsome in a black tux with a champagne-hued shirt to match my gown, that my heart soared to think this wonderful man was who I would spend my life with.

The reception that followed, held at the Hallston Lodge, was decorated in my favorite colors, pink and cream. Gram and Gramps danced the day away, on the same floor they had the very night when they first met.

"What went through your mind when you met Father Fargus?" I posed the question to Guylan as we danced to The Carpenters' "We've Only Just Begun."

"How amazing the past year has been," he said, drawing me close. "I mean, look around us, Nela. My parents, my siblings, Andy married to my sister, Sister Margaret again a part of the family... none of this would be as it is if—"

"If not for you," I finished the sentence for him. I pulled back to look into his eyes. "Guylan Sincloud, you are a magnificent man, and an even more magnificent Druid."

He smiled. "You're not so bad yourself, Nela Sincloud."

I beamed at his use of my new last name.

"Look at how happy your sister is with her husband. If not for you, this day would have been a sad one for her, having just buried the man she loved."

"How true," I whispered.

Guylan laughed. "And even Ronnie Fargus moved up the morality ladder, going from demon to disciple."

"The fact that none of them has the slightest inclination of what their lives once were astounds me." I looked again around the room. "They remember nothing."

Guylan leaned down to give me a gentle kiss on the tip of my nose. "It's best that way, babe. It will serve no great purpose for them to know the family secret."

"So true," I agreed. Everyone was much happier this way.

After the first round of dances, Andy stood up to make a toast. "I'd like to raise my glass to Guylan, my dearest friend and almost-brother. I am thankful for that day in 1985 when he came into St. Bernard's looking for Sister Margaret and found me as well." He raised his glass higher. "Thanks, Guylan, and bless you too, Nela. I wish you both much happiness and prosperity."

Xavior joined us. "Speaking of prosperity," he said, handing Guylan an envelope.

I watched Guylan slit the flap and pull out an impressive-looking document. His eyes widened as he read the text.

Xavior chuckled at his son's expression. "Remember when you advised me to invest in Microsoft?"

Guylan nodded.

"Well, that's your cut," Xavior said. "I planned it so each of my children would get a share of my profit on their wedding day. Your dividend is a bit more than the others, being you're the one who gave me the tip." He frowned. "I have to say I've been waiting a long time to give it to you, was getting a little worried you'd never marry." Xavior smiled at me. "I'm glad you finally found the right girl."

"It was just a case of waiting for her to grow up," Guylan said, handing me the certificate.

I read the amount of money saved in an account for us and swallowed hard. "I think I need to sit down."

"And I think I need a brandy," Guylan added.

Xavior laughed again.

After the reception, Guylan and I took Gramps and Gram back to my flat above the salon. Gram made sandwiches and we opened some of the gifts, then Guylan and I took them to the train station.

Gram smiled. "It's been a lovely day, Nela. Everything worked out perfectly."

"I've something to tell you," I whispered.

Gram moved nearer. "I'm listening."

"I'm expecting twins, Gram."

Her eyes brightened. "How far along are you?"

"Just eighteen days," I said.

Gram narrowed her eyes. "Nela, it's not possible to know..." she clipped her words and we both laughed. "I guess in this family, anything's possible."

"I'm having a boy and a girl, Gram."

"You even know their gender?"

I nodded. "Trust me on this."

"Oh, I do Nela; I do," Gram said, giving me a quick hug.

"Come on, Sophia," Gramps called, climbing up on the train step.

In our excitement, neither of us realized The Blessing Train had arrived. And another year would pass before I'd get an answer to that important question...*what's it like to be dead?*

"Hurry and get up, Sophia," Gramps called again, holding out his hand to her.

Gram kissed me and headed for the train, reaching for Gramps' hand.

"Jump up on the step, Sophia," Gramps urged.

Gram reached for his hand.

"Hurry and get up...hurry now...get up, Sophia...get up..."

Epilogue

October, 1930, Anglewood, New York

"Hurry now and get up, Sophia," her mother called.

She opened her eyes to find herself in her bed, the one she occupied on Cutler Street, upstairs from the bakery her family owned. She looked around the room at her things: the dresser with the statue of the Infant of Prague on it, her dolls lined up on a nearby shelf, the yellow-flowered curtains hanging from the window. She was home, in her own bedroom...but how could that be?

She sat up abruptly and stared at her hands, felt her face, ran her fingers through her long hair. Then she raised her gaze to her mother, holding little Angelo in her arms. "Mama, how did you get here?" She shook her head to make sense of it all.

"What do you mean, child? I live here, with you and Papa, your brothers and Nawna downstairs."

"No, that can't be," she argued.

Her mother frowned. "You are talking *assurdita*, nonsense."

"But I'm all grown up...dead even," she said, swinging her legs off the bed and looking down at her tiny feet. She wiggled her toes, bent her knees, and took a step forward.

"And that is the last time you eat two helpings of fried dough before bed," her mother warned. "Too much greasy food makes you dream strange, crazy things.

Sophia frowned. "Then, that's what it was, just a dream?"

Her mother comforted a crying Angelo by moving the infant over her shoulder and giving him a pat on the back. "I would say that's the case, since you are here, standing before me in your nightgown, which you'd better replace quickly with your dress."

"But everything was so, so...real," she mused.

"What will feel even more real is the wooden spoon on your behind, if you do not get a move on. Your papa is in need of your help and is waiting for you." Vincenzo teetered through the door, the stench of his soiled diaper filling the room. Her mother sighed. "Go to Nawna, Sophia. Let her give you breakfast. By the time I clean Vincenzo and feed Angelo—"

"I know, I know, it's how it happened before, Mama," she interrupted.

Her mother shook her head, reached for Vincenzo's hand and headed for the door. "I don't know what you're babbling about, Sophia."

"Mama, wait...can I take piano lessons?"

Maria Pettrocini turned. "Now, what has brought that on?"

"I want to learn. I have to learn. Everything counts on it."

"Humph, we have had that old piano sitting in the parlor for years and you have never showed one bit of interest in playing it."

"Well, now I do. And I know who can teach me...Mrs. Calafano, down the street."

"Oh, I don't know, Sophia. Right now, with a new *bambino*, there is so much we have to pay." Maria tightened her grip on Vincenzo's hand, before he could start to run around the house with messy pants.

"I know how much Mrs. Calafano loves the bread you bake, Mama. She's always coming into the bakery and bragging about the taste, how it melts in her mouth even without butter, and saying how she'd give anything to enjoy such a luxury more than once a week. I bet she'd teach me for trade if Papa gave her a loaf a few times a week."

Maria inclined her head in thought. "Such an exchange would not break us."

"Then you'll ask Papa?"

Maria smiled. "I will ask."

Sophia returned the smile. "Do you think he will say yes?"

Maria squared her shoulders. "I will make sure he does, if it is what you really want."

"Oh, it is...it is, Mama. But how can you make sure Papa will agree?"

"A good wife, Sophia, makes her husband think she listens and obeys his every word. A smart woman lets her husband believe all that goes on in his house is his idea, and a most clever woman keeps such power to herself." Maria narrowed her eyes. "I will explain better when you are older. For now, never you mind. Keep what I said between us and leave Papa to me."

Sophia bounced downstairs to Nawna's apartment, her heart racing and her spirit soaring. She caught her grandmother looking at the cedar wood box. "I know what you're doing with that, Nawna."

Nelana shut the lid and sat back in her chair. "Do you, now?"

She nodded. "I had a dream last night and know all about it."

"And what did you dream, my *bambina,* granddaughter?"

Sophia made a face. "I am not a baby anymore," she said, then went on to explain some of the vision to her grandmother.

She received a cunning smile. "Dreams can be very interesting, no?"

Sophia searched the elder woman's face. "It's what you wanted to happen, wasn't it, Nawna?"

Her grandmother folded her arms across her chest. "You are smart, Sophia. But just because you saw what you have, it does not mean you can act so brazen or jump ahead."

"I don't understand."

"You have been privileged to know more than any of us has a right." Nelana sighed. "You must learn to let it all unfold in its own time."

"Why is it so important for everything to be the same, Nawna?"

"*Equilibrio*, balance, child...we must not upset the balance. It is not for us to do. Now, sit and I will make your breakfast so you can go and help your father. Saturday is a busy day for my poor Antonio."

"You and I both know who will be the ones to change things."

Her grandmother only nodded and went about making something for her to eat.

In the bakery, Sophia found her father washing the large front window, readying it for a new display, as she knew he would be doing. She caught herself from going over to the candy jar and filling it with peppermint sticks before she was asked. She waited for Antonio to instruct her in making sure the lids were tight.

Everything has to be the same.

The October afternoon was unusually warm, and she was just about to go for a glass of lemonade, but hesitated a moment, eyeing the front door.

Would the caped man come, accompanied by the little red-haired girl?

Everything has to be the same.

Overwhelmed by wonder and anticipation, she headed for the lemonade. Her heart leapt with hope when she heard the bakery door open.

Turning back, she smiled ...ready for the rest of her life to begin.

Meet Roberta DeCaprio

Roberta C.M. DeCaprio is a freelance writer of all genres in romance and women's mainstream fiction. A prior "sexuality" columnist for *A.B.L.E.D. Magazine*, and former assistant editor for *Independence Today* newspaper (both publications dedicated to the needs and rights of the disabled), Roberta has insight into the problems other physically challenged people face due to her own walking impairment.

She has won awards for her poetry, becoming published in several anthologies. A graduate of the Writer's Digest School and Cornell Cooperative Extension, Roberta also held the office of newsletter editor (2002 to 2004) for Capital Region, her local chapter of Romance Writers of America, interviewing well-known published authors.

A mother of two and grandmother of four, Roberta shares her upstate NY home with two dearly loved rescue cats, Mikko and Misha, and her artist/screenplay writer husband with whom she's collaborated on a script for a 24-hour film race, and a sitcom that has won the attention of a producer.

To view Roberta's back list of novels, and read excerpts from her books, check out her website at: www.rcmdecaprio.com

Other Works From The Pen Of

Roberta DeCaprio

Coma Coast - We all know love comes from the heart, but what happens when it's all in your mind? On Halloween night, Finna Tarellie travels home via Old Coast Road. Swerving to avoid hitting a woman standing in the center of the road, Finna crashes her car. Lifted from the wreck by the mysterious woman who speaks telepathically, Finna is told she is chosen for a special mission and must right a terrible wrong. That mission will take Finna on an incredible journey through unexplained phenomena, and into the arms of the man she not only saves, but is destined to love.

The Vanity - What do you do after looking into a mirror if the eyes looking back aren't your own? After purchasing an old mansion, during renovations Jules Wheaton finds an antique vanity walled up in a partition. Upon her discovery, the evil presence trapped in the mirror is unleashed...waiting to haunt and possess her. Will Jules be taken over by the monster within the looking glass, or will her husband's love be strong enough to save her?

Letter to Our Readers

Enjoy this book?

You can make a difference

As an independent publisher, Wings ePress, Inc. does not have the financial clout of the large New York Publishers. We can't afford large magazine spreads or subway posters to tell people about our quality books.

But, we do have something much more effective and powerful than ads. We have a large base of loyal readers.

Honest Reviews help bring the attention of new readers to our books.

If you enjoyed this book, we would appreciate it if you would spend a few minutes posting a review on the site where you purchased this book or on the Wings ePress, Inc. webpages at:

https://wingsepress.com/

Thank You

Visit Our Website

For The Full Inventory
Of Quality Books:

Wings ePress.Inc
https://wingsepress.com/

Quality trade paperbacks and downloads
in multiple formats,
in genres ranging from light romantic comedy
to general fiction and horror.
Wings has something for every reader's taste.
Visit the website, then bookmark it.
We add new titles each month!

Wings ePress Inc.
3000 N. Rock Road
Newton, KS   67114